D0188853

A LETHAL LESSON

THE LANE WINSLOW MYSTERY SERIES

———————

PRAISE FOR THE LANE WINSLOW MYSTERIES

"The 'find of the year' . . . With the feel of Louise Penny's Three Pines, the independence and quick wit of Kerry Greenwood's Phryne Fisher and the intelligence of Jacqueline Winspear's Maisie Dobbs, this mystery series has it all!" —Murder by the Book, Texas

"Relentlessly exciting from start to finish." —*Kirkus Reviews*

"Whishaw spins an engrossing tale of murder, . . . British spies and local Canadian constabulary while deftly braiding the many story threads into a twisty plot." —*Shelf Awareness*

"Charming . . . with solid characters and nice puzzle plots . . . perfect for a mental getaway." —*Globe and Mail*

"Think a young Katharine Hepburn—beautiful, smart and beyond capable. Winslow is an example of the kind of woman who emerged after the war, a confident female who had worked in factories building tanks and guns, a woman who hadn't yet been suffocated by the 1950s—perfect housewife ideal." —*Vancouver Sun*

"There's no question you should read it—it's excellent." —*Toronto Star*

"A master of the genre." —*Wisconsin Bookwatch*

"In the vein of Louise Penny . . . a compelling series that combines a cozy setting, spy intrigue storylines, and police procedural elements—not an easy task, but one that Whishaw pulls off." —*Reviewing the Evidence*

PRAISE FOR THE LANE WINSLOW MYSTERIES

"Well-drawn, pleasantly complex characters and a clearly developed, believable, and intriguing setting . . ." —Historical Novel Society

"The setting is fresh and the cast endearing." —CrimeReads

"Fantastic . . . readers will stand up and cheer." —Anna Lee Huber, author of the Lady Darby Mysteries and the Verity Kent Mysteries

"Wonderfully complex . . . The post-war time period is particularly interesting and well captured." —Maureen Jennings, author of the Murdoch Mysteries

"Rich with intrigue, humour, murder and romance." —Kerry Clare, author of *Mitzi Bytes* and editor of 49th Shelf

"Exquisitely written, psychologically deft." —Linda Svendsen, author of *Sussex Drive*

"A series that's guaranteed to please." —Mercer Island Books, Washington

"Full of history, mystery, and a glorious setting . . . a wonderful series." —Sleuth of Baker Street, Ontario

IONA WHISHAW

A LETHAL LESSON

A LANE WINSLOW MYSTERY

TOUCHWOOD

Copyright © 2021 by Iona Whishaw

All rights reserved. No part of this publication may be reproduced, stored
in a retrieval system, or transmitted in any form or by any means, electronic,
mechanical, photocopying, recording, or otherwise, without the prior written
permission of the publisher. For more information, contact the publisher at:

TouchWood Editions
touchwoodeditions.com

This book is a work of fiction. Names, characters, places, and incidents are either
products of the author's imagination or are used fictitiously. Any resemblance to
actual events or locales or persons, living or dead, is entirely coincidental.

Edited by Claire Philipson
Cover illustration by Margaret Hanson
Cover design by Sydney Barnes

CATALOGUING DATA AVAILABLE FROM LIBRARY AND ARCHIVES CANADA
ISBN 9781771513531 (softcover)
ISBN 9781771513548 (electronic)

TouchWood Editions acknowledges that the land on which we live and work is
within the traditional territories of the Lkwungen (Esquimalt and Songhees),
Malahat, Pacheedaht, Scia'new, T'Sou-ke and W̱SÁNEĆ (Pauquachin, Tsartlip,
Tsawout, Tseycum) peoples.

We acknowledge the financial support of the Government of Canada through
the Canada Book Fund and the Canada Council for the Arts, and of the Province
of British Columbia through the British Columbia Arts Council and the Book
Publishing Tax Credit.

PRINTED IN CANADA AT FRIESENS

25 24 23 22 21   1 2 3 4 5

For Mary Wiens Miller,
who educated and brightened lives in her own
one-room schoolhouse in Saskatchewan in the 1940s

PROLOGUE

"GET OUT." THE DRIVER'S VOICE was compacted with rage. The car was stopped in the middle of the road. Only the fan of light provided by the headlights made any inroads in the utter darkness. Any trace of that night's half moon was obliterated by the swirling snow. At near midnight, in these conditions, it was unlikely any traffic would be on the road.

"What?" The man was drunk. He couldn't make out what was being said to him.

"Get out!" Shouting now, the driver leaned over, opened the door, and pushed hard at the man. Unable to help himself, the drunk man tumbled out onto the bank of snow that had piled up on the side of the road. He watched the car disappear around the corner toward Castlegar, the last red shred of its tail lights vanishing behind the bend. He stood, bemused, and then turned and began to trudge back to town. In an unconscious imitation of driving, the man stumbled across the road to walk on the right-hand side.

The river roared below him in the blackness. He shook his head as if to clear it, but the driving snow that blew onto his face under his hat countered his efforts to understand what was happening. He wondered suddenly where his car was. He tried pulling his hat off to see better, but that only covered him in snow and didn't alleviate the darkness. It occurred to him that he'd left something at home, and he tried to remember what it was. Not the car. How would he have gotten this far without the car? In the same instant he remembered, the road was lit blindingly by the headlights of a car coming from behind him, heading toward Nelson. His spirit buoyed in this one illuminated moment, and everything made sense. He would get home, be welcomed. He put out an arm to stop the car. He wanted to turn to face it, but he felt dizzy. The engine revved, sudden and deafening; he could hear it behind him and frowned. The sensation of being thrown into the snowy air made him feel full of light, as if the angels had come. In the darkness of the next moment, he was not aware of landing. He did not hear the blunt, hard sound of breaking, nor the muffled scream from somewhere. He had no sensation of bouncing or rolling. He knew nothing of sliding like a broken doll and resting in the snow far below. He did not hear the roar of the car disappearing, or see the lights blink out. He, indeed, would never hear or see anything again.

CHAPTER ONE

Wednesday, December 3, 1947

WENDY KEELING WAS AS HAPPY as she could ever remember being in her mostly unhappy life. She had ushered the children outside after they had put their lunch things away, and she could hear them now, shrieking in the snow, releasing all that pent-up animal energy they had accumulated during the morning. She would try to get them all on to arithmetic in the afternoon. She would start with a puzzle they could tackle in pairs. She walked up and down the short rows to make sure all the crumbs and jam smudges were off the desks, checked inside to make sure no one had hidden a sandwich away, and then looked at the clock. They had five minutes still before they had to come in and remove their piles of now no doubt soaking outer clothes.

Taking up a piece of chalk, she drew six glasses on the board and indicated with a line that the first three were filled. Then she went outside holding the school bell and rang it, calling, "It's time, ladies and gentlemen!"

Under the cries of protest, she stood on the porch, her arms crossed in front of her, looking benignly implacable and saying nothing. Even after only a few days, they knew the routine. Line up in front of the stairs and be allowed in quickly. The door was kept closed to keep the heat in until they were all ready to come in at once.

"What are we doing this afternoon, miss?" asked Rafe, one of Angela Bertolli's boys, turning to give a little shove to someone trying to usurp his first-place spot in line.

"Rafe!" Miss Keeling gave a warning note, and then smiled. "It's a great afternoon for arithmetic. Okay, every-one present and correct?" Seeing that the jostling group contained the number of students she expected, thirteen, Miss Keeling swung open the door, and watched the muffled group clamber up the stairs and into the classroom. She turned and put her head in the door. "Coats and scarves up! In your desks by the time I turn around."

She looked again at the now-quiet yard, with its trampled snow and two nascent snowmen, and was about to come in when she saw a red knitted scarf hanging on a branch of a short spruce tree at the south side of the school. Edith. Her granny had knitted it for her, Edith had told her. She was about to call the girl to come and take responsibility for her scarf, when she thought better of disrupting the complications of removing outer clothes and rubber boots. She closed the door and went down the four stairs and stepped into the snow, wishing immediately she had her rubbers, and made for the scarf.

When she saw the black car, parked halfway down the hill, the clouds of white coming out of the exhaust, she

4

frowned. The car was not moving, but the engine was running. Sunlight reflected off the front windshield, showing only the snow and trees around it, making it seem, she thought whimsically, as if she could see into its mind. Who was in it? It was almost as if someone were watching her, or the school, or more worryingly, the students. But who? She didn't recognize the car. She was going to wave, but then thought, Someone has come up the wrong road and is even now looking at a map. If that person was lost, she'd not be much use to them. She'd only come to the area a short time ago herself.

Even with the door closed, she could hear the banging and laughing of the children in the little kitchen room, boots being pulled off and hurled under the coat-rack bench, and she turned back to retrieve the scarf. When she looked down the road again, she saw that the car was slowly beginning to back away. Then, in some trick of the light, the windshield stopped reflecting the peaceful world it looked out on, and she could see, for the briefest moment, the shape of the head inside turned away to look out the back window, right arm over the seat, gloved left hand on the steering wheel, as the driver backed the car nonchalantly down the hill.

She lurched up the steps, not daring to look again, some atavistic superstition urging her to ignore what she had seen. It was a bad reflection, it was nothing, a lost stranger now pulling silently back to the main road. Do not look, it seemed to be saying, because looking will make it real. But competing with that desperate hope was the cold hard nub of the truth, deep in her gut. It had been too good to be true. Somehow, they had found her.

5

CHAPTER TWO

Friday, December 5

ROSE SCOTT LOOKED AROUND HER cramped bedroom. Even with the sun reflecting off the snow outside, the tiny bedroom window looked out only on the dark woods that pressed against the back of the cottage. She folded her Sunday dress carefully, preparing to put it into the suitcase that lay open on the bed, and then stood up to stretch out her back.

She felt vaguely bad about lying, but no one would care. She'd be away from here and everyone would think she'd gone off to a fairy-tale ending. At the moment, "happily ever after" meant anywhere but here—anywhere he wasn't. Even knowing she'd be safely away, the thought of him released a flood of sickening anxiety. She jumped at the sound of the telephone, its ring shattering the silence of the cottage. Should she tell Wendy about him?

She picked up the instrument that was on the desk in the tiny sitting room. "B 228, Rose Scott speaking." She could feel her heart beating in her throat.

"Oh, hello! I was looking for Wendy, Wendy Keeling. Is this her number?" A pleasant, friendly female voice.

"Yes, that's right. She's not here just now. She teaches at the school. She should be home by five or so. Can I give her a message?" Relief washed through her. For Wendy.

The woman on the other end of the line hesitated. "I'm her oldest friend, and I've just come up and thought I could surprise her. Would it be a bother if I stopped by this evening after she comes home?"

"No, of course not. Do you know how to get here?"

"I'm coming from Nelson," the woman said.

"Right, well you'll drive about twenty-five miles and just before the road takes a sharp rise, you'll see three little drives that go toward the lake, on your right. We're the middle one."

Rose put the receiver back on the cradle and leaned against the desk and shook her head, uttering a mirthless laugh. Wendy. Young, much younger than her, attractive. Could she become a target? But at least she had friends, evidently, and maybe that would protect her. She returned to the bedroom to continue her packing and then hesitated. Should she have asked the caller her name? She shook her head. By tomorrow, none of it would matter. At that moment, Rose could not think that she had a single friend in the world.

———

Monday, December 8

ELEANOR ARMSTRONG, THE King's Cove postmistress, slid the noisy wooden kiosk window up at Lane's knock and propped it with a stick. "Good Monday morning, my dear. Nothing in today, I'm afraid. The weather seems to have kept the boat docked up in town. Poor Kenny managed to drive all the way down to the wharf through the snow and had to come all the way back empty-handed. Did the inspector get off all right?" Lane thought of Eleanor and Kenny Armstrong practically as replacements for her grandparents, who were far away in Scotland. The Armstrongs ran the tiny King's Cove post office, and she basked in their good nature and enduring affection.

"Yes, he put the chains on yesterday afternoon. I've told him on no account to come home tonight if this continues." Lane hadn't liked telling her new husband to stay at his little house in Nelson, but one had to be sensible. In a way she'd never imagined possible before her wedding, she'd become quite used to having him at home at night. She'd been fearful that she'd miss her solitude once she married. Not a bit of it. She had all day to be solitary when he was off in town police inspecting.

That morning she had watched him back out of the gate, turn deftly in the thick, new fall of snow, and drive off, his chains clanking softly on the blanketed road. She had tidied the kitchen, and then had stood looking out her French doors at the lake below, shrouded, like everything this morning, in whiteness and mist. Nothing had moved along the water. She had wondered if it ever iced up the way the rivers of her childhood had. Lane had grown up as part of a British community alternately in Riga, Latvia, and the seaside resort of Bilderlinghshof, and she had adored the winters of her childhood. Snow always lifted her spirits.

8

She'd heard Kenny's truck struggling along the road on the way back from the wharf, where he normally met the steamboat four times a week to pick up the mail. She'd shovelled her way along the path between her house and the post office, and then propped her shovel against a tree and walked the rest of the way in the track left by Kenny's bright red Ford.

The truck provided the only splash of colour at the moment, with the clouds grey and low, and snow piled over everything, obscuring all but some glimpses of the dark green of the surrounding pine forest. The little wooden room that made up the post office was attached to the Armstrong cottage, and at the moment, though out of the immediate elements, it felt like a deep-freeze.

Eleanor grinned at Lane and cocked her head toward the inside of the cottage just past where she stored all the business of the post office. "Come on. Come have a cup of tea. I doubt anyone will attempt the trip this morning. The wireless has promised no let-up in the snow. I'm just making some Christmas cake."

Lane banged the snow off her boots on the stair and, stepping inside, leaned down to unlace them. She immediately had a face full of Alexandra, the Armstrongs' young West Highland dog, who wriggled excitedly and licked Lane's ear.

"Hello, darling! What do you do in all this snow, eh?" She toed her boots off and picked up the dog, who continued the face-licking campaign. "Gosh, it does smell lovely in here!"

"I haven't started baking yet. I'm on the last stages of

mixing. I bet it's the fruit soaking in brandy that you smell. His nibs is just bringing in some wood."

Lane pulled off her wool tartan jacket and sat in her usual chair, wondering if there was anything more divine than the smell of brandy-soaked raisins in a snug and cheerful cottage on a winter's day. "Maybe I should attempt it?" she said.

"Nonsense. I'm making enough to feed an army. It's shocking that I left it so late. I usually have them soaking away in the pantry by the end of October. It's already gone December 8. I can't think what it will taste like. I don't know what came over me this year. All the excitement of your wedding, I expect. Have you thought of trying to make shortbread?"

"You're so kind not to point out my ghastly deficiencies in the kitchen. Could I manage shortbread, do you think?"

"Certainly, my dear. You just have to remember not to handle it too much. Did you find Lady Armstrong's cookery books in the attic? It'll be in one of those."

Lady Armstrong, who had lived in the house Lane now owned, was Kenny's deceased mother, and it was generally assumed in King's Cove that she still haunted the place. Lane had reason to be relieved that the ghostly Lady Armstrong had the sense not to do her usual trick of opening the attic windows during this bitter cold spell.

"I found one of them. I've been using it to learn the basics. Honestly, I don't think my father ever imagined a world without a cook. My sister and I were brought up to be absolutely useless in the kitchen. It's quite quaint to be sorting out what is meant by a 'gill.' I've just interpreted it as 'some,' and hoped that after I've added 'some' milk to something it ends up the right consistency."

Alexandra jumped off her bed of folded quilt and gave a welcoming bark at the sound of Kenny on the steps.

"I thought I saw you plowing through the snow like a Laplander. What a day!" Kenny dumped the load of split wood into the woodbox, said a few words to Alexandra, and took off his scarf and thick woollen sweater. "I hope the lines don't go down."

As if to prove the system was so far withstanding this heavy onslaught of winter, the Armstrongs' phone rang. Lane was stirring sugar into her tea, thinking of the short-bread biscuits made by her parents' Latvian cook, who had learned to make them to please her English employer when Lane was a child, after her mother had died. They had always made her think of hardtack, or some other impenetrable military biscuit. It was a revelation when she first met real shortbread in England during her Christmas breaks from Oxford.

She came to with a start. It was two longs and a short, her ring pattern on their party line telephone system. "Oh. I think that's mine. Do you mind?"

Kenny waved her through to the sitting room where the instrument sat in splendour on a doily on a side table. The little-used room was about twenty degrees colder than the kitchen.

"KC 431, Lane Winslow speaking."

"Horrors! Can you believe this? I've been here for five winters and I still can't get over it. This is the worst by far!"

"Hello, Angela. Did you get the children off to school?

11

Oh, I can hear you haven't." Angela's three boys all seemed to be shouting at once in the background.

"I tried. Once you get onto the main road it's not quite as bad as long as you have chains. I struggled up the hill to the school and the place was as dark and cold as a grave. I had to bring them all back. On the way down I met Mrs. Laurie from that cottage near the lake and told her not to bother. We both agreed that it was funny that we hadn't been telephoned to say school was closed. Only about six or seven families send their kids there."

"I'm sure you secretly like having the boys around," Lane said, smiling. "Don't they have a new teacher?"

"Oh, yes. Have had for a little more than a week. Miss Scott is off to be married. She's well over thirty. It was about time we got someone younger, though I will say, the boys were terrified of Miss Scott. They never misbehaved with her. I wish I had some of what she has!"

"No, you don't. You don't believe any more than I do that children ought to be terrified into submission. Anyway, they learn, don't they?"

"Well, they can all read, if that's what you mean, and do a little arithmetic. And they do like the new teacher. She seems to be terribly kind."

"There you are, you see."

"I suppose they can learn anything else they need once they're up at the high school. But that's still a few years away. Oop, they're off!" Lane heard a crash and a wail in the background as Angela rang off in a hurry to deal with whatever emergency had arisen.

"The teacher at the Balfour school hasn't turned up

and didn't phone anyone, so Angela's got the boys all day. I know she'd been planning to paint today. From the background row, I don't get the feeling she'll get much done!" Lane sat down and looked gratefully at her cup, which was being refilled by Kenny. Eleanor was up at the counter with an enormous bowl and was stirring the contents with some difficulty.

"I met the new teacher," Kenny said, dropping a bit of toast on the floor for Alexandra. "Miss . . . Miss. Damn. Something to do with the navy. Keeling. That was it. I stopped by Bales's store on Friday to gas up the truck and pick up some things for her majesty here, and Miss Keeling was in there. She was sent out by the government right away, she told me, when Miss Scott announced her plan to marry. In fact, I think she's staying there. At Miss Scott's, I mean. Of course, it's a cottage for the local teacher, so it's not really Miss Scott's. She's not marrying anyone local, and there seems to be some sort of holdup in the wedding proceedings, so they both are staying there for the time being."

"You're a veritable fountain of knowledge. I only sent you to the store to pick up flour and treacle," Eleanor said. By this time, she'd given up trying to mix the fruit with a spoon and was up to her elbows, mixing with her bare hands. "Anyway, I'm happy to hear poor Miss Keeling isn't there on her own. It must have been very lonely for Miss Scott, all that time racketing about in a cottage by herself. Mind you, I don't know how Miss Keeling will be managing that mob of Angela's, and I hear a couple of the other families have rowdy children as well."

"Angela says her boys already like her because she's kind, so they are not complete strangers to finer feelings," Lane said, watching with a sense of deep contentment as Eleanor continued the mysterious process of creating Christmas cake. She was now sifting flour and spices onto a metal tray. Then Lane sat up, her brow furrowed. "I wonder if Angela has tried to phone Miss Scott's place? What if there was some sort of trouble and one of them has had to rush the other to town?"

A quick call to Angela established that she hadn't phoned the teacher's cottage, and that Rafe had fallen and was having a bad scrape attended to, and would Lane mind telephoning for her? Lane put a call through to the exchange, which was situated at the back of Bales's store on the Balfour hill. It was manned by Lucy Prevost, who was on duty and in good form.

"How can I connect you?" Lucy said with pert professionalism. And then, "Is that you, Miss Winslow?"

"Yes. How are you, Lucy? No trouble getting in to work today?"

"Oh, not me! I love a good slog through the snow! Who would you like to speak to?"

Lane could hear in Lucy's voice that she was dying to ask about the honeymoon. Lucy was known to eavesdrop on people's conversations and had followed Lane Winslow almost from the moment she'd arrived, what with the murders and the thrilling romance with Inspector Darling of the Nelson Police. Lane had come to King's Cove to get away from the violence of the war, after a career with the Special Operations Executive in intelligence in London, and almost immediately had come to the notice of the local police when a body was found in her creek. Since then she had applied her considerable skill and knowledge to helping the police with several other murders.

"Please put me through to Miss Scott or Miss Keeling, the teachers," Lane said firmly, not about to indulge the telephonist's worst instincts.

"One moment, please."

After a lengthy pause in which there was absolute silence, Lucy was back on. "Nope. The line is still dead. I'm not surprised, mind you, in this snow."

"What do you mean, 'still dead'? How long has it been down?"

"I don't know. Maybe since Saturday? I know it worked Friday."

Lane rang off and stood thoughtfully for a moment before going back into the bustle and warmth of the Armstrongs' little kitchen. "You know, I wonder if I hadn't better go along and make sure everyone is all right. The phone line seems to be knocked down, and I don't like it that Miss Keeling didn't turn up at the school. I don't know where she's from, and she may not be used to these conditions. She could have run her car into a snowbank or something."

"Should I come with?" offered Kenny.

"No, no. If something is amiss, I can contact people from the store telephone. No point in two of us floundering about in this stuff."

The trip out onto the main road to Nelson was eased somewhat by the fact that both Darling and Kenny Armstrong had left tracks for Lane's little car to travel in, and the main road had become densely packed and quite negotiable with chains. She didn't encounter any real difficulty until she reached the drive down the hill, past Bales's store, to the teacher's cottage, which was a good two hundred yards from the lakeshore on a slight rise. It was clear no one had been on it since this last heavy fall of snow the night before.

She drove slowly down the narrow drive, and as she rounded a small stand of trees, the green cottage came into view. The cottage had an air of having been abandoned, its green paint incongruously cheerful in the almost arctic landscape around it. No smoke from the chimney, no lights, no sign of traffic up and down the steps. It took her a moment to register that there was no car parked next to the house, though there was evidence that one had been there at some prior time. Did Miss Keeling have a car, or did they share the one Miss Scott always drove? Regardless, there had clearly been no traffic to or from the cottage since at least the previous afternoon, if not longer. Undecided about her next move, Lane turned off the engine and sat in the sudden silence, looking at the front door. Why would both teachers go away and not let the parents know there would be no one at the school today? She should go knock, just in case.

The snow came up over the tops of her boots, and she could feel it settling down inside them. The soft pitted mounds of new snow on the porch indicated there'd been a good deal of coming and going on the porch before the snowfall. She knocked on the door, calling out, "Miss Scott? Miss Keeling?"

She looked around and down toward the lake. Neighbours were far enough away, across fields and stands of trees, that they were barely visible. They would certainly not hear if anyone were in distress. Almost as an afterthought, Lane turned the doorknob as she was about to go back down to her car. The door creaked open as if it had been expecting her. She knocked again, looking into the darkness through the crack she had opened.

"Hello? Miss Scott? Is anyone here?" Hearing nothing, she pushed the door open, and even in the murky light sifting through the closed curtains, she could see that things were very much amiss. Books had been thrown to the floor, a chair knocked on its side, and a small wooden table overturned, broken crockery on the floor where it had slipped off in the melee. It was at that moment that she heard a faint and agonized groan.

CHAPTER THREE

"**H**ELLO?" **LANE CRIED IN ALARM.** She pulled the curtains back so that she could see better, saw no one in the shambles of the sitting room, and rushed to what she assumed was a bedroom door. She pushed it open. The bed was made, a clean chamber pot visible under it, and the room was empty and appeared undisturbed. She had no time to register what this might mean. Pushing open the next door, she saw with horror that a woman was on the floor, lying partway under a quilt she had evidently pulled off the bed.

"Miss Scott!" Lane stooped down and put her hand on the woman's shoulder. "What happened? Where are you hurt?"

Miss Scott's eyes fluttered momentarily, but she could not seem to open them. She made a sound like attempted speech, and then lay still, wheezing, her breath coming with difficulty.

Lane looked frantically around the bedroom, which she

saw had also been knocked about, and pulled a folded blanket from the floor where it had fallen, adding it to the quilt around Miss Scott. It was clear the teacher could not get up. With infinite delicacy Lane lifted the woman's head and positioned a pillow under it. The side of Miss Scott's head felt ominously sticky. With a lurch of anxiety, Lane saw there were smears of dark blood on her hand.

"There. I'm going to phone for an ambulance, Miss Scott, and I will try to make something hot for you to drink." Lane was reluctant to leave her, even for a moment. "I'm just going into the kitchen to telephone and see about that drink," she said again, trying for a tone of efficiency and confidence she was far from feeling. Propping the bedroom door open, so that Miss Scott would know she was nearby, Lane looked around the battered sitting room. There was a small wooden desk in the corner. The phone had been knocked onto the floor. She restored it to the desk and then lifted the receiver and clicked several times. It was dead, just as Lucy had said.

Swearing under her breath, Lane pulled at the cord. It came away in her hand, dangling uselessly where it had clearly been pulled violently from the wall. She leaned back against the desk, her hand over her mouth, beginning to take in the enormity of the situation. It looked very much as though Miss Scott had been attacked. She had to get her to the hospital. Could she get her up on her own and down to the car? She tried to imagine negotiating those slippery front steps with the dead weight of a woman unable to move. She went out onto the porch and looked about. Which neighbour was closest? She could see smoke rising above the stand of trees just to the south. Someone was home there, at least, and she could but pray that they would be on the telephone. She had a momentary panic at the prospect of finding the neighbour had no phone and having to drive from house to house till she found one. Why wasn't every house on the telephone? It was 1947, for God's sake! She could drive up to Bales's store, but that would take a good fifteen minutes there and back in these conditions.

Back inside she saw that the house was equipped only with the wood cooking stove so common among the houses up and down the lake. It would take ages to light it and get a kettle to boil. She rinsed her hands and found a glass in the cupboard above the sink and ran some water into it. A quick glance through the cupboards revealed no brandy.

Relieved to find Miss Scott still breathing, she said gently, "Try to drink a little water, Miss Scott."

The eyes fluttered again, and a slight movement of the head suggested the woman was trying to lift it. Lane tucked her hand underneath the pillow and gently raised Miss Scott's head to an angle where she might take a sip without choking. Miss Scott swallowed desperately in tiny gulps until water ran down her chin. Lane put the glass down and wiped her chin with the edge of the quilt.

"Your phone is down. I'm going to have to go to your neighbour to phone for an ambulance. The people on the other side of the trees, do they have a telephone? Can you nod or shake your head?"

Miss Scott's eyes moved under her closed lids, and Lane thought she could see the imperceptible movement of the head signifying, what? Yes? No?

"They do have a phone?" Lane tried again, nearly in despair. But instead of another attempt, Miss Scott's head turned heavily sideways and lay still.

With horror, Lane said the teacher's name and put her fingers to her neck. She can't have died, Lane thought desperately, she just can't. She focused on her fingers and felt a wave of relief. There was a faint thrumming. She had passed out.

How long would it take for Lane to drive next door, perhaps only to find there was no telephone? Miss Scott was not a large woman. She was relatively short and quite slender. Could Lane lift her?

She flew outside, found a shovel half buried and leaning against the wall by the porch, and hurriedly scraped the snow off the steps. Then she got into the car and drove it as close to the house as she could.

She could not imagine how she managed it, as she turned the engine on and set the heat up to high. Especially with her own recent injury, a bullet-grazed rib that objected strenuously to the bending and heaving required to get Miss Scott into the car. The ache was a reminder of the day she'd been shot by a bad-tempered killer while on her honeymoon in Arizona just the month before. Was there someone equally lethal watching her move Miss Scott to the hospital? Trying to still her anxiety, she backed carefully away from the house and onto the drive up to the main road with Miss Scott, wrapped in the quilt and blanket, laid out on the back seat with the pillow under her head. She prayed the teacher would

21

not die. It had been plain from the condition of her clothes that she had lain for at least a day and night, maybe longer, abandoned in the near freezing cold of the unheated cottage.

What had happened in there? She saw again the over-turned sitting room, the bedroom ransacked. It must have been a robbery. Such a situation was almost unthinkable. A violent robbery like that, the householder left for dead. There had been murders in the area, to be sure, usually stemming from some personal history of the individuals involved, but they, on the whole, did not present a threat to the population in general. A random robbery and attack would raise fear and anxiety in everybody. She'd been in the area under two years herself, but no one had ever mentioned a violent attack on a householder during the course of a robbery, including her police inspector husband.

She glanced at the rear-view mirror. The bundle that was Miss Scott still lay securely on the back seat. Then the real anomaly hit her. Why was the second bedroom completely untouched? It didn't make sense. Someone breaking into the house, pulling out the phone line, knocking out the woman—if that was what happened, they would mean business. They would ransack the whole house, not leave one bedroom untouched. Had they been scared off by something? But no. Of course not. Anyone scaring them off would have rescued poor Miss Scott.

She was frustrated, after an agonizingly slow drive of nearly an hour, to find that the ferry into town was just pulling up to the opposite side of the lake. It would have to unload cars going into town, load up cars coming out. "Damn!" she said aloud. She turned off the engine and jumped out of the car to open the rear door and check on her patient. She could still hear the faint hiss of her stertorous breathing. A truck pulled up behind her. The driver was smoking a cigarette, filling his cabin with smoke. Lane gave him a wave and got back into the car.

"We'll be there in no time, Miss Scott. We'll soon have you right as rain." She wanted to add, "Then you can tell us what happened," but in the event that somehow Miss Scott could hear and understand what she was saying, she didn't want her alarmed just at the moment by what must be a horrible memory.

Finally, the ferry docked with a loud clanking of chains and the metal ramp being let down. Even the short trip across the lake seemed interminable. Lane made her way along Nelson Street as quickly as she dared, and up the long, curved drive to the hospital emergency entrance. She ignored the man who told her she couldn't park there, that it was for emergencies only, and ran into the hospital. She explained what she could about the condition of Miss Scott and watched, relieved by the cleanliness and efficiency of it all, as a gurney was rushed out, and Miss Scott was rushed in, disappearing with her medical entourage through the green double doors to help.

"I'll just get my car out of the way and come back," Lane said, when the receptionist asked her to help with the paperwork. And when she'd done what she could of the paperwork, she decided to head straight to the police station. Darling had been complaining that things were rather dull at the moment.

O'BRIEN, THE DESK sergeant, looked up when Lane came in, kicking snow off her boots. "Good morning, Mrs. Darling. Come to report a crime, have you?" Not for O'Brien any newfangled notion of a wife keeping her maiden name. He smiled genially, and then realized that she looked troubled. "Shall I call the inspector, or will you go up?"

"Thanks, Sergeant O'Brien. I'll go up, if that's all right. I think I have come about a crime."

O'Brien peeled himself off his usual stool and gallantly opened the gate for her. "Upstairs to your right," he said unnecessarily. Before Lane had become the wife of Inspector Darling, she'd had a number of occasions to make the same trip over various cases she'd been able to help the police with, including one that had entailed her spending two nights in the jail cell herself.

He watched her go up the steps and shook his head. She really was the most beautiful woman. Waving auburn hair and hazel-green eyes, and a kind of vitality he suspected she'd never lose, if she lived to be a hundred. Then he harrumphed back onto his stool, but not before winking at Constable Terrell, who was occupying his corner desk, writing a report. "She's at it again," was all O'Brien said, and then he pulled the newspaper out from under the file he kept handy to make himself look busy.

Lane found both Sergeant Ames and Inspector Darling in Darling's office, conferring over a document that lay between them on the desk. Ames leaped up at her knock, smiling happily. "Mrs. . . . Miss Winslow. Good morning!" He consulted his watch. "It's just gone afternoon. Good afternoon!"

Darling rolled his eyes. Ames was an absolute slave to his wife. He wondered if Ames would ever get over his eager-puppy reaction whenever he saw her. He too rose and said, "Ames was just leaving. Do sit down."

Ames picked up the document and waved it cheerfully. "I was, actually. Just leaving, I mean." With what could almost be a slight bow, Ames left them.

"You know, you shouldn't come round getting him all riled up like that. It'll take all afternoon for him to settle back to work." Darling waved at the empty chair and sat down himself, an expression of concern settling on his face. "Why on earth have you driven all the way to town in this? Not that I'm not ecstatic to see you. It's been all lost dogs around here."

Lane sat, putting her handbag on the floor beside her. "I'm sorry, darling. Something has rather happened."

"Rather happened? By the expression on your face, I'd have said it was worse than that. I do so hope you've not come to tell me someone has turned up dead."

"Not quite dead, no. It's Miss Scott, the retiring teacher from the Balfour school. I went down to the teacher's cottage to see if everything was all right—no one turned up to teach today, you see—and I found Miss Scott collapsed on the floor, the cottage ransacked, and, oh, of course, Miss Keeling, the new teacher, gone, or at least not there. There was no car, and I'm pretty sure Miss Scott had a car. Now, I wonder if Miss Keeling went for help?" Lane shook her head, realizing at once that the lack of tracks or footsteps in the new snow made that less likely. Then where was Miss Keeling? "Anyway, I managed to get her to the hospital here because their phone line had been cut, and she'd passed out and I didn't think there would be time for me to be running around looking for someone with a phone to get an ambulance up the lake." Lane knew she was sounding a little garbled. "I'm sorry. I'm speaking in a jumble. I am quite flustered about poor Miss Scott. I do hope she'll be all right."

"It's hard to believe that such a beautiful woman could be such a harbinger of misfortune." Darling sighed. He got up and went to the door. "Ames, get in here. And bring a chair. And your notebook." He sat and looked at his wife, his head tilted. He said, almost to himself, "What an appalling thing to happen. Poor Miss Scott." He shook his head. "You know, you are fulfilling every exaggerated complaint I make. First, you are producing a serious crime just as lunchtime is approaching, destroying one of the bright spots of the day, and you're here about a nearly dead person. With your track record, the poor woman has probably died on the operating table by now."

"Don't be silly, darling. Ah. Here's Sergeant Ames." She moved her chair over to make room for Ames.

"Now then, start at the beginning, slowly," said Darling.

Lane went over the events of the morning, slowing down from time to time to try to remember every detail of the cottage. "I don't know how long she had to lie alone in that cold room. It must have been absolute torture if she was conscious the whole time. Now let me think. There was a suitcase on the floor. I didn't really make note of it at the time, but I remember it now, because it was lying open near Miss Scott's feet. It had clearly been packed, because clothing was sort of falling out of it. I couldn't say if it just fell off something and snapped open or someone went through it. She was leaving to get married, I think."

"And you are certain there was no one else in the house. Miss—what is the other one's name?—passed out in another room?"

"It's a tiny cottage with a sitting room, a small kitchen and two bedrooms, and a minute bathroom. I was in every room, including the bathroom to get a washcloth. Unless Miss Keeling is lying under the snow somewhere outside, there was only poor Miss Scott there."

Darling picked up the telephone receiver when it appeared that Lane had relayed all she could remember. "O'Brien, put the paper away and send Terrell up here."

Having dispatched Ames to get the car ready and Terrell to the hospital to check on the condition of Miss Scott, and interview her if possible, Darling turned to Lane.

"I had been planning to come home this afternoon. Thanks to you I may have to work late into the night. Well done." He stood up and came around the desk to kiss her.

"I know, darling. I'm sorry. I heard on the wireless there's another big snowfall coming by late this afternoon. You might not have made it home anyway."

Darling took his hat and coat off the rack. "Very comforting. I was joking about being bored, by the way. There was no need to arrange any special crime for me. We might even have had time for a lunch at Lorenzo's. And you're staying out of this one!" He leaned over and kissed her again. "If there's going to be more snow, you'd better get home yourself. I'll phone later."

"Righty-ho," Lane said, both to the strict instruction to stay out of it and to the instruction to get home. She'd stop at the supermarket on the way out of town and pick up something nice for when he did get home.

CHAPTER FOUR

Wednesday, December 3

"**M**iss K, what's this word here?" Wendy Keeling turned away from Gabriella and looked at the back of the room where the two boys in grade five sat. Randy had his head tilted and was watching her expectantly and impatiently.

"You must call me by my full name, Randy. Miss Keeling. And put up your hand if you have a question."

"But you weren't looking back here, and my arm would have fallen off waiting." He looked around at the gratifying giggles of his classmates.

"Now then, what word? Did you know it, Samuel?"

The boy she addressed, who had been reading with Randy, shook his head. They were such a contrast, she thought. Randy, loud, confident, abrasive, but curious, and Samuel, painfully shy and almost unable to look anyone in the eye. She wondered about his family life. She was sure she'd seen a faint bruise on his cheek. But if there was a puzzling word, she'd expect Samuel to be the one to know it.

Randy pointed at the word.

"I bet I would know it!" One of the Bertolli boys called this out from where he sat, leaning on the back of his seat, watching the proceedings at the back of the room.

"Thank you, Rolfie. Turn around, if you please. I expect that sheet of arithmetic to be done when I am finished here." She turned back to the word in question. "Do you think you could figure it out by what is written around it? Read me the whole sentence."

By three thirty Wendy Keeling was making sure the children were bundled up and ready to leave. Mrs. Bertolli was standing at the driver's-side door of her panelled station wagon with one foot inside the car, waiting for her boys. She waved cheerfully, and Miss Keeling waved back, almost relieved by the reduction in noise and motion of the three Bertolli boys all leaving at once. They were lively and energetic, but, she reflected, they enjoyed school and seemed almost excited about learning. Though she suspected their mother of being indulgent, she knew their father was a composer who taught music at the school in town. The whole family seemed kind, energetic, and creative. The old saying, which annoyed her in its simplicity, nevertheless held here: The apple doesn't fall far from the tree. She firmly did not think about what it meant about the fractured tree she'd fallen from.

The cars had gone, and the children who usually walked to their nearby homes down the hill near the lake had disappeared around the bend of the curved road. She turned back inside to begin planning for the next day. The wood in the stove was burnt down to glowing coals, so she might just get an hour's work in before the stove went cold.

She nearly jumped out of her skin when, instead of a schoolroom blissfully free of children, she saw Samuel, still at his desk, apparently reading. "Goodness, Samuel, what are you still doing here? Don't you usually walk home with Gabriella?" She realized that she'd seen Gabriella marching off down the hill on her own.

Samuel put his finger on the spot where he'd stopped reading. "My mom is away," he said.

"Oh. But your dad is home, isn't he?"

"He doesn't come home till after it's dark."

Miss Keeling frowned. "Ah, you have to be home on your own, is that the trouble?"

Samuel shrugged and pretended to read again.

"Where has your mother gone?"

"I don't know. She just left. It was after when my birthday was."

After his birthday? If she remembered the student card, Samuel's birthday was in late September. She tried to remember. Had Rose Scott told her about this? She would ask when she got home.

"I see." Wendy Keeling swallowed and pushed away an uprush of memory, surprised by the strength of feeling it engendered. Her mother leaving was not necessarily the same thing as Samuel's mother leaving, she reminded herself. She squatted down and looked at him.

"I have to do about an hour's work, and then, if you like, I will take you home. I could talk to your father to see if we could arrange for you to go home with another student and stay there until he comes home every day."

Samuel stood up and shook his head violently. "It's okay, miss. My father wouldn't like that. I'll just go home now." He closed the book and pushed it into his desk and strode to the kitchen area with the wooden coat pegs and took his coat. It was threadbare and too short for him.

Wendy Keeling stood and watched him. "I'm happy to take you there." She looked back at the stove, the warmth of which she would be sorry to walk away from. "Come. I'll drive you down." She could just as well do her work at home. Miss Scott would understand. She must have faced situations like this more than once during her tenure.

Samuel stood at the door and looked back at her. "I can go by myself." Then he was out the door, closing it loudly.

The teacher could hear him going down the steps. Something made him afraid. She walked to the window, watching him walking in his heavy, rough boots along the tracks left by the cars of the other parents. She wondered if she should insist, but she could hardly wrangle a reluctant boy into her car, and he'd made the trip countless times, no doubt many of them on his own. She realized that it was not his physical safety she was thinking of but his emotional state.

She went back to sit at the teacher desk at the front of the room and took up the reader to begin looking at what could be done for the next day's lessons. She opened the book and her eyes filled with tears. She set the book on the desk and stared unseeing through blurry eyes at the title of the chapter.

How could she meet the sadness or loss of this child, or indeed any other she was to confront in her career? She was scarcely able to deal with her own sense of abandonment, and worse now, this sudden return of constant fear.

———

Vancouver, September 1932

WENDY IRVING, A grade-three student at Seymour Elementary School, climbed up the steps of her house, happy because the sun was shining still, and it was warm enough to take off her sweater. It was as she was undoing the buttons that she realized she had left her metal lunch box at school. She stopped in front of the door and looked back down the street toward the school, holding her green sweater so that most of it was on the ground. Should she go back? Her mother would be mad. She threw her sweater into the corner of the porch and was about to turn and run back when the front door opened and her father stood looking at her. She could smell the smoke of his cigarettes wafting out from inside the house.

"Where do you think you're going?"

She stopped and looked anxiously at her father, who seemed murky in the darkness of the house. "I forgot my lunch box. I was going—"

But her father pushed the screen open. "Get in here."

Once she was inside, she tried to understand why her father was still in his pyjamas and bathrobe and why the house was dark when it was so nice outside. The cord of his robe had slipped most of the way through the loops and one side was dragging across the floor. Later she would remember that she felt a kind of silence in the house, as if some force she couldn't define had left it.

She followed her father into the kitchen, thinking her mother would be there, as she always was. He stood by the sink and lit a cigarette, tossing the match into the sink, where it hissed briefly.

"Your mother's gone."

"Did she go to visit Grandpa?" Why was her father still in his pyjamas?

"Don't ask stupid questions! She's not coming back. She won't be here to make your breakfast and lunch and whatever the hell else she did. You're going to have to pull your own weight."

Wendy watched her father fearfully. She tried to imagine what "pulling her own weight" meant. He was usually busy and was never home to put her to bed and didn't like to read to her, but she had never seen him like this.

That night, Wendy held her worn teddy bear and prayed in the darkness. She whispered urgently to the bear that he should too, because he used to be her mother's bear, and he might have prayers that would work better.

The first phone call came in mid-October. Her father wasn't home. It was the school principal.

"Is this Wendy? Is your father there, please?"

"No. He . . . he's not back yet."

"Do you know what time he gets home? Is he at work?"

"I think so. He always comes home later." There was a silence at the other end of the line. Wendy's heart was pumping so that she could feel it in her chest.

34

"It's six thirty now. Can I speak to—is there someone else I can talk to? Who is looking after you until he gets home?"

"Nobody has to look after me. I can do everything," Wendy said with a touch of anxious defiance.

There was sigh. "You tell him, please, that he has to phone me at the school or, better yet, come in. Do you understand?"

"Yes." Wendy waited to hear if he'd say something else, but she heard only the click of the receiver being put down on the other end.

"THIS IS BULL. We're going to go live with my brother. He's got a wife and kids. She can at least look after you, since you can't seem to manage yourself. You know why I got called? They said you were dirty and your clothes weren't ironed."

Wendy sat on the worn mauve couch in the living room and looked at the floor. She didn't know what to say. She didn't know how to iron.

"Can I take my bear?"

"You take whatever you can carry. I'm not carrying nothing of yours."

The train journey took almost two days. Wendy slept under her coat on the seat beside her father, who slept sitting up, his head wedged by the window. They ate most of the food that he had brought in a cloth bag. A loaf of bread, some apples, and there was also a can of meat, but he didn't open it. He talked very little, not even to say, "We're here," when they pulled into the station at Williams Lake. He simply got up and yanked her suitcase off the rack above their heads and dumped it on the seat beside her, then took his bag and pushed open the door of the compartment. When they stood on the road outside the station, he finally spoke. "He's not here, just like I thought."

Wendy stood next to him and tried to see where the town was, but she only saw a few houses. She could hear what she thought was water somewhere. It was already getting dark. She put her suitcase down, put the bear on top of it, and buttoned herself into her coat. Her socks had fallen down to her ankles and she could feel the cold air on her legs.

A black truck pulled up and a man wearing a thick green tartan jacket and a black hat with earflaps opened the window, waving. "You made it, then. We'd best get on. It's an hour on the road and my headlamps don't work."

Wendy's father slung both bags into the back of the truck resting against the cab and then lifted her up and put her on the bags. He got into the passenger side and closed the door. She heard her uncle say, "She'll be cold back there." She didn't hear her father's reply because the truck started and bumped along the road away from the station. They never went through any town that she could see. Just some houses and a store with a gas pump. There was a man on the porch smoking, watching them go by. He threw his cigarette butt onto the ground and shook his head and went into the store. She could see the light spilling out the door and then disappearing when he closed it.

She cowered back into the corner and pulled up her socks, and then pulled her yellow dress as far as it would go down over her legs. Her hair flew as if there were wind coming from all directions. She wanted to brush it away from her face where it was whipping into her eyes, but she didn't want to take her hands out of her coat sleeves where she had shoved them to keep warm.

Every bump on the road seemed to elevate her off the suitcase she sat on. She began to imagine she was Ali Baba, flying on a magic carpet, in the dark, with the wind blowing her hair. He would be able to see the earth below him, so she closed her eyes and imagined they were flying over a big city.

When they stopped finally, after a climbing and winding drive, Wendy sat still and waited. Her father and uncle got out of the truck at the same time and her father came around to the back.

"Get up," he said. He waited till she was on her feet and reached for their two bags and started for the house. Wendy, stiff from the cold, leaned down and picked up the bear where it had dropped. The screen door of the house opened and a woman came out.

"Is that the girl?" she said. "Poor mite. Looks like she's frozen to death."

"She's fine," her uncle said. "Tend to her."

Wendy felt herself lifted out of the truck and put on the ground.

"You look like you could use a meal," the woman said, leading her inside. The door opened directly into a kitchen. Wendy could immediately feel the heat of the stove. A black and tan dog struggled up from a tattered rug and looked at her, wagging his tail tentatively, and then sat on his haunches as if the effort had been too much.

"He's old," the woman said. She unbuttoned Wendy's coat and pushed her into a chair on the end of the table nearest the stove. "The two little ones have already gone to bed," she added, as if Wendy had asked after them. "You don't talk much, do you?"

Wendy managed to mutter a thanks when a bowl of dark soup and a piece of bread were placed before her. Looking surreptitiously across the table to see if there was butter, and seeing none, Wendy picked up the bread and bit a piece off. It was soft and fresh, reminding her how hungry she was. She and her father had run out of the bread and fruit he'd brought that morning.

The woman left the room with a tray of the same meal and Wendy could hear the voices of her father and uncle talking in another room somewhere. She looked around the kitchen. It's dark light, she thought. There was some sort of lamp hanging on the wall by the door and another sat on top of some shelves where dishes were piled. Everything in the kitchen lay in a kind of murky golden shadow. She tried the soup. It tasted strange, but she decided it was good, and began to lap it up quickly, slurping it off the big spoon she had been given.

She was about to say something to the dog when the door opened and the woman came back and looked at Wendy's bowl. "You don't turn your nose up at good food, anyhow. I made up a bed for you with the children. I'll show you what to do tomorrow. Can you read any?"

Wendy stood up to follow the woman, taking the teddy bear under her arm. She loved reading. She always took lots of books out of the library at school. "I read lots of books. Are you my aunt?"

"So, you do talk! I thought you were some sort of mute. Aunt Hilda. And you won't be having that thing with you. You'll have the Lord with you." To Wendy's dismay, her aunt reached out and took her bear and tucked it under her own arm. In the dark, after the door to the bedroom had been shut, Wendy lay on the mattress on the floor, the blankets pulled tight against her with both her hands. She could hear one of the children snuffling in a crib nearby. What had Aunt Hilda meant by showing her what to do tomorrow?

CHAPTER FIVE

———

"A NYBODY COULD DO ANYTHING OUT here," Ames said. "There's not a single neighbour near enough to hear if there's trouble." He'd always been a little mystified at people living so far from town, especially at this time of year. The weather had turned sunny and very cold, freezing the surface layer of snow. Dark clouds were beginning to bank over the mountains on the south side of the lake. The promised new snowfall had not yet begun. Inspector Darling and Ames had crunched down along the narrow road to the teacher's cottage in the maroon police car and stopped about fifteen feet from the house. Darling had suggested this as they might be better positioned to see who had come and gone from in front of the house, but it was clear that whatever might have been visible had been obliterated by Lane's car, which had pulled up in front of the house and then backed up and driven close to the door, leaving a complex pattern of tracks. She had said that it looked by the snowed-over indentations as though there had been activity before the snowfall. They could still see traces of these. There had evidently been a car parked at the side of the house up against a chicken-wire fence, but it was impossible to say when it had last been there because of the overlay of snow.

"Another remarkable observation, Ames. Bring the camera. We can take some shots of the inside. It's apparently been turned over." Darling went up the stairs carefully, sliding each foot back and forth a little to check the grip of his shoes. The steps Lane had cleared and walked on had become icy. He pushed the door open and looked into the chaos, waiting to go in until Ames arrived with the camera.

"Quite a mess. Were they looking for something, or just wanting to upset whoever was here?" Ames asked. A sudden shot of sunshine exposed by the passing of a cloud made the house momentarily less murky than Lane had found it, but Ames thought he might still need a bulb. He fit one into the camera and took a shot of the sitting room. The room exploded in light, crystallizing, Darling thought, the energy, or was it rage, that had gone into creating this havoc.

"Books are pulled out of the shelf, cupboards opened. That suggests searching," observed Darling. "But the table is overturned; whatever dishes were on it are smashed. That looks more vengeful, or an attempt to frighten whoever was here." He could imagine someone in a fury, demanding to know where something was hidden, while one woman, or two, if the missing Miss Keeling had been here as well, cowered by the bedroom door. "Miss Keeling is gone, and the car as well," he said. Had the two teachers had

41

an argument that had gone terribly wrong? Ames took another photograph of the kitchen area and then moved to the bedroom. "This must be where Miss Winslow found her," Darling said, standing cautiously by the bedclothes that trailed onto the floor. "She said she was lying on the floor next to the bed. She'd been conscious enough at some point to pull at the bedspread and cover herself with it. The bedspread isn't here. Lane must have wrapped her in it for the trip to the hospital." Darling eyed the dresser. Drawers had been pulled out and upended and clothes lay everywhere. The suitcase Lane had described was there, open, clothes and a pair of shoes tumbled about. "It really looks as though it was a search of some kind. What could two not-at-all-wealthy country teachers have that someone would want?"

"Not a very luxurious life, that's for sure. I saw an outdoor privy. They have a plumbed sink and tub in the bathroom. You'd think whoever built it would have finished the job. It must be miserable in weather like this." Ames held his camera down by his side and shook his head, as if he thought it a shame to capture any more of the sad shabbiness of this life.

Stepping over some scribblers that had cascaded across the floor, as if the teacher had been doing her marking sitting up in bed when she was surprised by the intruder, Darling left the room and went to the second bedroom. "Here's a puzzle for you: look at this room."

Ames walked to where Darling was standing in an open doorway and glanced at him, and then at the room. Darling wore an expression Ames was used to, the space between his eyebrows slightly furrowed, thoughtful, serious. He conveyed a concern for the principals in whatever case they were working on, even before he knew who they were. His inspector face. Ames had seen Darling once, smiling at something his wife had said, and had realized at that moment that there was a side to his boss he wouldn't have believed possible: Darling relaxed, given to an easy smile, his innate kindness not buried as it usually was but given full rein. A Darling, he thought fancifully, made possible by Miss Winslow. But he appreciated the worry his boss took into every investigation, the concern about who was being hurt by the situation, who could not be saved, whether there would be justice in the end. He'd never been the type of man who reached the end of a case and shut the book with satisfaction and said, "Well, that's done. Let's go for a drink." Ames suspected Darling ruminated long after a case closed about whether he'd done enough.

"The whole thing is a puzzle at the moment, sir, but I take your point. I'll take a picture just to show the contrast."

"You anticipate my every need. What's it about, then? Does whoever it is find what they are looking for in Miss Scott's room and not need to go any further? It really looks like Miss Keeling, assuming this is where she slept, has gotten up, dressed, made the bed, packed up whatever she had, and left. Where was she off to, then, and did she leave before any of this happened?"

Ames chewed his bottom lip and shook his head. "Or," he suggested, "the intruder panics and hits Miss Scott on the head and, realizing what he's done, runs off. That doesn't tell us about Miss Keeling, though." Darling conceded the point with a nod and a shrug.

"We'd better hope Miss Scott is up to a conversation soon. I'm uneasy about this Miss Keeling. What do we know about her? Has she done this and made off with, say, a roll of money Miss Scott kept in a tea tin somewhere?"

"If Miss Keeling was living here with her, wouldn't she know where she kept things like that? Why would she need to turn the house upside down?"

"Because, Ames, people typically don't tell people they don't know very well where they are keeping their money hidden. My understanding is that Miss Scott was about to leave to get married—hence the suitcase—and Miss Keeling had arrived inside the last week or so to take up her post." Darling moved through the untouched room. There was no wardrobe. A wire had been strung between two nails to serve as a closet, and one lightweight summer dress hung on it. Otherwise there were four empty wire hangers, two of which lay on the floor, as if clothes had been hastily yanked off them. The chest of drawers by the bed yielded one drawer with school supplies: some pencils, a packet of pen holders, a box of nibs, two bottles of ink, and some new exercise books. The only clothing was a pair of socks and a pair of blue wool pants. Where were the rest of Miss Keeling's effects? The room was certainly suggestive of a hasty removal. He imagined a frantic Miss Keeling hurling things into a bag, leaving things behind in her hurry. Fleeing?

"It sure looks like she left in a hurry," Ames said, giving voice to Darling's thoughts. "If that doesn't look like guilt,

I don't know what does. Was she here long enough to get to know someone here, or did some bad actor she knew from before come to help her rob the cottage?"

Darling shook his head. "This, and many more things to be found out. That school is up past Bales's store at the top of the road. They'd buy some of their food there, presumably." He made his way to the kitchen. There was a small GE fridge that looked at least twenty years old. The icing unit was on top of the refrigerator.

"We had one of these when I was really little," Ames said. "It set my father back quite a bit of money. I guess whoever furnished this cottage picked it up at a junk shop for a song." He opened it. "Half bottle of milk, plate of margarine, some carrots, the nub end of some sort of dried-out pot roast. That's not going to last past one meal." On the counter there was a bowl of eggs, a new tin of cocoa, and a small bag of flour that looked to have been cut open and then sent flying so that flour was spread across the counter, onto the floor, and into the sink. A similar treatment had been meted to a bowl of sugar, which now lay on its side, its contents having been flung across the counter and onto the floor, where it now crunched underfoot. Ames lifted the lid of a green metal breadbox and discovered a heel of brown bread that was beginning to curl. The floor of the kitchen revealed that the cupboards had been opened and swept clean of their contents. A smashed jar of marmalade, a box of crackers, a box of salt, a metal tin of bicarbonate of soda, and several tins of vegetables and corned beef lay scattered on counter and floor. A drawer containing cutlery had not been turned out, but merely disordered, as if whoever it was had picked up the few knives, forks, and spoons and thrown them back into the drawer willy-nilly.

MEANWHILE, TERRELL WAS having almost as much difficulty getting information as Ames and Darling were. The woman at the front desk at the hospital had shown great reluctance to accept Terrell's bona fides. She clearly had never encountered a Black police officer before, or indeed, any person much different from herself.

"I see," she'd said. "What is it you want, again?"

"I have to learn about the condition of a Miss Rose Scott, who was brought in here earlier today, or even better, actually talk to her to find out what happened to her."

The receptionist picked up Terrell's warrant card and looked at it again. "I will have to speak to your supervisor."

"I beg your pardon? My supervisor? My supervisor is out at the scene trying to understand how Miss Scott was attacked. Could we perhaps start with *your* supervisor?" Terrell kept his voice pleasant with some effort. The situation was resolved when a doctor strolled through the swinging doors, an unlit cigarette in his mouth and his hands in the pockets of his white coat. He sensed the contretemps at the desk.

"Is there a problem, Miss Saunders?"

"This gentleman claims to be from the police and wishes information about one of our patients," Miss Saunders said reprovingly, casting a poisonous glance at Terrell, and handing over the warrant card.

"Right," the doctor said. He looked at the card and

offered Terrell his hand. "Constable Terrell, is it? I'm Dr. Arnold. How can I help?"

Relieved to be in the hands of someone competent, Terrell explained his mission again.

"Oh, yes. I saw that case come in. She's been moved to a room in our intensive unit upstairs. Dr. Edison is looking after her. Quite a bad bang on the head. Thank you, Miss Saunders!" he finished brightly, indicating Terrell should follow him through the doors.

Once into the inner hallway, Dr. Arnold smiled in a confiding manner at Terrell. "You'll find Dr. Edison an absolute force of nature. We're all quite terrified of her." He winked. "Here we are."

Dr. Edison sat at a desk in an upstairs ward, apparently making notes. She stood up, sighing, and looked with interest at Constable Terrell. She was very tall, fair hair pulled into a chignon, and had an angular, serious face. She looked to be in her late thirties.

"This gentleman is Constable Terrell from the police, and he is wanting to find out what we know about your patient." Dr. Arnold smiled at Terrell, shook his hand again, and said, "I'll leave you with the squadron leader, then? I'm off to the mess hall. Missed my lunch."

"Constable," she said by way of greeting. "I can tell you more or less what's wrong with her, but not how she got that way." Dr. Edison was tall enough to look at him directly, and he sensed a kind of no-nonsense power about her.

"Anything would be better than what we have now," he said.

"Where was she brought from?" Edison asked. "She suffered from exposure apart from anything else."

"A cottage up the lake, close to Balfour. She was found by a woman from King's Cove who had gone to where the teachers are billeted to find out why no one had turned up at the school this morning. It's not clear how long she'd been lying there, but the cottage was sacked and had no heat. Could have been there the whole weekend, I suppose."

"That would explain it. Well, I can tell you she was hit on the rear right side of her head, the occipital area, just here." Edison pointed to the back of her own head. "The blow itself was not terrible. She could have just been knocked over, say, but she also suffered a stroke, possibly as a result of the shock, or some internal trauma because of the blow. Or she had the stroke first and fell, banging her head. She's been in and out of consciousness, I'm afraid, and I don't know what she remembers, if anything. You might not get much out of her. It's a good job she was found when she was. Wouldn't have lasted another day."

"A stroke? A woman as young as that?"

"Strokes are not confined to the elderly. She might have had some underlying condition, a weak heart. These are not always detectable and, as you point out, are rarely anticipated in a woman in her late thirties."

"I see. Do you think I might have a word?"

"If she is awake, yes, but only a brief one. I expect she's a little confused. Just along here."

Dr. Edison led him down the hall and into a mostly darkened room. She leaned over and said very gently, "Miss Scott? Are you awake?"

The patient stirred slightly and opened her eyes very slowly.

"Miss Scott, might you be well enough to have a word with Constable Terrell here? He'd just like to know what happened."

Miss Scott closed her eyes and lay still, as if she had gone off to sleep again. Then she opened them and turned her head marginally in the direction of Edison and Terrell. "A constable? Is something wrong?"

Terrell sat next to the bed so that he wouldn't loom over her and addressed her very gently. "Miss Scott. I'm Constable Terrell. You've been brought into hospital. Do you remember what happened to you?"

Miss Scott smiled and shook her head very slightly. "Happened to me? No, no, nothing has happened. The children are all well. You needn't have come out all this way."

Terrell glanced at Dr. Edison, and then turned back to Miss Scott. "It was no trouble at all. You look very tired. I'll come back another time, shall I?"

Miss Scott looked at him and cocked her head, smiling again. "You're so like my brother, so kind. I am a little tired, so I'll turn in. So kind." She closed her eyes, and this time did go into a deep sleep.

"It's as if in her mind she's at home and has gone to the bedroom to rest. She seems to have very little consciousness of where she is, or that anything has happened to her," Terrell said.

Dr. Edison nodded. "I'll give the station a call tomorrow if she seems in better shape. She may not be all that befuddled when she's had a rest and the medications settle down."

Terrell stood up, looked at Miss Scott again, and went into the hall with the doctor.

"Can you find your way out?" she asked.

Terrell smiled and touched the rim of his hat. He turned to leave and then turned back. "Squadron leader?" he asked.

"I ran a medical unit in the air force during the recent show. I'm afraid Dr. Arnold can't get past his fascination with the idea of a woman doctor."

"I know exactly what you mean," Terrell said. He touched his hat again and made his way out of the hospital feeling somewhat uplifted by his conversation with Dr. Edison. So much so that he smiled and raised his hat to the icy Miss Saunders on the way out the door.

IN SPITE OF Darling's prediction of snow for the afternoon, the skies had cleared, and Lane found herself driving home in brilliant sunlight, which set everything around it to sparkling. She knew Darling and Ames were on their way to the cottage, picking up the case, and so she felt free to enjoy the sun. It was so mood altering that Lane had to chide herself for feeling quite so elevated when poor Miss Scott was barely clinging to life. As she climbed the hill toward Bales's store, at the peak of the road before it descended again toward the lake and curved around the cove, she thought she would stop in and find out what Fred Bales knew. Kenny Armstrong had said he'd heard Bales mention the new teacher.

A green Studebaker was pulled up at the pump, and Bales was feeding it gas. He was encased in a dark maroon wool jacket with his face nearly obscured by his wool hat and scarf. He looked up and gave Lane a wave as she stopped the car. His breath came in white clouds. Gas bubbled in the glass pump.

Inside the store, Lane walked up and down the shelves looking for something to buy that she hadn't picked up in town. She settled on a couple of Cadbury bars and then stood at the counter waiting for Bales to finish with the customer outside. She passed the time chatting with his black Labrador, which had abandoned its usual position on the road outside the store for the warmth of the blanket beside the counter.

"Whew! I thought it was bad when the damn snow wouldn't stop. This is almost worse. It's freezing out there." Bales came through the door, stamping his feet and unwinding his scarf. "Lucy said Miss Scott's phone is down. I've been waiting for the rest of them to go. That snow on the wires is starting to ice up."

"It's worse than that, I'm afraid. Her phone line was deliberately pulled out. I had to rush poor Miss Scott into town to the hospital. It looks like someone ransacked the cottage and hit her on the head."

A rustling and then a chair scraping in the room behind the cash counter produced Lucy herself, her earpiece still on her head, the wire dangling where she'd pulled it out. "That's awful! That accounts for the calls!"

"What accounts for what calls?" Lane asked. "Hello, Lucy."

"Miss Winslow. The calls. I told you, there were two calls Saturday morning, asking to be put through to her number."

"Oh, you did, yes. But the line was down, you said."

"Yes. I don't know who it was. A man, though." She lifted her finger with a sudden recollection. "Oh, and someone did call Friday afternoon, so the phone was working then. A woman. I didn't listen, of course, so I don't know who it was," she said primly.

Lane and Bales eyed Lucy with skepticism, and then a honk from outside took Bales out to a customer.

"I didn't, Miss Winslow. It was very busy Friday afternoon," Lucy said, defensive now.

"You're quite sure? Nothing?"

"I swear it. All I can tell you is that it was a woman on Friday, who got through, and a man two times on Saturday when the line was down."

Lamenting the irony that now, when they could have used a little eavesdropping, Lucy had been too busy to behave in what everyone believed was her usual manner, Lane asked, "The same man both times?"

Lucy adopted a thinking position, her hand on her chin. "I think so. He had a slightly high-pitched voice. He sounded like it was urgent, especially the second time. He must have wanted to make sure the line was actually dead. He sounded upset. In fact, he had a coughing fit. I don't know why, but it always makes me think germs can come down the line at me, because they're coughing right in my ear. Anyway, that was a bit later and the call wouldn't connect."

"How far apart?" Lane asked, ignoring Lucy's whimsical germ theory.

"How far apart what?"

"Between the two calls?" She tried not to sound impatient, but Lucy could be obtuse.

Lucy looked slightly offended. "Okay, keep your hair on. I'd say the first one was at around ten thirty, the second one maybe three minutes later."

"Whom did he say he wanted to talk to?" Lane asked. It wouldn't be usual. One usually just gave the phone number. Hers, for example, was KC 431.

"Nobody, he just gave the number."

"So the lines were fine Friday, and so were Miss Scott and Miss Keeling, presumably," Lane said, more to herself than to Lucy. Was there anything else she ought to ask? It was possible, given the calls, that the police would be interviewing Lucy. She would go home and make a note of what Lucy had told her. "Thanks, Lucy," she said as warmly as she could. Lucy couldn't help being curious, and it was a trait Lane could hardly censure in someone else, considering her own inclinations.

Bales came in, the bell on the door jingling loudly, a miasma of gas coming in with him. There was a noise from the switchboard and Lucy hurried to the back to take care of it with a wave at them.

"Coldest day of the year and everybody needs gas," Bales said, pulling off his hat. His black hair stood at angles and he brushed it back with his hand. "Just the chocolate bars?" he asked, slipping behind the counter.

"Yes, thank you. You've met Miss Keeling, haven't you?"

"Yes, she's been here a couple of weeks already, I think. Very nice young woman. Oh. I should have asked, was she hurt too?"

"No. She wasn't there." Bales rested his hands on the

open drawer of the cash register and looked puzzled.

"Not there? How so?"

"Just, not there."

Bales frowned. "Now let me think. When was the last time I saw either of them? I definitely saw Miss Keeling on Friday. She stopped by here on her way down from the school. Had to pick up eggs and a little bag of flour because she wanted to make pancakes for Saturday morning, she said."

"So, she was in a cheerful frame of mind?"

"I think so. She laughed about the hijinks of the children and was happy it was Friday. She did sound a little thoughtful at one point because she said, 'If only all children could be happy, eh, Mr. Bales?' Nice woman. You can tell she really cares for the kiddies."

"Does she have her own motor car?"

"No, she usually drives that old thing of Miss Scott's, but she was on foot on Friday. Said it was a great way to shake off the day. She did mention she was going to buy the car off Miss Scott when she goes off to get married or get a second-hand one of her own."

"Does she usually drive to the school?"

Bales shook his head. "No, actually. When she arrived, the two of them went to the school together a couple of days last week. Showing her the ropes, I guess. Was on her own most of this last week, I think. I understood Miss Scott was off to the prairies somewhere on the Sunday. Her fellow lives out there. Yesterday, that would be."

CHAPTER SIX

"HAVE YOU HEARD? SOMEONE BOUGHT that dreadful old place up the hill past the Yanks' place." This astonishing revelation was made by Alice Mather to Eleanor Armstrong and Gwen Hughes in the post office, just about the time Lane was talking to Bales. The steamboat had finally made it to King's Cove and dropped off the nearly empty canvas bag of mail, well past tea time. Kenny had seen the boat plying up the lake toward King's Cove and had hurried down to meet it.

Stifling a desire to say, "How would you know that? You never come out of your house," Gwen said, "Who?"

"I didn't interrogate the bloody people, did I? They stopped at the gate and asked where it was. I told 'em," Alice retorted.

"It doesn't follow they're buying it," Gwen protested.

"Oh, it's bought, trust me. They're fixing it up. They had a van. Some sort of fix-it company."

Eleanor, sighing imperceptibly at the hazards of trying

to get any sense out of Alice Mather, said, "If it is being fixed up, presumably someone is going to live in it, then."

"That's what I'm saying," Alice said, nodding her head impatiently.

"It would be nice to have a new family here. Maybe some children for those boys of Angela's to play with," Eleanor said.

"Axe murderers, like as not," Alice said, putting her mail under her arm and pushing the door open.

"*She's* hardly in a position to judge," Gwen said a little peevishly when the door had banged shut at Alice's departure. Alice had been known to take up a rifle and go about shooting at what she claimed were cougars when she was having one of her "turns." Alice's husband, Reginald, assured them all that he'd put the rifle beyond her reach, but no one was convinced.

"That's not entirely fair, Gwen. She's never actually shot anyone," Eleanor said.

"She nearly shot one of Angela's noisy dogs. Can't tell the difference between a cougar and a collie. I'm terrified she'll come up our way one day and pick off one of the spaniels."

"Still, let's say her information is good. That will be a turn-up. I can't imagine anyone wanting that ghastly old place, especially since—" Eleanor stopped herself. It was still a matter of some sensitivity that a human skeleton associated with that house had been found in the Hugheses' root cellar the previous spring.

This seemed to set Gwen off on another train of thought. "Quite. I suppose Miss Winslow, as she appears to still be calling herself, is too busy for us all now that she's married to that policeman. I don't think she's been up to ours twice since she got back from her honeymoon." She liked Miss Winslow, and resented slightly that she'd been, as Gwen felt, taken out of circulation by the inspector, however handsome.

"I don't think it's as bad as all that. Her evenings are taken up, of course, but her days are her own. She was here earlier, but she rushed off to see if the teachers at the Balfour school are all right because no one turned up this morning and the phone is down at the teacher's house. Poor Angela has those boys all day. Here. You're the only one with any mail today because you didn't come in last week."

"Well, they are 'poor' Angela's boys." Gwen nodded her thanks and pulled her wool hat lower on her head and lifted her handful of letters by way of salutation. "Best get off. Mother will be wanting her tea."

Eleanor glanced at the clock in the interior of the mail room. Tea indeed. Lane had been gone a good while. She was surprised not to get a call to bring them up to date about the teachers. And now the possibility of a new resident at King's Cove. There was much to contemplate.

LANE PULLED THE car forward so that Darling could park the car he'd rented until he bought one for his commute into town, when, if, he got home that night. She turned off the engine. The house looked beautiful. A white house set in billows of sparkling snow. Like something from "The Snow Queen." She frowned, trying to remember scraps of the story. She had heard it as a child from one of her governesses and had been enchanted by the idea of a queen who ruled over the beauty of winter. Alas, the queen had turned out to have an icy heart. She remembered her own disappointment at hearing that. There'd been something about a mirror too, a cursed mirror in which people could only see bad things in themselves. Highly metaphorical, she was sure.

Inside, she was just hanging up her jacket, scarf, and wool hat, and anticipating the burbling of the boiling kettle on her electric stove, when it came to her. She'd been so preoccupied with the condition of Miss Scott that she hadn't registered that the bathroom mirror at the teacher's cottage had a spiderwebbed crack in it. Why would someone have broken the mirror? There was nothing in the bathroom but a sink and a bathtub. Someone in a fit of rage?

Darling had shovelled some coal into the furnace before he'd left, so the house felt warm, especially after the crystalline cold outside. She was thankful every day that when Kenny Armstrong had decided to sell his mother's house, he had fitted it up with a modern kitchen, though he himself saw no reason to get a newfangled stove in his own cottage kitchen. The wood one had always been just fine, an opinion that appeared universal in King's Cove with all the residents except Angela, whose magnificent log house had also been updated with a bright, modern kitchen.

Taking up the pile of paper she always kept handy, along with a jar of sharpened pencils, on her little writing desk in the corner Lane quickly made some notes about her conversation with Lucy. She would organize her pot of tea and then phone Darling with what she had learned.

DARLING, AMES, AND Terrell sat in Darling's office. It was gone four. Darling was drumming his fingers on the desk and leaning away, looking out the window. Elephant Mountain was a great white behemoth across the lake, the late-afternoon sun beaming off its surface. It offered nothing, so he turned back. "Three whole policemen, most of the day, and not a whole hell of a lot," he said.

"Sir," said Terrell, attentive. He was pleased to be in on a confab.

"Friday afternoon, based on the information we have from Mr. Bales, who called in earlier under my wife's instructions, Lucy, the irrepressibly nosy Balfour telephone operator, put a call through to Miss Scott from a woman. She, Lucy, did not remember the exact time. We should find out from her how long that call was. She claims she did not listen in. Too bad, in this case. Ergo, someone was able to answer the phone then.

"Saturday mid-morning a man calls twice in quick succession, perhaps not trusting Lucy's assertion that the phone line to the cottage is down. So let's say someone arrives at the teacher's cottage sometime after that Friday call, either that evening or the next morning, ransacks the place looking for something, pulls out the phone line, hits Miss Scott over the head, finds what he or she is looking for, and leaves. Is it the woman caller? Is that woman caller in fact Miss Keeling, calling Miss Scott, or someone else calling either of them? If it's a burglar, not related to the call, does Miss Keeling go with him? Hide? Run away in the mayhem? Not very sporting, leaving Miss Scott, but understandable if Scott is already down and she's next.

Only where is she now?" Darling said.

"Or alternatively," began Ames.

"Yes, exactly," Darling said. "Or alternatively, Miss Keeling is in league with the robber, knows there is something of value, decides this is the time to get it, threatens Miss Scott, and, when she doesn't talk, hits her over the head and tears the place apart looking for whatever it is. She finds it and runs off, leaving Miss Scott to her fate. We still have unanswered the question of who the Saturday caller is, or if he even has anything to do with all of this. It certainly suggests this happened either Friday after the first call, or sometime before the ten-thirty call on Saturday."

"In a way," ventured Terrell a little hesitantly, "the latter scenario is the more likely. According to the doctor, Miss Scott was not hit all that hard. It was the stroke that did the damage. So Miss Keeling, frustrated, but not wanting to really hurt Scott, hits her and tears the place apart. Or maybe she's already torn the place apart and threatens Miss Scott, who tells her where to look, and then hits her or pushes her, to give herself time to get the thing and run off with her accomplice."

Ames nodded grudgingly. "And it would account for the second bedroom not being searched. There surely must have been a second vehicle driven by the assailant. He would not have arrived on foot, if he was going to rob and assault Miss Scott. As Miss Winslow told you, sir, they only had one car between them, and that is now missing, with, perhaps, Miss Keeling at the wheel, in a bid to steal her car as well."

Darling nodded. "Most immediately we need to find

Miss Keeling, double quick, and we need Miss Scott to pull herself together and tell us what happened. Constable Terrell, get on to the provincial Education Department first thing in the morning and find out what you can about this Keeling woman. Sergeant, let's see if the Mounties can get a bead on Miss K, and we'd better get a bulletin out to them to be on the lookout for her."

"HOW IS SHE?" Lane asked. Darling had made it home and was hanging his coat on the coat rack.

"No change. She's not woken up much since Terrell had a brief word with her, but she seems stable enough. I don't really know what a stroke does to someone. She was a bit addled when Terrell talked to her. Didn't seem to have any idea anything had happened. I only hope it does not permanently erase their memories." He took off his hat, hung it up, and then reached for Lane, kissing her and nuzzling her hair. "How are you?"

"Perfectly splendid, as you can see. It comes of not having anyone hit me on the head and try to rob the house."

"No one would dare. They know you married a policeman." Darling said this and immediately wished it were true. Lane's propensity for inserting herself and her curiosity into dangerous situations was something from which he feared no one could protect her, least of all himself. She would be very affronted by any move on his part to suggest she limit her activities on the grounds that she was now his wife and he was protecting her. She'd been an intelligence officer during the war, parachuting into France to do who knew what; she'd never been allowed to tell him. He hardly felt it seemly to suggest in any way that she was incapable of looking after herself.

When they were sitting down to a dish of meatloaf and boiled buttered potatoes, Lane asked, "Any word on when a new teacher can come? I'm worried about the children."

"You know, this is very good. Mrs. Anderson, my housekeeper, used to make something she called meatloaf, which had no resemblance at all to this. Hers was more along the lines of a brick."

"Thank you. Credit Angela. It's an American specialty, apparently, though it certainly has French antecedents. Now I think of it, it's not unlike a good country pâté. I imagine it will be good cold in a sandwich tomorrow. Now what about the children? I wonder if I should offer to go along and teach them till someone is sent out?"

"You?"

"Don't say 'you' in that tone of voice. I have a degree from Oxford, you know. There must be something they can learn from me."

"You can read Shakespeare to them," Darling suggested mildly. "Something useful." He picked up the bottle of wine and held it over her glass. "More wine? You'll need it."

THE RESIDENTS OF King's Cove were unequal to resisting the urge to see what was going on at the old Anscomb house, so named because of the last family that had ever lived there. It had been abandoned before the Great War, sometime in 1913, leaving behind a reek of sorrow, poverty, and failure. Only Lane and the police had been in the house since, and it still had the detritus of the unfortunate

62

family, along with, as Gladys Hughes said, mouldering walls and rising damp.

Consequently, Gladys's middle-aged daughters Mabel and Gwen found a reason to walk the dogs there, strolling past the Bertollis' and then continuing up the hill until the fix-it van was visible. They could see that a large pile of rubbish was accumulating on the overgrown lawn.

"I suppose they'll want to fill our garbage dump with that lot," Mabel said. "As if it wasn't full enough already."

"Why don't they just take the whole place down and start again? It's an absolute horror, that place. I'd forgotten it was still on the market. I know Lane said it was offered to her, along with the Lady Armstrong house. Get rid, I say."

"I don't know," Mabel said. "It's probably got good bones. Waste not, want not."

Gwen turned to look at her sister. "Is that some sort of joke? How can you talk about bones after what we've been through?" She turned back to the house, and muttered nearly under her breath, "You've been through, more like." The finding of a child's skeleton in their own root cellar the previous spring had unleashed all the pain of an episode in Mabel's adolescence she would sooner forget.

Mabel coloured. "What are you saying? That any of that was my fault?"

"No, I'm not saying anything was your fault. Anyway, didn't you go in there when we were girls? Get out of there, you stupid dogs!" The spaniels had plunged into the underbrush beside the road, shaking piles of accumulated snow off the bushes. "Having them find a carcass is all we need!"

"I never went into the house. I was terrified of Mr. Anscomb and was sure I'd catch something horrible. Bob had a shed he lived in. I went into that," Mabel said. "For a moment. The old man found me and sent me packing." She had never told anyone about that visit.

Gwen turned and looked at her sister with a raised eyebrow and then looked back up at the activity by the van. A man came around the side of the house and threw some boards out onto the growing pile and caught sight of Gwen and Mabel. He brushed off his gloves and lifted his hand in a friendly wave, and then turned to go back into the house.

"Can we have a look inside?" Gwen called, ignoring Mabel swatting at her arm.

The builder smiled but shook his head. "Sorry. Orders. Place is locked up. Just clearing out this lot."

ROBIN HARRIS DECIDED he'd take his tractor out of the barn where it wintered over and make the slow, noisy trip up to the old Anscomb house to have a look. It took a couple of tries to get the thing going, but, belching smoke, it lumbered out of the barn and down his driveway.

Gladys, who had stopped at the post office to drop off some letters to be mailed, was walking back along the road rather than the narrow, steep, snow-covered path that climbed directly from the Armstrongs' to her house. She heard the racket and arrived at the intersection in time to see Robin, wrapped up in his grimy winter jacket and a hat with the earflaps tied down tightly under his chin, bumping up the road. He had a floppy, hand-rolled cigarette hanging out of the corner of his mouth, as usual.

"Now, what the devil is he doing?" she asked out loud. Maybe her daughters would know. They'd been out with the dogs, and she suspected they'd have made for the abandoned house. Was that what he was up to as well?

Robin trundled right up to the Anscomb house and parked on the road in front of the van. He surveyed the scene and then heard the banging around the back of the house. It was true, then. He climbed down and, putting his hands in his pockets, strolled toward the pile containing splintered boards, an old bedstead, and some broken chairs heaped up outside the house.

"Where do you think you're going to dump that lot?" he asked by way of greeting. The builder had a wooden box with a chipped enamel basin tilted into it and had thrown it onto the pile. He pulled off his woollen hat and wiped his brow.

"Afternoon," he said. "You live around here?"

"None of your bloody business," Robin said. "What do you think you're doing?"

"Natives are friendly, I see," the builder said. He nodded at the house. "Just doing my job. Fixing it up for the new owner. Getting rid of the rubbish now and bringing in materials. You should get along like a house on fire with the new owner. Of a friendly disposition like yourself."

"What new owner?" Robin asked, ignoring the dig.

"Wouldn't be happy to see me standing around gabbing, so I'll wish you a good day."

Being treated breezily by the builder did not improve Robin's mood. Swearing under his breath, he got back onto his tractor and, after a couple of false starts, made his way back down the road. He could have gone down the narrow one-way that led directly to his own house, but instead he elected to turn right, past the Bertolli cabin, and head to the post office. The Bertolli collies were barking to raise the dead off the front porch just through the rise of leafless birch trees, and Angela came out to have a look.

Seeing it was Robin, far from his usual haunts in the winter with the tractor, she raised her arm and waved vigorously. "Hello, Robin!"

He didn't hear the greeting over the noise of his engine, but he saw the wave, so on a whim he stopped the tractor at the drive and waited for her to come to him. He hadn't any real use for the American Bertolli family, but this was a special case. He watched dogs and mistress come down the stairs and wade through the snow on the path until they reached him.

"How are you, Robin? You don't usually put that thing on the road in the middle of winter."

"Someone's bought that place," he responded, scowling. "Some upstart. Bound to be trouble." He didn't, strictly speaking, know the newcomer was bound to be trouble, but he hadn't mistaken the builder's meaning about the personality of the new owner.

"You don't know he's an upstart. He might be a nice man with a family. Maybe some kids." Robin could hear Angela's three shouting to each other somewhere behind the house.

"We don't need any more kids. Why aren't yours in school?"

"The teacher didn't turn up yesterday, haven't you heard?

Apparently Miss Scott, the old teacher who was leaving to get married, got knocked on the head and the new one disappeared. We have to wait for a new teacher."

He hadn't heard. "That's what comes of having all sorts coming in from outside. We'll all be murdered in our beds in the end."

"But, Robin, why should the new people murder us in our beds? They'll have a nice renovated house to live in."

Robin harrumphed and pulled out his little metal box of cigarettes. He didn't offer one to Angela. Neither prospect was appealing: a murderer or a family with more children.

"Should have set that house alight after the Great War. A misery of a place." He lit his cigarette and tossed the match into the snow.

Angela tilted her head noncommittally and said, "Well then, let's hope it's a nice new family."

"You don't know what you're talking about," grumbled Robin. He started up his tractor without another word. Angela watched him retreating up the road, black smoke trailing out of his exhaust chimney, and shook her head. Whoever it was could certainly not be worse than Robin, she thought.

CHAPTER SEVEN

―――――――

Vancouver, July 1923

DENISE IRVING STOOD ON THE street outside Woodward's Department Store where she worked, and waited for the streetcar. She tried not to feel self-conscious in the queue. After all, no one could guess just by looking at her.

When the car stopped, she waited her turn and then found a seat near the back, next to a large man in a dark suit. Perfect. Even on the nearly impossible chance of her being seen, she would be invisible to anyone on the outside. Heat poured in the windows and seemed to emanate from the man, who was smoking. She was glad of her light tea dress. She had bought it in the ladies' department and had been keeping it in her locker at work.

Impatiently she counted the stops, feeling her heart turn over. She had thought when love finally came into her life it would be a joyful matter. That she would feel young and fizzy, filled with the carefree laughter of two people sharing a special joke. That it would provide warmth, comfort, and refuge. What she felt now was far from that. What she felt instead was a sick anxiety and powerful, draining longing. What if he was not there? What if he was, and Zeke found out?

This thought caused her to look anxiously out the window, past the large man's paper. But the street in this part of town was full of the bustle of business: men in suits, women in dark, serious hats. She unconsciously touched the brim of her own hat, as if to bring it down farther, shading her eyes. She felt herself smile at that. She was like a child who covers her own eyes and thinks no one can see her. This momentary relaxation only released a flood of anxiety. At Granville she got off and walked purposefully up the hill toward the hotel, hoping the aura of sweat and cigarette smoke from the man on the bus would dissipate.

He'd said he would meet her at a corner table in the Palm Court.

The doorman who opened the brass and dark oak door wore white gloves. She tried to pretend she belonged there, had a room somewhere with a view of the water. She glanced at the doorman, and he looked friendly, as if he opened the door to all kinds of people and made no judgment.

"The Palm Court?"

"Just through there, madam. Lovely at this time of day." He smiled and touched his hat.

He was at a corner table. He stood up the moment he saw her, as if he too had been in the grip of anxiety. He took her gloved hands when she sat down, and looked down at them, stroking her fingers.

"My father would kill me," he said. His dark eyes

conveyed sadness, as if they knew, before even he did, that their enterprise was fated for tragedy.

She'd be killed, too, she thought. Her husband would come home from wherever he was, most of his paycheque gone, his mood fractious. He would demand things, the length of his list of expectations directly proportional to his own sense of powerlessness. Her money, her body, her labour.

"It's beautiful here," she said.

"You're beautiful. Denise. It's a name I dream about now. I've ordered champagne. And then tea. And then we can dance. The orchestra will start in a couple of minutes." He punctuated these sentences with little silences, as if she might say something. Finally she did. He was so young, and so beautiful.

"I'm all for dancing. And champagne. Is your father likely to see us here? I'd like to think you will survive our first real date."

The man smiled, exhaling, as if with relief. "My God, I do love you. Here we are." He leaned back slightly while the champagne was poured and thanked the waiter with a nod. The waiter bowed, giving his head a tiny twist of acknowledgement. "To us!" The young man said this almost gaily, holding his glass out toward her. But Denise had seen that acknowledgement from the waiter.

"Do they know you here?" she asked, anxious again.

"Oh, do relax. I'm the scion of a great family on a date. The point is, they don't know you."

"So they are used to you coming in with women."

"No, they are used to me coming in with my father and

his cronies. I work for him, you know. He's a bootstraps kind of man. I work in the mailroom, just like the cliché. I can't normally afford to bring anyone here. But I wanted something beautiful for you. You're . . . extraordinary to me."

He looked so stricken as he said this that she gave way entirely to her desire to believe him, to believe in this new miracle.

She smiled and held up her glass. "To us, then," she said. She hadn't told him she had a husband, but she thought he must know, if only because of the way she insisted she meet him, rather than having him call on her at home. Perhaps not. It wasn't that usual for a married woman to work, but she, like many, removed her ring as she went in every morning. She hadn't believed him when he told her that the perfume was for his mother. Looking at him now, she realized he had probably been telling the truth. And that he was in love. She should allow herself to be in love too, she thought.

They ate little sandwiches and danced. She could feel his arm around her waist, pressing, reassuring, and closed her eyes. When she opened them, he was looking at her, uncertainty gone.

"You know it was meant to be," he said. "You can't doubt it."

"I'm married."

He nodded. "I know that, but you don't care about those old-fashioned bourgeois notions."

In a room on the fifth floor, with a view of Stanley Park and afternoon sunlight glinting off the water, he held her as they both lay facing the window. "Why even go back? Stay here with me."

"You're impractical. Follow your logic through. There would be a divorce. Your name, your father's name, in all the papers. Bourgeois notions they may be, but flout them and any chance you have at a career would be doomed."

"I love the way you say 'doomed,'" he said, laughing. "That long 'oo' sound. So resonant of the end of days. Tell me about your husband. What's his name?"

She turned and looked at him. "Zeke. Why does he have to come into it?"

"Not a soft or reassuring name. I assume he's a bastard or you wouldn't be here. Is it short for Ezekiel? That would be a name that screams biblical disapproval."

She turned back to gaze at the sky. "It is Ezekiel. His family belongs to some sort of religious group. Very strict. No dancing, no drinking. He came here to get away from them, and now he drinks enough for all of them. He doesn't care to be happy."

"Why in God's name did you marry him? You're beautiful, educated. You could have had anyone. You could have had me."

"I was convinced by his desire to be his own man. I felt his sincerity. I don't think I ever experienced sincerity before that." I couldn't have had you, she thought but didn't say. Some society girl would have him. She was sure there must be something in the works even now.

ONE AFTERNOON, ON an early September day, they met to sit on a bench at the beach and eat ice cream. School

72

was in and the beach was quiet, waves lapping gently on English Bay.

"We're like normal people," he said. "Like a couple sharing an ice cream on the beach."

"We are sharing ice cream, but we are far from normal." Denise put a hand to her mouth suddenly. She had wanted to do this without crying. "I'm pregnant," she said, pulling herself together. She didn't look at him. She looked across the bay. His silence was what she had expected. She was now, she supposed, someone who "knew the ways of the world," and this would go as expected. "I don't expect you to concern yourself. I brought it on myself. It does mean the end, of course. We cannot go on pretending the world doesn't exist. It turns out I do believe in the old bourgeois notions. I am married, so this baby will have a home and a family." She looked at him finally. That is what "dumbstruck" must look like in real life, she thought. "We won't have a fuss. I'll be leaving my job soon and you can return to your life."

"You cannot, you *cannot*, imagine that you can stay with that man, and have a child of mine brought up by him?"

"Don't be dramatic. What will you do? Be the correspondent in a public divorce and then marry your pregnant lover? I should think your father really would kill you. And Zeke would demand the child, think it's his. It would be given to him. You know what the courts are like."

She amazed herself with her own practical sangfroid. She did not say what she felt: that leaving him would be the end of all happiness for her, the end of her delusion that love would conquer anything at all.

THE SCHOOLHOUSE WAS freezing on the Tuesday morning. Frost had gathered on the inside corner of the five long windows. Like morning in a Scottish country house shooting weekend in December, Lane thought. It was still almost dark when she arrived, hoping to start the fire in the stove and warm the place up by the time the children got there. After supper she'd got hold of as many students as she could through a sort of telephone tree of the few parents she knew, to say the school would be open. Angela had agreed to let the local officials know that Lane would provide temporary instruction and reassure them with her degree from Oxford. If there were misgivings, Angela would say that Lane was just providing care for the children until the situation was resolved.

Lane flicked on the light switch and was relieved that the four bowl-shaped light fixtures that hung in the centre of the ceiling from the back of the room to the front all worked and brightened the place up considerably. Fourteen desks were lined up facing the blackboard, and several more were pushed against the back wall, obviously unneeded. A low bookshelf between the two north-facing windows had a neat pile of exercise books, some readers, and some copies of the *Nelson Daily News*, at which Lane nodded approvingly. Miss Scott and Miss Keeling were clearly interested in teaching the children some practical skills. Three wooden trays sat on the top of the bookcase. One contained rows of ink bottles, another pencils, and a third red pen holders and boxes of nibs.

"Right," she said out loud. "Time to get the stove going." Her words seem to flatten and disappear in the frigid air. Happily, Miss Keeling had brought wood in from the shed at the side of the school and piled it, along with kindling and some rolled-up newspapers, in the woodbox next to the stove. Lane had brought matches with her, just in case she found the place less organized than it proved to be. It made her think again of Miss Keeling. According to Angela, the children liked her. While Lane held loosely to the idea that if dogs and children like someone, they can't be all bad, she cautioned herself not to jump to conclusions. After all, there had been no dog to confirm the judgment. Perhaps Miss Keeling was only good at making herself seem agreeable, while looking for the chance to steal Miss Scott's life savings, for example.

Reminding herself not to compensate in the other direction, she realized that Miss Keeling must have taken the teacher training provided by the province, or she wouldn't have been assigned to the job by whoever it was that assigned teachers to tiny schools like this. Good, so she wasn't a complete imposter, and the room showed a very tidy turn of mind. One thing seemed certain: Miss Keeling clearly expected to come to school on the Monday. The preparation of kindling and wood and homework for the various grades of the students on the blackboard showed this.

With the fire making no inroads on the chill, Lane was obliged to keep her coat on. She tried a door on the north wall near the teacher desk. It opened into a small kitchen sort of room with a sink and, to her enormous relief, an indoor loo. She had seen only an outhouse at the teacher's cottage and had harboured an anxiety that she and the children would spend the day popping in and out of winter clothes to visit the outdoor privy.

There was a cupboard with some glasses lined up, a kettle that must be used on the wood stove, perhaps after the students had left, and a second cupboard that contained rudimentary first aid equipment: a bottle of Mercurochrome and one of iodine and a little yellow metal box of Band-Aids. It was here, as well, that the children were meant to hang up their coats. There was a bench along the wall opposite the sink, with pegs above it. And finally, there was a door to the outside. It was a relief to see a second exit in case of a fire or some emergency.

Wondering if children ever got burnt on the stove, Lane went and collected the exercise books, and now feeling just about able to remove her wool coat, she sat down at the desk and set them up in a pile ready to read. Out of curiosity, she pulled open the shallow centre drawer in the wooden desk. An attendance book, some regular pencils and two red pencils, some pens, and loose lined paper. The upper drawer on the side of the desk revealed a box of chalk and some clean erasers. In the second drawer there was a neatly folded black hand-knit cardigan. She lifted this, and underneath she saw an envelope from the Department of Education, Province of British Columbia. Inside it, a letter addressed to Miss Wendy Keeling congratulated her on her assignment to the rural school located at Balfour, British Columbia, at an annual salary of $1,128. Someone had circled the salary in pencil and written, "$285 less than a man!"

Realizing she didn't know much about the average salaries for various professions, Lane thought this sum a little small. It was less than $100 a month to live on. A man would be doing little better when it was averaged out across the year. She remembered the bank teller in Nelson telling her that her inheritance, nearly $20,000 when converted from pounds, was the equivalent of a number of years' salary for him.

Lane folded the letter and put it back into its envelope and lifted the cardigan to slide it back underneath. She was about to close the drawer and get stuck into looking at the exercise books to see what lessons the children were doing, when she found she couldn't close the drawer completely. She opened it and then tried to close it again, but something was certainly preventing it from closing. With a sigh she stood up and pulled the drawer all the way out and then saw that a wad of paper had somehow escaped the drawer and been jammed between the back of the drawer and the desk. She took it out and unfolded it. It proved to be an envelope that had been tightly folded and perhaps thrown in the drawer and forgotten.

It had no addressee, but it had been opened and there was a folded letter inside. She unfolded it and gasped at the directness of the communication. "You aren't fit to be around children. Don't think your wicked secret is safe. You won't be there long."

The exercise books forgotten, Lane reread the letter, printed in pencil in big block capitals, as if the writer had borne down on the lead. She turned the envelope over, hoping to find some clue about the sender or, she realized, even about the receiver. Had this been directed at Miss Scott or Miss Keeling? Was it sent by a man or a woman? Her instinct, she thought regretfully, was that it was a woman, but then she chided herself. Men could be hateful in print, after all, though she thought their methods would veer more along the lines of abusing a person directly to her face.

She looked at her watch and realized the children would be descending on her in less than an hour. She went to put the letter in the drawer, and then thought better of it. This letter, and even the announcement of Miss K's appointment, ought to get to the police. She looked along the walls of the room and realized there was no telephone. Who the devil doesn't put a phone in a school?

Well, she didn't have time to leave her post to make a call, but she would ask Angela, when she dropped her boys off, to put in a call to the police station and mention—what? She couldn't, she felt, share this evidence, if that is what it proved to be, with anyone but the police. Of course, she could ask Angela to tell them that there may be evidence at the schoolhouse. That would bring one of them out. For all she knew, they were already planning on a trip to the schoolhouse, depending on what they learned from Miss Scott when she regained consciousness.

She didn't want the police going through the drawers while the children were there, so she kept the letters in her handbag to hand over when they came.

By the time she heard the first car door slamming outside, Lane had ascertained that the children were in roughly four grades, and their lessons were all over the map. All the exercise books had a section for penmanship, and she had thought that after the introductions, she might safely provide time to improve handwriting, a skill only two of the children seemed to be mastering at a high level.

On the blackboard she had written the first and second stanza of Wordsworth's "Daffodils," judging it sufficiently visual for children to cope with, and something she had off the top of her head. The car door, and the high voice of a child saying, "Goodbye, Mommy," made her stomach lurch and she admonished herself for a coward. You've jumped out of airplanes carrying weapons to the French Resistance, she reminded herself. These are little children.

CHAPTER EIGHT

———

DARLING WAS LOOKING GRIMLY AT the headline in the *Nelson Daily News*: "Balfour Teacher Near Death, Second Teacher Sought by Police." The article that followed, while adhering to the factual rules of journalism, skated near the edge of implying that the second teacher was responsible, with its suggestive wording of "Miss Wendy Keeling, about whom little is known . . ."

The knock on his door roused him from dark thoughts about journalists and how they bent public opinion and got in the way of investigations. "Come!"

"Sir, we've had a call from Mrs. Bertolli up at the Cove." Ames was holding a piece of paper on which he'd made notes. "She didn't want to bother you directly," he added, answering Darling's unspoken question about why the call hadn't been put through to him.

"Yes, Ames. What is it?"

"Your good wi . . . er . . . Miss Winslow asked her to call. Apparently she found something in the desk at the school that might be of interest. Can I ask, sir, why is Miss Winslow going through the desk? You don't usually like to involve her in your cases, not that you can ever keep—"

"Ames, I'm in no mood for your impertinence."

"Yes, sir, sorry, sir. Anyway. She has something and she thinks one of us ought to have a look."

"If you must know, in the temporary absence of a teacher, she has agreed to take on the job until someone turns up."

"Wow! She's brave. But no surprise, eh, sir? That's Miss Winslow all over."

"I think she's utterly mad." Darling rolled up the newspaper and tossed it into the trash can by his desk with a definitive thud. If Lane thought it important enough to have a call put through, "What sort of thing did she find?"

"Mrs. Bertolli didn't say. In fact, she said that of course she had no idea since it wouldn't be appropriate to share information with anyone outside the police. But she did say that Miss Winslow thought it was important. Do you want me to go out?"

Darling nodded. There was no point in his making the long drive. He was hoping to be Johnny-on-the-spot when the hospital called through to say Miss Scott was able to talk. His early-morning call to the hospital had confirmed that she had "stabilized," whatever that meant, but was unconscious, though they were feeling optimistic.

Ames stopped by Terrell's desk downstairs to see if he wanted to come along, but he found him still on the phone.

"Well, can you put me through to someone who does know something?" he was saying. He looked up at Ames, who was dangling the car keys, and shook his head. He put his hand over the receiver and whispered, "Bureaucracy." Then he turned back to the phone. "Yes, this is the police. Constable Terrell of the Nelson Police, yes."

LANE'S MORNING WAS stuttering along. The children were variously skeptical or excited. The Bertolli boys were excited and traded on the fact that they knew her and she had solved a murder. Lane found herself grateful that they appeared not to be in possession of the full menu of her involvement with the law. Other children seemed to resent an interloper. "Where is Miss Keeling? Is she dead?"

When she had invited them all to sit in their usual seats, and had read out their names, checking them off as Miss Keeling had done in the register, she found she had one missing. "Does anyone know Samuel Gaskell?" All the children put up their hands tentatively. Lane looked at the register. "Gabriella? Do you know if he is sick today?"

The little girl shook her head and glanced nervously at the boy sitting next to her. Lane couldn't tell if the girl meant that Samuel wasn't sick, or she didn't know, but there was certainly something nervous about the children's response to his name. Deciding that would have to be good enough, she said brightly, "Thank you, Gabriella. Now then, I see that you were given homework. How does your teacher check that you've done it?"

Philip put up his hand. "We put our homework on our desk, and the teacher walks around and puts a check in her book."

"Thank you, Philip. Could everyone do that, then?" While the noise of children opening their school bags and taking out homework unfolded behind her, Lane sought the attendance book and saw there was a column for homework checks with Monday, December 8, ready to be marked off. She made an entry for Tuesday and then walked solemnly by each desk, glanced at the work, and put a check mark next to the student's name. Only a boy called Randy had not done his. Lane didn't want to embarrass him by asking, and had just decided she would bring it up later when all the students were occupied with the poem, when he said, "I forgot to write it down, miss."

Lane nodded. "Thank you, Randy. Maybe there'll be a moment later for you to catch up. Would you mind handing out everyone's exercise books? Who would like to hand out the ink and pens?"

There was another anxious shuffle, and then Philip Bertolli put up his hand and said, "Only the big kids get ink, miss."

"Ah. Well, raise your hand if you normally work in ink." Several children responded. She was about to ask Philip to hand out the ink, when Randy spoke up. "What about the prayer, miss? We don't do nothing till we pray the Lord's Prayer."

"Oh, of course. Thank you, Randy."

He nodded, looking important. Perhaps his reminding the new teacher about the Lord's Prayer made up for not having done his homework.

"And who leads us in prayer, Randy?"

"You do, miss." He nodded at the other children and they all stood up, folded their hands in front of them, and put their heads down.

"Oh, of course." Feeling slightly hypocritical, Lane began. "Our Father . . ." All of the children joined in, pulling Lane to the preferred speed of very slow and well articulated. ". . . Forever and ever, amen."

"Right," Lane said, when the correct booklets and equipment had been handed out. "I thought we would begin with a little penmanship today. I've put two verses of a poem by a famous English poet called William Wordsworth on the board. It's about daffodils. I thought it would be fun to remember the yellow of daffodils in the middle of all this snow. You can copy down the poem in your very best writing, and then we can talk about it."

A hand went up. "My pencil isn't sharp."

Lane looked around and spotted the pencil sharpener attached to the top of the low bookshelf. "Off you go, then, and sharpen it."

This invitation elicited several more blunt pencils, so the children lined up and the room was filled with the sound of wood grinding.

Lane leaned back on the teacher desk and smiled at Rafe, who sat at the forward-most desk.

"I'm good at arithmetic," he said.

"That's splendid," Lane said. "You can help me get everyone organized when it's time for the lesson."

"Everyone is at a different level. Me and him," he pointed at a boy also sitting at the front, "are at the same level, because we're in the same grade. And Ralph is with Gabriella and Samuel, and Philip is on his own because he's better than anyone, even though he's only in grade five." Wondering how Miss Keeling, or Miss Scott, or any of the miss or mister anyones, managed such divergent needs and levels in these small schools, Lane took in a deep breath and told herself, One thing at a time. Penmanship first; take cues from the children. The local board could not be long in assigning a proper teacher.

The pencil sharpener was finally silent, and the children back in their places. "Can anyone read what I have written on the board?"

There was a shuffling, then Gabriella spoke up. "Samuel is the best reader, miss."

"That's very nice of you to say so. Since Samuel is sick today, would anyone else volunteer?"

Finally, after an agonizingly long silence, Philip Bertolli put up his hand. "I guess I could, Miss Winslow."

"Splendid. Have a go." Philip stood up and began, "I wandered lonely as a cloud, that floats on high . . . I don't know that word . . . or?"

"O'er. It's a kind of old-fashioned shortcut for saying 'over.' Carry on, you're doing very well. Read to the end of the stanza, and we'll see if someone else can read the second one."

Philip, thus encouraged, proceeded to the end, and sat down.

"Why doesn't he just say 'over'?" asked Randy. "It's easier to understand."

"You make a good point, Randy. The poem is over a hundred years old and poets then tended to use special language when writing poetry."

Gabriella volunteered the second verse, stopping firmly at the end of each line, though she balked immediately at "continuous." "I know what it is when I read it to myself, but I never had to say it out loud," she said, to stifle a giggle from one of the boys.

"Thank you, Gabriella. That happens to all of us. I often encounter words in reading that I'm not really certain how to pronounce."

Gabriella folded her arms with a satisfied nod at the giggler.

That done, Lane instructed them to write the poem down, using the lines in their scribblers to write as neatly as possible.

"We usually do special circles and lines to practise," said Rafe, holding up his book to show that, indeed, there were exercises completed before each writing assignment.

Lane contained a sigh. "Good, then let's do the exercises first. How many lines do you usually use for the exercises?" By the time the children were on to writing out the poem, Lane was wondering how she would make it through to lunch, never mind the end of the day.

"WELL, I DON'T like the sound of it," Gladys declared over lunch, a meal of chicken soup with bottled peas and carrots from their root cellar and great slabs of bread and butter. Mabel had baked the day before. They sat at their kitchen table enjoying the warmth of the wood stove upon which the soup had been produced. The white blankets of snow mounded over the flower beds outside the long bank of east-facing windows added to their sense of snugness. The two cocker spaniels were lying on the bench where the wood was kept, watching the lunchers hopefully, and the cat was curled up by the stove. "The way Robin was talking, that builder seemed to be suggesting that the new owner was nothing to write home about. And the van wasn't local."

"Trust Robin to get the wrong end of any stick," said Gwen. "I'm sure he's perfectly nice. Maybe he just likes to keep himself to himself. That would suit most of us down to the ground."

"If he keeps himself to himself, it doesn't matter if he's nice or not," suggested Mabel, in rare support of her sister.

"What if he's got some hare-brained scheme to log the place like Sandy had?" asked Gladys. "Life here wouldn't be worth living."

Sandy Mather, the unpleasant only son of Reginald and Alice Mather, was serving time out on the coast for second-degree murder. He'd had plans to log his father's property and had been in the process of trying to buy up some of Robin's property for the same purpose, when he was arrested.

"I'm actually interested to see what that builder does with the place, especially if he's not local. He might be a fancy big city man from Vancouver," Gwen said, rolling her napkin up and sliding it back into its ring. "I'm going to tackle the linen cupboard. Everything needs a bit of an airing. The sheets felt damp last time I changed the beds."

"I'm having a nap," said Gladys. Mabel would have been happy to retreat to her bedroom with a book but thought she ought to be doing something if Gwen was airing the linen. She took the dishes to the sink and unwound the rope that held the drying rack over the stove.

While Gwen tended to the linen cupboard, Mabel stoppered the sink, filled it, and took up the soap saver and whooshed it about in the hot water. The whole business of someone moving into that dreadful house was completely unsettling and reminded her uncomfortably of one of the greatest follies of her life. If this person proved to be someone who wanted to make a complete nuisance of himself by upending everyone with a logging enterprise, it really would be too much.

AMES HAD RETURNED from Balfour with the documents, only to find Darling had gone out to the hospital, so he called O'Brien and asked him to send Terrell up. "Any luck with the education people?" he asked.

"The chairman of the local board was extremely upset," Terrell said. "He'd had a call from Mrs. Bertolli saying Miss Winslow would be happy to look after things until someone turned up. It's apparently not that easy to find a teacher mid-year. Miss Keeling had extremely good references and had, in fact, taught briefly at some community on Vancouver Island called Saanich. I think he felt he ought to be in charge, because it took some persuading to get him to give me the contact he had at the department in Victoria, but I got it out of him finally, on the proviso that I tell them Balfour needs a teacher double quick. Victoria confirmed that Miss Keeling had been a top candidate. She'd attended Normal School and even had a couple of years of university. Nothing known to her detriment."

"Hmm," said Ames. "What do you make of these, then?"

Terrell read through the two papers and bit his lower

lip. "This notice of posting is obviously Miss Keeling's, and what I find interesting is that she is not happy with her salary. The remark she scribbled here about a man making more makes her seem a trifle rebellious, though I suppose it's a good thing to be rebellious about. The other one—poison pen. Do we know that it is hers? It could have been sent to the other teacher, Miss Scott, who, after all, got hit on the head."

"You know what I wonder?" said Ames. "I wonder if this is the only one. I'm sure Miss Winslow, having found this, would have searched the rest of the desk, but we didn't search the house for anything like this, did we?"

They heard the familiar tramp of Darling coming up the stairs.

"Boss?" said Ames.

Darling stopped at the door and began to remove his hat and scarf. "Bloody waste of time," he declared. "Miss Scott is awake, all right, and at least seems more on top of things than when you spoke with her, Constable. She can speak enough to ask what she's doing in hospital and remembers absolutely nothing. Doctor says she seems okay otherwise, but they're keeping her in for a few more days. Knows she's a teacher, knows where she lives, how old she is, and the like. Didn't seem to remember she was getting married or anything about her fiancé, and there you are." He caught sight of the letters lying on the desk. "Any luck there?"

Ames briefed him on the contents and gave a précis of their discussions. They were interrupted by the phone. It was O'Brien. There'd been an altercation at the Legion, and they wanted the law down there to apprehend the culprit, whom they'd temporarily locked into a cupboard.

Darling looked at his watch. "At this time of day? He must have got an early start. Terrell, you can go see to that. Ames, you'll have to find time to go back to the cottage and see if there are any more notes. Tomorrow, first thing."

CHAPTER NINE

——————

MABEL DROPPED THE UTENSILS FROM lunch into the water and was reaching for the dish mop, when a movement at the top end of the driveway caught her eye.

She put the mop down and narrowed her eyes trying to see more clearly. Someone appeared to be approaching the top of their driveway in an enormous black car; she didn't recognize it. As she watched, the person drove about a car length past the fence that marked the beginning of their spacious yard, surveyed their property, glanced briefly at the house, and then backed away, executing a quick turn. The car disappeared around the corner to the road leading down the hill. Hurrying into the boot room, Mabel pulled on her wellies, heavy jacket, and scarf, and took up her walking stick. Followed by the excited spaniels, she marched across the garden, the dogs romping onto the icy snow, and up the long driveway.

Whoever it was had disappeared down the road and onto, she assumed, the main road. She could hear the car faintly in the distance. The dogs began to bark, looking into the empty orchard adjacent to the road. She walked toward the road and looked along the length of it. Who the blazes drove a car like that?

Wondering if it was remotely possible that their conversation at lunch might have conjured the hapless Sandy, the only person who had been known to skulk around on other people's property, Mabel shook her head and started back to the house.

Gwen came to the door to watch her kicking the snow off her boots. "What have you been playing at?" she asked.

"Someone in a huge black car drove right into our driveway, pretty as you like, gave us the once-over, and then drove off, if you must know. It gave me quite a turn. I thought for a moment it might be Sandy. They haven't let him out, have they?"

"After a year? I doubt it."

"Who else would sneak about like that?"

"You don't know it was someone sneaking. It could be someone just got lost. After you've finished the dishes and we've hung up the sheets to air, let's pop down to the post office and see if anyone else has seen anyone. Don't tell Mother just yet. She'll only accuse you of imagining things," Gwen said, with a tone that suggested she was wondering about that herself.

"WE'LL HAVE TO canvass the neighbours," Darling said. It was the end of an unfruitful day. "Miss Scott remembers nothing. The Education Department knows nothing against Miss Keeling. It was miserable on Friday, and

Saturday for that matter, depending on when this all happened. Most sensible people would have been indoors. I'll stop by the immediate neighbours of the teacher's cottage on my way in tomorrow morning."

Darling got up and stretched, reaching for his coat. It was already dark outside, though it was only 5:30. He had a momentary thought about 5:30 PM in the summer, still a long day left to enjoy. Now it felt as though it was long past his dinnertime already.

Ames nodded. "Do you want me to meet you out there?"

"No. You're fine. We'll organize where we go from here when we get back here tomorrow." Downstairs he met Terrell, who was just heading out.

"Ah, sir. The man from the Legion. A bit too much to drink. He's sleeping it off in a cell. I'll charge him with mischief in the morning. He isn't up to understanding much now."

Darling nodded. "Good man. What's his name?"

"Frank Dixter. He works at a heavy-vehicles garage just up the road to Castlegar."

"Not one of our regulars. And, happily, not the garage we take the car to. Right, well, see you tomorrow."

While Darling waited for the ferry to make the trip up the north shore of the lake, a faint dusting of snow began to fall, the still-small flakes dancing in the ambient light of the street lamp and the headlights of a car pulling up behind his. He thought about Terrell and wondered where he lived, and if he cooked, or had a room with a nice motherly landlady. Ames, he knew, didn't cook but had a nice motherly mother who looked after him. Though Darling had met her once, he had never set foot in Ames's house. He had a vague feeling it was up the hill from the station somewhere on the east side of town. It was, perhaps, his own very new domestic arrangements that sent his mind off in this direction. Private life, he thought, was blissfully private. He had no real wish to know how the men under him lived, and he abhorred the thought that they might know, or even think, about how he lived.

Of course, it didn't stop him from mildly abusing Ames on the subject of his continuing to live with his mother, but the sergeant seemed to take it in good part. After all, he wasn't married, and his mother didn't seem to interfere in his life much, though he assumed she hoped he would marry soon. He shifted into gear as the last vehicle came off into town and smiled in the darkness of the car. Ames looked likely to remain a well-cared-for bachelor for some time unless he could regulate his love life.

Terrell was different. He was young, certainly, perhaps not much older than Ames, but he was less boyish, somehow, more serious and earnest. He'd been in the war, that was part of it, but Darling wondered if another part of it was the need to not stand out, an impulse to excel at his job to reduce the amount of prejudice he must experience. Or maybe Terrell just had the makings of a damn good policeman and was of a naturally serious disposition.

I'm no psychiatrist, Darling thought. I ought not to go around assigning motivation for people's behaviour when I know nothing about them. He was sure Lane would have gotten to the bottom of Terrell after an hour of knowing him.

Ought he to treat Terrell differently? All the crew of his Lancaster bomber took a certain amount of ribbing from him, regardless. They had been an excellent group of men, and he had been their commander. The ribbing was a way, perhaps, of softening that power of absolute command invested in him by the air force. He could see, looking back, that if he'd left any single man out of this relationship, that man might have felt isolated, not part of the crew. A continued formal courtesy to Terrell might also make him not feel part of the crew at the police station. It was likely that Terrell just wanted to be treated like any officer on the Nelson Police force, and not have to constantly salve other people's feelings about his background. Terrell, after all, was Terrell. Anything that might trouble others about him was their problem.

DARLING AND LANE had washed the dishes and now sat in the armchairs pulled up to the Franklin wood stove with pre-bed whisky in hand.

"It surprised me to suddenly remember today that the mirror in the bathroom of the teacher's cottage was cracked. Did you notice it when you went through the house? I don't think I took it in because it must be the door of a cabinet, and nothing had been pulled out or messed about in the bathroom. I was thinking about an old fairy tale about a cruel snow queen who cursed people to see bad things in a mirror when they looked at themselves."

"'The Snow Queen,' of course. The whole thing makes sense now. Why didn't I think of that? We should be able to get on with the arresting tomorrow," said Darling, reaching over to stroke her hair, its chestnut colour highlighted by the flicker of flames in the stove.

"You laugh now, but you'll be laughing out of the other side of your face when I solve the whole thing. The teacher's bathroom mirror, if I may explain more thoroughly without further heckling from the audience, was cracked, but not completely broken. The rest of the house was really knocked about, things swept off the counter and broken, things thrown everywhere and so on. But the bathroom only had that cracked mirror. It made me think of someone looking at it and cracking it angrily with a hairbrush, as if she didn't like what she'd seen." The hairbrush image seemed suddenly clear to her, as if she remembered it from somewhere.

"Well, if it was Miss Keeling in her guise as an assault and battery expert suddenly looking at what she'd become, I suppose," Darling said. "Good grief. We've gotten through the whole of dinner and I didn't ask about your first day as teacher. How did it go?" Darling suddenly felt his neglect acutely. He'd come in, sniffed about at the dinner arrangements, and launched into his day. They'd had a long discussion about his thoughts about Terrell, to which she'd said, "Of course you must treat him as you do anyone else. I, and the other women I worked with, spent a good deal of the early days of the war being treated either derisively or with kid gloves because people were worried about our being women. It's annoying, apart from everything else. It leaves room for people to assume you can't do as good a job, for example, or, alternatively, are getting special privileges. Later on, it was much better. There was a war on, people knew what we could do, and we all mucked on together, pretty much as equals. Some never got over it, of course, but lots did. If Terrell is a good policeman, and everything you tell me suggests he is, he should come in for all the usual treatment you mete out to everyone else, God help him." Darling had seen the absolute logic of this.

Lane told him about her day at the school. In truth she'd come home exhausted, but, at the same time, stimulated. She'd surprised herself. Never having been exposed to children particularly, aside from Angela's boys, who formed a self-entertaining society of their own, she was pleased to discover she really quite enjoyed them. They were unguarded, in a way. You knew what you were getting, unlike with adults.

"They were really very helpful. I was stumbling about trying to pretend I was in charge, and at every turn there was a reminder from one of them about what the normal classroom routine was. It seems children are quite conservative and like to see the regular way of doing things maintained."

"How do you know they weren't pulling your leg?"

"No, they weren't. I was told that not everyone was old enough to use ink, that we must say a prayer at the beginning of each day, and that we were to do penmanship exercises before copying anything from the board." She paused. "I find it hard to believe anything ill about Miss Keeling. The children, all of them, really like her. That means, I think, that she is a very genuine person. Children would know instantly if someone was pretending to be something they weren't."

"You put an awful lot of faith in the wisdom of children. I should have thought they could be duped like anyone else.

In fact, they are sometimes, by people who wish them ill."

"Yes, of course." Lane thought for a moment, feeling her own naïveté. Darling's police experience must have included some dire examples of this. "In this case, it's a feeling, I suppose. They believe they have given their trust to someone who is trustworthy, someone they know really likes them and won't hurt them. It is clear from what Angela said that Miss Scott ruled with a kind of benevolent dictatorship, but the way the students talked about Miss Keeling, it seems as if she was more relaxed, but still in charge, if you know what I mean. The grown-up in the room."

IN THE MORNING, Darling slowed down at the turnoff that would lead to the teacher's cottage. Though he did not like to admit it, Lane's mirror observation had stuck with him. It was an anomaly, like the bedroom that had not been ransacked. The violence of the destruction in the rest of the cabin suggested that whoever did it would have smashed the mirror hard enough to knock all the glass out. Unless of course it had been cracked all along. That was the trouble with investigating this sort of crime. You never quite knew what you had to take into account.

Instead, he drove forward to the next road and bumped down on the icy snow and pulled up before a modest house, the front door of which opened onto a large porch facing the lake. It must be lovely to sit out there in the summer, he thought, rapping on the screen door. In the silence he turned and looked out toward the lake. The sun was finally beginning to throw light on the mountains across the water.

It looked like the beginning of another sunny, icy day.

He heard the inside door open, and he turned and touched his hat. Obscured slightly by the screen, a woman in a green bathrobe and a turban covering bobby-pinned curls asked him cautiously what he wanted.

"Inspector Darling, Nelson Police. We are investigating a situation that occurred during the weekend next door, and I'm wondering if you heard or saw anything unusual between, say, Friday afternoon and Sunday night?"

"Them teachers," the woman said.

"What is your name?" She looked like someone who was past having school-aged children.

"Mrs. Merchant." She glanced in the direction of the cottage. "Don't see much from here. That man on the other side, his house is built closer. No doubt he sticks his nose in."

Darling looked as well. A solid bank of aspen would obscure the cottage in the summer, and even with the leaves off for the winter, it was difficult to see the cottage clearly. Its front door faced the road, not the lake.

"In what way?"

"He's a nasty piece of work. Sue, that's his wife, made a run for it, but he wouldn't let her take the child." Unpleasant, to be sure, but this wasn't moving his particular business this morning forward.

"Do you know either of the teachers, Miss Scott or Miss Keeling?"

"I don't have no kids in school. I don't involve myself in things that aren't nothing to do with me."

Belying, Darling thought, her apparently intimate

knowledge of the marital troubles of . . . he realized he hadn't asked the man's name.

"What is the name of the neighbour on the other side?"

"Gaskell. He works the Nelson ferry."

Darling took out a card and held it up. Only then did Mrs. Merchant open the door an inch and he slipped it to her. "Can you telephone if there is anything you remember?"

She looked at the card. "Why? What's happened to them?"

Darling touched his hat. "Thank you, Mrs. Merchant."

GASKELL'S HOUSE WAS rundown. That it had been painted once was evident, but the little paint remaining was peeling, and the yard was full of rubbish: a rusted barrel, some sort of engine parts, just showing under their cover of frozen snow. The stick of a broom or mop was thrown onto the surface of the snow. The house looked empty. No smoke from the chimney. Gaskell must be at work, and the child at school. He'd leave a card. He climbed the stairs to the narrow porch. A rusted chain attached to the house suggested there might have been a dog once. He shuddered. A beastly life for a dog. The curtains were all closed. He took out a card, unscrewed the cap of his pen, and was about to write a note asking the occupant to contact him, when he saw the curtain move and a small face stare out at him. Darling smiled encouragingly and then knocked on the door frame. The curtain closed. He wondered if he'd scared the child away, but then he heard someone struggling with the door.

A little boy stood in the doorway, holding a tattered quilt

around his body. He looked at Darling but said nothing. He was pale and slender.

"What's your name, then?" Darling asked, squatting down to get at eye level.

"Samuel." Not Sam. Samuel.

"I'm Inspector Darling, from the Nelson Police, Samuel. Would you like to see my card?" He pulled it out of his inside pocket and held it up to the screen door. The boy pushed the screen door open and looked at the card.

"My father isn't home," he said. But Darling scarcely heard him. Not only was the boy undernourished and unkempt, he had a black eye that was beginning to turn ugly shades of blue and green. It looked a good three or four days old. If his father had given him that, he might clam up if he asked him about it.

"Not at school today?" Darling pitched his voice in a friendly tone.

"I was sick."

"I see. Who is looking after you?"

The boy hesitated. "I'm okay now," he said finally.

"Can I come in?" Darling asked.

Samuel opened the door and held it. The house was freezing. The door opened directly into a kitchen with a tiny table and three chairs. A window above the sink faced out toward the lake. No beauty seen through it could make up for the cold and disarray inside the house. A box of cereal lay overturned, and clearly empty, and a jar of peanut butter sat open with a spoon in it. There wasn't much left. An empty milk bottle stood on the table by a glass.

Darling saw no fridge and continued through a narrow

door to a sitting room. The bleakness was intensified by closed curtains and an ancient, dirty, and worn area rug. Blankets were piled on a collapsing brown sofa and a book lay turned over on the top of the pile. *Robinson Crusoe*. Darling picked it up.

"Are you reading this?"

Samuel nodded. "I got some other books, but I read them all. This is my favourite one."

Darling looked at the fly-leaf. "To Darling Samuel, with love from Mother." He looked around the dark room. "Is your mother at work?"

"She's gone right now. She's coming back. She left at my birthday."

"Oh! When is your birthday?"

Samuel smiled. "September 10. I turned nine."

Blimey, Darling thought. It was December. His mission to discover if anyone in the house heard or saw anything at the teacher's cottage was abandoned. "And your father? Is he at work? He works at the ferry, doesn't he?"

The boy was silent for a moment. "He never came home. I was scared some of the time."

AMES AND TERRELL were having breakfast at the café. "I always eat the same thing every time. Scrambled eggs and toast and some coffee. I'm afraid April thinks I'm a little predictable in my habits."

"Sounds good to me." Terrell smiled. "Except I take a little less sugar in my coffee, sir."

Ames smiled. "You, my mother, my ex-girlfriend. Everyone has something to say to me about the sugar. I saw

Dixter leaving this morning. Didn't like our hospitality?"

"I feel kind of sorry for him. He has a whopping hangover. He never even said goodbye."

"I bet his wife won't be too happy either. Drinking in the Legion seems to be an occupational hazard. Someone usually has to get tossed out. I heard that in the thirties there was a huge donnybrook and the then boss got a good punch in the solar plexus. I'd like to see someone try that with Darling!"

Terrell smiled. "No kidding! What do you think about this teacher business?" he asked. They were sitting at the counter where they could see the cook's head bobbing up and down behind the window. Two plates were put up, but April was seeing to someone in a booth.

"It's hard for me to imagine a young woman bashing someone over the head and running off. But I guess it happens." He could imagine that under severe enough provocation Tina Van Eyck, the mechanic at her father's garage near Balfour, could do it, but he still resisted the thought that women could be violent in that way. After all, Tina had had a lot of provocation the month before in a recent murder case he'd been in charge of, and she hadn't knocked anyone's block off. He shook his head. It had looked like things might improve in that quarter. For reasons that baffled him still—and had made him a bit of a laughingstock at the station—she had brought him flowers after that case in November. It wasn't a romantic gesture, really. She'd asked to see him, thrust the flowers into his hand, and said, "Thanks." He had tried a couple of times to invite her out, but she had put him off. He was beginning to feel it didn't pay to be soft on a hard girl.

"Sir?"

"Sorry. A million miles away." Only twenty. Should he try driving out there one afternoon? That hadn't gone at all as he had hoped last time. "Oh, thanks," Ames said. April was winking at Terrell and pushing Ames's breakfast toward him.

"You know, I'm wondering if Miss Keeling was also a victim. She's a good decade younger than Miss Scott. Maybe the assailant kidnapped her." Terrell didn't say for what purpose, and Ames didn't ask.

"You're suggesting a random sort of attack by a stranger. A man knows there are women alone, robs the house, knocks out the older teacher, and carries off the younger one. The thing is, there's that threatening note directed at one of them. I'm headed out after breakfast to see if I can find any more."

"Good point, sir. I'm not surprised Miss Scott didn't remember the assault, but I'll tell you what surprised me: Darling said she remembered everything else about her life, but not that she's getting married."

Ames piled eggs on his toast. "You think that's significant?"

"Isn't that an important thing? Especially when you're her age and you think you might not ever marry?"

April was standing by the coffee machine waiting for it to fill. She looked at them and shook her head.

Ames saw her. "What?"

"Men always think women want nothing in life but to get married." She turned and poured three cups of coffee for the noisy group at the booth. "What did we fight a war for, anyway?" she added on her way past them with the tray.

Ames chewed his lip and looked at Terrell. "You fought the war. I missed it. Is that what you fought for?"

Terrell breathed in the scent of his unsweetened coffee and gave a little speculative nod. "Maybe, in part."

April interrupted any further speculation. "Would you look at that! I never thought I'd see the day."

Both men turned in time to see Inspector Darling coming into the café with a little boy who looked like he could use some breakfast and a good wash.

Ames leaped up. "Sir?"

Darling lifted Samuel onto the seat next to Terrell. "Samuel, this is Constable Terrell, and this is Sergeant Ames. The constable is going to make sure you get a good breakfast. A big mug of coffee for me, please, April." Darling collapsed beside the boy.

"Are you real policemen?" Samuel asked. "Can I have hot chocolate?"

April, a look of distress in her eyes, leaned forward and said, "You certainly can. Would you like some scrambled eggs and . . ." she turned to the kitchen, where the cook had stopped proceedings to watch what was unfolding at the counter, and mouthed something. He gave a small nod. "And pancakes?" April finished.

ON THE WAY back to the station, Darling responded to Ames's unasked question with barely compressed rage. "He'd been left there, on his own, no heat, little food, and for who knows how long. Possibly since Friday, and it's now Wednesday. When I asked him why he hadn't

105

telephoned someone he said he mustn't because it would make his father angry. He says he did hear something next door, as it happens, sometime in the evening after he got home from school. He saw a black car leaving, because it had got stuck in the snow and its engine was revving, and he went to look out the window."

"On his own, in this cold?" Ames glanced back at the café, seeing only the reflection of the street on the window.

"You might well ask. He told me there had been food in the house, but he'd certainly eaten his way through most of it. We're going to have to talk to child protection. Apparently it's not the first time. There's a local family that took him in once because their child went to play with him and found him alone. He said his father got angry and told him not to go begging at other people's houses."

"No mother?"

"Mother left a couple of months ago, if what he says is accurate. He's a very intelligent little chap. Reads widely of all everyone's favourite children's books. I expect that's the mother's doing. I brought some along. He has a bag in the car."

They pushed open the door of the station. O'Brien lumbered off his stool and approached with a sheet of paper. "You're not going to like this, sir. Hit and run. Victim deceased."

CHAPTER TEN

———

SERGEANT AMES STOOD IN THE doorway of the teacher's cottage and looked around the scattered room, as if trying to see it with new eyes and put a little distance between the violence that must have happened on Friday or Saturday and the bleak emptiness of the abandoned cottage now.

He would start with the untouched room. It looked as though the occupant had cleared out, so there would be less to find, and he could check it off his list. He closed the front door. He wanted to take his heavy wool coat off so it would be easier to move about, but the unheated cottage was icy.

Sweeping his gaze across the room, he saw again the little stool by the bed with a lamp. He imagined Miss Keeling, if this was her room, reading before she went to sleep. Reading what? He lifted the coverlet and looked under the bed, and he was surprised to see what looked like a small bible by the back leg, as if it had fallen to the floor as its owner had drifted off to sleep. It was at some remove from the chamber pot, he was happy to see. He went round to the other side and leaned over to retrieve it. Bible or no bible, Miss Keeling was right in the middle of this, he was certain.

Trying to imagine what sort of conflict the two teachers would have had that could escalate to this destruction, he was about to set the bible down when he realized it might be inscribed to its owner. He opened it. There, in a careful, almost childish hand, was the name W. Irving, and nothing else. He put the book down, made a note in his notebook, and as a last measure lifted up the mattress to see if anything had been left under it. Finding nothing, he turned to the bedroom where Miss Winslow had found the nearly unconscious Miss Scott.

It was interesting that it was Miss Scott who was leaving and Miss Keeling who was replacing her. Miss Keeling's room looked barely used. No pictures on the wall, or personal items on the dresser. But, of course, it had been packed up and quit in what appeared to be a hurry. Miss Scott's was still full of only half-packed things, as if she was somehow reluctant to leave and was dragging out the packing process.

He started with the suitcase, open, and lying at an angle half off the bed with its contents spilling out. He gingerly lifted the clothes out and put them on the bed, searching for anything that might give even the remotest clue to what had happened here. Under those clothes that remained in the case, he found a slim leather document holder. It had a flap with two buttons, and he opened these. Pulling out a stack of about five sheets of paper, he looked at them one by one, placing them face down on the bed next to him as he finished. First was a certificate of professional teaching issued in 1936 by the Province of Manitoba to Rose Marie Scott. 1936. She must have been young. What was she now? There were several letters addressed to "My darling girl" from "Mummy." They dated to 1943. They were on blue airmail paper, until one more recent one dated 1946 that was very brief and announced the death of her father. He turned these over as well. He did not want to read Miss Scott's private mail if it was not necessary. She was making a recovery. She should soon, he hoped, be able to supply them with the information they needed. The next was an army discharge document. He nodded. She'd been in service. Had she made it overseas, or did she serve in one of the many domestically based outfits? Last, an envelope from the Western Union telegraph office. He opened the flap and extracted the folded paper and read: "Sorry, Rosie, just learned. Captain S. Corcoran confirmed lost Scheldt, October 1944. DB."

Ames turned this over, as if its bloodless message could be explained in some way. DB must be a friend of hers, he thought, and then slipped the telegram back into the envelope and replaced all the papers in the leather folder. Who was Captain Corcoran to Miss Scott? No nasty letters. He put the document case back into the suitcase and continued his search. There was nothing to be found under Miss Scott's mattress either. But of course not, he reasoned. People hid things they valued under mattresses, not things that were upsetting.

His search of the living room revealed nothing. He concluded that any other poison-pen letters must have been destroyed. He went to stand in the doorway of Miss Scott's room, and gave some more thought to what might have happened to her here. She had suffered a blow to the head, the doctor had said. Had she fallen and hit her head after being pushed by someone? Or had she been coshed? It made a difference. He could imagine some sort of tussle, say, between the missing Miss Keeling and Miss Scott, where Miss Scott had come upon Miss Keeling going through her things and moved to stop her, causing Miss Keeling to push her away violently. If she'd been struck by something, it seemed to him more plausible that there was an assailant who'd come deliberately to rob the premises or take away the missing teacher for some reason.

What did it mean that she hadn't been killed? Was the kidnapper/assailant/robber not worried about being identified later? Or did he, or she, seeing Miss Scott fall unconscious, think she had died?

He looked carefully around the room to identify something she might have fallen against. The bed was a simple wooden bedstead with plain bedposts that extended only about ten inches above the base of the bed. Ames looked closely at the two that were away from the wall. There did not appear to be any evidence of a head falling against them. He began to pick up the books and personal belongings that had been knocked off a small bookshelf that had fallen over, which had likely stood on the inside wall of the room. She could have been pushed and knocked it over as she went down. The blow was to the rear side of the head. This seemed more likely. The trouble was that Miss Scott had been lying with her head away from the shelf, unless she had fallen and somehow, perhaps trying to make her way to the bed, repositioned herself.

He closed his eyes, trying to imagine the scene. Judging by the mess in the main room, Miss Scott has run in here to get away, because the assailant is between her and the only door out of the cottage. He opened his eyes and looked at the window that was opposite the door. It was closed and latched. He tried the latch and found it very hard to turn. Had she rushed in here, hoping to escape by the window, and found out too late that she couldn't? It would have been a desperate gambit in any case; the window was small and had a screen on it that might have taken time to dislodge.

She'd been found alive, so if Miss Scott had been hit on the head, she might have been able to turn herself over, grab at the bedcover, and do no more. Perhaps she'd lain quietly until the attacker had left, and then tried to move, but had had the stroke, which, according to the doctor, had done the bulk of the damage. Running his hand along the bookshelf, he looked for some indication that she might have fallen against it.

He went back into the living room and again surveyed the chaos. What kept niggling at his mind was the question of who the poison-pen note had been for, and if you received such notes, did you keep them somewhere, or get rid of them? One certainly was kept, shoved into the desk drawer at school. Perhaps it was the most recent one. She hadn't had time to throw it away, and then she never got the chance.

It occurred to him that if Miss Scott was scheduled to leave, she would have emptied out her desk for Miss Keeling's use. That suggested the note had been addressed to Miss Keeling. But it had fallen behind the drawer, Miss Winslow had said, meaning it could have been Miss Scott's and she'd missed it when she was clearing out.

———

Manitoba, 1942

"YOU CAN'T POSSIBLY. I absolutely forbid it! It's not enough that your brother's gone, I don't suppose?" Rose Scott's father, who had been sitting with his paper by the fire, had only barely listened to his daughter's declaration, but when the full portent of it finally penetrated, he'd thrown down the paper and had stood up. He had his hands in his pockets, as if to keep himself in check.

"Father, I'm twenty-five. I don't see how you can stop me. I want to help. With my teaching, I have skills that will be of use. With Danny gone, I can't sit idly by. It's not right. I'm only really telling you as a courtesy."

Rose's mother had been in the kitchen and now stood at the doorway into the sitting room, one hand over her mouth, fearful of her husband's too familiar tone.

He lurched angrily toward his daughter and then stopped. Rose could hear her mother's gasp of protest. She stood squarely, as if she would fight him if he came closer.

Mr. Scott's face hardened into a blotchy rage. He took another step closer to her and raised his voice. "Courtesy? Courtesy? There is no courtesy in outright disobedience.

I am the head of this household and you do as I say while you live under this roof! Have you heard what they call women who go into uniform? Loose women, trash. Not on my watch, my girl, not on my watch. Have you thought about what this will do to your mother?"

Rose looked at her mother, who was now crying silently, looking at her daughter, appealing to her to stop, to make it right. But Rose gave a little shake of her head, and, full of the sorrow brought on by the finality of this moment, turned away and mounted the stairs to her bedroom. She had anticipated this. She had heard her father carry on about his disgust at women joining up. His declaration that the fabric of society would be torn up by women quitting their proper sphere. Released from the respectable bounds of family, they would be whoring about. Whoring. Rose remembered her shock at hearing the word said out loud for the first time, and by her own father. Consequently, she had packed her bag in advance and had it at the ready.

She came downstairs and put the bag in the hallway, took her coat and hat, and put them on. She could see that her father had returned to his newspaper, perhaps convinced she would obey him after all, or perhaps cutting her out of his life altogether. The expression on his face, she thought, was much the same either way. Her father had never admitted of a world outside his own view of things.

Her mother stood in the hall, watching her daughter settle her hat using the little mirror by the door, her misery mute and contained. Rose put her arms around her mother and hugged her briefly. "Goodbye, Mother. I will write to you, I promise. No. Don't come with me. I will wait at the station on my own."

She picked up the suitcase and turned to open the door, certain that her mother, always subservient, would have nothing to say at the constant tension that unfolded between herself and her father. But her mother had put her hand on her shoulder firmly, giving it a little shake, and had whispered, "You're a good, strong girl."

———

October 1944

THE GIRLS SAT on their beds in the barracks, waiting while the milk boiled on the little single burner for their nightly cocoa.

"I wonder what the men do," said Daisy, a short, plump blonde from Halifax. She was like an optimistic child. Always full of good cheer and curiosity.

"They get shot," said Rose. She said it as if it was lightly meant, but it hung starkly in the air for a moment.

Daisy hesitated and looked down, and then said, "No, I know." She, like the other girls in the room, knew about Rose's brother, Danny. "But I mean now. Do they make cocoa or do they have secret bottles of hooch they take out for what Daddy used to call a 'nightcap'?"

"I don't think military discipline allows for hooch, Daisy," Rose said, smiling now. She stirred the cocoa and doled it into cups. "Let's drink up and say our prayers. Antwerp tomorrow."

Daisy threw herself back on her bed, a hand over her

forehead. "I wonder if I'll see Rufus again."

"That's what you get for falling in love with a man called Rufus," Rose said. "Here. Sit up and get this down."

"Yes, Mother," Daisy said with charming sarcasm. "I don't know how you could understand, at your age."

Rose smiled again. "A woman of twenty-seven is not too old to fall in love, Daisy." Her smile belied the pang she felt. What would Daisy think about Captain Corcoran? What would anyone think? Stifling a rueful smile by drinking her cocoa, she asked herself, What would my father think? He would be proved right, after all.

In the dark, Rose lay on her side, her arms crossed on her chest, her hands tucked under her chin, a position that had given comfort all her life, and thought about Stigg Corcoran, Third Canadian Infantry Division. He'd only said there was a big push. He hadn't said more, but she had heard they were doing something near or in Holland, she wasn't sure which. She closed her eyes and all she could see in that inner darkness was a terrible, gnawing fear.

———

THE SKY HAD darkened again as Ames drove back toward Nelson, and he was happy to be going back before the next snowfall hit. The ferry was on the Nelson side when he arrived, and for some reason there was quite a lineup of cars waiting to go across. It was doubtful he'd even make the next one.

People had gotten out of their cars and now stood in small groups, smoking and talking quietly. It was clear something was up. Ames joined a couple of men a few cars down.

"What's going on?" he asked, pulling his collar up against a gust of wind. A definite smell of new snow. He wondered how Terrell was getting on with the boy, Samuel.

One of the men, dressed in a long overcoat with his hat pulled low, shook his head. "Apparently they are short-staffed. The guy who is supposed to start the shift today never turned up. Good thing there's no emergency, that's all I can say." He drew on his cigarette, and then put his hand in his pocket and pulled out the packet, offering one to Ames.

Ames shook his head and said, "Thanks."

"I saw your colleague in the Legion last evening. He was pretty good with that fool, Dixter, in spite of the insults being flung at him. You can always count on Dixter to take things too far. Not the first time he's gone crazy. Can't take his drink. I expect they'll ban him after this. The war, I'm told, though it's been thirty years. Usually his brother-in-law comes to get him before anyone calls you fellows. I gather that officer is new here," the man said, repocketing his cigarettes.

"Yes, he is." If the man had hoped to use this as an opening salvo for a longer conversation, Ames was sorry to disappoint him. He was cold and wanted to get back into the car.

The ferry lights finally came on and there was some sign of movement. Ames lifted his chin toward the other side of the lake. "Looks like there's some action." He touched the brim of his hat with a pleasant smile and returned to his car.

DARLING LOOKED DOWN the short embankment. They could see the river below them. They were a few miles along on the road toward Castlegar. A tire-shaped curve in the snow right near the edge of the road suggested a vehicle had come too near the edge and swerved back, but it was snowed over so it was impossible to tell what sort of vehicle it would have been. Cars driving along the road with chains all day had turned the road into a dimpled landscape of snow. The figure, which looked like a doll that had been tossed out a car window, still lay face down and was almost completely covered in snow.

"It's remarkable anyone actually saw him," Ashford Gillingham said. The police pathologist had accompanied Darling to examine the corpse at the death scene, something he was doing more now. It was his normal practice to wait until the body of a victim was brought to his basement morgue, but he'd been interested to learn that one could gather more information by seeing the body in situ. He had fallen into the job when he was still a family doctor and had been asked to do a post-mortem on a man who had been shot at a local mine. He had found it intriguing and had offered himself to the police on a more regular basis, and he was working hard to catch up on his reading about the latest approaches in forensic science. He now stood next to Darling, gazing at the shape of the body lying below.

"Nothing for it," Darling said, and began to sidle down the short snowy embankment.

"I've brought my camera, so I can take a few shots. They might help, though no doubt your caller is right, it looks like a hit and run. As he's off this side of the road, I'm going to tentatively assume he was walking toward Nelson." The two men whose task it would be to take the body into town stood by their van smoking and drinking coffee from a Thermos, watching the activity around the body below. They were still not used to seeing Gilly working at the scene, though he had gone out to see Mrs. Hughes's root cellar when human remains had been found the previous spring.

Darling had joined the pathologist. "Scruffy-looking fellow," he observed. "How long has he been lying out here, I wonder."

"Still in a state of rigor mortis, but that's not saying much. In these cold conditions it can last for days. We may only get a real sense of that when we find out how long whoever he is has been missing from the bosom of his family." Gilly leaned down and looked closely at the face from which he'd brushed the snow. It was now exposed because of the angle of his head. "There are some abrasions on his face, but possibly from his slide, or fall, down to this position. If he was hit by a car, I might expect a broken neck, or back, perhaps."

Darling stood up, looking along the edge of the road above them, and shook his head. "Whoever hit him didn't bother to stick around." His voice registered grim disapproval. He leaned down and fished in the one coat pocket visible and found only a few coins. What he did notice was the lining of the coat was torn and the coat itself was old and well-worn along the edges. The man had several days' growth of beard.

"He almost looks like a vagrant," Darling suggested. "If he was hit in the back, he won't have seen the end coming.

That's a mercy, I suppose. I wonder what he was doing this far from town on foot."

"I expect, from the lingering odour, we will find he'd been drinking," Gilly said. "Perhaps he'd had a skinful and was walking home."

"From where? Castlegar is miles in that direction, and he's going the wrong way if he was drinking in Nelson. If he has no identification on him and he is vagrant, it will be the devil trying to work out who he is. It would have been a long walk in this snow, no matter where he was headed." Darling waved his hand at the van to signal the men to begin the process of removal. "Unless you have anything more you'd like to look at?"

"Nope. I have a couple of snaps. Together with whatever I discover in the post-mortem, I might be able to make a fairly complete picture. Good luck finding the driver. With this coat, if he was hit in the back, it's unlikely to have left a convenient dent on a front bumper, but we'll see how hard he was hit."

CONSTABLE TERRELL, WITH his hand resting gently on Samuel's shoulder, stood on the front porch of the neighbours who had once taken the boy in. He removed his glove and knocked on the door. Mentally crossing his fingers, he prayed they would take him. The child needed to be somewhere familiar, near his school, rather than uprooted into town. He looked down and saw that Samuel was looking up at him, concerned. Terrell gave him a little wink and a smile.

Footsteps, and then the door was opened by a plump

young woman who looked puzzled at the sight of Terrell, but then burst into smiles when she saw Samuel.

"Hello, you!" she said. "Come in, come in. It's freezing out. It's already starting to snow again. It wouldn't do to have you out there turning into a snowman!" She pushed the screen door open and stood aside. "Look, Ed. It's young Samuel and a friend," she called into the kitchen. "And who is your friend?" she asked, bending down to unbutton the boy's coat.

"This is Constable Terrell. He's helping me. I met two other policemen, too."

Terrell had removed his hat and was standing on the mat in front of the door. He nodded and said, "Ma'am."

"I'm Julia Benjamin. Just call me Julie. This is my husband, Ed. Gabriella is upstairs reading. They have a temporary teacher at the school she seems to like who is encouraging it. Gabriella! Come see who's here! Samuel's come to see us," she called. "Samuel, let's hang your coat up, and you go upstairs to see Gabby. There's a good boy."

The three adults stood watching Samuel climb the stairs to meet their daughter, who took him by the hand, saying, "I wondered where you'd got to." Julia Benjamin turned back to Terrell, her expression worried. "What's happened? He's welcome here, he's a lovely little boy, but I don't want any trouble with that father of his. I'm assuming his turning up with a bruised eye like that, at our doorstep, with a policeman, means something is not right."

"Let's get the constable off the mat, shall we?" Her husband came up behind her, smiling and wiping his hands. "Come in. I've just made a fresh pot of coffee. We can sit down. I'm guessing we're going to need to be sitting down for this."

Terrell, extremely grateful for the offer of coffee, explained that Inspector Darling had found Samuel at home, where he'd evidently been on his own since sometime on Friday.

"On his own? He's all of eight or nine years old. That man's a bloody criminal! He oughtn't to be allowed to care for him," Julie exclaimed. "It's not the first time, either. My Gabby went over to see him earlier in the fall, maybe October, and found him alone. She brought him back here. She left a note on the kitchen table saying Samuel was with us. Well, didn't his father rant and rave at us, telling us he didn't take 'nothing' from 'no neighbours,' and threatening us. He's an uneducated boor. I can't even believe Samuel can be his son. The mother, poor soul, left, you know. We don't know when. But I expect she was getting some of what Samuel has on his face. She was terribly frail and beaten down, if you know what I mean. But I wonder if she would have left if she thought he was going to be left at home like this, on his own.

"The thing is," Terrell said, "the only thing we'd be able to do is place him with a family in town, which might take some time and would also deprive him of being in his own school with his own friends. He's putting a brave face on it just now, but he's going to need people who care about him, as you folks so evidently do, until his father comes back, when he begins to take in the enormity of being left like that."

Ed shook his head. "You don't need to ask, Constable.

The man's a brute, and no doubt about it. That kid deserves better. If I'm honest, I only wish we could keep him. Gabby loves him, and often said she wished she had a little brother she could care for like she does Samuel. But I suppose he'll have to go back."

"There will likely be charges of neglect and so on. The courts could deem his father unfit. A search would begin, will begin, in fact, for his mother. The preference is always for a family member."

Julia sniffed. "I know she wasn't strong, but what kind of mother would she be, seeing as she couldn't cope or look after him?"

"Now, Julie, we don't know the full circumstances. Anyway, we'll be glad to look after him. Is there anything you can do to keep that maniac from coming over here uttering threats? I don't really think he'd do much, but he frightens Gabby," her husband said.

"He frightens me!" Julia Benjamin said.

"I think there is something. We can get an injunction to keep him away from here and away from Samuel till this is resolved. I'd like to see the boy back in school. He seems pretty bright."

"As bright as a button. Loves to read and is interested in everything. It's a real shame."

"I'm very grateful to you both," Terrell said, rising and taking up his hat. "And the coffee really hit the spot. I'd best get on before the snow gets too bad."

"You're new, Constable Terrell. How are you finding everything?" Julia Benjamin asked.

"Thank you, ma'am. It's a small station and everyone has

been very welcoming. And Nelson? It's not too different from a small town in Nova Scotia." Enough said, Terrell thought. Every town had a percentage of people who were determinedly friendly, and those who scowled and pulled away. According to Ames, some people even scowled at the small number of Italians in town, so it might have more to do with people unwilling to be around anyone different from themselves. The Benjamins were determinedly friendly, and that extended to him and to lost children.

He buttoned himself into his coat and slipped on his gloves. "Thank you again for taking him. I think you're just what he needs right about now."

"Don't worry about a thing," Ed Benjamin said. "We'll take good care of him."

CHAPTER ELEVEN

TERRELL ARRIVED AT THE POLICE station late, just as O'Brien was going off shift. He'd been waiting for the night man to come on.

"Busy place today," O'Brien commented, placing his Thermos in the lid of his substantial lunch box. "I'll be glad to put my feet up."

Terrell was still in the grip of some despondency about the ultimate fate of young Samuel, and worried that his consoling words about the father being deemed unfit to care for his son might, in the end, be but wishful thinking. If Gaskell wore a suit and made a good enough case to a judge, he could regain custody of the boy.

"Feet up sounds good. Are the inspector and the sergeant here?" He took off his hat and shrugged gloomily out of his coat.

"Ames has been out to the teacher's cottage again, and Darling's been up the road collecting a corpse from a ditch."

"A corpse! A car accident?"

"More like a hit and run. He's upstairs if you want chapter and verse. I'll say good night." O'Brien took his coat off the row of pegs on the wall, each with the name of its owner taped above it, and took up his lunch box. He'd just opened the door when he closed it again, shaking his head. "I'll forget my own head next. The hospital called. What with the excitement of the body, it went clean out of my mind. I made a note." He tucked the lunch box under one arm and shuffled through the untidy pile of papers at his desk.

Terrell, who had been partway up the stairs, came back down and took the note. "Seems she's remembered something," O'Brien said.

UPSTAIRS, TERRELL FOUND Darling and Ames in conference in Darling's office. Darling waved him in.

"I hear you've been out at a hit and run, sir," Terrell began.

"First things first, Constable. How's the little lad? Were they willing to take him?" Darling asked.

"They were. A very nice, warm family, though they are worried that they will have to deal with trouble from the father. I did assure them that we could seek an injunction to keep him away for the time being, but I'm not completely confident that a judge will place a child away from the father, especially if he presents himself penitently. I'm afraid my experience in these matters has not been encouraging. My thought is we should try to find the boy's mother as soon as possible."

"Yes, you make a very good point. We'll put something through to the RCMP and put some ads in the papers and

125

hope for the best. At the moment we don't even have his father in hand, unless he's slunk home in the meantime," Darling said.

"He hasn't. I stopped by the house to see if he'd returned and made sure it was shut up."

"Good man. Ames here has been back to the house of the hapless teachers to have another look around, especially for more notes, but aside from a folder of legal whatnots and letters belonging to Miss Scott, he hasn't found much to add."

"It was a real nuisance getting back as well," Ames complained amiably. "I had to wait two sailings to get back into town because the guy who was supposed to work the afternoon shift hadn't turned up."

"Yes, I had a bit of a wait as well," Terrell said. "That explains it. Speaking of Miss Scott, sir, Sergeant O'Brien handed me a note saying the hospital had called. Miss Scott has remembered something, and would one of us call round?"

Darling frowned. "What time was this, then?"

Terrell looked at O'Brien's note. "He's written 3:10."

Darling looked at his watch. "Well, it's gone seven. Give them a call, will you, and say one of you will be around to see her first thing in the morning."

"Sir," said Terrell, turning to leave, a bit sorry not to hear more about the corpse.

"Hey, just a minute," Ames said suddenly. "Didn't someone say Gaskell works the Nelson ferry?"

"Yes, that's right," Darling said. "He must be on a real bender if he's missed his shift."

"Unless he's the dead guy," Ames said.

126

"OH, I DO hope this means Samuel will be in school tomorrow," Lane said. "I haven't met him yet, and I can see that some of the other children are worried about him, with good reason, apparently." Darling had described finding Samuel alone in his freezing house and Terrell's placing him with the kindly neighbours.

They were at dinner eating a perfectly palatable stew, assembled by Lane after some hints from Eleanor Armstrong, with some fresh buns provided by Mabel Hughes. "I really cannot go on depending on the neighbours to provide food. We're like stray cats, getting handouts of buns from Mabel and recipes and cookies from Eleanor. Harris even dropped off a little bag of non-worm-eaten apples at the post office for us."

"They are very good buns," said Darling. "Perhaps you could continue your lessons. Weren't you learning how to bake up the hill before you started finding bodies all over the place?" Getting no response but a face from Lane, he continued, "How was school today?"

"Gabriella told me she liked the poem about the daffodils and said she looked up the rest of it at home. Her parents apparently have quite a good library."

"That will be nice for young Samuel." Darling did not share his anxiety that the body of the man they'd picked up that day might be that of Samuel's father. There was no point, he argued to himself, until more was known.

"Anyway, she offered to read the whole thing to the class, and then little Amy said that there were very good poems in the reader that Miss Scott used to use. Here is that reader." Lane turned and pulled it off the counter near the kitchen table. "What do you make of this? It's part of a hymn by someone called Kingsbury: 'But a glad or grievous fruitage, waits us at the harvest day.' When is the last time you used the word 'fruitage'?"

"I confess I've never used it. But perhaps you can bring it back into vogue." He put his napkin down and fiddled with his glass of wine. "I don't care if we're stray cats. The meals here have been a hundred times better than poor Mrs. Anderson used to make for me at my solitary little house in town."

"Any news on the teachers?"

"Oh, yes. I quite forgot. Apparently Miss Scott has remembered something. O'Brien delivered the note he wrote after the phone call from the hospital in his usual timely fashion, so we won't know till tomorrow morning."

"That's good news. Nothing on Miss Keeling, I don't suppose."

"Not a sausage."

LANE OCCUPIED THE time she usually spent reading in front of the fire before bed looking through the spelling book with more determination and found some more respectable poems. She picked words suitable to the children's various reading levels, which they might use to make sentences, or even poems, though she balked at providing them the word "auger," which appeared in the list of suggested vocabulary words.

"I'm delighted to see how busy you are with school," Darling said, looking at her over his own reading. "It will keep you out of my hair. At work, of course. I look forward to every opportunity to hobnob with you here."

"You make me blush. I won't be out of your hair for long, I hope. Either the British Columbia education people will send someone, or you will find the elusive Miss Keeling and bring her back to do her job."

"Unless she's responsible for banging Miss Scott on the head. Such a person would not be a suitable model for young people," Darling said.

"I don't believe for one minute she's the one responsible. Not for one minute."

"I am not as sanguine as you. She's likely the only one who can tell us what happened, and she may very well be responsible for it. It is extremely frustrating that she seems to have disappeared without a trace. You never know about the dark underbelly of people's characters," Darling grumbled. Then he brightened and reached out to take Lane's hand. "You finished? I feel sleepiness coming on."

———

May 1939

WENDY LOOKED UP from the table where Verna sewed and Isaiah read. She heard the screen door open and her father's voice pitched respectfully, a circumstance so unusual that she felt a flutter of anxiety. The very fact that her father was there at all suddenly seemed ominous to her. "Elder Nathaniel," she heard, alongside the clang of the coffee pot on the stove, and the smell of the cake her aunt took out of the oven and spread raspberry jam on while it was still warm. She heard her aunt murmur something, and then chairs scraping. From where she was, she could see down the hall to one end of the table in the kitchen where her uncle sat.

"Have you finished that passage? Are you ready to read it out loud to me?" Wendy said, turning back to Isaiah. She wasn't sure why she'd elected to use the Bible for today's readings rather than the books hidden on a shelf behind the bed. There had been a sense of expectation in the house, as if someone important was coming. That often meant an elder. Best to be caught with the Bible.

He put his finger on the line and began, "That whosoever believeth," stumbling over believeth, "in me, should not p-p- . . ."

"Perish," supplied Wendy, glancing again toward the kitchen. Her aunt came around the table with the milk jug, and just at that moment stopped and looked down the hall toward the children's bedroom. She apparently had not expected to see Wendy looking along the passage at her, and she turned abruptly and moved away from the door.

The swiftness in her aunt's turning away from her made Wendy's heart leap into her throat. Something wasn't right. Her aunt looked guilty. It took all her effort to turn back to Isaiah and try to listen to his question.

"What does perish mean?"

"It means to die," Wendy said. She could feel her voice shaking, and she cleared her throat.

"Then we won't die," he said, with all the satisfaction of a seven-year-old.

"My rabbit died," Verna said, looking up from the handkerchief she was trimming.

"He didn't believe in Jesus Christ," her brother said, a little contemptuously.

Wendy toyed with the idea of explaining that everything dies, no matter what it believes in, and then, because she loved them, simply patted Verna on the head gently.

"Let's go outside," she said, impelled by a sudden feeling of claustrophobia in the dimly lit room. "We can see if any new flowers came up at the edge of the field."

Only too happy to go out, the children put on pullovers and together made for the mud room to get boots. Wendy did not look toward the kitchen and closed the interior mud room door so she would not have to hear the low voices murmuring over cake and coffee.

IT WASN'T UNTIL she was making sure the children were washing their hands for dinner that her aunt approached her in the kitchen. "You two go to your room and change. We have a guest for dinner."

When they had gone, protesting, their mother turned back to Wendy. "A blessed and joyful thing is to happen to you. The Lord has seen fit to select a fine man for you. He is a godly and a good man." She had taken both of Wendy's hands and was pressing them.

"A man?" She glanced past her aunt and down the darkened hallway. "But why? I'm barely sixteen!" Wendy felt bereft, betrayed by her aunt who had been so kind to her. "I can see even you don't think it's a good idea!" Far from looking joyful, her aunt looked defeated. Wendy could feel the tears starting up and beginning to roll down her cheeks. "Who is he? I don't even know him."

"It is your uncle's will, my dear. Yes, you are sixteen. You are a woman now. The Lord requires that women, who are sinful vessels, marry young so that they do not stray into temptation. I was fifteen when I married."

"Sinful? How am I sinful? I have obeyed you and looked after the children since I was eight years old."

Her aunt glanced toward the closed door of the living room, where the muffled male voices could be heard, and was silent. "Aunty?" Wendy implored, sobbing quietly now. She'd retrieved her hands and was wiping her nose with the back of one.

"You cannot understand the nature of sin, nor the temptations women visit upon men."

"My father used to drink most nights and for all I know he still does, and that is against the word of God, but I am the sinful one? Is that why he's here?" Her father had lived with them for only a few months when he had first brought Wendy to be cared for by her aunt and uncle, and then had returned to the city, saying he couldn't stomach the religious "claptrap."

"Your father was driven toward the devil because of the wickedness of your mother. You bear the burden of your mother's sin. It is best like this. Even he knows this. Go and make yourself ready. A clean scarf around your head, a clean apron. Wash those tears. You must present a joyful face to your new husband."

"It's not fair! Why should the men be in charge of every-thing? I've never done anything to deserve this!" Wendy whispered this angrily, seeing her aunt's fear that somehow their argument would carry through to the kitchen. She turned and went into the children's room to change.

Numbly Wendy sat at the table. She watched with a kind of horrified fascination as Elder Nathaniel ate. He took up his soup and then turned the spoon so that the front of it faced him, and tipped the soup in, as if he were feeding a baby. His hair was lank and a white strand hung over his eye. How old was he? He put down his spoon and wiped his mouth with his sleeve and leaned back in his chair. His eyes swivelled briefly in her direction and then he turned to her aunt.

"That was good, Sister Hilda. You run a quiet, godly house, I can see that. You know, my first wife, Martha, is getting old. The arthritis gets to her. She will be happy for the help. I imagine you've brought this girl up in all the knowledge you have." He turned then, nodding and smiling at Wendy. He did not show his teeth when he smiled, just curved his red, moist lips under his moustache.

My God, she thought. He is already married. She felt as if the blood were draining out of her, and she put her spoon down and clutched the edge of the table in case she fainted. She turned to her father. "Daddy?"

She knew already he would not answer, would drive away in the morning, or even tonight, and let it all happen. After an excruciating "chat" with coffee served in her aunt's best teacups, Wendy went in search of her father. Her skin still crawled from where Elder Nathaniel had held her hand, kneading it as if he were milking a goat. She found him sitting on a bench at the back of the house, smoking, watching the sheets she had hung for her aunt move in the breeze.

"Why do I have to marry that old man? Have you seen him? He already has a wife!"

"They've been good to you, haven't they? There's no law that says you can't marry at sixteen with your parents' permission."

"Is that why you came here? To give me permission? I don't want permission." She could feel tears starting up again.

"Look, it's for the best. He's old, I know, but he has a good-sized farm. You'll be taken care of."

She sat, watching the evening come on, her spirits already low and falling further. This was the time of day that she fell into a sadness she could not understand. The one thing she wanted to ask him was too terrifying to articulate: "Why am I sinful?"

Instead, through her tears, all she said was, "Please don't make me do this."

He stood up, threw his cigarette butt into the grass, and started toward his car. "You'll do as you're told. Your aunt and uncle cannot be burdened with providing for a grown woman."

LATER, WHEN HER aunt came into the bedroom to say good night to the children, Wendy waited until she was leaving, and then she slipped out the door behind her and whispered, "What do you mean my mother's sin? What does that mean?"

Her aunt only shook her head and looked fearfully down the hall toward the sound of voices in the front room.

Wendy could see she was angry. She had seen her aunt's

anger more and more as she'd grown up. Even stifled, it had etched the shape of her face into tight lines.

"Aunty . . ."

"Don't ask me. I can't even say the words!" She tried to turn and go, but Wendy caught her by the sleeve.

"Please, please. Is it the reason you're making me marry that disgusting old man?" She felt suddenly overwhelmed by rage and powerlessness. "I won't! I'll run away!" She let go of her aunt's wrist and turned to go back into the children's room, where her bed had been for the last seven years, tucked into the corner of the room, nearest the window.

She was not prepared for the violence of the next moment. Her aunt wheeled her around and slapped her. Her head ricocheted off the door frame. She felt rather than heard the sound that came out of her, an oof from deep inside. The only thing present in the next moment was the sharp pain at the back of her skull. Her aunt took her chin between her thumb and forefinger and pressed it hard, coming close to her.

"Your mother was a whore, who got you off another man and then abandoned you, left her husband to bring up another man's seed. Do you understand that? Elder Nathaniel can keep you from going the same way. You should be falling on your knees and thanking God he has seen fit to redeem you."

Her grip on Wendy's chin softened into a caress. "Please, child. You are old enough to understand. You must not try your uncle. He has taken you in, housed you, clothed you, fed you. You must be obedient, as you have always been taught." She took hold of Wendy's shoulder, clamping her fingers hard so that Wendy cried out. "Don't try to run away. They will find you, no matter where you go, or how long it takes, and they will beat you until you cannot recognize yourself. And you will still have to marry him, only your life will not be worth living." She let go of Wendy, and whispered, "Please, Wendy. Please."

CHAPTER TWELVE

THOUGH CHRISTMAS WAS ALMOST TWO weeks away, perhaps it was not too early to get the children involved in some sort of Christmas activity. They could read Christmas stories and make cards to take home. They could sing some carols. That should fill the rest of this week and a good part of the next one, Lane thought. Judging by the calendar one of the teachers had put up, the holiday would start at the end of day on Friday the nineteenth.

Standing in the quiet, almost ringing silence of the cold classroom in the pre-dawn dark, she knew she was grasping at straws. She had prepared some dictation and had found a little book of science facts for the younger children and a book of world history. She would have to look at these and perhaps find out from the children where they'd got to, and which students were on which level. Of course, she wouldn't be here that long. The problem was what to do now, in the short term. An essay! They could all attempt an essay on what Christmas meant to them. That would certainly be educational.

Hope renewed, she set about lighting the stove. That done, but with her thick wool jacket still on till the room began to warm up, she turned her mind to supplies. There must be art supplies somewhere. Though she had found some foolscap pads, ink, pen nibs and holders, pencils, and the children's copy books in the main classroom, as well as several copies of books of stories, grammar, science, and arithmetic, she had found no boxes of coloured pencils or coloured chart paper. She had not looked through all the kitchen cupboards, thinking that they would only contain plates and cups, and she had rejected the uppermost cupboard as being too high to be useful. Now she dragged a chair to the counter and climbed on it to reach the upper cupboard. Nothing. As a disappointed afterthought, she pushed her hand into the back, feeling the layer of dust, and struck something hard and metallic. Her hand recoiled. She could feel at once that it was a revolver. She clambered off the chair and went to the classroom to where her handbag sat on the desk and extracted her handkerchief.

Carefully she reached in with the handkerchief and found the handle of the revolver, slid it out of the back of the cupboard, and carefully held it flat in her hand. It immediately struck her that it was not dusty. She wrapped the revolver in the handkerchief and put it on the counter and then reached up again into the back of the cupboard, feeling the space carefully with her hand, but there was nothing else, only the thick layer of dust coating that came away on her fingers, which she brushed off on the back of her jacket.

Lane hurried back into the classroom to look at the clock. The stove was beginning to do its job. She took off her jacket and hung it on the hook beside her desk and then she sat down, her hands flat on the desk in front of her. The children would not be there for a good fifteen minutes still.

One of the teachers had brought a gun into the school, and relatively recently. Why? She could imagine someone deciding that a revolver might make them safer in that cabin, especially when only one person lived there. Had Miss Scott owned the gun, and then, when Miss Keeling had moved in, thought it might be safe enough to be without it? But why move it to the school where any of the older, more curious children might find it? It was an act of absolute folly.

It would have to go back into the cupboard for the day, and Lane would call the station as soon as she got home. With this plan firmly in mind she returned to the kitchen and pulled the edges of the handkerchief away to look more closely. It was a Webley, certainly pre-war vintage. She was tempted to break it to see if it was loaded but decided against it. Darling could do it. They could drive back to the school as soon as he got home and retrieve it. Anxious now about the day's lessons, and glad she had spent the evening before preparing dictation and spelling work to start off the day, she rewrapped the gun, climbed the chair, and pushed the weapon into the back corner of the cupboard, where she'd found it. And not a moment too soon; she could hear the first car toiling up the road toward the schoolhouse.

She took a few deep breaths and had begun to write the day's activities on the blackboard when the stomping of snow off boots was followed by the door being opened. She turned. It was Gabriella Benjamin and a slender pale boy she had not seen before. This must be Samuel.

"Good morning, Gabriella. Who do you have with you?" Lane put the chalk down and walked to the back of the class prepared to shake hands.

"Good morning, miss. This is Samuel. He doesn't like to be called Sam."

"How do you do, Samuel. I'm Miss Winslow. You've been away. I'm very glad to see you." Lane offered her hand, which the boy took shyly before pulling his hand away. "I think I heard that you like to read. Is that so?" Lane asked, helping him out of his coat. He was alarmingly thin.

He nodded.

"He reads all the time. He's our best reader. He knows all the words the other students don't," Gabriella said with a formal and almost proprietary air.

"That is splendid. Then you will be enormous help to me. I'm quite new, and I need lots of help with the younger children. Where do you normally sit, Samuel?" She had seen with a flutter of dismay that he had the remnants of a black eye.

"He sits over here, next to me, where Randy has been sitting. He can go back to his regular seat. Samuel is staying with me right now. He gets to read all the books we have."

Gabriella was guiding Samuel to his desk.

"That must be fun. What's your favourite book?" Lane asked, hunching next to his desk.

"I'm reading *Robinson Crusoe*."

His voice was clear in a way Lane had not expected. A survivor, she thought. It was in his eyes and his voice and it belied his now fading black eye, scrawny body, and clean but threadbare clothes. She suspected Gabriella's family had cleaned up what little clothing he'd come to them with.

"One of my favourites," she said. She rested her hand for just a moment on his arm, and then stood up to greet the other students, who were beginning to tramp up the stairs.

AT NOON, THE students, having finished their lunches, crowded into the kitchen area and noisily stowed their metal lunch boxes. Then the tussle of climbing into outdoor clothes began. Lane leaned on the door jamb, watching them wrestle with scarves and boots, leaning down from time to time to help with the buttoning of a coat. She opened the back door and watched them tumble down the stairs and called out, "I'll be out in a moment! Stay right where I can see you."

Closing the door with a sigh of relief at the sudden diminution of the high-pitched shrieking that is the sound of children everywhere, she reached for her own coat and overshoes, and wished, not for the first time that day, that she could have worn trousers, the only reasonable garb on such a piercing, snowy day. She walked back into the classroom to check the stove and was surprised to hear the shuffle of a page turning.

"Samuel! You don't want to go outside to play with the others?"

"I just want to read my book," he said. His head lay on his outstretched arm, and he was holding the book at an angle. He sat up, as though he thought he might be in trouble for resting his head on the desk.

Lane approached and sat in the desk next to his. "Still *Robinson Crusoe*?"

"I've almost finished it. I love the part at the end. I've read it lots of times before."

"I know what you mean," Lane said. "I hate to put a book down when it's near the end." She jumped when a snowball slammed the wall. If they are starting with snowballs, they really will want watching, she thought. She was about to get up when he spoke again.

"I thought there would be a new student here."

"Did you? Why? Do you know of someone who has moved nearby?" Lane asked.

"No, but I saw that car a couple of times. It was the same one that was at Miss Scott's." Samuel had turned the book over, and now turned to glance out the window.

"You saw the same car here, at the school?"

Samuel nodded. "I guess so. It was stopped just down where the big tree is. The last time I saw it I was walking home, and I tried to look inside to see if there was any children."

"But there weren't any?" Lane was curious now.

"It was hard to see because the windows were shut. It was sort of like a mirror. I could see myself. Then when I saw the car at Miss Scott's, I figured they were going to talk to her, or Miss Keeling, about their child coming to the school."

"Well, that's disappointing, isn't it, when you expect to meet an interesting new student? When did you see the car at Miss Scott's?"

"Like I told the inspector policeman, the one with the brown hat who took me into town, it was the day my father went to work, except he didn't come back. I got to eat pancakes at a place in town with the policeman."

"That sounds just lovely," Lane said, smiling. "Did you tell the inspector about seeing that same car here?" Samuel turned his book back over, just as two more snowballs in close succession hit the school.

It'll be the windows next, Lane thought with alarm, pulling her gloves on.

"He didn't ask me about that."

"I'm going to leave you in charge of the classroom, and you can stay and read. I'd better get outside," Lane said.

Outside, Lane's presence put a momentary halt to the worst excesses of the snow activity, and then when she didn't shout at them, they continued playing, but were slightly more subdued. She was relieved to see Philip and Rafe building a snowman with Gabriella. Three fewer children making snowballs. She stood with her hands behind her back, watching with delight the children just being children, illuminated by sunlight and the responding sparkle of the snow, and then she turned to look down the road that approached the school. What was the "big tree"? From where she stood, all the trees looked the same, and they'd all be quite big relative to the size of Samuel, certainly.

But then she remembered the snow-covered winters of her own childhood, and how she wandered for hours outside on her own, especially to the small stand of trees at the top of a hill near her house. She had loved that hill because she could look down at her house, the smoke curling out of its chimneys, the small figure of the gardener outside cutting wood. She pretended it was as miniature as a dollhouse, with tiny living people. She had known, she recalled, each of those trees as if it were a friend. She knew their shape, and the peculiarities in their bark, and which ones had birds in them. Perhaps a grown-up looking at them would just have seen trees, all looking more or less the same. She would ask Samuel after school about the big tree.

DARLING WAS STANDING in the morgue with one Arthur Begley, the supervisor of the small ferry works crew that ran the cable ferry between Nelson and the north shore of the lake. The corpse was exposed from the shoulders up, any expression on the face released by death, devoid of the tension of anger and disappointment that had shaped it in life. Even his unshaven, scruffy chin looked benign in death.

"That's him, all right, poor fellow. Gaskell. I mean, he wasn't the most pleasant person to work with, but he did his job. Drinking, no doubt?"

"Thank you, Mr. Begley. You are quite sure? Are you aware of any next of kin?"

Begley shook his head, turning his hat around in both his hands. "I heard a story from one of the other men that his wife had upped stakes. She was quite a bit younger than him. He has a kiddie, I know that. Bit old to be parenting a young kid on his own, if you ask me. I don't know who looks after him when Gaskell's at the bar."

And didn't think to ask, Darling thought. Samuel's condition was the consequence of the reluctance of anyone to get into anyone else's business.

"Do you know if Gaskell had a regular drinking place?"

"I know he's a regular at the Legion. He saw service in the first show. Now that I think of it, someone told me they'd seem him heading toward the Metro from there on Friday night, though that's a little fancier. Not his usual, I wouldn't have said."

"Was he a good employee? Reliable?"

Begley shrugged. "He came on time, anyway, and did his job. Didn't take too much sick time. Surly sort of fellow, if it's not wrong to speak ill."

"Surly?" asked Darling.

"Didn't get on with the other men. Didn't get on with anyone, as near as I could see." Begley looked again at the covered mound that was the last mortal remains of Gaskell and shook his head a fraction. "Maybe the good Lord will find a place for him."

"Thank you, Mr. Begley. Sergeant Ames will see you out. He is at the top of the stairs." Darling turned back to contemplate the corpse. Though he knew already it was futile, he wanted somehow to see something in that face, anything, that would explain how a man could leave a child to fend for himself while he went off drinking in the middle of winter, but all reasons were gone. Only the fatherless child was left.

Gilly had said the victim's pelvis and lower back had been broken by being struck directly from behind at speed. He had refused to commit to whether it might have been deliberate, though on the whole, because of the violence of the damage, he thought it was possible that it was accidental, that the driver had not seen him until it was too late and had no ability to slow down or swerve away in time, especially with the snow. Other than these injuries he could report that his hands showed the wear and tear of handling the ferry in all weathers, that he had broken his ulna in childhood, and that he had been cut quite badly on the upper part of his wrist, possibly within the last year, which had left a nasty scar. Otherwise, considering the amount of drinking he apparently did, he had been in relatively good health.

It had been difficult to ascertain with the snow that had fallen since the accident if the car in question had been equipped with chains. If it hadn't been, it wouldn't be surprising that the driver had lost control on that road.

The next thing would be having to tell Samuel that his father was dead. Darling never relished informing families, but it was worse having to tell a child. He'd only had to do it a few times in his career, but the incomprehension, the sheer inability of children to understand the final magnitude of death, was painful. They could only understand that their mother or father would never come back, and it opened a void of darkness and fear that had little to do with "mourning the loss of a loved one," as the funeral brochures put it with such saccharine detachment.

He turned to go back upstairs just as the door opened. "Phone call, sir. The boss."

Darling frowned. "What boss?"

"Your missus." Only O'Brien could get away with this and he knew it. Darling's disapproving expression only encouraged him.

"You sound like someone whose day has just taken a bad turn," Lane said.

"It has," Darling said, collapsing onto his chair. "That hit and run has been identified as that poor little boy's father, Gaskell. I don't even know how to begin to tell him."

"Oh, that's absolutely beastly! He's such a lovely little boy. He was at school today, with Gabriella. She seems terribly fond of him. Of course, nothing can take away the shock of losing a parent like that, but I think her being in his corner is something."

"Yes, I expect you're right."

"Could you telephone the parents ahead of time to let them know that you're coming? That way they could be somewhat prepared." Lane pitied Darling, listening to his silence at the other end of the line. How often were the police obliged to make this visit and give this news? How much worse to have to deliver it to a child who effectively had no other parent! "I don't know, of course, how he will respond, but he has a kind of wisdom of a very old soul." But she wondered as soon as she said this if it were true, or just a comforting fantasy. She had, after all, only met him the once. He certainly had something that made him—here she paused in her thoughts—more resilient, perhaps. Still, children were, after all, children, however wise and tough.

"I'd best be about it," Darling said finally. "I'll see you when I get home."

Lane hung up the phone at her end, feeling the weight of sorrow for Samuel compressing her heart. Too late she remembered she was the one who'd called Darling, to tell him about the gun she'd found. She sat down and imagined Darling having to tell the boy this impossible news. What a dreadful part of his job!

For his part, Darling was trying to sort out how he would organize the awful business. He would make the call to the Benjamins before he left and then stop there on the way home, he decided.

He poked his head into Ames's office. "Why are you still here?"

"Stuff to finish up, sir. Any word on our corpse?"

"The worst, I'm afraid. It's Gaskell, that little boy's father. I'm going to telephone the Benjamins first to break the news. Thank God he's with that family. They seem like pretty decent people."

"Yes, sir. I'm sorry."

"You won't have time to be sorry, Ames. I want you to get out to the Legion, Gaskell's usual drinking place, and see if you can get a bead on who he was with on Friday night. Did he leave with anyone? Did anyone leave right after him? If you get no joy there, try the Metro. Someone saw him heading that way."

"The Metro, sir? That seems a little high-class for him."

"That's why it's interesting. Would a dishevelled single man like him go alone to the Metro? Or would he go with someone, and if so, whom? Or was he meeting someone there? Or even hoping to meet someone there?"

CHAPTER THIRTEEN

"I JUST HAVEN'T THE WILL FOR it," Lane said. She was in the Armstrongs' kitchen. "It's so frightful. What kind of Christmas will that little boy have now? Though I'm sure it would have been no picnic with that father."

"It is dreadful," Eleanor said, "but he will have the best Christmas that kind family can make for him."

"From what I understand, his place with that family is not even a sure thing. They've agreed to take him, but the government might decide to carry him off somewhere else, to complete strangers, or even send him to some sort of orphanage. Do they have those here?"

Eleanor drank her tea reflectively. "I suppose they have something on the coast or at some of the bigger towns. But surely no one would want to take a child from a family that wants him?"

A skeptical "Humph" escaped Kenny as he leaned over to pat Alexandra, who lay on her bed at his feet.

"And what if they only agreed to take him on the

understanding that he would go back to his father when things had settled? I mean, they may not be prepared to keep him, even if they are allowed to. It is an added burden to a family," Lane said. "Now that he's dead, I'm sure there's a bureaucracy out there that grinds into action when something like this happens. I'm really afraid that what is right is the very thing that will not happen."

"Let's keep a positive outlook. You may be surprised. Are they any closer to finding a teacher?" Eleanor gently tried to move the conversation away from the tragedy of Samuel Gaskell's situation.

"Well, certainly no one tells me anything. I'm assuming I'll be there one morning, struggling to teach arithmetic, and a teacher will sweep in and take over." Lane looked at her watch. "He must be on his way back soon. I'd better get going. Poor dear, it must be absolutely the worst part of the job."

Alexandra leaped up when Lane stood and watched her as she put on her coat. Lane smiled. For all the world, Alexandra's face seemed to be saying, "I'm here if you need me," as if she understood that something sad was afoot with the humans.

Lane stooped down and rubbed the top of the dog's head, and she was rewarded with happy tail wagging. "I really ought to get you a little friend," she said. As she stood up, Eleanor, who'd been busy at the counter by the sink, thrust a cake tin at her.

"Just a bit of the walnut cake. We can't eat it all. It'll be a little something for afters."

The kindness in Eleanor's voice filled Lane with gratitude

and she went into the darkening afternoon full of the juxtaposition of human kindness and human tragedy, all playing out together on this eternal snowy landscape. The icy air hit her with a refreshing wallop after the almost overwarm air of the cottage kitchen. As she approached the path to her house through the stand of birch, now leafless and white like the snow around them, she could hear the strain of a car changing gears as it tackled the hill. She hurried the last distance to the house and put on the kettle. A whisky toddy would certainly be a start. It was then that she remembered that she had meant to tell Darling about the revolver in the cupboard, and what she was certain it meant. It would be, she feared, a long night.

———

June 1939

THE TRAIN STATION at Williams Lake was nearly empty. Wendy had no idea when a train would be leaving. The man in the ticket booth looked up when she knocked on the window to get his attention.

"I need a ticket to Vancouver." She could feel her voice shaking. It must be obvious that she was running away. But the man pulled his watch out and waved it at her.

"No train till morning. You're a bit early, or a bit late." He chuckled.

Wendy relaxed a little and pushed money toward him. "How much money does it cost?" She'd taken money from the jar where her aunt kept it in the pantry. She was a thief as well as a runaway, she thought.

"You don't need that much." He took a small amount and returned the rest. "I'm about to close up the station. You better go home and come back in the morning. You people don't travel much. In fact"—here he peered up at her through the grill—"you look a little young. You supposed to be on your own?"

"I'm visiting an aunt." She was going to add the name of a place, but she didn't know one besides Vancouver.

"All right. Well, here's your ticket. Now run along home. Train'll be here at eight. It's coming overnight from out east."

Wendy took the ticket and walked out of the station as if she were going to walk up the road, but instead turned and ducked along the side of the station building, and then found a space at the back of the station facing the tracks. The main platform was built on sturdy scaffolding so that under it there was space just big enough for her to hide in. She sat on her small suitcase, the same one she had packed when she was a child to come here. She had been pulled away from everything she knew to a new life with her aunt and uncle, and now she prepared to wait out the night to begin a new life again. Her long skirt and wool stockings would help to keep her warm overnight.

She had been there no more than an hour when she heard a truck around the front of the station on the road. Her blood froze. She knew that truck. She pushed herself farther under the platform and held her breath. She could hear someone running, and then banging on the door of the station.

"It's closed. No train until tomorrow. What if she left

on this morning's train?" Her uncle's voice.

The second voice was the elder's. He spoke more quietly. She strained to hear. ". . . A ride going east, maybe."

"When I find her, I will strangle her for the shame she's brought on my house! I should never have taken her in. You are a saint to want to take her on!"

"I suppose we could call the authorities? Anything could happen to her if she's gone into the wilderness."

"Then it would be righteous judgment. I don't have truck with the police! When I want to do justice, I do it according to the word of the Lord. Tomorrow we will ask if she boarded the train. She'd be like to go back to the city. It's all she knows." Wendy heard no more, as her uncle's voice dropped, or he'd arrived back at the truck.

She heard the doors of the truck slamming. The sound was final, loud in the quiet afternoon. She folded into the tightest ball she could and waited, the sound of the river now her only companion.

VANCOUVER FELT LIKE a wall of noise. It was a world so unlike her old one that she could scarcely remember who she must have been as an eight-year-old. She stood on the platform and tried to recapture what that had felt like. Nothing came. Her childhood was an alien world to her now. Someone jostled her and she turned to look. It was a man, his face hidden under a hat. A woman followed him, hurrying, calling out for him to wait up. The woman sounded peevish. And then they were swallowed by the station door, taking their lives with them.

The Vancouver station was full of people, their coming

and going a heart-pounding blur to her. She could not have imagined so many people in one place. And all of them seemed to have purpose, direction. Wendy went and sat on the bench against the station wall, pressing her back to the wall as if it might protect her, and looked at the train that had just dropped her off. She pushed her suitcase so that it was behind her feet, hidden by her long skirt. She had thought only of getting away, but never of what she would do when she got here. She had spent the time on the train alternately sleeping and wondering when they would catch her. She had peered anxiously out at each station the train stopped at, thinking they must know now she hadn't gone on yesterday's train, and must have followed in the truck, but each station was only full of strangers who stared at her, then quickly looked away. As the train had travelled farther away from Williams Lake, her immediate fear had begun to dissipate, and instead she had been over-whelmed by an exhausted sleep.

When most of the people had left the station, she went to the ticket booth and leaned in to speak to a man with a dark blue cap who was looking down at some papers.

"Excuse me. Do you know of a rooming house near here? Well, anywhere, really."

At the sound of her voice he looked up and peered closely at her. "You look a bit young," he said.

"I'm eighteen," she lied. "I've come to go to secretarial school." She hoped there was such a thing.

"Just go down that way, along Cardero. You'll see signs." He waved his hand toward the door.

She thanked him and turned to go. "Good luck," she

heard him call after her as she pushed open the door onto the street. The skepticism she heard in his voice was drowned by the noise of traffic.

After passing several houses with signs, losing her nerve at each one, indeed, losing her nerve at every moment on the street, startled by every stranger she passed, she stopped in front of a dark gabled house with a tiny, neat garden behind a fence. "Lady Boarders" said the sign.

A tall woman dressed in tweed with an olive-green cardigan over her shoulders answered her knock. Her hair was tightly curled and held in place with a fine net. She looked at Wendy for a long moment before she spoke.

"Yes?"

"I'm looking for a room. I . . . I don't have very much money, I don't think." That was one of the features of Wendy's life. She had no idea about money. Her uncle went into town to buy supplies, and they had chickens and milk cows and a garden. Wendy had never left the farm.

The tall woman frowned at her, and unconsciously glanced down the street and then back at the young woman in her strange clothes. "Where have you come from?"

Fearful now that she would be in trouble because she was young, or that the woman would think she had run away from home, Wendy said, "I came from near . . ." She hesitated. If she said Williams Lake, she could be traced if her uncle changed his mind and the police were set on her. "Vernon. I've come to find work. My family . . . needs the extra money."

The woman shook her head and opened the door wider. "You'd better come in. You don't look like you should be out on your own. As it happens, I need some help around here. You can stay in return for some housekeeping. As to you getting a job—" The woman looked her over, shaking her head again. "You're going to have to dress like a normal person. You can put your bag there for now."

In the kitchen, the woman filled a kettle at the sink and put it on the stove with a clatter, turning a knob. "I'm Mrs. Franklin. I have four other young ladies here. Three of them are going to school. Can you read and write?"

Her face flushing, Wendy stammered, "Of course." Did she look like someone who couldn't read?

"Well, that's something, anyway. What sort of work were you thinking of?" The water in the kettle was beginning to heat up, making a hum. As Wendy watched it, it triggered something far back in her memory. "We had a stove like that, that you just turn on with a knob," she said suddenly. "When I was a child. I remember now!"

"My word," Mrs. Franklin said quietly, pulling a tin of tea out of the cupboard.

"I'm sorry. I was thinking that I could teach school. I like children." This statement was a surprise to Wendy, but now that it was said, she saw that it must be true.

"You have to do a darn sight more than like children. You have to have training, get a certificate. You have to have a high school education, for starters. You don't look like you've ever seen the inside of a public school."

"Oh." Wendy sat back and was silent. Then she remembered the inside of her school. The long hallways, a picture of the King in her classroom. Other children sitting in rows around her. A smell of orange peels. She felt almost overwhelmed with the flood of memories. "I did go to school. Here in Vancouver. I was in grade three. Then I had to go live with my uncle and aunt."

"A grade-three education. Splendid," Mrs. Franklin said. "After you have a cup of tea, I'll show you to your room. You'll be sharing with Mary McCardle. We'll have to see about getting you some proper clothes, and I'll show you your duties."

It was only then that Wendy looked down at her clothes. The long, loose dress, the apron, the thick wool stockings, her heavy boots. They weren't like anyone else's. She had been so fixated on her escape that she hadn't noticed how different she looked from everyone else. In what other ways was she not like everyone else?

———

DARLING HAD DECIDED not to call the Benjamins from work, feeling he needed to build up to it, and was on the phone now, from home, to Julia Benjamin. Lane could hear the long silence at the other end of the line when Darling had broken the news about Samuel's father. Finally she heard the voice, far away, tinny, hesitant, saying something.

"Yes, of course. You are right. I'll be there first thing in the morning, if you can keep him back." The woman's voice again, pitched suddenly higher. "No," Darling said, "I don't think we need to worry about that just at the moment. It's very, very good of you. It will make all the difference to him just now."

"She's right, of course," Darling said as he hung up.

"It is not the sort of news you deliver to a child before bedtime. They were worried that this might cause him to be moved somewhere, to a relative. I sincerely hope I'm right that it is not something to worry about just now." He sighed and shook his head. "I don't know if a nine-year-old child even understands death, really. Anyway, they are keen to keep him there."

"Thank God for that," Lane said. She had begun to make supper and moved back toward the kitchen, but instead of taking up the task of slicing carrots again, she sat down, her hands folded in front of her. Did a child understand death? She had been five when her mother died. She still remembered being told of it, her grandmother holding both her hands. She remembered feeling a kind of dread whenever she was near the room where her mother had been sick, and then never seeing her again. Had she thought her mother would come back one day? "He's nine. I don't know what a child that age would understand. I was five when my mother died. I can't remember what I understood, only that there was a kind of darkness."

"I was sixteen when mine died. I'm not sure I even understood it then. I mean, you know what 'dead' means, but you can't comprehend the massive absence the person leaves behind," Darling said.

Lane let this sit for a moment, and then took up the knife and moved the carrots into place, then paused. "If there were other relatives, wouldn't they have come out of the woodwork before now? It sounds as if that poor child has been living an extremely marginal life with that inept brute since the mother went away."

"Unless they didn't know about his situation. We've instituted a search, of course, but it becomes more urgent now. We can add Samuel's relations to the list of missing persons we're trying to track down," Darling said.

"Speaking of missing persons, I made a discovery today. Two, actually. I believe either Miss Keeling or Miss Scott was afraid of someone. It's the reason I telephoned you, but of course this dreadful business of Samuel's father put it right out of my mind. I found a pre-war Webley revolver high up in the kitchen cupboard at the school that I'm pretty sure was put there recently. There was no dust on it, but plenty of dust on the shelf. I nearly jumped out of my skin when I found it, and I wondered who would bring a gun into a school, and why. It seems to me to be an act of desperation. But Samuel, actually, said he'd seen a car several times parked down the road a bit from the school, as if someone was watching. Maybe one of the teachers thought she was being watched. Maybe one of them *was* being watched. He thought it was the same car that he'd seen outside the teacher's cottage."

Darling frowned. "Where is the gun now?"

"Wrapped in my handkerchief and back in the top cupboard. I was hoping we could nip over and pick it up. I don't want that thing in the school!"

———

June 1939

WENDY STOOD IN the room she'd been shown to. It was dark because the flowered curtains were closed, and it had a

159

smell she could not quite identify: something pungent, like the remedy her aunt spooned into water for the children when they had tummy upsets. Mrs. Franklin had gone for sheets and a pillow slip for the unmade bed. Wendy opened her bag and took out the small bible, now the only thing she had from her mother, and placed it on the bedside table. She sat on the bed with her hands folded, looking at it. She had often wondered what happened to the teddy bear she'd had. That had been her mother's too. Something in it was wicked, it was ungodly, her aunt had said. She was ungodly. Her heart was pounding with a sudden upsurge of fear. What had she done? She had run away from home, from a sacred obligation to marry and escape from her mother's sin. Her sin. If they found her! She felt her breath catch with fear at that final warning about what would happen if she were caught. The silence of the room offered nothing in the way of comment. She put her bag at the foot of the unused bed and turned to look at the room. Whoever the other girl was, she was very neat. Her bed was made, and a three-drawer dresser had a hairbrush and a comb lined up side by side on a little pink cloth. A small jar of Pond's face cream stood next to them. She longed to open the jar and smell the cream, but she could hear Mrs. Franklin closing a door somewhere outside in the hall.

Next to her own bed was another dresser, and it, like the other one, had a mirror hanging on the wall behind it. Wendy approached this and looked into it. Reflected back at her was a face she scarcely recognized, hair pulled back and hidden under a scarf tied tightly at the nape of her neck.

There were no mirrors in her uncle's house. It was to prevent sinful vanity. How did she know that? Had she asked once, when she'd first arrived? Her hand went up to her forehead and then down again.

"You see what I mean about your clothes," Mrs. Franklin said, coming briskly through the door with a pile of bed linen. "You can't possibly go about looking like that. Now then. Make your bed and settle in. The bathroom is down the hall. We have a bathing schedule for all our young ladies that you will see posted on the wall. You will be bed four."

Wendy turned guiltily away from the mirror and accepted the linen that Mrs. Franklin put into her hands.

Nodding at the bag Wendy had put on the floor, Mrs. Franklin asked, "Is that full of more of this sort of thing?" She pointed at Wendy's clothes.

Wendy nodded. "It's what we have. We make them." She stopped. It had been in her mind to add "as God intended."

"Good for you. You can sew. I can put you to the mending. I have a few bits of clothing that my young ladies have left behind. Let's see if we can get you looking less like a girl off a wagon train. Now, you get settled and come down when you're ready." She walked to the window and pulled the curtains open decisively, turned smartly out of the room, and shut the door, leaving Wendy in the heavy silence with her new and unknown self.

CHAPTER FOURTEEN

—————

"WHAT I REMEMBER, YOU SEE," said Miss Scott, "is that she wasn't there." It was Friday morning and Ames had gone to the hospital first thing at Dr. Edison's call. She reported that Miss Scott now seemed clearer about her circumstances and it might be a good time to interview her. He was relieved to see she had no roommate.

"I see," said Ames. "You mean Miss Keeling." He had his notebook out and was wishing hospitals didn't smell of something that made him want to breathe stingy, shallow breaths. A combination of something they must use to clean—Lysol? Bleach?—with a chemical overlay of strange medications. Miss Scott's bed was by a window that looked west, and now offered grey morning light filtered through the icy mists that hung over the town. Ames was feeling that vague repulsion the healthy have for hospitals.

"Yes, I think so. Miss Keeling. Yes." Miss Scott, who was propped on two pillows into an uncomfortable-looking position, neither fully lying down nor fully upright, put her hand to her brow, tenting her fingers over her eyes as if to draw out some clearer memory.

Ames was silent for a moment, unsure how to pursue the problem of Miss Scott's obvious uncertainty about what she remembered. "Someone came to your door, but Miss Keeling was not there. Had she gone out shopping?" Perhaps some appeal to the ordinary would work.

"I don't know, you see," Miss Scott said. "I was packing to go home. I couldn't find—" Her forehead furrowed. "I couldn't find her. That's it. I didn't know the voice, so I knew it must be for her, but I couldn't find her, I told them that."

"When you told the nurse that you remembered something, is this what it was, that a man had called asking for Miss Keeling?" Ames asked, trying to anchor her statement.

Miss Scott was silent. "Miss Keeling was gone already, you see. I had been in town. It was so cold, you see. And when I came back, she was gone. Her clothes, everything. She didn't leave a note. There was just the bathroom mirror. That's it."

Ames was developing an urge to count how many times Miss Scott said "you see." He didn't see at all.

"Was this Saturday morning?" And what did she mean about the bathroom mirror?

Her face lit up. "No, Friday, you see, because I thought at first she hadn't come home from school. You see, that's what I remembered! I told her I didn't know where she was."

Ames made some notes, trying to make sense of the gist. "When you say you 'told her,' do you mean Miss

Keeling? When she came home you told her you hadn't known where she was?"

Miss Scott looked at him, suddenly confused. "No, I don't know."

"What did you mean about the bathroom mirror? Had something happened to it?" Ames asked. But even as he said this, he remembered the crack in it. Was this what she meant?

Miss Scott reached for a glass of water by her bed and sipped at it, splashing the contents onto her covers. She looked as if she'd exhausted her last bit of strength. At that moment a young nurse, her dark hair in a neat bob under her cap, came into the room and took up the unprotesting patient's wrist, frowning at her wristwatch.

"That's it, Sergeant. She'll have to rest now. Have you everything you need?" She spoke with an authority at odds with her youth.

Not even remotely, Ames thought, getting up and slipping his notebook into his pocket. "Not quite, I'm afraid. Can I come again later? I think she was close to being able to tell me more about the assailant. It's critical that we get that information."

Tucking the covers more securely around Miss Scott, whose eyes had closed, the nurse shook her head. She put her hand on the back of Ames's shoulder and guided him out into the hall. "Head injuries are unpredictable, Sergeant, and people with them can't be bullied into giving information. We will let you know when you may return, if that is all?" She tilted her head primly in a way that conveyed an air of unequivocal dismissal.

Realizing he should have got her name, Ames stepped back out of the elevator he'd been shown to. "I'm sorry, can I have your name?"

She had already gone behind the counter and looked up when Ames spoke. She really was quite pretty, Ames thought.

"Sister Davies, but I will not be the one who contacts you. Good day."

Ames got into the car and shuddered. Here was another woman who appeared to disapprove of him. Making a mental note to avoid dating Sister Davies, should the opportunity ever present itself, Ames drove slowly down the hill, relieved that the city snowplow had made it up this hill, thinking about what Miss Scott had had to say. Really, when you thought about it, there was not much in it that you could hang your hat on, with the possible exception that Miss Keeling had decamped some time prior to the assault of Miss Scott. Well, it would all go into the hopper. Sooner or later it might all begin to make sense. Her main preoccupation seemed to be that Miss Keeling had not been there when . . . what? When she got home from going into town. Was that at night? In the afternoon? He suspected Miss Scott might be very mixed up about the times things happened. But then again, she had been very clear that it had been Friday. So say she'd been into town on Friday and had come back and Miss Keeling had been gone. Did that put Miss Keeling out of the running as the assailant? Not completely.

As he pulled the car into its spot in front of the station, he wondered how Darling was getting on with the hit and run and telling that poor boy about his father. Ames's visit to the Legion and the Metro had yielded exactly nothing.

Ames knocked on the door of Darling's office. It was ajar, and he could see Darling standing by the window with his hands in his pockets, his inevitable pose when cases became difficult. "Sir?"

"What is it, Ames? You'd better have good news," Darling said, turning away from the window. "More bloody snow!" He sat down with a sigh.

"I'm not sure if it's good or not." Ames took out his notebook and sat down heavily, making the chair scrape loudly.

"Please, sit down," Darling said with a wan smile.

"Sir." Ames smiled briefly. "Miss Scott doesn't seem like she's all there, I must say, but what I got out of her possibly takes Miss Keeling out of the picture, or not." Ames went on to explain what he'd got in his interview at the hospital. "Unless Miss Keeling cleared out her things with a view to coming back later to demand whatever it was from Miss Scott and then do a runner. In the event Scott refused to tell her, so she trashed the place and made her getaway."

Darling nodded and rubbed his chin thoughtfully, and then folded his hands in front of him. "I'd love to take the elusive Miss K out of this mess. It would simplify things if we could just assume she went off for her own reasons, angry about her pay or what have you. Unfortunately, your Miss Winslow has found something that puts that in doubt."

"Sir?"

"She has found a revolver hidden away on a top shelf at the school, and put there recently, Detective Winslow says, because the gun is not dusty while the rest of the cupboard is, and furthermore, that young Samuel Gaskell saw a car parked just down the road from the school several times, and furthermore, he told her that the car looked like the same one that was outside the teacher's cottage late last Friday afternoon. So no, I don't think we can drop Miss K just yet."

"Wow!" Ames leaned back in his chair.

"As you say. We don't, of course, know for certain that the gun belonged to Miss Keeling, or Miss Scott, or, indeed, some previous teacher. It's being dusted for prints. You're going to have to get a kit and pop back up to the hospital and get Miss Scott's prints for elimination."

"Just this minute, sir? I was more or less given the bum's rush out of there by a pretty ferocious nursing sister who said I was tiring her patient."

Darling gave him a look that suggested he was a blatant coward to be afraid of a nurse, and that he'd better hop to it.

"What about the Legion and the Metro?"

"Oh, right. He wasn't at the Metro on Friday night, at least no one saw him there, though he sometimes puts his head in before he decides if he's going in. He was, apparently very much as usual, at the Legion for much of the night. He has a specific corner he sits in, and he usually drinks pretty heavily, and then, God help us, drives home. He talks to a few of the people that the bartender pointed out to me, so I had a chat with them. They certainly remembered him being there, but one person thought he might have seen him leave a little earlier than usual, when the bartender told him he was cut off. The funny thing about Friday is that he didn't have his car. He said he'd left it 'somewhere,' he didn't seem to remember where. And here's something, sir. Someone seems to have given him a ride, because he was seen getting into a car, which no one could remember the make or colour of. No one, by the way, seemed very sad to hear he'd died, though they all said they were sorry for the little kid."

"Good. That narrows it down. Interesting about the car. I wonder where he left it? And, critically important, who gave him a ride. That person was the last one to see him alive."

"I did ask, sir, if anyone there had taken him home, but no one admitted to it, anyway. I think that shows how much his colleagues give a damn. Not one of them offered to drive him, or even thought twice about how he'd get home. He walked off into the night and they went back to their business."

Ames paused on his way out the door. "Oh, I forgot. About Miss Scott. She mentioned that crack on the bathroom mirror. She sort of implied she saw it when she found Miss Keeling gone. That means it might not be part of the trashing done by the man who came there. And that, by the way, is all I got before she faded and I was ushered out."

"Go back to the man who said he saw Gaskell getting into a car. Find out anything he might have remembered about the car. Maybe in retrospect he will have remembered something useful, like who was driving the damn thing."

———

Monday, December 1

"WHERE'S MY MONEY?" Gaskell said it quietly. He and Art Mackenzie were standing by the dock at shift change, smoking.

Uttering an imprecation, Mackenzie threw his cigarette into the snow. It was cold, he was just starting his shift, and he didn't need this.

Gaskell reached over and shoved Mackenzie hard. "I want my money. I've asked nicely."

"That's right. Your usual tactic. Bullying. You can bully that kid and your wife, but you aren't going to push me around." Mackenzie pulled his hat down and turned to go.

"What's that you said?" Gaskell's face seemed to go crimson with rage.

"You know how I know?" Mackenzie said, turning back to Gaskell and leaning close. "Know how I know? She told me, crying, looking for comfort, nestled up all sweet in my arms." He was nodding. "And you can go to hell. I don't have your money, and I doubt I ever will." He knew he'd landed a blow. Gaskell had taken a step back and his mouth was opening and closing as if he'd lost the power of speech.

The strike, when it came, was surprisingly fast. They were standing in snow, dressed in the voluminous winter garb they needed to be out in this weather on the deck of the ferry. Mackenzie was taken aback by Gaskell's speed and rage. He had barely begun turning to go back to the ferry when he felt his head snap back with the crack to his chin, and he staggered backward, trying not to lose his footing. A second blow hit him in the solar plexus and this time he did go down, gasping for breath. He flinched as Gaskell surged up to him.

"I'll kill you, Mackenzie. See if I don't," he said in a strangled voice. "You won't know what hit you. You have a week to get my money, and if you ever mention my wife again you'll be sorry."

"Hey, everything all right here?" Their shift supervisor came on the scene just as Mackenzie was getting up, still trying to catch his breath. "Could you two sort this out later, maybe? Mackenzie, you're due on. We've got cars piling up."

Gaskell turned without a word and made his way up the street away from the landing.

Mackenzie watched him disappearing up the road. "He is a horse's backside," he said, shaking his head.

"You're no saint yourself. Now get to work."

———

AMAZINGLY, THE WEATHER had warmed up just enough to render the roads and streets a slushy mess. On the byways of King's Cove, this typically took on a muddy characteristic that left deep splatters over the backs of cars trundling up and down the roads. Lane had watched Darling's car disappearing up the road with an unhappy Darling at the wheel. He would be stopping by the Benjamins' to talk with young Samuel.

Lane readied herself to go to the school, telling herself not to forget the tin of lemon and oatmeal cookies Eleanor Armstrong had given her for the children. It might, she had said, cheer them up a bit, if, and she did not doubt it, the news of Gaskell's death was already out. Lane wondered, as she walked through the melting snow with books and the tin of cookies, how Samuel was coping, and if she ought to say something to the other students.

She would make some hot cocoa for after the lunch playtime and bring out the cookies then. They could talk about Christmas and then perhaps they could spend the afternoon making cards. She had purchased all the stationery supplies Bales had in stock.

Samuel had come back to school a little later in the morning, much to her surprise, Mrs. Benjamin explaining that he hadn't wanted to stay at home. The children, who had indeed heard the news in that mysterious way children had of knowing things, had kept a sombre mien when Samuel was about. Lane had taken him aside and told him how sorry she was about his father, to which he had nodded and said, "Thank you, Miss Winslow." He had been about to go back to his seat, where Gabriella was laying out his work in as protective and motherly a fashion as could be imagined from a child, and then he said, "I have to go back to my house because I have to get my things, because I am going to keep staying with Gabriella."

"That is lovely, about staying with Gabriella," Lane had said. "Will her mother go with you to help?"

He had nodded solemnly and gone to sit down. The cookies and cocoa had been a big success, and the children had thrown themselves into the card making with much energy and laughter. While they were working, Lane had placed a piece of string across the blackboard so that the children could hang their cards until the last day of school when it was time to take them home.

It was Samuel talking about going home to get his things that put Lane in mind of the teacher's cottage. She was certain it had been left in the appalling state she had seen it in when she had found Miss Scott. It was the first time it occurred to her that she had no idea who might be deputized to clean it up. After all, in spite of Darling's glum outlook at the lack of progress on any front, which he had regaled her with over dinner the evening before, sooner or later a teacher would be coming along, and it would be a shame for her, or him, to have to cope with the cottage in that state. Consequently, when the last child had left, she tidied the classroom, banked the fire, made her way down the hill to the Balfour store, and went in to use the phone.

Mr. Bales was stacking some cans of peas on a shelf when she came through the door. "Afternoon, Mrs. Darling," he said, relieved to be away from the box of cans. "Need some gas?"

"No, I'm all right there. I'm just wondering if I could phone through to my husband. I was thinking that the new teacher might come any day and it would be nice if the cottage were tidied a bit. I may pick up a couple of cleaning supplies as well."

Bales's black Lab had gotten up and was now inspecting Lane's knees with interest. Bales inclined his head toward the phone sitting on the desk behind the counter. "Just get her to put you through."

Lane stooped down to have a quick word with the dog and then went around behind the counter. "Hello, Lucy, do you mind putting me through to the police department in town?" she said into the doorway to the exchange where Lucy was hurriedly putting her earphones down.

"Certainly, Miss Winslow," she said, performing some

172

mysterious procedure with jacks being plugged into sockets. "It's ringing through now." Lane smiled. Lucy had obviously been listening in to some conversation. Lane supposed she could hardly be blamed. It no doubt helped pass the time, though Lane could see she also had a paperback book face down on the console. A seedy-looking volume called *Stolen Love*, with a cover to match.

"Hello, it's me. I just had a thought. Would you mind awfully if I went to tidy up the teacher's cottage? Either Miss Scott will get better and go back, or the new teacher will come, and it's a frightful mess."

Darling considered. She had a point. They'd been back once since the initial search for evidence, and there appeared to be little more to find. "I suppose there's no harm in it."

"I mean, is anyone else going to do it? Who is usually in charge of this sort of thing?" Lane asked.

"Usually the householder, when all is said and done, but as you point out, there's really no one to do it. Miss Scott will no doubt need recuperation time before she goes off to get married." Darling stopped. "It's very funny, now that I think of it, that no one has come forward claiming to be the bridegroom and demanding to know where his fiancée is."

Lane wanted very much to ask if they'd received any word of Wendy Keeling. She was becoming increasingly worried about why she might have disappeared but was very conscious of the presence of Lucy just around the corner, no doubt primly reading her book. "That's good then. I'll pick up some scouring powder and some sponges and have a go at it now. No, before you say it, we don't need to worry about supper. Angela has invited us over.

We can discuss the goings-on up at the old house. Can you pick up a bottle of something on your way home? I'm just at Bales's store now and will go right down to get started. Bye now," she finished brightly.

Ah, Darling thought, hanging up the phone on his end. She's as intrigued as I am, no doubt, about the possibility of a missing fiancé to add to the confusion, but she was probably being closely monitored by Lucy the telephonist.

LANE BUMPED DOWN the road to the teacher's cottage. She would have another hour of daylight, and perhaps she could get the furniture upright at least, and then maybe tackle the cleaning the next day. The cottage had electric lights, but she thought she'd like to get home before it was dark. She would be back the next day, after all. The snow that had been on the steps had melted after being trampled on by her and various police officers, leaving the unpainted and greying wooden steps exposed. Taking up the box of cleaning supplies, Lane started up the stairs and then was startled by a loud wet noise coming from the side of the house.

She smiled at her own jumpiness when she saw that it was just a huge mass of snow that had slid off the roof under its own melting weight. Once inside, she put the box of supplies on the counter and turned to look at her task. This proved to be difficult to assess because the inside of the cottage was so dark. She pushed open the kitchen curtains as far as they would go, and then those in the living room, and then tried the lights, but they barely made a dent. It was absolutely freezing in the house, and

Lane did not take off her coat. Perhaps she would warm up as she got moving.

She went to the kitchen stove and lifted the lid. Miss Scott must have thought of starting a fire because there were twisted scraps of paper inside and a few bits of kindling had been put on top. That Friday had been cold. Did this mean that the assailant had come very early, before she had had time to light the fire? That might be helpful in terms of establishing a time, if Miss Scott herself still could not quite remember. Lane was about to put the lid back in place when one of the papers caught her attention. It had writing on it in very dark pencil.

Careful not to get soot all over her coat sleeve, she put her hand in and pulled out the paper and unrolled it, flattening it on the surface of the stove. She recognized the hand immediately. It was the same one as had written the note she'd found in the teacher desk. "Miss high and mighty. The whole world will know what a whore you are. I'm right behind you."

CHAPTER FIFTEEN

"I MEAN, SIX OF THEM. THAT seems like overkill," Lane said. She and Darling were walking together up the road toward the Bertollis' house, she with her arm through Darling's, and he with a bottle of wine tucked into his overcoat pocket. In spite of the melt, it had become damp and cold as the afternoon had worn into early darkness. Lane was happy to be in warm wool pants and her sage-green turtleneck, as well as her thick jacket. Her rubber overshoes reached her ankles and she hoped that the path from the road to Angela's door would not be full of slush. Should she have worn her wellingtons?

"The notes certainly bespeak a person who is obsessed with Miss Scott or Miss Keeling," Darling said. "Actually, as we've found more of the notes, I'm now inclined to believe they were intended for Miss Scott. Miss Keeling has only been here a couple of weeks. Surely that's not enough time to excite the ire of some local. Besides, I'm increasingly convinced Miss Keeling is very far from being the victim here. Too much points to her possible involvement in what happened to Miss Scott. As to the notes, they're from a woman, I would have said."

"Would you? How curious. Because men can't write full sentences? Isn't that a bit like that nonsense cliché that poison is a woman's weapon?" She considered what her own initial reaction had been. "I confess, I thought that myself, but it's not useful to assume those ridiculous clichés are true. Women poisoners, women poison-pen writers. It might lead you quite astray."

They had reached the turn at the top of the road where the Mather cottage sat, smoke curling from the chimney, and the two front windows lit up. What were they doing of an evening? Lane wondered. Not talking, she guessed. Such a bitterness existed between Reg Mather and his wife, Alice, that she could scarcely imagine them spending any time in the same room together. She pulled closer to Darling, thanking whatever stars had been responsible for throwing them together.

"I draw your attention to the very last case of murder we had here on the lake," Darling said. "The one that ended with Ames getting a posy of flowers from Tina Van Eyck. By the way, I wonder how that is going?"

"Don't try to change the subject. Against one woman using poison to rid herself of, say, a bothersome man, there are doubtless scores of men doing the same thing up and down the country. It's neat, for one thing. No blood to cope with, no bashing resisting victims over the head. Why wouldn't anyone with a murderous bent use it? Why do you think the notes are from a woman, particularly?"

"All that focus on the perceived immorality, calling her a whore and so on. It suggests jealousy, or that the writer feels her own marriage threatened by this single woman floating about unattached in decent society."

"Piffle. You have a grim view of how women see each other. I spent the whole war working with women and we had none of that. We just got on with our jobs and helped each other. So much is made, and rightly so, about the deep comradeship of men at war, but you would have recognized the exact same instinct among women. We are not a different species entirely, you know."

Darling smiled in the darkness and kissed her cheek. "I'm relieved to hear it, else we might not be able to procreate."

They walked on in companionable silence, past a field that lay in impenetrable darkness, toward the cheerfully lit Bertolli cabin. Simultaneously, the collies began to bark and the front porch light was turned on. They could hear David telling the dogs to shut up with good-natured impatience.

Lane stopped and turned to Darling. "But you know, this means the gun is not necessarily Miss Keeling's. Much more likely to be Miss Scott's, if she's the one who was getting the notes. What if the notes in the stove are only scratching the surface? What if she'd been under this sort of pressure for some time, and had become afraid that whoever it was would confront her one afternoon when she was alone at the school? That 'I'm right behind you' is chillingly sinister. There is no way to get help, really, if you're under attack alone. No telephone, and only the one narrow road down the hill."

The dogs had been settled and Angela had directed

David to supply Lane and Darling with drinks while she went off to the kitchen. They were sitting on a sofa in front of an enormous fire that threw dancing golden light along the walls.

"Any news of your potential new neighbours up the hill?" Lane asked.

"I don't see much, I'm afraid, but Angela tells me they were quite busy bustling up and down the road in vans and trucks. And then it all stopped. Typical builders. With any luck, they won't start up till after Christmas. They keep the dogs agitated when they're barrelling up and down all the time," David said, leaning back, cradling his scotch on his chest.

"It's absolutely frightful!" called Angela, poking her head around the door. "I'm getting like everyone else in King's Cove. I don't want anyone new moving here. It was blissfully quiet and then suddenly we're in a construction zone. It's peculiar that I haven't heard a thing for a few days. That's contractors for you! They've probably left the place an absolute shambles and then gone off. I must say, whoever bought it must be absolutely loaded! The expense of refurbishing a wreck like that! And someone said the vans aren't local, which must double the cost."

"Has anyone been up to see it?" Lane asked, ignoring Darling's "Here we go again" look. "I'm busy tomorrow, but if no one's working on it we could go up Sunday and have a look."

"Splendid idea!" Angela said. "Oh, damn, I think I've burned the carrots!" She disappeared back into the kitchen.

Dave topped up their glasses entirely unnecessarily, and

then asked, "How are you finding teaching, Lane? You are effectively the village schoolmistress now. The boys, by the way, love you. Philip said you gave him an important job. He's quite puffed up about it."

"He's been wonderful; between him and Gabriella, I'm just about able to cope with the younger children. He's been helping with their arithmetic. It's the spread of ages and skills—they're all over the map. I don't know how people do it. I've been having a wonderful time, except for the ghastly business of one of the boys losing his father in a hit and run. He's practically an orphan now, and he wasn't much better off before, given his condition. But he's gone to live with Gabriella's family and they're helping him cope. I'm not sure I'm cut out for it. I admire you no end, driving up to town every day to teach. With any luck a new teacher will be along soon."

"Not before January, I shouldn't think," Dave said. "A natural time to assign a teacher would be after the holidays, and they may feel with you there and only a week left of school, they can wait. I must say, the boys really liked Miss Keeling. Perhaps she'll come back."

Perhaps, Darling thought, but said nothing. He was relieved when Angela called them to the table.

"You know, Darling, you want to be careful driving the lake road at night," David said, between mouthfuls of pot roast. "One of our teachers lives out toward Salmo, and he hit a deer that bolted onto the road the other night. He was lucky, not the deer obviously, our teacher. It bounced on the top of the hood and made a mess of the car. He had to put the thing out of its misery. Now I wonder if he took it home. I forgot to ask him." David took a reflective sip of wine.

"He had a rifle?" Lane asked, momentarily horrified at "putting the thing out of its misery."

"Good grief, yes. He's a hunter, though I think he prefers more sport and less vehicular damage."

———

August 1939

WENDY SAT OPPOSITE a man behind a desk. He was older, with thin hair and spectacles that he peered over, giving him an air of disapproval. Her face flushed in her anxiety. She still felt exposed and uncomfortable in the clothes Mrs. Franklin had found for her, and she nervously pulled the hem of her flowered dress lower to cover her knees. She had conceded to giving up her head scarf but had insisted on her hair being pulled tightly into a bun. She had never worn a hat, and the flowered straw hat that Mrs. Franklin had helped her pin on felt like something she must try to balance, lest it slide off.

She had been asked if she had any experience with children. It came into her mind to say she had herself been a child once, and this too caused her to blush at its wild inappropriateness. "I was in charge of two young children, and I taught them to read and do arithmetic. We used the outdoors to learn biology."

"They did not attend school?"

How could she say that they were not, any of them, permitted to leave the property? That her aunt had insisted on their learning to read, even though her uncle had railed at the potential exposure to sin that literacy might engender. Her aunt had persuaded him that one day when they needed to interact with the outside world on farm business it would be best if they could read and cipher so as not to be cheated.

"The school was too far to go to. My aunt and uncle were not wealthy enough to afford a car." This was true as far as it went. Their one truck was patched together and battered by the local roads, and at least a decade and a half old.

"I see. Well, teaching two children is not the same as teaching a room full of children, Miss—" Here he looked down through his glasses at the paper before him. "Keeling. What makes you think you would be able to handle children, some nearly as old as you, in a rural school? Farm children who may be quite strangers to the discipline more common to our urban children?"

"I have always wanted to teach school, Mr. Sanders. Even when I was in grade school here in Vancouver, before my mother died and I had to leave to live with my aunt and uncle. I believe I have a God-given ability."

Mr. Sanders sniffed. "Well, you certainly don't lack in confidence, I'll say that. I will allow you to sit the exams for entry into Normal School and we'll see where we go, shall we? Please bring a proper piece of identification. Do you have a birth certificate?"

Wendy felt her face flush again. She had never heard of a birth certificate. She nodded and got up to leave.

Cambie Street was alive with noise and cars when Wendy emerged from the Normal School. She stopped on the steps and looked down the street toward the city, pulling her cardigan around her. The unfamiliar handbag, left behind by one of Mrs. Franklin's girls when she had married, a bit worn but quite usable, hung on her arm.

She had told two lies already: that her uncle could not afford a vehicle, and that her mother was dead. And now she had to get identification. She had made up the name she had written on the paper for the secretary to show the man. She had no idea how she would get a birth certificate. She must have had one because she was born in Vancouver. Her father would know, but she could never seek him out lest he return her to her uncle. The man had said she needed identification. She thought about the children she had been living with. It was suddenly clear to her that they probably had no birth certificates. Her uncle had often railed against the government, sent census takers away, said they had no business in the lives of honest God-fearing men. She was certain her aunt Hilda had said the children had been born at home. Could she tell the man that? How many more lies would she tell, let loose from the restrictions of her uncle's house? She wondered if it was true after all, that without strong male guidance she was naturally and irredeemably sinful.

If she was sinful, then her aunt, who had been good to her and given her warmth and purpose, must be a veritable Jezebel, with her secret cupboard of books. Her aunt, who wore long dresses and thick stockings, and talked of sin, had nevertheless seemed to Wendy to be a kindred spirit, long before she could have understood those words. Now, looking back, she saw that the books were an anomaly that fairly shouted. She had been told in the strictest confidence that she was to read the books and use them as the basis for teaching the children, but to never let her uncle know where they were hidden. But she could not forget the fearful warning her aunt had delivered when she had declared she would run away rather than be married. It was clear that she was on her husband's side, when push came to shove.

A truck pulling up to a traffic light slowed in front of her, and Wendy felt the old panic and turned quickly to go east along Twelfth Avenue. She had never been fully free of the fear that they would come and find her. She could scarcely comprehend the enormity of the sin she'd committed by running away.

Even now, after several months, when she stepped out of the rooming house, she looked both ways, searching the street, fearful that her uncle or the elder would be there, venturing out timidly only when it was clear they were not.

Calmer after walking several blocks, she began to think about the exams. Mr. Sanders had said it was highly irregular to accept a student who had not completed grade twelve. Had he been convinced by her tale of being home-schooled because of the isolation of the farm she lived on? In a way, she thought, it was perfectly true. She had schooled herself. Her thoughts drifted to her mother, as she walked down Main Street toward the rooming house downtown.

Sometimes at night she thought she remembered what her mother had looked like, especially her deep blue eyes, and then it was gone. Why had she left? Wendy had thought of forgivable answers and unforgivable ones. Had her mother been threatened or beaten by her father when he was drinking, or had she left because she'd found someone else? Or had she left because she couldn't be bothered with the work of bringing up a child? It dawned on her with such force that she nearly stopped in the middle of an intersection and only moved on as other pedestrians pushed past her. How she had endeavoured to be good every moment of her life since then, so that she would not be abandoned again. Running away from her uncle's was her first rebellion. It terrified her, and yet it made her feel an almost surging sense of power.

She arrived back at the rooming house and called as she came in the door. "Mrs. Franklin? I'm home. They're going to let me take the exams."

Coming from the kitchen, her landlady smiled. "That is good news. You must have done a good job of convincing them you could pass them."

"I don't even remember what I said, I was so terrified! I'll just run upstairs to put away my hat and then I'll come down and get at the laundry."

"Before you go, a couple of men came to the door. They were looking for someone named Wendy Irving. Now, I think they were looking for you." She eyed Wendy meaningfully.

Wendy went white and sat down hard on the stairs, her hand over her mouth. "Oh my God, oh my God."

"Don't fret, dear. I didn't let on. I didn't much like the tone they took, if you must know. I think they were going up and down the street to every boarding house. I quite truthfully told them I don't have a Wendy Irving here. I watched them and sure enough, they went down to Mrs. Gregor's across the street. They have no idea where you are. You're perfectly safe. But I think it's time you told me what's going on, don't you?"

"They must have asked the conductor in Williams Lake where my ticket was for, and then asked the station man here if anyone had seen me. He told me to come down Cardero to look for the boarding houses." Wendy could feel her heart pounding out her fear.

"There you are, you see? If they don't find you at any boarding houses, I hardly think they're going to be able to scour the whole city."

Wendy was unconvinced. "What did they look like?"

"One was quite old, I'd say in his sixties, but looking much older, and the other was a bad-tempered fellow of about fifty."

"My uncle and the elder." Wendy closed her eyes and shuddered.

"Look, come off of those stairs and into the kitchen. The laundry can wait. We'll make a cup of tea and have a bit of cake and you can tell me why a sixteen-year-old had to run all the way from Williams Lake to hide in Vancouver."

Between sobs, Wendy told Mrs. Franklin the real reason she had fled, and even shared her fear that she would be damned, if they didn't catch her first.

"Nonsense, my dear. This is 1939. No one can force a sixteen-year-old into a marriage in this day and age. If they tried it, I'd have the police on them. And you mark my words, if they don't find you, they'll give up."

For the first time Wendy wondered why. Why was she being forced to marry? "He already has a wife. No doubt beaten down by doing his bidding her whole life. I wonder if he gave my uncle money. I think I heard them arguing, my uncle and aunt, I mean, about the farm not doing well."

"Bigamy on top of it all!" Mrs. Franklin declared. "Well, you're well out of it. How attached are you to this lovely hair?"

"Why?" Wendy took a strand of her hair that had fallen out of her bun.

"Because it's time to put that nonsense of a life behind you. We'll cut your hair, bob it. Annie's a hairdresser, she'll see to it. We'll get you some proper clothes that aren't just hand-me-downs. And you're smart as a whip. You'll pass those exams and go to that school, and you'll never look back."

Wendy went up the stairs, still dazed, hardly knowing what she was feeling. She sat on her bed. She had not known there were laws to protect her. She suddenly felt her own ignorance. If she was going to live in this world, she would have to know everything she could. She would study, read the papers, find out about the laws, make new friends who could help her. And not, under any circumstances, let any man interfere with her life. She felt a new determination. She would get to take the exams, and she would pass them. She stood in front of her mirror and instead of avoiding her own reflection as she usually did, she looked at herself as she took the pin out of her hat, and placed hat and pin on the dresser. Her image shimmered in the mirror, her hair pulled away from her face. Without thinking, she pulled her hair out of its bun and let it fall around her face and onto her shoulders. This was her, now. Wendy Keeling. That other girl left behind forever. She would build her house around this girl. When her roommate got back, she would ask her to cut and perm her hair.

———

MISS SCOTT'S RECOVERY now included walking sedately up and down the hallways of the hospital for a few minutes a day, though she found she still had little memory of why she was there. Sometimes in her dreams she felt the opening of a great black chasm full of fear, and she woke up gasping. They had upped her dose of sleeping pills, and the fear that sometimes followed her into the day receded a bit.

She had found books in the little reading library, but her head hurt after only a few pages, and the nurses had pulled the books away from her saying reading was a no-no. She had tried to write to her mother, but the effort made her vision swim, and the enormity of telling her mother she was in hospital was too much. Her mother needed her. It was wrong in every way for her to need her mother.

After her breakfast of milky porridge and lukewarm tea, Miss Scott got carefully out of bed and shuffled into her slippers and dressing gown and made for the smoking room. She had been visited by no one but the various policemen, and had no one to bring her cigarettes, and in any case had been told she was not to smoke. She couldn't see why, really. What had smoking to do with a head injury? Reasoning that being among smokers would be almost as good, she went into the common room and found two people, only one of whom was smoking.

Sighing, she sat down near the window, crossed her legs, and looked out at the snowy landscape of trees lining the edge of the parking area, with Elephant Mountain, white and imperious, just visible behind them. She had no real idea how long she'd been in hospital. She wondered where Wendy Keeling was, and why she hadn't come to visit, and then realized that of course she must be with the children at the school. She frowned. There was something about Wendy. She struggled to remember, felt a wave of panic, and then gave up. She looked at the other two people in the room: one an elderly man with flying tufts of white hair and days of unkempt beard growth around his moist mouth, and the other a woman who was feverishly puffing on a cigarette and turning the pages of a magazine. *Life*, Miss Scott saw, no doubt some old pawed-up issue. She picked up a copy of the *Nelson Daily News* lying beside her and looked at the date. So, it was close to Christmas. She felt a pang of anxiety. She should be home with her mother. She shouldn't have to cope all alone with the work on the farm in the winter. She was about to put the paper down and go back to her room, when a headline caught her eye. "Hit and Run Victim Identified." She read further and then stood convulsively, feeling suddenly as if her head would burst from the pressure, crying, "No, no, no, no!"

"CONSTABLE TERRELL? THIS is Dr. Edison at the hospital. I thought I'd better let you know that Miss Rose Scott has had another relapse and possible stroke, and I'm afraid she's back with me upstairs."

"Oh. I'm sorry. Is there any sense of what caused it? I

mean, are you liable to have more strokes once you've had one?" Terrell asked. He pulled his notebook forward on his desk and wrote, "Miss Scott, stroke."

"Not necessarily. However, between the head injury and a possible heart abnormality, there is plenty of possible cause. And though it is not popular to say so, there was some work done on smoking before the war in Germany that suggested smoking is bad for the heart and lungs, and Miss Scott is a smoker. We've kept her away from cigarettes to avoid the coughing, but she has been visiting the common room where you can count on there being lots of people smoking. That's where we found her, in fact, clutching a copy of the *Nelson Daily News*. There's a paper that doesn't usually knock someone over, but there you are."

Terrell was silent for a moment, writing. Had something been in the newspaper? "Would any sort of sudden shock cause her to have a stroke? I was wondering about the paper. Do you recall which day the paper was from?"

"I would have said no, but in fact the patient who raised the alarm said that she had been reading the paper and suddenly stood up crying out the word 'no.' Perhaps she had seen something. I'll see if I can track down the paper. If we know of something that would give alarm, we'll be able to keep it from her. She will be with me for the next while anyway and she's having no disturbance, even a visit from you. Is that clear?"

"Yes, Dr. Edison, but if you could track down the date of the paper, that might be helpful. I'm afraid we have very little to go on just now, and something that alarmed her may be helpful. Perhaps she saw a picture of the man

190

who attacked her, or something that might give us a lead."

"Right you are. I'll do a bit of sleuthing myself at this end and call you back."

CHAPTER SIXTEEN

SATURDAY DAWNED UNPROPITIOUSLY GREY AND delivering an icy rain. Lane woke up to find Darling reading beside her.

"I've lit the fire and put on coffee. I think I hear it blipping now," he said, putting his book down and leaning over to kiss her.

"Aren't you a good husband! It smells divine. Gosh. Look at the day. I'll be off after breakfast to finish up at the teacher's cottage. I must say, nature could have obliged with some decent weather to support my good works. What are you doing today?" Lane sat up and reached for her dressing gown.

"I had thought it would be a perfect day to sit by the fire and read. I wish I'd known before I married you that you are so unrestfully ambitious. I suppose I'd best do what I understand rural husbands typically do. I'll go up to the barn and split a pile of firewood." He put a bookmark in his Steinbeck; he'd read *The Grapes of Wrath* on their honeymoon, and with a background primarily in English writing, he thought he'd best keep going with Americans. "If you're sure you wouldn't like a bit of a lie-in?" he said with an endearing touch of plaintiveness.

"Don't try to tempt me away from my duty! Come, the coffee smells divine, and I have some bacon to go with Gladys's eggs."

Darling had no sooner buttoned up his grey tartan flannel shirt than the phone in the hall rang. He waited. Two longs and a short. "I'll get it," he called. He looked at his watch. It was already nine thirty, though it felt, because of the dim weather, much earlier. "KC 431, Winslow-Darling residence."

"Ah, sir. I'm sorry to bother you at home. It's Constable Terrell."

"Bully for you, Constable. What's so important I'm being kept from my coffee?"

"Sir. I got a call late yesterday from the hospital, Dr. Edison. You know, she works in the special care part of the hospital. It appears Miss Scott had another stroke. It is possible it was triggered by reading the paper. It turns out it was the December 12 issue, yesterday's. I've got hold of one, but I can't immediately see what she might have seen to alarm her."

Darling could smell the bacon wafting up the hall and hear the uplifting clatter of plates being handled. "What do you mean 'triggered'?"

"Oh, sorry, sir. I mean she apparently was reading the paper in the smoking room, and, according to someone there, stood up suddenly saying 'no' several times and fell over, presumably from the stroke."

"Right. Well, I don't know what can be done at this juncture. I have this week's papers here. I'll give it a look-see at this end. You on your own there?"

"Weekend staff, sir. Though Sergeant Ames is upstairs doing paperwork. Thank you."

Darling hung the earpiece on the phone and went in search of the papers piled on the window seat. Muttering as he looked through them, he said, "Aha!" as he found the right one. "I have something else to do," he said, going into the kitchen. "I'll be going through yesterday's paper to find out why Miss Scott keeled over after reading it."

"Good God! Really? Poor woman. I'm so glad she's in the hospital where they can keep an eye on her. Right. I'm off."

LANE PULLED THE car up to the front steps. The deserted cottage looked even more dismal than usual, though the sleet that had been falling out of the looming sky was beginning to let up. It almost looked as though the little house had shrunk further from the pummelling. With a sigh, she buttoned the top button of her jacket, adjusted her hat, and got out of the car and went around to the trunk to take out the supplies she'd brought from home. Bucket, cloths, a mop, and her container of Old Dutch scouring powder, because the one she'd bought at the store the afternoon before was not, she felt, going to be enough. She put them down on the porch, balancing her mop on the wall, while she opened the door to the house.

Just before she went in, she looked in the direction of

Gaskell's house, what she could see of it. She wondered about the hit and run. It must have damaged the car that hit him in some way. David had just last evening told a story of a teacher hitting a deer at night. It was obviously a more common hazard than she had imagined. She herself had seen them in her headlights, leaping up the embankment along the Nelson road, having crossed in front of her. It struck her now what a wallop a car, and the driver, for that matter, would receive hitting a deer. How different would a car that had struck a deer look from one that had struck a man?

Inside, Lane, having picked up most of the things slung around the sitting room and kitchen the afternoon before, started the serious cleaning in the easiest room, the one she assumed had been Miss Keeling's. She got to work stripping the bed and making a pile of washing to take home, which she set by the door. She also took the two garments that had been left behind. She could keep them, in case Miss Keeling came back, or pass them on to charity should a new teacher be assigned. This room was straightforward. A sweep and a mop, and she'd remake the bed once she brought the sheets back.

Miss Scott's yielded more complex problems. She flipped the light switch and found the low-watt bulb provided little added illumination. She shuddered. She loved light. Sunlight, bright electric light. How could someone live in this murky semi-darkness? Even the window gave only a little light as it was small and looked out onto the patch of dense, looming evergreen woods at the back of the house.

There was Miss Scott's half-packed suitcase, and a quick

look in her dresser showed that she must have intended to pack another suitcase, as two drawers still contained clothes. She opened the second, as-yet-unfilled suitcase. Hoping there would be enough room for all the clothes, she set about packing the rest of them. Should she take them home so that they would be ready for Miss Scott when she got out of hospital?

It suddenly occurred to her, as she gathered up hairbrushes, combs, boxes of pins, and a jar of face cream, that Darling had been puzzled about there being nary a word from Miss Scott's fiancé. Had Darling said that when interviewed she hadn't remembered she was off to be married? Hadn't Bales said she'd been meant to leave that Sunday? If she was going home first, the fiancé would have had no reason to become alarmed, but if she was going straight to wherever he was, he should have been heard from by now. These thoughts deepened the real mystery of Miss Scott. Was she really getting married? Or was she planning to run away? If those poisonous notes were for her, Lane thought, she had every provocation. Looking at the condition of the cottage and knowing Miss Scott was in dire straits in the hospital, it seemed clear she had left running away just a little too late.

And that begged the question: If the notes were from a woman, as Darling seemed to assume, would a woman have come in, wrecked the cottage, and attacked Miss Scott? Surely the teacher would have had more of an ability to fight off a woman?

Having cleared the dressing table, she took the large doily off it and wiped the surface with a damp cloth, giving the edges of the surface a quick swipe. She replaced the doily and went to the kitchen to rinse the cloth and nearly missed it: a dark ferrous red stain on the cloth. She hurried back to the bedroom and turned the light back on. She was certain that there had been nothing on the surface of the dresser, so after looking at this she ran her hand gingerly along the edge. There! A slight irregularity, like food dried on a surface. Snatching her hand back, she leaned in to look more closely. It was right on the corner and barely visible against the dark wood in the dim light, but what was on her cloth was assuredly dried blood. Had Miss Scott struck her head on this? It was a low dressing table. If she'd been pushed, from which angle? Lane stood experimentally where she thought Miss Scott might have been standing to hit the back of her head on this corner of the dresser.

She contemplated the dresser, imagining the scene, the assailant following Miss Scott into the room. Perhaps she'd made a run for it and had tried to close and lock the door of the bedroom, but he, or she, had pushed through. Miss Scott, her back to the dresser, her front to—here Lane stopped. Her front to the wardrobe? She remembered that when she'd first found Miss Scott she'd wondered if she'd hit her head on the bedstead but had seen no evidence of it. That would have made sense because the bed was directly opposite the door into the bedroom, and a frightened, backing-up Miss Scott, who was pushed, would have hit her head on some part of the bed. The dresser, on the other hand, where she'd found the blood, was behind the door. Perhaps the blood was from something else, after all. A scrape, a cut finger.

It didn't change anything, really. Someone had still come in, made a mess of the house, pulled out the phone cord, and either hit or, more likely, pushed Miss Scott so that she fell and got a concussion. Just a curiosity, really, but she thought it would be helpful to the police.

She worked until about one thirty and then went outside with the bundle of bedding, placing it and then the suitcases into the car. She had got through a good amount of scouring, powder washing the chamber pots, doing the bathroom sink and the bath, and scrubbing the kitchen sink and wiping up the mess of flour and sugar off the counters and floor. She'd washed two milk bottles and stacked them neatly by the sink and had removed whatever would not last another month from the fridge and given it a good cleaning as well. She could stop at the King's Cove dump on the way home.

As she was dumping the garbage, she imagined again the assailant tearing the house apart looking for whatever it was he, or she, expected would be there. Looking in cupboards, under the sink, lifting the mattresses. Now that was odd. The mattresses did not look as if they'd been moved. She'd check with Darling when she got home. Perhaps they'd straightened the mattresses during their initial runs through the cottage.

Of course, she realized, driving slowly down the rutted garbage dump road toward Bales's store, she was overthinking it. Obviously the person had found whatever he'd been looking for and could stop searching and get on with the business of fleeing. Or kidnapping Miss Keeling and fleeing. Where *was* Miss Keeling? Could Darling be right that she was in league with the assailant?

TERRELL REREAD THE front page of the newspaper. Luckily, he'd found it with its crossword still not done, piled on the front counter where O'Brien usually sat. "Holy mackerel!" he exclaimed. How had he not seen this immediately? He wondered if it was worth disturbing Darling again. But perhaps his boss had made the self-same discovery—and hadn't taken so long about it.

"Holy mackerel, what?" asked Ames, who had been coming down the stairs from his office.

"I think it's the article about the hit and run where they've identified Gaskell. She'd know he's the father of one of her students."

"Of course!" Ames said, taking the paper from Terrell. "Poor little Samuel. I'm sure she must have felt sorry for the kid. If he went to school dressed the way he was when Darling picked him up the other day, I'm sure she must have worried about him. Seeing this, she'd realize how devastated he would be. Didn't he already lose his mother?"

"Yes. She apparently decamped early in the fall, or late summer. I asked the RCMP, but they haven't traced her yet. I also asked, by the bye, if there's been anything on the missing Miss Keeling. I called this morning to tell the inspector about Miss Scott's condition. Should I call about this? It's Saturday and he did sound a little impatient. He said he was going to look through his papers there."

Ames shrugged. "He'd sound like that even if he'd especially asked you to call him back. The truth is, he doesn't really take the weekends, necessarily, so he might like to hear. No harm in showing him you're alert and on the job."

"You again," Darling said into the telephone receiver.

"What now? Not enough to keep you busy in town?"

"Yes, sir. It's just that I think I may have discovered what startled Miss Scott in the paper." He glanced up to where Ames was leaning against a desk with his hands in his pockets, looking amused.

"Startled, you call it, do you? Well, go on."

"There's a headline about the hit-and-run victim being identified as Mr. Gaskell. Miss Scott wouldn't have known he'd been killed, but she'd know he was that little fellow Samuel's father. I can see where she might be upset."

"Hmm. The question is, why would it give her a stroke?" Darling said after a short silence.

"She's in a weakened condition. Perhaps—"

But Darling interrupted. "Yes, all right. Since you aren't a doctor yourself, unless you've been keeping something from me, perhaps you could check with Edison at the hospital."

AT A LOOSE end and unwilling to get started just yet on the pile of wood waiting in the barn for his attention, Darling remembered that there was apparently another cookery book somewhere upstairs among the effects of the late Lady Armstrong. He had not yet fully explored the house, and he had to admit he felt in his heart it was Lane's house, and not yet theirs. He went up the creaking stairs and opened the door to the attic and was immediately hit by the icy cold of this shut-off and completely unheated part of the house. But at the same time, the attic was suffused with light, albeit the cold blue grey of the ice and rain pounding the windows that faced south toward the lake. He'd been here only once, the summer he had met her, when she had spread paper across the floor and was mapping out the events that had led to her arrest after a man had been found dead in her creek. His heart warmed at the memory. Then the room had been bathed with sun, the windows open, letting in the fragrant flurry of warm summer air, and Lane had been beautiful and serious. He saw her now, earnest, kneeling over her map, the sunlight reflected off the waves of that wonderful hair. He must have been well on the way to being irretrievably lost. He recalled now that in the summer there'd been no door. Perhaps Kenny Armstrong had put one in. He was happy to see it now corralling all that cold away from the rest of the house. The attic was enveloped in a deep icy chill. He quickly scanned the wooden boxes that had been pushed under the eaves. There were dishes stacked with old newspapers around them, some boxes with fabrics, perhaps clothes or table furnishings, other boxes with old-fashioned heavy photo albums. Seeing a box with books, Darling pulled it forward and began to take them out.

"Aha!" he said into the cold. He pulled out a weathered cookbook by someone called Fannie Farmer. Not much minding what was in it, as long as there were recipes, he seized it, pushed the box back under the eaves, and, with a final look out the windows at the unrelenting rain, hurried downstairs to the warmth.

Deciding it would be more fun to look through the book with Lane, Darling put it on the table and donned his jacket to make the trip to the barn, where he spent the next hour chopping wood and conveying it to the pile next to the Franklin stove. Then he went downstairs into the basement to shovel some coal into the furnace. Having engaged, as he saw it, in these manly activities, Darling stood in the hallway looking out toward the door. The weather really was beastly. He was about to turn back to put the kettle on when he saw Lane's car pull up to the gate. Things were looking up.

"When are you proposing to do their laundry?" he asked when he had heard her plan.

"I'd better do it more or less now. Who knows when the new teacher will come," she said, as she hung up her wet jacket.

"You heard Bertolli. They're unlikely to post a new teacher till January. Come, I've produced a fresh pile of wood, put the kettle on, and am ready to try to do something really useful, like learn to make shortbread from the cookbook I found in that ice house you call an attic."

"Thus shattering forever any impression of the dour inspector," Lane said, smiling. "I've done whatever I can with the place. Oh. I've also brought Miss Scott's two suitcases here, because who knows when she'll get out of hospital. They're in the boot. There's no hurry now. I'd kill for a cup of tea. And while we're having tea, I can tell you about the very strange thing I found that might solve the mystery of the blow to Miss Scott's head. Or might not. Right. Well, I'm changing out of these clothes. Have tea and newspaper at the ready. And is there any of that cake left?"

Settled at the table, with her hands around a mug of tea, Lane related her finding of the blood on the corner edge of the dressing table.

"It's a good question. How does this alter the situation?"

Darling mused. "It suggests the assailant may not have had such murderous intentions. Perhaps she got in his way, tried to get him to stop, maybe grabbed his arm, and he pushed her away. The fact of the matter is, if she doesn't remember something, we're probably never really going to know. The aggravating part is that we have no idea if something was taken, if that was the intention of the attack on the cottage in the first place."

"I wondered if it was the note writer. In fact, it even crossed my mind that she wasn't getting married at all, but just running away, only she left it too late. If the note writer did it, I think you'll agree that it's more likely to have been a man hounding her than a woman. Poor Miss Scott! She's trying to recover while the police are ghoulishly hanging about waiting for her to be able to tell them what happened."

"Are we ghoulish, do you think? More ghoulish than, say, you, excited because you've found a blood-stained dressing table? As you know, I had a call about Miss Scott this morning from Terrell because she'd collapsed after reading the paper. I perused our copy of yesterday's paper, and Terrell found one as well at the station. He just telephoned to say he thought he might know what it was. And you know, I think I won't tell you, and see if you can guess. I thought he was quite clever, actually."

"But I bet you didn't tell him so," Lane said.

"Certainly not. It doesn't do to swell the heads of underlings."

Lane had, of course, guessed, but then, Darling reasoned, she was seeing little Samuel every day. Now they sat, tea,

203

sandwiches, and the last of the cake consumed, fulfilling their original plan for the day, reading by the fire. She put her book face down on the arm of her chair. "Oh, I meant to ask you, when you went to the cottage that first time, were the mattresses on straight? Only I just couldn't imagine someone tearing a place apart looking for something and not going straight for the mattresses. People always hide things under mattresses."

Darling skewed his mouth sideways in an effort of remembering and then shook his head. "I know Ames looked under them to see if any notes had been shoved there, but that was after our initial visit. I don't think they were askew, now that you mention it, though I concede your point. Perhaps he found whatever he was looking for before he needed to look under mattresses."

"Of course, you're right. That's just what I came to as well. I just thought it odd it wasn't the first place they'd look." Lane took up her book, and then put it down again. "You know, after hearing David's story yesterday evening, I now imagine the whole road is littered with dead deer. I wonder what happens to them all."

"It's quite a serious business," Darling said. "People have been killed hitting wild animals, especially at night. They shoot out of nowhere and there's no time to react."

"I've been thinking," Lane said, "it will make it harder to find the car, if there are so many out there banged up by animals." She sighed. "There are so many loose ends." She cleared a space on the little table between their chairs. "You have Scott over here, recovering from a bang on the head and a stroke. And somewhere out of the picture you presumably have a missing Keeling. It is difficult to imagine they are not related, but then we learn that Keeling may have left before the attack on Scott. However, it's quite conceivable that she only left to meet up with her confederate and returned again with him to attack Miss Scott."

"I consider this an unhealthy occupation," Darling observed. "Then what?"

"We have artifacts, if you will, all around the business. There are poison-pen notes, one at school and five found in the stove at the cottage. Can we assume more? A campaign of intimidation by someone? I think we can. But against whom? And then we have a revolver hidden at the school, and, if young Samuel is right, several sightings of a car that seems to be watching the school, well, not the car, obviously, someone in it. The same car that was at the house on the Friday, again according to your Samuel. What am I missing, so far?"

Darling rubbed his chin. "You have, and I think it can only be irrelevant and an actual genuine coincidence—something I don't allow for normally—the fact of Samuel's father being killed on the highway."

"I mean, if I were to draw these out on a map, there would be disparate and possibly entirely unconnected bits and pieces, and a raft of questions. Who was in the car? Who attacked Scott? Same person? What were they looking for? Where did Keeling go, and why? Was she the attacker? Or is she a victim, kidnapped? And where is Scott's supposed fiancé? Oh, and not incidentally, how reliable are Scott and young Samuel? She's recovering from a concussion and a stroke, and he's nine years old. Do we know, by the way, when he saw that car? Because if it was Friday, someone could have taken Miss Keeling away that night, and could it be the same person returning later to complete the job on Scott?"

Darling was making a move preparatory to speaking when Lane added, "And why was Miss Keeling's room not messed about? And there's the question of why the assailant didn't look under the mattresses if he was looking for something valuable. Finally, is there any significance to the bathroom mirror being cracked?"

Darling mused, "I'm not sure Samuel actually said he saw the car there on the Friday. I'm wondering now if I assumed it. Damn. He's our only witness to a car being at the cottage, and he's no doubt in a bad way over his father. Another thing to add to the hopper: Miss Scott has not mentioned in any of her interviews that she was going to marry. In fact, she said at least once that she was going home to Manitoba to help her mother, so your theory about her doing a runner might hold water, perhaps to get away from whoever was persecuting her with notes, or worse."

"When you say 'or worse,' what are you thinking of?"

"Well, I mean, someone is stalking her, you could say. If it was a man, had he already attacked her before and she just hasn't been able to tell us?"

"Yes, but I say, wouldn't she have warned poor Miss Keeling?" Lane asked.

"Yes, she could have. Perhaps she did. She can't seem to remember much, and Miss Keeling is gone, so no one to tell us. But equally she could have been ashamed of it, feeling somehow she'd brought it on herself."

CHAPTER SEVENTEEN

Wednesday, December 3

MISS KEELING WOULDN'T HAVE NOTICED, except that Samuel was staying late at school again, finding reasons to drag out his departure long past that of the other children. She had been so close to asking him, but then she thought she really knew. His father would be away at work on the Nelson ferry, and Samuel would be alone until he got back. Under those circumstances he would almost certainly be too proud to complain. She stood now and watched Samuel walk down the road, eating the extra scone she had brought for just this purpose. Shaking her head and resolving that she ought to talk to someone about him, she was just turning away to prepare for the next day's classes when she saw the car.

It was backing slowly down the hill. Samuel stopped and was looking at it, and then it disappeared from her sight, and Samuel walked on.

She was not prepared for the flood of panic that assailed

her so powerfully that she had to sit down and hold the edge of the desk. It was nonsense. Someone lost. She tried to focus on the details of the car to still the rampant beating of her heart. It was an older model. Dark blue, maybe, or black. Some sort of red insignia on the front. The real trouble was that she'd seen it before. It wasn't someone lost. It had been stopped at the top of the road to the cottage. When? Two days before? She'd given it no thought then. She'd seen it when she was carrying wood from the shed, and she had dismissed it completely as belonging to a local. She certainly didn't recognize all the cars of the parents yet. People were always pausing at roads looking for addresses because they were so poorly marked. She looked around the classroom trying to restore a sense of the normal. She would mark papers, prepare lessons, write on the board, make sure the fire was damped, and drive home to where Miss Scott was preparing supper. They would chat about the children, and she would imagine what it must be like to be leaving to get married. And she would close her eyes, happy about her assignment here at the Balfour school. Happy, free at last. Her own woman. After all, no one had ever come, just as Mrs. Franklin had predicted.

It was useless. She got up abruptly and paced.

She should have asked for an assignment in the far north, or in the Peace River country. Now look at her! So nervy that she had got a revolver, which she had never told Miss Scott about. She could never use it, she knew, but she had bought it before she left the Island, thinking it would make her feel safe. She would bring it the next day, stow it somewhere secure. She walked around the classroom, opening and shutting the desk drawers. No. A child could find it. In the kitchen she saw the high cupboards. In there. If the car came back, if someone got out of the car, she would just have time to get it.

———

SUNDAY UNFOLDED IN a way Darling had always imagined Sundays might, if one was with someone one loved. A slow getting up, a shivering run downstairs to heave some coal into the furnace, and a return to bed until it took effect. Sitting in the kitchen in thick flannel dressing gowns, looking out at the change from the icy rain of the previous days back to snow, with thick mugs of coffee in hand and bacon cooking.

They had perused the Fannie Farmer cookbook and found pancakes, which were now staying warm in the oven. Lane dropped eggs into the frying pan and then rummaged around in the cupboard until she found the can of treacle.

"At last, a use for this! Mabel tells me it is a must in ginger cake, but I've yet to attempt that. Theirs is so delicious I'm afraid to try."

"Should we have dressed for breakfast?" Darling asked, with the air of a man who has no intention of budging.

"I am dressed," Lane objected, pushing her auburn hair away from her face with a spatula-laden hand.

"Do that again, and you won't be for long," he said. He wondered when he might tire of her cheekbones and that fall of hair.

The remains of breakfast before them, Lane said, "Angela

and I are going up the hill to look at that house and see how the builders are getting on. Want to come along?"

"That's all right. I'll do the washing up and keep the home fires burning. And I have to finish this book. It's due back at the library this week." He waggled the Steinbeck at her.

"I HAVEN'T HEARD a thing," Angela said, coming down the stairs from the porch, "so I expect the workers are gone till tomorrow and we can have a good look. We can get to the road through the back here." The Bertolli collies had stationed themselves, one in front, one behind, apparently bent on herding Angela and Lane through the yard to the road and up to the construction site.

Snow had begun to fall in tiny exploratory flakes, and the sight of it lifted Lane's spirits to no end. She had loved the long snowy landscapes of her childhood home in Latvia. When she had moved to England to attend Oxford it was, she reflected, what she most missed. It was an irony, she always thought, that all her English relations living in Latvia idealized and missed the English summers. Here in King's Cove, she thought, she could have both.

As they walked, Angela asked, "Are you still enjoying your stint as a teacher? You must have a real talent for it," she added. "The children love you."

Lane smiled. "And I love them. It's really my first experience with children, and I don't think I expected it to be such fun. Although, I was thinking how hard it is in some ways. I don't just mean trying to sort out all the different levels of lessons and trying to be an expert on everything.

It's the emotional part. I think I'm finding it's very easy to get attached, and that's mostly lovely, because they are lovely children, but when one of them has an unhappy home life, and you can see it right on his face . . . I don't know. I feel quite powerless and wish so much I could help. Like little Samuel. Not only was he abandoned occasionally, but I'm certain he'd been struck. And now on top of it, his father has died. It's heartbreaking."

"Absolutely dreadful! The boys tell me that he's staying with Gabriella, so that must help. The Benjamins are awfully good people. I know I shouldn't speak ill and all that, but that Gaskell was a dreadful excuse for a human being. Nobody liked him. Last year at the Dominion Day dance he got absolutely pie-eyed and made extremely loud, rude remarks to poor Miss Scott. Loud enough for the whole place to hear."

"Oh? What sort of remarks?"

"I think I put it right out of my mind. I just remember he was disgusting. Honestly, a more blameless and self-sacrificing woman would be hard to find!"

At the top of the road, the dogs abandoned their charges and ran into the yard, which was still full of lumber and tools under canvas tarpaulins, and sniffed earnestly at the new smells.

"It's going to be very nice," Lane observed. "It looks like they might add another floor. That will lift that gloomy overhanging roof that keeps the sitting room dark all year long."

They followed the dogs into the yard and around the back. The kitchen had been enhanced by the addition of new larger windows and a porch.

Peering in the window, Lane exclaimed, "Oh, too bad!"

"What?" Angela asked, joining in the peering.

"There used to be a nice wood floor in the kitchen that a little sanding could have really spruced up. They've covered it up with linoleum."

"Yes, but quite nice linoleum," Angela said. "It's a very pretty green, that floral sort of design. It'll be handy in the kitchen."

"Trust an artist to find the bright side. They have a fancy electric stove. Now then." Lane pulled away from the window and looked around the yard. "What have they done with the old wood-burning number that was there? I mean, the house was a ghastly mess when I was in here last spring. No one had been in it since before the Great War, but I would have thought a wood stove could still have some use." She gave a cursory look around the yard, and then wondered if they'd simply thrown it in the woods behind the house. She stood back and looked at the house. Even the work it was undergoing seemed unlikely to lift the pall of sadness she associated with the house. "It's still hard not to think of this as a place of tragedy, what with that little child."

"I suppose you're right, but what house hasn't had someone die in it, when you think about it? Our cabin already had most of the additions when we bought it a few years ago, but it was once an old settlers' cabin. People must have died in droves there." Angela pushed her hands into her pockets and started back toward the road.

"I suppose you're right," Lane said, "though 'droves' might be an overstatement. Even if whoever is building it is only planning to use it for the summer, I hope it's a cheerful, happy family that can change the fortunes of the sad place."

"Now who's being an optimist? It's all right for you. You're two miles away. You won't hear the fast cars driving up and down the roads, taking the noisy family you so fondly envision to the lake to swim and have drunken late-night picnics. Where have the bloody dogs got to?" Angela turned back toward the house, calling, "Lassie? Sandy? Come on. We're going home."

Lane, who could hear the dogs barking at something, waited on the road, looking up past the trees into the sky, where the first tentative flakes of snow had been replaced by larger, fluffier models that promised a lovely white cover over everything. She sighed with contentment, thinking of nestling down by the stove for the rest of the day with her lessons for the children. She turned at the sound of Angela's voice.

"What on earth are you up to? Come away, you beastly animals!"

Lane started toward the house, meeting Angela and the two dogs, who seemed reluctant to leave. "What is it?"

"They were digging and sniffing along the edge of the house there. No doubt a dead something, speaking of things dying. I'm sure the work on the house has scared out all the rats and God knows what living there. Why *will* dogs go after carcasses? It's disgusting."

"IT'S A RICH Vancouverite!"

"What is?" Mabel asked. The temperature had dropped,

and the snow was falling in earnest. Reg Mather was with her in the post office alcove, waiting for Eleanor to pull up the window. Both were muffled in scarves and hats. They could hear Eleanor in the background calling out, "Coming! No, Alexandra, no one needs you right now."

"That work at the house up the road. I was talking to the workmen last week, and they told me they'd discovered a rich city dweller was behind the whole business. Summer home sort of thing. That's all we need. Strangers in and out. Good stand of trees there going to waste."

Mabel abhorred Reg's views on stands of trees but had long ago stopped worrying about it because Reg, in her view, was too bone idle to start cutting underbrush in his garden, let alone logging stands of trees. "Why wouldn't they buy one of the houses on the lake? That's where the summer holidaymakers ought to confine themselves. Ah! Good morning, Eleanor. You hear what Reg is saying?"

"I was saying," Reg interposed, irritated at having his story whipped away from him, "that the fixing up of that house is being directed by some rich bastard, begging your pardon, who wants a summer home. Utter nonsense. We don't need that sort of carry-on up here. Respectable families willing to put their backs into things. That's what's wanted. We'd be better off if people stayed away altogether."

Mabel uttered a sound like a punctured tire and turned to Eleanor with a "Yes, like him!" expression on her face.

"Lane came here, and she's been a great addition. We don't know these people won't be the same," Eleanor said, reaching up into the wooden cubbies to collect the Hugheses' mail for Mabel.

"Completely different. She's not a summer visitor. She lives here. She redeemed herself by putting down roots and marrying," Reg pointed out, completely oblivious to any opinion the eldest unmarried Hughes daughter might have about what constituted being redeemed.

"In my view," Mabel said, "if whoever it is is only going to be here in the summer, they'll be out of our hair for the other three-quarters of the year. We're all too busy in the summer to pay attention to holidaymakers, anyway. We're about to be enveloped in snow again. I'd best get back."

"Oh, dear," said Eleanor, looking out into the yard as the post office door opened and then closed on Mabel. "It makes travel up to town so difficult, all this snow. I feel sorry for Dave Bertolli and the poor inspector, having to go all that way every day."

"See, that's another thing. Why can't people stay put? We didn't used to have to rush up to town every five minutes in the old days. We got whatever we needed every week on the steamboat. We grew vegetables and fruit and ordered what we couldn't grow."

"The world is changing, I expect, Reg. You can't say life wasn't a struggle. It's rather nice to go up to town and shop in the nice new supermarket and see a film. And people must go to their jobs," Eleanor said mildly, if a little pointedly. Lane was always so generous about offering to take Eleanor to town, and she had to confess she rather liked the diversion.

"That struggle made us strong. How do you think we won the war?" Unwilling to discuss any war with Reg, who

215

had participated in neither one because of a "gamy" leg, Eleanor smiled. "Do give my regards to Alice. She makes the loveliest sugar cookies. I do hope we'll see some at the Christmas service this year!"

CHAPTER EIGHTEEN

October 1947

HARRY DEVLIN AND HIS WIFE, Serena, waited on the pier, wrapped in thick jackets against the late October morning cold. The boats moored along the length of the pier made a gentle knocking sound against the rubber bumpers and each other with the quiet oscillation of the water. The sun was breasting the low hill before them, and already shone a splash of golden light on the autumn trees making their last declaration in explosions of red and yellow surrounding the lodge. The fishing holiday had been Harry's idea, but Serena had to admit that the glow of the trees in the early morning cold was uplifting. And it was nice to get away from her husband's cohort. Besides the maid, his only aide on this trip was his secretary, Michael, who had elected to stay at the lodge to deal with a briefcase full of correspondence he'd brought along.

"Happy, darling?" Harry turned to her and put his arm around her shoulders.

Serena smiled and nodded.

"That's my girl! It'll be good to take a few days away. I know it's been a little overwhelming. You've been a good sport about it all. It's a bit of nonsense anyway. I don't know how I was persuaded into it, now that I'm out here away from everything. I'm bound to fail. Instead, life should be like this: simple, elemental." He took a deep breath of the crisp air and squeezed her shoulders.

He was, she thought, like a Nietzschean superhero: tall, full of self-centred confidence, so sure of his own rightness. He seemed to have no awareness at all of the struggle of life for ordinary people, or really, how many people and how much work it was taking to get him elected. Serena was tempted to make a sarcastic remark about the "simple and elemental" activity in getting them to the island with two large suitcases, a trunk, a private secretary, and a maid for only a weekend away. Money, as she had often observed, could buy quite a lot of high-grade "simple."

"If you don't mind, darling, I won't fish. Could you get the boatman to drop me off at the picnic site? It's going to be a lovely day. I have a nice warm rug, a good book, and, if that fails, my little paintbox. And I'm thinking of buying a little property for us. A real getaway far from anything. We could find a nice little lake somewhere easy to get to. You're much too busy, of course, but I think I could have quite a lot of fun with it. I've even brought a notebook to sketch out some ideas for a cottage." She held up a leather bag.

"If you're sure, darling?" Harry tried to hide his relief. She was a lovely woman, but not very sporty. He'd have liked to leave her behind altogether, but it was increasingly important that they be seen together being happy and engaged in activities the average voter would understand. He knew Michael would be alerting someone from the press who would be up to photograph them before day's end. A large fish held aloft and his pretty blond wife beside him were just the thing. This by-election had come up suddenly, and he'd been unpersuaded at first. He was not, after all, a particularly political animal, but Serena had been so convincing that he had agreed to run. The local Tories had leaped on the idea. He was ideal. Intelligent, good-looking, the leader of a major business empire, well liked, and he had a beautiful wife. It seemed to him that he'd given his entire life over to the people running his campaign. All its demands seemed to put everything out of his mind. He suppressed a little upsurge of guilt. He was away so much that he realized he'd almost lost a sense of their life together. He was relieved that she had a project and that the whole election would be over before Christmas. A cabin somewhere on a lake would keep her busy, and happy, he was sure, as she would only want the most luxurious fixtures and furnishings.

"If you're sure, darling, about not fishing. I promise not to be too long."

"Absolutely sure. I imagine the lodge elves are already over there starting up the fire and making coffee." She turned at the sound of booted footsteps on the pier. "This looks promising."

It wasn't a man they were waiting for, as it turned out, but a woman. She was a grizzled-looking specimen, Serena thought, closer to fifty than forty by the look of her, dressed in men's clothing, hair pulled back, and a cloth cap low over her eyes. It was just as she was about to turn away and prepare to climb on board that Serena saw what fine eyes this woman had. Intense blue, undiminished, despite her age. She must have been a beauty once. She mentally shook her head. Country life.

"Morning. My name is Deedee. You can call me Dee." Her voice had the texture of soft gravel. She walked past them and threw the fishing rods she'd been carrying into the boat and then pulled a folded scrap of paper out of the breast pocket of the thick wool shirt she was wearing over a turtleneck sweater. "Mr. . . ." she read, "Harry Devlin." She stopped and looked at him and then turned away quickly toward Serena.

"Let me help you on, Mrs. Devlin. You like to fish?"

Serena took her hand. "Not much, but Harry loves it. In fact, I was wondering if you could drop me off at the picnic site. I'll spend the morning there, if I may. Would that be a bother?"

"No, ma'am. I believe they've set out some chairs and whatnot so you should be quite comfortable. Sir." She pulled her cap low and nodded at Devlin as he got on board.

Dee went to the outboard and sat down, looking at the backs of the two customers, and shook her head. What were the chances? She'd been following his career. President of his father's company and now Tory candidate for parliament. Beautiful young wife. She pulled the cord and the engine sprang into life. No embarrassing faltering with this outboard motor. The lodge provided the best of everything for its wealthy, often famous, clients. The sun blanketed both sides of the river now, and though the air was still chilly, it would be one of those glorious October days, warm enough to sit in shirt sleeves in the early afternoon.

Serena stood on the beach across the river where she'd been deposited and put her hand over her eyes to watch the boat pull away, the outboard churning up the sparkling water. Her husband sat facing forward, fiddling with a rod, and Dee, one hand on the tiller, looked out toward the shining length of the river.

"I HOPE YOU don't mind," Serena said to a young man already on site, placing a grate over a firepit. The sound of the boat receding downriver faded into the background. "I'm not much of an angler. Could I just sit in one of these chairs and enjoy the whole thing from here?"

The young man leaped to help her put the chair exactly where she wanted it, on the sunny point near the water, overlooking the sweep of the river, with the lodge just visible along the opposite bank. He could not recall a prettier woman coming to the lodge. Blond, her hair swept and curved into a bun, a beautiful tweed hat framing her face. Pale blue eyes, an oval face, and perfect skin.

"You're so kind," she said. She'd remember to tip him generously when they decamped after lunch. She sat down and stretched her legs, prepared to enjoy this respite from the fuss of getting Harry elected. She closed her eyes and felt the warmth of the strengthening sun on her lids. Unbidden, the matter of children came to her mind. She had been somewhat successful in pushing this unhappiness far away, but the by-election had opened up the wound. Her husband's political handlers had lamented more than once that there ought to be a couple of kids to complete the look of the all-Canadian family. She took a deep breath and exhaled, trying to let the morning work its magic, but the pain, once remembered, lingered, making her feel as if she was recovering from some long-ago illness.

She knew it was her. She'd gone secretly to her doctor when a few years had gone by and no children had materialized, and he'd confirmed that it was unlikely she would ever be able to conceive. A deep part of her believed that it was some sort of cosmic retribution for the kind of family she had come from. Of course, Harry didn't know the full extent of it, and her education and European finishing school, her clever brother with his law degree, had all done their job of lifting them, fresh smelling, into society. But she never felt fully free of the taint of it. And of course Harry had been deeply disappointed about the children, though he had gallantly worked hard to cover that disappointment. He had never blamed her, but she knew. It was a disappointment nothing she did could ever quite erase.

With a slight groan of impatience for once again allowing herself to go down this road, she reached into her bag to take out her sketchbook. She knew that her feelings of guilt were slowly transforming into a kind of constant irritation with her husband, and she found herself resolving to try to be a better person. The work on the cottage would help, give her an outlet.

The sound of a suddenly raised voice from across the water caused her to look up, furrowing her brow, and she leaned forward to hear better. The only vessel on the river just now was the boat Harry was in. It was quite far downriver from where she sat, but she could see the two figures on it. Putting her hand across the brim of her hat to further block the sun, she saw that Harry had turned and now sat facing the woman at the outboard. She could hear their voices, earnest, suddenly lowered, carried over the water, but could hear nothing of what was said. Were they arguing over where to go? She saw her husband suddenly reach out his hand toward the woman. She made some movement and he abruptly took it back.

Serena sat back, perplexed, watching. They were still talking. She could make no sense of this interaction. For a wild moment the thought came to her that Harry had come here to meet a lover, and she flushed. Certainly that old cat could not be his lover. Then, what?

With deliberate grace, Serena got up and walked to the fire where the young man had set up a table and was unfolding some chairs, and was now stopped, watching her approach. "So, tell me about your work at the lodge," she said, smiling sweetly. He looked like he might be inclined to gossip.

——

November 1939

THE NIGHTCLUB WAS smoky and noisy. Harry Devlin was well beyond tipsy, but he excused himself because he was drinking champagne in a convoluted attempt to both defiantly celebrate the loss of his latest girlfriend and drown his misery about it. His father's impatient demands that he needed to marry and "get on with his life" were an added irritation he could do without. He lit a cigarette and leaned back in his chair, squinting to enhance the murkiness of the scene before him. He was at the point of feeling a kind of elation where nothing and everything looked marvellous. The girls on the stage, scantily clad and generously proportioned, the satisfied complacency of the groups of men and women at the tables who smoked, drank cocktails, and talked and laughed, ignoring the stage show. Everyone looked jolly.

His companion tapped him on the shoulder, bringing him out of his reverie. "You want to look over there, Devlin. A cure for all your ills."

Harry put out his cigarette and languidly directed his attention to where his friend was pointing at a table on the mezzanine just above them. He felt a jolt that made him feel as though he'd sobered up instantly. There sat undoubtedly the most beautiful woman he'd ever seen, her blond hair pulled back on one side and curling under in a sleek pageboy that reflected the candlelight. Her gold satin dress flowed down her body like, he thought, liquid. And most importantly, she appeared to be very angry with her date. She was collecting her purse and pulling her pale fur coat around her shoulders. As she stood, her date reached out to stop her, but did not get up.

"Don't wait up," Harry said, rising. He manoeuvred through the dining room between the tightly packed tables and kept an eye on her progress along the mezzanine. He was at the bottom of the stairs waiting as she came down.

"Miss, let me get you a cab."

"I'm quite capable of getting my own cab, thank you." She glanced at him. "Haven't I seen you before?"

"You have the advantage of me. I have never seen you before. If I had, I would never forget you. Harry Devlin." He offered his hand, which she took passively.

"Serena Lee. You're that businessman."

"I don't know if I'm *that* businessman, but I do have a business. Where do you live?" The doorman had opened the door and they were moving onto the street before she answered.

"I tell you what. You can hail the cab and I'll tell him where to go." She smiled.

"Fair enough. What was wrong with your date?"

"He was an idiot. I don't like idiots."

Devlin nodded. "He certainly was. He made no attempt to follow you when you left. Ah. Here we go. Here, my card." He opened the door to the cab so she could get in, and then bent down. "I'd like to see you again, Miss Lee. I hope it is 'Miss.' I would be devastated to learn that the idiot is your husband."

"He's not. And we'll see." She closed the door and said something to the driver.

Devlin patted the roof of the cab and then stood on the sidewalk watching it drive up the street. Yellow Cab, number twenty-eight. She'd be worth a fling, he thought. He went back to his table and was pleased to see another bottle of champagne was being put into the ice bucket.

"You're back. Bad luck," his companion said, leaning over with a lighter for the cigarette Devlin dangled between his lips. "I'm not surprised. She's not known for being easy to get."

"You know her?"

"Not exactly know her, no. Know of her. Her family is a mixed bag. They run a couple of clubs in town, including, if I'm not mistaken, a piece of this one, but also two high-priced restaurants. Mostly on the up and up."

"Mostly?" Devlin asked. It would be a shame to discover that he was attracted to a local moll.

"Oh, she's fine, if that's what you're worried about. Nothing known against her. She's their attempt to get into society. I even heard she went to Switzerland to some school and has a degree from UBC in something ladylike, like philosophy. No, it's some of her younger male relations that have a reputation. You need muscle to run clubs, and her uncle likes to keep it in the family."

"How do you know so much? I've never heard of her before now."

"I met her at a dinner party thrown by that Tory politician, Grant, the wife made me go to. I was sorely tempted, I can tell you. She looks very good in candlelight. But . . ."

"Your wife," Devlin concluded.

"Yup. But you don't have a wife, and it's time you settled down. She's smart and she's connected. Who knows, maybe she'll drag you kicking and screaming into politics."

"Ha! Very unlikely. I'd make a lousy politician. Anyway, I don't care who she's connected to, she's jolly nice looking and, if I'm not wrong, didn't seem entirely uninterested."

———

MISS SCOTT OPENED her eyes. Someone had her arm and was tucking it back under the covers. She made a sound. Her mouth felt dry.

"You awake then, dear? Yes, I know. You must be thirsty. Here you go." The speaker held a straw to her lips and Miss Scott sipped, feeling an almost desperate relief. "I'll just go get Dr. Edison. She wanted to know when you woke up."

The straw was pulled away, and Miss Scott closed her eyes and concentrated on the feel of the cool water on her parched throat.

The room was dim and silent, until she began to vaguely hear sounds coming from somewhere else, outside the door. A metal cart wheeled by, a phone rang. Quiet voices. She had an idea she'd been dreaming. She turned inward and was assailed by a sense of disruption. Clothes being thrown. Books cascading. Breaking things. A feeling of panic. Falling.

"Ah! Miss Scott. Awake. Splendid."

The brisk voice cut through the murky images. Her arm was taken again, and she could feel gentle pressure on her wrist.

"We had a bit of a scare. Can you answer a couple of questions?"

Miss Scott had no idea if she could. She moved her lips and a sound came out.

"Excellent. Now then. Anything hurting right now?" She shook her head. "Headache?"

Miss Scott considered. No.

"Do you remember what happened?" the doctor asked.

She was sitting on the edge of the bed. Miss Scott felt

comforted by that. She tried to push away the murky memory of the clothes cascading onto the floor. She'd been in the hospital before. She remembered that. She looked away from the doctor and toward the window. Not this room. She shook her head.

"You were in the smoking room. Good thing you were in the hospital. We were able to get you up here quickly. We suspect another small stroke. You passed out, you see."

The patient nodded, trying to imagine herself in the scene the doctor was describing. Quite clearly and suddenly she remembered the window and someone smoking. She remembered wanting a cigarette. She nodded again, more firmly.

"Oh, splendid. You do remember. Good sign. Not too much damage. We're going to keep you quiet for a few days. No books, no reading of any kind." The doctor smiled.

Small details seemed to be taking on an overwhelming importance, like that window she just remembered, and now the doctor's smile. What was in that? Something knowing, as if it was meant to be a secret between them. She nodded again, and then heard herself say, "Water."

"Certainly." The doctor reached for the glass and inserted the straw into Miss Scott's mouth. "You're talking. Excellent."

Miss Scott closed her eyes and drank, feeling the water fresh and sliding in her throat.

A noise in the hallway outside, someone running an equipment cart into the wall, made Dr. Edison turn irritably toward the door of the room. Probably a candystriper bumbling about, but it was noise and she wanted her patient quiet. The sudden sputtering of that patient made her turn back in alarm. Miss Scott's eyes were wide, and she seemed intent on coughing the straw out of her mouth. Water ran down her chin. She appeared to be staring at nothing. Alarmed, Dr. Edison remembered this look on enlisted men who came in with battle fatigue, a kind of shock that took hold and did not diminish.

"There, there, it's all right. Just someone being clumsy in the hall." She had replaced the glass on the side table and wiped the water from her patient's chin and neck. To her immense relief, Miss Scott seemed to recover. She closed her eyes and lifted her hand slightly, as if to dismiss the doctor. "That's the stuff. A little sleep. I'll be in in the morning. We'll keep a good watch on you overnight. It should only take a couple of days to have you back where you were before this little incident."

Dr. Edison rose. Miss Scott could feel the lightening of the space on the bed where she'd been sitting. She could hear her go into the hall, issue quiet instructions. But inside she could feel the blow, hear it over and over, and she could feel the tears sliding down the side of her face.

———

Monday, December 15

THE DAY DAWNED crisp and white. Lane stood looking through the French doors at the gentle waves of snow that covered everything, the sun just hitting the tops of the mountains across the lake. She was holding a mug of coffee and inhaling the smell. Coffee smelled better than it tasted, she thought, taking a sip. She turned back to the table and added another spoon and a half of sugar. Darling was in the bath. He'd said he only wanted coffee and he'd pick up breakfast at the café. He wanted to leave early in case the trek into town was difficult and slow.

Both cars had chains, and Lane was happy she had only to go the four or so miles up to the school. She had decided she would tell the story of *A Christmas Carol* to the students. Darling had warned her against it.

"You'll frighten all those little children with Jacob Marley and all those ghosts. I wouldn't recommend it," he'd said upon hearing her plans the night before. "It gave me nightmares as a child."

"You must have been a very delicately nurtured child. I loved it. And anyway, these children are hardy British Columbians."

"I was not delicately nurtured. I was brought up by wolves and obliged to fend entirely for myself."

But it had given Lane pause. One could not, after all, project one's own view of things onto everyone else. She would give the story some context, lay some ground-work—what did Christmas mean to them, what was on their Christmas dinner table, and so on—to direct their attention. Her difficulty, of course, was that from a very young age she had felt herself adrift and alone in the big house she shared with her father and her little sister, who both seemed to need only each other, and the servants and parade of governesses that had drifted through her childhood. When she wasn't having lessons, or playing outside or in the garage, her favourite places, she was in the library, reading whatever was there. She supposed now that they would be considered adult books. Really, the closest there'd been to any concession to children had been *A Christmas Carol*. She'd found it quite delightful. By telling it, instead of reading it, she thought, she could spare these children, who might have quite different sensibilities, the most frightening moments of the story.

With a sigh she swigged back her sugary coffee and heard Darling coming down the hallway, already suited up in overcoat and hat. "Off then?"

"I am. I shall need a kiss to equip me to deal with the environmental conditions. And you, please drive carefully and try not to frighten the children. I still very much doubt the soundness of your plan. If I had my way, I'd cancel school today."

"Why? You're not closing the police station, after all."

"That's because, in weather like this, criminals strap on skis and keep at it," Darling said, taking her in his arms and helping himself to the required travel kiss. When he was gone, she rebelliously boiled water for tea, which, in contrast to coffee, smelled of nothing much but tasted lovely, and would be delicious in a Thermos when she had a roomful of frightened students to deal with after she'd alarmed them with Dickens.

CHAPTER NINETEEN

"THANK GOD FOR CHAINS," LANE said out loud in the
snow-quiet and deserted early morning, pulling her
car alongside the school into her usual spot. The school
was like a picture postcard, pristine snow billowing
around it and on the roof, the sun sparkling off every
surface. Lane sat and looked at it through the car window
and shook her head. Beautiful, impractical snow. The
realm of the Snow Queen. She, an ordinary human with
a taste for warmth and not slipping, faced a good deal of
shovelling and fire lighting before she and all her little
charges could feel comfortable.

She took up her bag and Thermos and stepped into the
snow, glad she'd worn her wellies, and carried her pumps
to put on inside.

But her thoughts of the Snow Queen persisted as she
went about making the school welcoming. Perhaps "The
Snow Queen" was a better story for the children, after all.
She tried to remember the whole thing, but she was stuck

on the magical mirror that made anyone looking into it see only the bad in themselves and forget all the good. It broke, she now remembered, into a million pieces and showered onto the earth like grains of sand. It got into people's hearts and made them destructive and bad and unhappy.

Now, that is interesting, she thought, waiting for the newspaper to catch fire and light the kindling to combat the cold that hung like an icy cloak inside the schoolroom. The story spoke to an idea of duality: people had both bad and good, and in forgetting the good, one acted on the bad or was perhaps pushed, if not quite to act on the bad, to feel badly about themselves, and to become unhappy.

That broken mirror came again into her mind. That little crack, as if someone had looked into it and seen only a reason to despair. Rising early, she had stood with her cup of tea looking at the new snow in the garden and had thought of her own broken mirror, trying to capture what it meant now in her life, a little fearful that no matter how happy one was, one might not be able to escape one's past.

The kindling caught and crackled, and she felt cheered again at the sound. She watched the fire a little more until the larger pieces of wood began to catch, then she closed the stove, double-checked the flue, and went to sit quietly at the desk she now thought of as hers. She opened her bag and pulled out her own reflection on the Snow Queen, read it silently, and, not particularly happy with it, made some marks on it before she tucked it back away.

After a Night of Snow,
And the burying billowing mounds of white

That cover all that shattered glass,
I get a brief respite.
I've left behind the rattling past
For some other better day
All my faults abandoned
Where they lay.

I see only these gleaming curves now
But in the thaw,
Under every greening bough,
In the flowering
Of all Spring's charms,
Those telling shards might all be waiting,
revealing and unharmed.

October 1933

COOK SHUFFLED HER to the chair against the wall and said good-naturedly, "It's your birthday, Laneke. Thirteen years old! Not such a beauty as your sister because you never smile, but lovely nonetheless. I am making a special cake. It is meant to be a surprise, but I can't keep it from you, my sweet! Run upstairs. I am sure your papa and sister are happy for you today."

Lane felt a sudden heaviness in her chest. The kitchen was warm and bustling; upstairs she would meet with her father's cold discontent, her sister's everlasting superiority. Prettier, more cheerful, more interesting. She wished she could be with her grandmother. She smiled briefly at Cook.

They would be with Grandmama soon, because Father would be going away again.

She climbed up the back stairs rather than going up to her room through the sitting room, where her father sat working. Masha was coming down with a mop and a bucket.

"Not this way, miss," she said in Lettish. "You know that. Why are you so disobedient? Your sister, at least, does what she is told."

Lane reversed her steps and instead went up the stairs that led to the sitting room. Her father was bent over some papers at his desk, and her sister played with the cat in front of the fire.

"Happy birthday," her sister said with a touch of sarcasm.

Lane nodded. "It's good to know you are so happy for me," she retorted and moved across the room.

Her father turned, slamming his pen down. "You are not to be rude to your sister. She wished you a happy birthday. You could be gracious."

Lane froze. "Yes, Papa." She glanced toward her sister, who still stroked the cat and watched the scene with her head slightly tilted.

"She doesn't mean it," her sister said at last.

"How old are you?" her father asked, his voice modulating slightly.

"Thirteen, Papa," Lane said. She wished she did not feel this aching fear whenever he addressed her.

"Thirteen and as disagreeable as ever." He sighed, turning back to his work, and Diana looked at Lane and smiled.

Her father spoke again suddenly, turning to look at both of them. "I'm sorry to say I will have to leave this afternoon. I cannot be here for supper. Cook is preparing a cake, I believe, so you will have to enjoy it without me. Diana, can you ready my bag as you always do?"

Lane watched Diana get up and go to her father, put her pudgy arm around his neck, and kiss his cheek. "Yes, Papa. Just the way you like it." She did not waste another second on her sister but turned to go into the hallway where their father's leather shoulder bag hung on a hook by the door.

"Is there anything I can do, Papa?" Lane could feel her voice faltering, alone now with her father. Putting her arm around his neck and kissing him was unimaginable to her.

"No, thank you." He got up and began to push papers into an envelope. Then he turned and looked at her again. He seemed to be attempting a smile, as if to soften his words. "You are not to be rude to Cook. She has no doubt gone to a lot of trouble for you, all right?"

Lane looked down abashed, amazed that her father did not know that it was Diana and not she who was rude to the servants, treating them with a supercilious air and ordering them about in a way Lane found unimaginable.

"But I—"

"No one is interested in what you think. All I ask is for a little cheerful good nature from my daughter. Instead I get this sullen, sulking face day in and day out." He shook his head and sighed, pulling on his gloves. "Now, your grandmother will want you both tomorrow. I will have the car. Anton will drive you in the cart." He reached out, almost as an afterthought, and patted the top of her head and said stiffly, "You will have a good birthday, Lanette. I am sorry I'm missing your cake."

Lane stood in front of her mirror in her room. Masha had come in and offered to put her hair up, like a grown-up, now that she was thirteen, but her head felt alien where her father had touched it.

"There is no point. Papa is not here. We are eating alone. Anyway, I'm ugly. Go put Diana's hair up. She always acts like the grown-up in this house."

———

LANE BEGAN TO pull herself away from this memory, which in truth made her feel ashamed. What a sullen, unpleasant child she must have been! But one thing stood out. How had the mirror got broken? Had she hit it with her brush? Had Masha still been in the room with her? She only remembered sitting fearfully in front of the mirror, her face a jagged broken reflection in the cracked glass, knowing how much trouble she would be in. She could see clearly, suddenly, that no matter how hard she tried to be good, she wasn't good at all. She was sulky and angry.

"SIR, I'VE FOLLOWED up on locating Miss Keeling's people. The RCMP and the Vancouver Police are working on it. Wait, before you say anything," Ames said, raising a hand and looking down at his notes. He was leaning against the door into Darling's office. "She did graduate from Normal School in Vancouver in 1942. She was very young, apparently. She was about nineteen when she left, but she was a good student according to the records."

"Did she have an address on file?"

"Yes. And I called one of my pals from the Vancouver Police, and he went to have a look at it. A rooming house for young women. Apparently the woman who ran it is retired and living with a daughter. I've asked him to track her down and see if she remembers anything about Miss Keeling's family. I've got someone looking into birth records in Victoria now."

Darling sat back and pursed his lips thoughtfully. "If she's the one who attacked Miss Scott, she's probably unlikely to go back to family, were we even able to find them. I wonder if she'd seek shelter with an old roommate."

Ames moved into the office and sat on the chair opposite Darling's desk. "What I find so strange is that everyone who knew her liked her, and she was by all accounts a great favourite with the students. On top of that, we know she was a good student, despite her age. She completed three years of Normal School, which means she must have started when she was sixteen."

"Your point, Ames?"

"Well, what I'm thinking is that she seems, on the face of it, an unlikely sort of person to suddenly become violent. I'm wondering if whatever she was running from all those years ago finally caught up with her. Why is a sixteen-year-old living in a rooming house? Because she can't, or won't, live at home. What if she was running from whomever it was, and in his frustration, he tore up the cottage and struck Miss Scott when she didn't know, or wouldn't tell him, where Miss Keeling had gone?"

"I'm wondering if Keeling is even her real name. I know Terrell has been trying to trace her family and can't find anything before her engagement with the Normal School. The Mounties have come up with nothing, so far." Darling sat up straight and moved a pile of papers an inch or two to the right. "Before you go constructing a novel with your speculations, find out what you can from the retired landlady. And maybe Vital Statistics will come up with something, though unlikely, if Keeling is an assumed name. In the meantime, Miss Scott has had a relapse, and we still don't have a bloody clue who ran down Samuel's father."

AMES GOT OFF the phone with his friend Constable Blake, whom he'd met while studying for the sergeant's exam in Vancouver, and glanced at his watch. They might have a lead to follow up. Blake said he'd call back either later that afternoon or the next day. Nearly one o'clock.

"Sir, I'm thinking of going down to the café for lunch. Care to come, or can I bring you something?"

"Nope. Yes. Bring me a sandwich, ham, no cheese. Take Terrell. He's been working on the Miss Scott angle today. You can talk shop. And don't be all day about it!"

Ames, knowing full well that the inspector was unlikely to give him money just that moment for the sandwich, put on his overcoat and hat, and clattered down the stairs whistling. The snow was falling now in big flakes, and as annoying as it was for the traffic crawling along Baker Street, it was lovely. Christmassy, he would have said.

"You're in a good mood. Who is she?" O'Brien said, looking up from his post by the telephone. Remarkably he appeared to be filing things, instead of bent over the crossword.

"None of your impertinence, O'Brien. I'm going to the café. Can I bring you something?"

O'Brien looked at his watch. "At this time of day? No, thank you very much. I ate at twelve like normal people. He's not moved from his desk." He jerked his head in the direction of Terrell, who had just gotten off the phone and was making notes. "Could probably use a bite. Take him with you; he's looking peaky."

Wondering how the vibrant Terrell could in any way be described as "peaky," Ames went over to his colleague's desk. "Come on, lunch."

"Yes, sir. Good idea. I'm famished. I just—"

"Nope. Now."

They were seated in a corner booth and could see the pedestrians in rubber overshoes and snow-sprinkled hats making their way along the street. A good mood prevailed. April beamed at Terrell, and Terrell beamed at April. Ames brushed his hand through his sandy hair and contemplated breaking the habit of years and ordering something different.

"What's on today?"

"Really?" April said. "Patty melt, if you must know, but—"

"I'll have that, just to prove that whatever you were about to say is completely wrong."

"Well, I'll be. You, Constable?"

"This vegetable soup looks good. Grilled cheese, no ham."

"Which reminds me," Ames said, "we have to take something back for the inspector. Ham, no cheese."

"The weather is a good metaphor for what we are dealing

with now," observed Terrell when April had gone off to get coffee for them. "Everything is covered up. It's hard to discern what's underneath."

"Good grief. If I wanted to have lunch with people who use the word 'metaphor' I would have asked Darling," Ames said. "But I think I see your point. Someone does a hit and run on a snowy road in the dark, and as far as I can see, we have no real way of finding the culprit."

"Exactly. And Miss Scott gets a bang on the head and can't remember anything, and Miss Keeling, who might not be called Keeling at all, disappears, and it's not clear whether we should be alarmed about it, because she's taken her things with her, which could mean she's either in danger or on the run. It's not like a regular case where someone's been killed and we line up all the people who could have used the person being dead and pick the most likely suspects and their possible motives like they do in books. Sooner or later that leads to results, apparently," Terrell said.

"Yes, true. Even outside of books it can lead to results. The one corpse we have is Samuel's father, but that was a hit and run. As unpremeditated as you can get. The only crime here is the run part. In weather conditions like we've been having, the driver might not even have been driving dangerously." Ames held the sugar dispenser over his teaspoon.

Terrell watched Ames dumping sugar into his cup and raised his eyebrows. "Let's, for the sake of argument, say that the hit and run was deliberate. How could it have happened? Who would want it to happen? Why?"

"I see you raising your eyebrows at my cup. I need the energy. It's cold and we're getting nowhere. Okay, for the sake of argument: He's a pretty unpleasant man, at least as far as his child is concerned, and the teachers and neighbours as well. He says they're interfering when they express concern about Samuel being neglected. So theoretically teachers could want him dead, though that's a bit extreme and not teacher-like behaviour, as he's the only parent Samuel has, and what they care about is Samuel. He also was away from home, leaving the kid alone, and out at the bar after work. According to Gilly he had been drinking heavily. Perhaps he annoys someone at the bar, and they follow him and kill him. Except, of course, he's gotten a ride with someone somewhere. And no one has come forward to say they gave him a ride."

Terrell was thoughtful. "A man like that could have any number of people lined up to kill him. But he was alone at the Legion on Friday and headed to the Metropol and didn't get there. We could find out who might have had it in for him, certainly. Maybe the person who gave him that ride. Certainly he was on the wrong side of town for someone who lived north, up the lake."

"Our ad in the papers and on the radio asking the driver to give himself up has netted exactly nothing," Ames said. "It hasn't pushed the culprit to come out of hiding, but I suppose we can still hope that maybe someone he's confessed to about it will come forward."

"Possibly, though we better hope he didn't confess to a priest. Also, we are assuming it's a he. Could have been a she."

"True. Thank you, April," Ames said as lunch was delivered to their table. He watched her as she retreated. "I'm operating on a kind of prejudice that women don't drive around in the snow late at night."

"Yes, sir. I operate under the same prejudice. But I wonder if we should. I mean, Miss Van Eyck would drive any time, I bet. What if it's a woman rushing a sick child to a hospital?"

"Wouldn't someone like that be responsible enough to report that they'd hit someone?" Ames recognized the truth of what Terrell said about Tina. He couldn't tell if he admired her for it, or if it alarmed him.

"Hmm. I don't know, sir. I think lots of people would be very afraid to do that, at least right away." Terrell munched reflectively on his grilled cheese.

"Raising the possibility that someone may still come forward. In the meantime, what about the clues we *do* have? Take the letters. I can't help believing that the nasty letters are connected to the debacle at the teacher's cottage. Someone sends poison-pen letters, and then escalates. Begins to stalk, for example. We have the suggestion from Samuel that a car was parked during the day near the school. If the letters are sent to Miss Keeling, she runs away, and the man, in a rage, bonks Miss Scott on the head and smashes the cabin up. If only Miss Scott could remember what happened!" Ames said.

"And if the letters are sent to Miss Scott, whoever it is comes to the cottage and is free to attack her because Miss Keeling is already gone. Somewhere. What if she's gone to meet the letter writer and is in league with him? Or has been kidnapped already by him, to get her out of the house so he can have at Miss Scott?"

Ames made no response to this and fell to looking out the window. He could see people moving along the inside of the sidewalk where the roof overhang provided a drier walk. They had packages and seemed, to a man and woman, cheerful, chatting and laughing. The Dade Hotel had put some coloured lights around the entrance. He should think about finding a little present for his mother. Then, before he could stop it, the thought came to him that he ought to find something for Tina Van Eyck. Mentally saying, "Damn," he pulled his gaze away from the window.

"The case, sir?" asked Terrell, who had not missed his sergeant's sudden distraction. Ames shook his head.

"No, Constable. Christmas. The annual 'What the hell should I get Mother?' conundrum. And anyone else who feels they deserve something: the paper boy, the garbage collector."

"Ah!" Terrell smiled. "Any ideas?"

"Nary a one. Take Mother. She doesn't need kitchen stuff, and she must have cupboards full of scarves and gloves that I bet she never uses."

"My grandmother always says you should get a little something someone wouldn't spend money on for themselves. I gave my mother a subscription to *Life* magazine. When I was there earlier this year I went to the market with her, and I saw her leafing through a copy on the stand in the drugstore, and when I went to buy it for her she said it was a terrible waste of money, but I could tell she loved it."

Ames nodded thoughtfully. "That is an excellent idea.

I know Mother loves the *Canadian Home Journal*. I could get her the current issue and stick a note inside about the subscription."

"I'm glad I could help. Anyone else I can provide guidance on?" Terrell asked, raising an eyebrow in a way Ames thought a trifle pointed.

"Certainly not. Back to work." He raised his hand for April, who came over with the bill and Darling's sandwich. "I'll get this," he said.

It was only on the walk back that something filtered into Ames's consciousness. "Irving!" he said.

"Sir?" asked Terrell.

"Irving, in the bible. The name written in the fly-leaf of the bible was 'W. Irving.' I'll call my chum in Vancouver back. I bet her real name was Irving."

CHAPTER TWENTY

November 1947

"I'M NOT INTERESTED IN GOD, so you take yourself off," he shouted at the woman who had called through the door and was still knocking. His voice was hoarse. He lay back down again.

The Hotel Lux, a dilapidated effort along East Hastings Street, was the last stop for the desperate. His fellow denizens consisted of vets from two wars who had returned to a world they no longer understood. For many, it was the same world they had left, and they had hoped their service would alter their circumstances but it never did. For others the world they had left could not accommodate their altered personalities, and so they ended up at the Lux, living day to day. He himself had never made much sense of the world after getting back from Europe in '19. He was relieved he had no family now to strive for so he could focus on just keeping himself going, though it had surprised him that he found himself thinking of Wendy often. He knew she had been better off without him, even with his mad religious brother. His brother's wife was a good woman. She would have made sure the girl was all right. It surprised him to think how a child could grow on you, even one that was not your own. He tried not to think of how he had treated her after Denise had told him the truth, but that was not so easy, now that the drinking had stopped. He wondered if he should try to see her again, make things right.

Unlike the other men in the hotel, Irving did not drink, and he had, since quitting his brother's house all those years ago, eschewed any part of the life he had lived before. It was a kind of penance, and the anonymity of his existence suited him perfectly.

The knocking was more persistent. The woman spoke again. "Mr. Irving. I must speak with you."

The voice sounded like that of a younger woman. With irritation he got up and walked the short distance to the door in his stocking feet and pulled the chain, opening it just wide enough to see that the woman was indeed young, and extremely well turned out. His surprise at this caused him to open the door a little wider, and she used the opportunity to push her way in.

There was a small table by the single window in the room, and she took up the only chair that was beside it and folded her expensively gloved hands on her handbag.

"What the blazes do you want?" he asked. He wanted to sit down, but there was only the bed, and he did not want to put himself into a subordinate position to this woman. She might be some sort of social worker.

"I'll get right down to business. You needn't ask how,

but I understand you have a daughter. I wish to be in touch with her. I would be obliged if you could provide me with her address."

He was stunned into silence by this. A daughter? How could this woman know such a thing? "Come, Mr. Irving. I haven't got all day. I will of course pay you." Here she opened the handbag and extracted a billfold and began to remove bills from it. "I can see that you could use a little help. I am happy to provide it."

"Who the devil are you, to come here throwing money around?" She had turned her face so that the light from the window shone on her profile. For a second he almost thought he recognized her from somewhere, but she was certainly not someone he knew or had ever known. She must be only slightly older than the daughter she was trying to find.

"That really is none of your concern, Mr. Irving. I need to get in touch with your daughter, Wendy. She might have changed her name, as you must know, or do you? So she has either married or wishes to remain out of sight." She stood up and put the bills on the table. "If you would oblige me."

"I will not oblige you. You can get the hell out of here and take your money with you." Irving took up the cash, thrust it into her hand, and opened the door.

"You may come to regret this decision, Mr. Irving," said the young woman imperiously, as she swept out into the hallway, her fox-fur stole as out of place in this establishment as she was herself. "I will find her, you know. It's quite within my power. I know where you lived, where she went to school, and that you removed her from that school in

'32. I know you moved her to Williams Lake. In fact, I've tracked her down to a rooming house quite near here. I have a lead on one of her roommates, who, I'm sure, will not turn her nose up at a little extra cash. Need I say more? I will find where she is now. You'd save me a lot of time if you just told me what you know." She stopped in the doorway. "One last chance. The money is yours."

"Please leave," was all he said.

Irving stood at the door, listening to her footsteps recede down the two flights of stairs, and then he hurried to the window to look down to the street. He saw her emerge from the front door and stand for a moment, looking at the street, and then walk toward a long sleek car that began to slowly move in her direction. The car, a Rolls-Royce, stopped. A uniformed driver got out and came round to open the rear door. She refused his hand and got in. The car slid down the street toward the centre of town. Irving turned away and thought about his daughter. She'd certainly not wanted anything to do with him the last time he'd tried.

It was then that the penny dropped, and he remembered where he'd seen his visitor: on the front page of the *Vancouver Sun*.

———

BACK AT THE station where he was waiting for his lunch, Darling's thoughts were travelling along the same lines as those of his subordinates. The only real handle we have on any of the teacher business is the letters, he was thinking. He reached into the inbox where he kept his manila file folders neatly piled and pulled out the letter Lane had found at the school and the other singed ones she had fished out of the stove. They were ugly, and in combination with someone lurking at the school in a car, he could understand how a teacher in an isolated schoolhouse might be terrified and decide to arm herself. And the circumstances of Miss Keeling having disappeared still pointed, in his mind, to the idea that the letters might have been aimed at her. He took up the letter that had been most damaged by the fire. The usual invective and name-calling and then—his head jerked back and he squinted to see better. Not having any luck, he took the letter to the window and tried to make out the crude pencil markings that had been nearly obliterated by the heat browning the paper. "You can't hide . . ." That part was clear enough, and then, "I know . . ." When? What? No, "who," surely. You can't hide who . . . you are? I know who you are?

So, who was Miss Keeling? Darling sat down again and chewed his lower lip briefly. Whoever she was, Ames had now traced her story back as far as a boarding house in Vancouver. If she started Normal School at the age of sixteen, could they assume that was when she'd arrived at the boarding house? That was very young to live away from family, but not unheard of. If the family was poor and could not afford to feed all the children, sending the oldest to make her way on her own was plausible. Had she changed her name? Certainly they could not trace her further back than the rooming house in Vancouver. Vital Statistics had produced neither a birth nor a marriage certificate. Was she running from something even then? In this context it would be useful to find out why she'd left her first teaching assignment on Vancouver Island. And, according to Ames, the Vancouver Police might still come up with something. He made a note on the file, and turned his thoughts back to Samuel's dead father. Just as Ames and Terrell had done over their sandwiches, he bemoaned the fact that they were very unlikely to find the driver unless that driver, driven by guilt or fear, turned himself in. And where the hell was his sandwich?

―――

November 1947

"SIR, THERE'S A gentleman here to see you. He will be a constituent in the riding you are contesting." Michael Perkins, Harry Devlin's meticulous secretary, who wore double-breasted suits and firmly combed-back hair in the style of the mid-1920s, pronounced the word "gentleman" with a suggestion of distaste.

Devlin appreciated his secretary's exactitude, but not his evident class consciousness. He said with friendly impatience, "Yes, go on, Perkins. Show him in."

"Please step in," Perkins said, casting a look at his boss that said, "Don't blame me."

The man who stood before his mahogany desk was, thought Devlin, clearly not a businessman, and yet he could not quite peg him as a labourer. His clothes were a mismatched shabby blue jacket and brown pants. He wore no tie, and his hair was a little overlong. He was well into his fifties and looked like someone who had barely recovered from a personal disaster, the loss of a job, or perhaps he was a veteran of the Great War who'd never quite found his feet again.

"Please sit down, Mr. . . ."

"Irving. Ezekiel Irving. I'll stand, thank you. I won't be here long." Something in Devlin surged at the name "Ezekiel." It took him a moment to realize it was a wave of fear. "As you wish. How can I help?" Devlin folded his hands on the desk and leaned forward, affecting a friendly smile. This man would be asking for money, he thought, feeling that familiar stiffening of a resolve to keep the number reasonable but not ungenerous.

"I read in the papers that you would be giving up all this"—Irving waved his hand to encompass the huge, wood-panelled, seventh-floor office with the views of English Bay—"to run for public office. And since we have a personal connection, I thought I would stop by and have a chat."

Devlin felt his head jerk almost imperceptibly, but he maintained his smile, adding to it a slight pulling together of the eyebrows. "I see?" he said, but left it hanging as a question. The bitter drops of misgivings were beginning to collect somewhere inside him.

"I hope you do," Irving said. He walked over to the large window to the right of the desk, his hands in his pockets, and looked across at the view. A large ship was making its way toward the harbour in the strait. "I'd never give up an office like this," he said.

"Mr. Irving," Devlin said, glancing toward the office door, wishing now he'd heeded the broad hint Perkins had provided. He had a buzzer that would bring his secretary back into the room. He suspected Perkins was parked by the door, at the ready.

"Yes. I know. I do know, actually. I know you slept with . . . I was going to say my whore of a wife, but I'm trying to let bygones be bygones, and that your child, whom I was forced to provide for, is grown up now. I mean, I assume she is, somewhere. She ran away when she was sixteen."

Devlin sat back, trying to comprehend the full import of the moment. "What do you want?" he said finally.

"That's right. Reduce everything to money. People like you never learn, do you? You throw money at things and assume that makes them disappear. Nothing disappears, my friend. You shovel it under and it grows roots. No, I don't want money. I just thought you'd like to know that your wife came to see me."

Frowning, Devlin said, "What? My wife? I don't—"

"Understand. I know," Irving interrupted. "Believe me, I didn't either. I don't really know how she found me. I suppose the wealthy have people who do that sort of thing. She was looking for your daughter. Unfortunately, I couldn't tell her anything. I don't really know where she is just at the moment, and if I did, I wouldn't tell her." Irving turned his hat in his hand and shrugged. He took a step closer to the desk, where Devlin sat unmoving, watching him warily. "If I were you, I'd keep my eye on her. Your wife, I mean. I can tell by the look on your face you don't even know what she's up to. What she's up to is looking after your political career. She knows that news of a love child getting out is a career killer if there ever was one."

"You're talking absolute rubbish. Now what do you want?" Devlin pulled open a drawer and began to look for something.

Irving nodded. "I can see why your wife thinks she has to look after you. You don't seem very bright. More bad taste on the part of my ex-wife, I guess, after me, of course. I don't want anything. I'm just warning you about what's going on out there. You obviously didn't care two ticks about your daughter, and I confess, I didn't either, I was so angry about my wife. I did the best I knew how, because Wendy was an innocent child and didn't deserve to be around someone like me who couldn't care for her, so I took her to my brother's family. I didn't see until too late that was a mistake as well. I was happy, if I'm truthful, when she ran away from that sanctimonious old goat."

Devlin's head was swimming and he struggled with the unfamiliar force of something between fear and rage. He could make no sense of anything after "your wife."

"I think you'd better leave," he said, trying to sound aloof. He went to press the bell to get his secretary back into the room.

Irving raised his hand to stop him. "I'm just saying this. Life has given me a few hard lessons, and one is that that girl turned out to be pretty bright, and I admire her, you know, for getting away. I know I couldn't. I was a drinker. I guess that's why Denise went for a charmer like you. I'm pretty sure about this: Wendy knows nothing about you. No one ever told her I wasn't her father. I'd get your wife to back off if I were you. She'll only draw attention to a problem you don't even have. You know, I spent some time in the library having a look-see at anything I could find about your wife. The back issues of magazines were helpful. Fashionable woman. But the back issues of newspapers were more revealing. Dodgy family. Are you aware of what kind of family she comes from, or did you just go for the shiny exterior? Here's the thing. If something happens to that girl, I will be back."

———

"THERE AREN'T REALLY ghosts, are there?" The question was asked with a slight giggle that did not cover up young Randy's underlying anxiety. They had arrived with some relief at the Ghost of Christmas Present, and Lane had built in a little discussion time after the day's episode.

Lane smiled. "Only in stories. During the time when Charles Dickens wrote this story, people tended to believe in ghosts. Now we know they are safely between the covers of books." She slid the bookmark into the book, as she might the conjured ghosts, and closed it firmly. She'd decided on reading and telling alternately so that the children still got the advantage of hearing some of Dickens's language. But then, feeling she hadn't listened properly to the child's anxiety, nor perhaps that of the other children who had not asked the question out of fear of looking silly, she said, "Is it something you worry about?"

Philip put up his hand. "My mother said there was a ghost in her house when she was a little girl. She said she actually heard it." Lane's heart sank. She could hardly

255

contradict stories from the children's parents, but she didn't want to leave them all going home to nightmares.

"Now, that is interesting. Has anyone else heard about ghosts from parents or family?" Five children put their hands up firmly.

"My grandmother told me about a ghost," said Amy.

"And was she afraid of the ghost?"

"I don't know. I don't think so. Maybe when she was little."

"How do you think stories about ghosts might come about?"

Rafe put up his hand. "Maybe because they get told in families. Like maybe Mommy's grandmother told her, but maybe her grandmother heard it from her grandmother."

Lane nodded thoughtfully. "So, passed down in family stories?"

Gabriella raised her hand. "I used to be afraid of the dark. If I heard a noise, like a tree branch scratching the wall outside, I was scared that someone was there. I put my head under my pillow."

"You know, I think we all are afraid of things in the night, even grown-ups. I know I am sometimes. It is possible ghost stories happen because people are afraid in the dark and worry that someone is there. Anything else? Scrooge thought it was just indigestion, that something he'd had at supper made him have bad dreams."

"What if you found out that someone died in your house? Wouldn't they be a ghost?" Rolfie.

"No, that's silly. If you live in an old house someone probably did die there." Philip.

Philip sounded so like his mother, she thought. "Okay," Lane said. She was going to have to draw this to a less alarming conclusion. "It seems to me that in spite of being frightened of ghosts, or things in the dark, everybody is still safe. The sun comes up and our fears don't seem as scary. Even Ebenezer Scrooge. The ghosts frighten him, but after these first two ghosts, he is still safe in the end, right in his bed. In a way, they are his imagination helping him to understand why he is such an unhappy and mean person, so not really ghosts at all. Now then. Let's get out our writing implements, and I would like you to write a little paragraph about what you think Scrooge has learned so far about himself."

Lane sat back, mentally fanning herself for having gotten out of a sticky situation and thinking she might not carry on with the Ghost of Christmas Yet to Come. She really should have gone with the Snow Queen.

"Excuse me, miss. I forgot to give you this note. It's from my mother to say why I was away last week. I was sick." Randy handed Lane a crumpled paper.

"Oh, thank you. I'm glad you're feeling better. What was wrong?"

"I think I ate something bad. I was throwing up and stuff."

"Then I'm doubly glad you're feeling better, and I hope it didn't give you any bad dreams!" She looked at the note, and then realized the teachers must store them somewhere to mark in the attendance book.

"Miss Keeling and Miss Scott had a clipboard for the notes," Randy said, as if reading her mind. "It's hanging over there."

"Thank you, Randy. That's helpful. Now off you go to do your paragraph." She'd already seen a tendency in Randy to put off any writing task as long as possible.

"Over there" turned out to be on the side of the desk itself, where a nail had been driven for the purpose. She hadn't seen it before because that side of the desk was pushed close to the wall. She pulled the clipboard off its nail, and sure enough, there was a little collection of notes on all sorts of paper, written with all sorts of instruments.

She lifted the clip and pulled them out. Had these not been put into the attendance record? She glanced up at the class and was gratified that all of them seemed to be occupied with writing. No time like the present. She pulled the ledger out of the middle drawer where she'd put it after the attendance call and then began to go through the notes. Most, she was relieved to see, were dated. She put a small *e* by the *x* for any day a student was absent, which she saw was the form, and assumed it meant "excused."

Randy, not unexpectedly, got up to sharpen his pencil. He was old enough to be writing with an ink pen, but he had told her that he had trouble writing and that Miss Keeling let him carry on with a pencil. Anything that keeps him writing, Lane thought, and got back to her task. She picked up the next note and stared at it. When realization hit her, she felt her heart give an anxious beat. She knew the hand. Crude, ungainly words in pencil, the message brief. "Sam was sick for two days."

TERRELL HUNG UP the phone and finished the notes he had started. He went upstairs and presented himself at Darling's door. "Sir?"

"Yes?"

"Sir, I put in a call to the district where Miss Keeling taught on Vancouver Island. Near a place called Saanich. I talked to the woman who is teaching there now, a Miss Fleming. She took the job after Miss Keeling left, but she did talk with her. She gave no reason for having to leave, but she seemed 'jumpy.' She was in a bit of a hurry to finish handing over the reins.

"Apparently Miss Fleming asked her if she was all right, and she just said something like, 'I'm fine. I think there's someone here I just don't want to see.' Miss Fleming assumed it was a beau of some sort that hadn't turned out well. She said she'd been worried it might have been trouble with one of the parents, but they all turned out to be lovely people. She said she couldn't understand why anyone would leave the school, because the students were great and the parents very kind, bringing treats and Christmas presents and the like. Sounds like she was afraid of something."

"Yes, it does indeed." Darling reread Terrell's notes after he had left. So, she was so afraid of someone that she left an otherwise ideal post and accepted a job pretty far off the beaten track, only to find she was plagued by the same thing here? This opened up the possibility that whoever it was had come after her, found where Miss Keeling was teaching, and she'd somehow seen whoever it was and fled. The person then burst into the cottage and, in a rage at not finding Miss Keeling, turned over the place and attacked

Miss Scott. Or, had found her and torn the place up because Miss Scott had put up a fight to protect her colleague, so he'd hit her and carried Keeling off. The missing clothes were an impediment, though. A kidnapper would not hang about packing things.

No sooner had Terrell left than Ames popped up in his doorway.

"I followed up on the Irving idea, sir."

"Irving?" Darling was mystified.

"In the bible I found, sir, in what we assume was Miss Keeling's room. The fly-leaf had the name 'W. Irving.' It occurred to me at lunch that perhaps that had been her name. Vital Statistics. There was a Wendy Irving born April 15, 1924, to a Denise and Ezekiel Irving."

"It doesn't necessarily follow it's the same woman. She could have borrowed the bible, picked it up at a used bookstore, swiped it from a hotel. However, keep at it. Full points for picking up on that."

"Sir." Turning back to his own office, Ames gave a brisk and businesslike nod, to cover how pleased he was to get the rare praise from his boss.

Darling sat back and stared out at Elephant Mountain. Is it, he asked himself, that we have two teachers running from things? The same thing?

CHAPTER TWENTY-ONE

LANE CHECKED HER WATCH AS she left the school. It was after five and already nearly dark outside. Darling should be back within the hour. She had gone through all the children's writings about what Scrooge had learned and had enjoyed them so much she was tempted to take them home to share after dinner. They ranged from "He learned you shouldn't eat bad stuff before bed because you get nightmares. That happened to me" to "He shouldn't have been so mean when he was young because he would end up being sorry later" to the very touching "If you end up being treated really badly by your father when you are little, you might end up forgetting how to care. Someone should have been nicer to him to make up for his mean father." That was Gabriella.

She left the paragraphs, reasoning that the students might not want them shared about without their permission, and put the note from Samuel's father into her bag. She double-checked the door on the stove and turned out the lights. Outside in the dark winter silence, the cold air cooled her cheeks and soothed her slightly jangled nerves. Snow was falling gently, and she found herself hoping Darling had gotten home first and would have started up the fire.

It was not to be. The house was dark. What had occupied her thoughts on the way home was that there ought to be a telephone installed at the school. She had wanted to telephone Darling the minute she found the note and realized its significance, but further, if anything happened to one of the children, with only one adult on hand, the teacher would be faced with the decision of driving off to get help, leaving perhaps the older children in charge, Philip and Gabriella, say, or sending one of the children running down the long hill to the store to get Bales to call for help.

She hung up her coat, shivered at the cold, and wondered who would be in charge of a telephone for the school. She had just coaxed the fire in the stove into a proper blaze and was contemplating an omelette for supper, when she saw the welcome headlights of the returning husband.

"Hello, darling," she called from the kitchen. "Omelette do you? And Gladys gave us a jar of beets."

Darling by this time was leaning in the doorway looking at her, undecided about gazing a bit more or kissing her. Instead he put his hands in his pockets and nodded speculatively. "You're proposing to feed me a beet omelette? Very unexpected. What sort of wine would you recommend with that?"

Lane advanced and kissed him, slid her hand out of his, and walked past him into the sitting room. "Look, I found something today." She pulled the note out of her handbag and brought it back into the brighter light of the kitchen.

Darling read it, turned it over and back, and asked, "What am I looking at?"

"A sick note for Samuel, written by his father. Handwriting identical to the poison pen received by Miss Keeling or Miss Scott."

"Blimey! It was Gaskell!" he said, sitting down. It was an expression he'd brought back from his time in Britain as a fighter pilot.

"Blimey indeed," said Lane. "It was Samuel's unpleasant father who got the wind up about one of the teachers and was peppering her with horrible notes. Whoever the notes were intended for, he's now dead."

"Those are not necessarily cause and effect," Darling said slowly. "After all, his death was a hit and run a good thirty miles from here. But," he conceded, "he is dead. And it's Miss Keeling who is missing, after all, and clearly left in a hurry. Terrell learned today, by the way, that she apparently left her last post on Vancouver Island because she might have seen or interacted with someone she really didn't want to see. Gaskell could have found out something about that and have begun the poison-pen campaign against her. But before we go racing down that road, you should get on with that beet omelette, and we can discuss it over dinner. I'm famished."

Rather pleased with herself for having created what she was sure could be described as a well-balanced meal from the limited ingredients on hand, Lane produced a cheese omelette along with a salad of beets with some grated carrot and a little oil, with buttered wheat toast on the side.

"Omelette's delicious," Darling said, "though I still wonder if you shouldn't have risked the beets." He leaned back in his chair. "If Samuel's father is the poison-pen artist, then he can't have been the same person she didn't want to encounter on faraway Vancouver Island. And if Miss Keeling was the intended victim, it increases by at least one the number of people who want Gaskell dead. Both teachers might have been at least relieved, if not positively joyous, if he disappeared. But from what we know now, Miss Keeling might have had a completely different enemy, as well."

"Ah," said Lane, toying with her glass of wine. "Horrible for her to come here to get away from an unpleasant character and meet the same fate here."

"Let's say she displayed what some might have termed dubious morals and incited the locals in both places."

"No, let's not say that. We are making her responsible for being harassed, very unfair under any circumstances, but very much so where there is no evidence of her being anything but wonderful, at least from the children's point of view, though I do concede that her running off muddies the waters. No. His notes, if they were directed at her, suggest to me a hatred born out of envy and malice. Perhaps he made a play for her and she rejected him."

Darling shrugged and nodded. "It would fit in with what we know about him. His wife left him; he was neglectful and unkind to his boy. I wouldn't put what you suggest past him. If we follow that logic to its conclusion, however, she's run him down on a snowy road and done a bunk."

"Stopping only to beat Miss Scott about the head and tear up the cottage? No, a man like that must have lots of enemies. What about his workmates?"

"Those fellows usually man the ferry alone, but as it happens, he doesn't get along with most of them. On that night, he'd evidently been drinking and was given a ride away from town in the wrong direction. He could have been followed by someone from work or the Legion and been run down, though that begs the question of why he was on the road on foot. He apparently was alone at the Legion earlier that night. Or is it exactly what it seems? It's dark, it's snowing, and it's an accident, except that the driver speeds away, and is only now a criminal. What if Miss Keeling, whom we know to have been independent from a young age, and is probably of a determined nature, learns of the notes, sees that Miss Scott is in a state about them, and goes after Gaskell that night? She knows if she takes any drastic action against the parent of one of the students she will have to leave, so she packs her bags, ready to disappear. Maybe she doesn't even intend to kill him, just have a word, and it all goes wrong."

"But then who is knocking Miss Scott out? If the notes are intended for her, he may have taken his animosity to the next extreme, but that means he's not on the highway getting run down. By anyone."

"No, but look. He's a known quantity. He goes to the pub every night after work and gets drunk. We're just assuming Gaskell's back at the ranch beating up Miss Scott. His normal behaviour is to go drinking directly from work. We make it too complicated if we try to fit him into every part of this. Miss Scott is being attacked by someone else. Someone who is trying to rob the cottage, plain and simple."

Lane got up and moved the dishes to the sink, and then fetched a piece of foolscap from the writing desk by the window.

"Okay. Here's Miss Keeling. Let's say the notes are for her. We do this and this and this—and end up with a dead man." She wrote the sequence of events Darling had outlined with arrows connecting them. "But what if the notes are for Miss Scott after all? Let's put her here and see what happens. To start with, Miss Keeling just arrived a few weeks ago, but Miss Scott has been here all along. Lots of time for her to have annoyed Gaskell. She could have objected to the way the boy was sent to school, dirty, hungry, neglected. He doesn't like being confronted with his failures. What if he's been making passes at her, and she's rejected him. And—" Lane turned to him, excitement animating her face. "And the car!" she finished.

"The car?" he asked. He was still focused on the arrows she had drawn. This mapping out of the circumstances of a crime had intrigued him in the past, and his mind had conjured up several scenes of Miss Scott being propositioned. Before Miss Keeling's arrival, she was alone in an isolated cottage, with Samuel and his father as her nearest neighbours.

"The car. Where is Miss Scott's car? His car is missing, and so is hers."

"Yes, but look here, Miss Scott is found Monday morning near death, and it's likely she's been there the whole weekend. When did she have time to go around hitting

266

people with her car? It's more likely that Miss Keeling has the car somewhere. Unless Miss Scott did the hitting. She has plenty of reason to." Darling leaned back and stared speculatively at the ceiling. "And then she ditches her car, comes home, dusts off her hands, puts on a sweater, and makes a cup of chocolate, pretty as you please, and then gets knocked out and robbed and left for dead. Natural justice, certainly. However, it still raises one or two questions."

Lane smiled sweetly and said, "No, she parks her car, Miss Keeling takes it, and . . . well, all the rest of it. But I know what you mean. Miss Scott must have cared for her students. It's unlikely she'd be keen to leave one orphaned, even to get rid of Gaskell. Come. Fireplace, feet on grate, a bedtime whisky. When we've sorted the details of Friday, we can discuss Ebenezer Scrooge's visit to the schoolhouse today."

Darling was more than happy to fall in with the plans, for he saw that his conversation with Lane was going to be more work for him.

"He didn't have his car. We don't know why. He went to work in it on Friday morning as usual, parked it . . . where? I'll detail one of the lads to find out where he usually parked. Perhaps the car's still there. If not, where is it? So then he walks from the ferry all the way to the Legion, spends the evening drinking alone, and then leaves alone to go to the Metropol, only maybe he's just going in that direction to pick up his car, gets picked up, and the next thing we know about him is that he's a few of miles out of town, not toward Balfour, but on the other side, on the Castlegar road, getting killed. Only he's not walking *to*

Castlegar; according to where we found him, he's walking *back* to Nelson. Why? And as Eeyore asked, wherefore?"

"Where we've lost him and the mystery ride-giver is somewhere between Castlegar and Nelson. Is he so drunk he staggers out of the Legion, begins walking, he thinks, toward the ferry, where he'll either pick up his car, or even imagines he's going to walk all the way home? He realizes whoever is giving him the ride is going the wrong way, asks to be returned, the driver says no, so Gaskell asks to be let out. Now he has seventeen miles to walk in the snow. Conditions would have killed him if the mystery hit-and-run driver hadn't. And why does he take a ride with someone going the wrong way in the first place? Is he too drunk to know what he's about?"

Darling adjusted his feet on the grate and sipped his whisky. "We've got nothing but whys on this case. Gilly did say he had a lot of alcohol in his system, so he could definitely have been in a muddle. Let's move to the safer ground of you frightening the children to death with Dickens."

Lane told him of their delightful essays. "They really are full of wisdom. I suppose I'm in danger of idealizing children, but what I see is that they are honest and say things the way they see them. They are untrammelled by complicated expectations about how they ought to think."

Smiling, Darling said, "Maybe we should get a couple of them on the job of solving this. No one has taught them how they ought to see things, so they might see them more clearly, is that your thinking?"

"To be honest," Lane said, "I'm thinking about whether I should go on with the story. The Ghost of Christmas Yet to Come is extremely unpleasant. Sure to give nightmares with that hooded black cassock and bony pointing finger and reminders that we're all going to die."

"Yes. I see your point. But think of the Greeks. Catharsis. You frighten people and afterward they feel better."

"Better than what? Than before you ever frightened them at all? No. The Greeks are no help here, I'm afraid. Perhaps a good night's sleep will show me the way."

"Stopping only to consider a child of our own, since you seem so keen on them?" Darling asked.

DARLING HAD JUST settled down at his desk when his phone rang. "Darling."

It was O'Brien. "Sir. We have a call from up the lake, three miles this side of Balfour. Car tipped off the road into the top of his field. Wouldn't have seen it, but he went up to check on his younger apple trees to make sure they'd survived the snow. Looks like the driver cracked it up and left it. Gave me the plate number. British Columbia two—"

"Yes, thank you, O'Brien. I'll leave you to track down the plate. Did he say how it was cracked up?"

"Grill completely smashed, hood damaged. He said it looks as though it ran into a tree. He was concerned it might have been one of his trees, but they seem all right."

CHAPTER TWENTY-TWO

"GILLY. I HAVE AN INTERESTING proposition for you. Do you think that you could identify whether a specific car had hit Mr. Gaskell if I offered you one to inspect?" Darling asked. He'd asked Ashford Gillingham to stop by his office. He had also dispatched Terrell to see if he could find out where Gaskell had abandoned his car. It might even be Gaskell's car he was proposing to show the medical examiner.

Gilly made a considering "hmm" sound and then said, "Absolutely not my field of expertise. But I'm happy to go along for the ride. I don't have to be at the hospital till this afternoon."

"Come along, then, if you have the time. It's out near Balfour." Darling took his hat off the hat stand and pulled his overcoat on.

"I'm better with bodies, you know," Gilly said while they waited for the ferry. "How did you find this car, anyway?"

"Called in by a concerned citizen. He was worried that

the car had crashed into one of his trees and had been left to clutter up his upper field."

"Ah. I'm surprised you're not telling me the perspicacious Miss Winslow found it. Good to hear you are having success in keeping your married life separate from your work life. Whose car is it, anyway?"

Darling primly ignored the remark about Lane. "No idea. O'Brien is going to track down the plate number. The car looks like it's been there for days. He said he hadn't noticed it because it was buried in snow. I'm missing two cars: Gaskell's, our corpse, and Miss Scott's."

"Isn't Miss Scott the woman who got clonked on the head and is in the hospital even now?"

"Yes. The whole thing is very unlikely. He was killed on Friday night under circumstances we can't quite understand, and she was hit over the head and left for dead, also on Friday night. It's the only car we have in hand, and it has the sort of damage we're looking for. And, it turns out, he was sending one of the teachers some very nasty notes. Poison-pen sort of things. We're not sure who they were aimed at, but it could easily have been Miss Scott, the teacher who was supposed to be leaving. Or there's a chance they could be directed at the new teacher, Miss Keeling. He was generally known to be an unsavoury character, and Miss Keeling has disappeared, and we suspect she was afraid of someone. It could have been him, or it could have been someone from her life before she got here."

Gilly settled in comfortably as the car pulled onto the ferry. "Ah. So now you have a connection between the dead man and the teachers. That is interesting, to be sure."

"Several connections. He's the unpleasant father of one of the students about whom they, no doubt, worried. And now we know him to be the sender of the poison-pen notes."

"I can certainly see the teacher wanting him out of her hair, but would a teacher go so far as to run a man down? It seems a bit extreme for someone entrusted with the education of our young," mused Gilly.

THE CAR, WHICH proved to be a ten-or-so-year-old Ford, had slid, or had been driven, off the shoulder of the road and down an embankment into packed snow and a small stand of apple trees. It was clear why it had remained hidden, as it was piled high with snow, except where the man who'd called the station had brushed off the licence plate. Gilly and Darling swept more snow off the hood to reveal the full extent of the dent, and then Gilly squatted down to take a closer look at the grill. It was completely smashed in on the passenger side. He was about to stand up, when he looked at the bumper.

"Grill's a mess, but they're just decorative, really. However, bumper's off its moorings as well. See here? It's pushed down a bit." He stood up and reached into his pocket and removed a small cloth retractable measuring tape in a leather case. First he measured the space between where the bumper ought to be and where it was hanging, and then stood and measured the dimensions of the dent as well as he could.

"I always carry it with me," Gilly said at Darling's inquiring look. Gilly walked around to the back of the car. "Well, you're the professional in this sort of thing, so

I'll be interested to learn what you have to say. I will say this much. I wouldn't have said it necessarily hit a tree." Gilly stood back and put his hands into his pockets.

Darling wouldn't have said he was an expert either, though he certainly knew it was his job to speculate. Big city police departments had forensic people who probably did nothing but this sort of investigation. He hoped very much that whenever there was someone held responsible and there was a trial, the evidence to convict would not hang on the condition of this car.

"No," agreed Darling. "On the other hand, no chains, and these aren't snow tires. It could have skidded, I suppose. I think the bumper would have a dent in it as well if it had banged into a tree, but it looks more like it's been knocked loose. Nor would I say something like a deer did that. They are much heavier and can be counted on to make quite a mess if they flip up onto the car and would likely have left traces of blood. It would be very handy to find coat threads on the grill. I'm sure Sherlock would. I'm going to say it is very possible this car would sustain damage like this if it hit a man of Gaskell's size. Now, that's not forensic proof, merely probability. The bumper is right here, at shin height. That's what causes this flipping onto the hood movement. And with the grill stove in like that I'd be very surprised if it didn't damage something inside the engine—radiator, fan belt, that sort of thing."

Gilly pulled a pipe and some tobacco out of his pocket and occupied himself filling, tamping, and lighting it while Darling walked around the car. It was tipped in a way that made this awkward. When he was next to Gilly, who was now pulling happily on his pipe, filling the air with the fragrance of good tobacco, Gilly said, "So, your conclusion?"

Darling chewed his lower lip and looked back along the road. No snow tires was possibly important. "Gaskell was hit more than twenty-five miles from here on the other side of town by a car that possibly didn't have snow tires. If the engine was damaged, it still might limp along this far. Van Eyck's garage is near here. I'll get him to tow it there. He can assess the damage for us." He smiled and rubbed his hands. "And then I'll get Ames to run out and deal with it. That'll fix him!"

"SO," SAID DARLING on the way back. "Whoever drove that car could have hit and killed Gaskell. If it proves to be Miss Scott's car, and I say that only because hers is one of two cars we have missing—it could be someone else's entirely—there is at least some shred of a motive. It does not explain how she herself came to be attacked on the same night. Unless Miss Keeling did both. Or Gaskell attacked Miss Scott and Keeling avenged her."

"Is she that sort of person, do you think?"

Darling explained the circumstances of the disappearance of Miss Keeling and the counter-circumstances of her apparently being extremely well liked by all who knew her, and therefore the least likely to be running people over and hitting them on the head. He added the fact that she had fled a posting on Vancouver Island for fear of being found by someone she didn't wish to see. "Anyway, that theory is weak. If she'd seen Miss Scott attacked, she would not have left her all weekend in a freezing house. She'd have got her to the hospital. Unless she thought Miss Scott was dead, and she rushed off in a rage to get him. Or, I did wonder if she did go after him that night, and Miss Scott was attacked in a simple burglary attempt."

"You've got all those nice young policemen and your clever wife, and you can't seem to get on top of this one." Gilly beamed amiably. "You can drop me off at the hospital."

Darling pulled into the parking area at the hospital and stopped the car. Had he better come in and see if he could question Miss Scott? She didn't know him and might not respond well to yet another person interrogating her in her shaky condition. Too bad, he decided crossly.

"I'll come in too. I might as well see if I can get anything out of Miss Scott."

Once inside, Gilly bade him luck and disappeared into the basement. Darling turned to the receptionist, showed her his card, and asked on which floor he would find Miss Scott.

"My goodness, she is popular with you fellows. She's on the third floor in the special care area. I doubt Dr. Edison will let you talk to her, but knock yourself out."

He arrived on the third floor and was directed to the nursing sister's station. He leaned over the counter and was about to ask to speak to Dr. Edison, when a tall woman swept out of one of the patient rooms and said, "Are you from the police? You've come very quickly! Thank you."

ANGELA CRUNCHED THROUGH the morning snowfall to the post office and was gratified to see quite a gathering outside the door, as if the brilliant sunny morning, so near Christmas, had inspired a desire to hobnob with neighbours. Sunny as it was, it was cold, and everyone was bundled up in an assortment of wool and heavy canvas jackets and swaddled in scarves and wool hats. Their breath came in wisps of cloud. She could see what had occasioned the crowd; Kenny had just arrived from his trip down to the lake to meet the steamer for the mailbag, and everyone was obliged to either go home or wait till it was sorted.

"Morning, Angela!" said Kenny, pulling the mailbag off the back of his truck.

"Good morning, Kenny. You're like Santa himself with that bag. Can I help?"

"No need. I'll get this in, and her majesty will get it sorted in no time. It feels like more than usual has been ordered from catalogues. Time of year!" Kenny strode to the cottage door and pulled it open. He was greeted by an explosion of dog, as Alexandra burst out of the house leaping and barking in excitement.

Smiling, Angela took her place among the gathered group. "Dogs always bark excitedly, as if they haven't seen you for a year," she remarked by way of greeting. She moved from one foot to the other, trying to stay warm.

"Yours certainly do, fifteen times a day," remarked Reginald Mather acidly.

Mabel and Gwen had both come down to join the throng and were standing close to the post office door. Gwen rolled her eyes at Reginald's predictability, and said to Angela, "We miss Lane since she's been off teaching at the school, though I must say, I admire her. I don't think I'd willingly submit myself to the tender mercies of children. They're positively barbarian!"

Angela shrugged agreeably. "My barbarians seem to like her. Philip said she's always interested in what they have to say."

"Sooner Lane than me!" Gwen said with a shudder.

"What's new up the road?" Mabel asked. "Have they finished the monstrosity yet? Summer visitors, indeed! They'll soon tire of being so far from the water and having to put up with Robin and his beastly tractor making a racket and belching smoke all over the place. Speaking of the devil," she added, as Robin and his tractor became audible at the top of the road.

"Actually," said Angela, suddenly thoughtful, "there's been no one there for a good week. I suppose they don't want to work in this weather, though now that you mention it, I could swear I heard a car going up that back road last night."

"Well, night is any time from four in the afternoon on these days. I thought I heard your bloody dogs at about one in the morning," Reginald said.

"Yes, you're right!" Angela said, with unfailing good nature. "It was the dogs that alerted me. Though, Reggie, they were in the house, so I'm not sure how you think you heard them. I woke up because the dogs were restless and that's when I heard the car. I'm fairly sure it was well after two, actually."

"Restless!" Reginald snorted. "Is that what you call it?"

"Now that's interesting," said Mabel. "I had a strange car drive up to the edge of our driveway yesterday, have a good look around, and then back out. Big black thing. Did you hear them leave again?"

"No. I don't think so. Mind you, if they left early in the morning, I wouldn't hear them. A steam shovel could be operating in the yard and I wouldn't hear a thing while I'm getting the children ready for school."

"Now why would someone be arriving at that time of night? If the construction has stopped, then nothing would be hooked up," Gwen said.

"Really, you lot are getting more and more like Miss Winslow, as she insists on calling herself against all human decency," said Reginald. "You'd all be better off minding your own business." He'd had to raise his voice to be heard above the tractor that had now arrived. "Turn that bloody thing off!"

Robin turned off the tractor and sat staring at the gathering with his eyebrows drawn together in a look of irritation. "What's going on?"

"Oh, nothing, Robin. We're just waiting for Eleanor to sort the mail. I think the steamer arrived a little late today," Angela said.

"Actually, Angela was just telling us that she heard someone heading up the back road toward the Anscomb house at two in the morning. Did you hear anyone drive into King's Cove?" Gwen asked.

Robin lived right at the turnoff, and if he was home, he was in a good position to see the traffic, rare as it was, turning up the road into the community. He had complained to Gladys over a cup of tea the week before about the steady stream of builders' vans and equipment trucks going past him and up to the house.

"I didn't, as it happens. Sleep of the dead." He turned to look at the post office door. "What's holding up the proceedings?"

Just at that moment Kenny came out with the dog and his wood basket. "All right, all done!" he said, and then he made his way to the woodshed around the side of the house.

Gwen and Mabel were first to the door and opened it just as Eleanor slid up the window with a friendly bang and gave them her toothy grin. "Something for you and Gladys. A big handful of Christmas cards. Some from the old country. It's wonderful you still have ties there!"

"Various sorts of cousins. Hardly know them at all anymore. I expect most of them are ninety if they're a day," said Mabel, taking the mail. "Have to keep up the whole charade of cards for form's sake, I suppose. Mummy likes it. You didn't hear. Angela said someone was driving up the back road at two in the morning." Mabel leaned forward as she said this, aware of the waiting group behind her.

"Goodness! I wonder what that means. Here you are, lovey. I know it's coals to Newcastle, but your mumsy did say she enjoyed my spiced biscuits." She handed Mabel a packet of cookies wrapped in greaseproof paper.

When it was Angela's turn to collect the mail for the Bertolli household, Eleanor handed over a larger bunch of cookies to accommodate the appetites of the three boys. "What do you make of it, then?" she asked.

"I'm not sure. I'm tempted to wander up there and have a look around, see if they have made any progress, though as I told the others, I don't think there's been anyone working there for at least a week. I don't know who would come there in the middle of the night last night. Still, if it's someone from Vancouver, it's a long way to drive, so they've arrived late and are sleeping over in an unfinished house. I wish Lane wasn't having to go into the school every day. She'd come along with me."

"Would you like me to send Kenny? He's as nosy as they come! You could pretend you were a delegation of locals coming to welcome them, and, if what you say is true, offer them a cup of coffee and a cooked breakfast," Eleanor suggested.

"No, that's all right. I walk the dogs near there anyway. But that's a brilliant idea. If there's anyone there, I can just welcome them to King's Cove and make sure they have everything they need!"

———

November 1947

SERENA DEVLIN PARKED her rented Chevrolet at the side of the road, though she doubted she'd be in the way if she parked it right in the middle of the road. It looked as if no one ever came along here. She threw her right arm over the seat and leaned so that she could look out the passenger window. The grassy track she was looking at extended into the woods. Clearly a vehicle had been driven on it, so perhaps she could risk it. She put the car in gear and turned onto the track and drove forward slowly.

She was rewarded after about two hundred yards by the appearance of a cottage, remarkably, she thought, painted a bright sky blue. An old battered DeSoto was parked at an angle in front of the cottage. Serena pulled up next to it and got out, surveying the yard. On the near side of the cottage, a small vegetable garden that had been outlined with what looked like discarded railway ties had brown and dying remains of runner beans on pole teepees and a few small, worm-eaten cabbages. Otherwise the surrounding forest and bush seemed to have been allowed to encroach.

As she approached the stairs, she saw the curtain move, and when she reached the third of four steps, the door was opened. The woman from the fishing lodge with the striking blue eyes stood before her, one hand on her hip, the other holding the door, as if uncertain whether to shut it or to open it wider. She was dressed in a faded plaid shirt and blue jeans. Her dark hair was pinned back on both sides, more a testament to convenience than fashion. Serena was surprised that close up, in spite of her weathered face, she looked younger than she'd imagined.

"Mrs. Devlin. I'm very surprised to see you here."

"You remember me," Serena said. "Can I come in?"

"Suit yourself." The woman held the door wider.

The door led directly into a little sitting room with an iron stove as its centrepiece. A neat pile of wood was in a box beside it, and a fading hand-braided rag rug in blues and greens occupied the space in front of the stove. A collapsing easy chair with a side table held a half-empty cup of coffee and two books turned over. Against a small window, a tiny kitchen table with one wooden chair suggested the woman's dining facilities.

Serena stood uncertainly for a moment and the woman

pulled the wooden chair forward. "Please, sit down," she said, seating herself on the arm of the easy chair.

As Serena turned to sit, she saw that the whole back wall, between the window and the door, was fitted with a bookshelf that was crammed with books.

"Thank you. I've come to ask how you know my husband. Your name is Denise Irving, is it not?" Serena asked. "I asked at the lodge."

The woman nodded and crossed her arms, then she made as if to get up. "May I get you something?"

"No, thank you." Serena sat with her hands folded on her lap, her legs crossed, causing her emerald-green skirt to fall gracefully. She had not removed her calfskin driving gloves. She waited, but Denise Irving did not speak. Instead she sighed, looked out the window, and then down at her hands.

"I saw the way you and he talked on the boat. I could see that you knew each other, and I just wonder how, you see."

"You didn't ask him?" Denise asked.

"I didn't. I knew he would lie to me. I suspect you are more likely to tell me the truth," Serena said this in a matter-of-fact way. She lifted her chin slightly as she spoke, in a kind of unconscious defiance.

"I read in the papers about your marriage some years ago. How I know him is immaterial in every way to you. I knew him twenty-four years ago. I had not seen him since '23. I imagine he was as taken aback as I was." Denise tilted her head slightly, as if trying to understand why this young, beautiful, and smartly dressed woman had made the trek out into the middle of nowhere.

"Were you lovers?"

Denise looked at her. She was certain that Serena must already know they had been. "Yes. He was young; I was married. It didn't work out. I don't understand why you've come to rake up such ancient history. Is it because he's running for office? Because if so, he must have had scores of lovers since me. You will exhaust yourself trying to track them all down. Let me reassure you now, I pose no danger whatsoever to you, or him, or his political aspirations, though I see he's running as a Tory. He must not expect my vote."

"There was a child." The bluntness of this declaration, the sudden chill with which it was delivered, caused Denise to stand abruptly and walk toward the window.

"I'm right, aren't I?" Serena insisted. "It turns out they are quite gossipy at the lodge."

"Again, I have to ask why it matters," Denise said, turning back toward her guest.

"Don't misunderstand me. I don't care about your sordid history or grubby affair, or your brat, but my husband cannot have in his background a child born out of wedlock. It would ruin him. I need to know that whoever that child is, he or she is not going to spring out of the weeds at the least opportune time."

Denise shook her head, her forehead contracted. Her voice caught, and she quickly controlled it. "You amaze me. Let me put your mind at rest. I have no idea where the child is, or indeed who she is anymore. I am certain she does not know the identity of her real father. My husband tossed me out, and I felt it better to leave her with him, since I was broke and had no place to live. In a weak moment I called her school a year later, just to get some news of her, and they told me he'd taken her to live with an uncle, his religious maniac of a brother. No doubt she was married at fourteen and is tethered to some ghastly farm and five children by now."

CHAPTER TWENTY-THREE

DARLING SAT BESIDE MISS SCOTT'S bed, waiting. When he'd first been shown in, Miss Scott had looked up eagerly. Dr. Edison had said, rather loudly, he thought, that here was Inspector Darling from the police. But moments later the patient had sunk into this state of lethargy. Miss Scott was looking down at the pale green coverlet and folding and unfolding it between her fingers.

"Miss Scott?" he said.

She shook her head. It was hard to tell if it was to clear her thoughts, or an expression of some decision not to talk after all.

"You asked for someone from the police to come and talk to you. How can I help?"

"Where is the other one?" she said, finally, her voice weak.

"The other which?"

"The dark one. I like him. He's kind." She finally looked at him but only sidelong, and only for a moment.

"Constable Terrell. Would you feel more comfortable

speaking with him?" Darling's heart sank. Miss Scott had so far shown a very uneven ability to remember things, and he was afraid he would lose whatever advantage he had if he did not find out quickly what had prompted her to ask to speak to the police.

"I can probably get him here in fifteen minutes. Would that be soon enough? I know you seemed very anxious to talk to someone right away." He was aching to ask her about where her car was, but he was afraid she might shut down.

Miss Scott lifted her hand, either acquiescing or dismissing him, Darling could not tell which, and closed her eyes. Quelling a muttered "Blast!" he went back out to the nurse's desk.

"Could I use your telephone?"

"Yes, of course. This one here will reach the exchange and you can call outside the hospital."

Tapping his fingers on the desk impatiently as his call was put through to the station, Darling looked toward the room where Miss Scott lay, burdened, he hoped, with something that might be of use in solving the question of who hit her. Finally, O'Brien came on.

"Nelson Police Station."

"Put that paper down and get Terrell on the line, and quickly."

"Certainly, sir. I mean, I would, but he's gone next door to the café to get a sandwich to bring back to his desk," O'Brien said. Darling closed his eyes and shook his head. If O'Brien had seen this show of impatience, he would have responded by becoming more stolidly and reproachfully respectful. "Then kindly go and get him. Tell him he is to drop everything and come to the hospital to speak to Miss Scott instanter. He can eat sandwiches on his own time."

"Yes, sir. Of course, sir. But the phones—"

"O'Brien." There was enough warning sounded in this one word.

"Righty-ho, I'm on my way."

When Darling returned to Miss Scott's room, she appeared to have drifted off to sleep. Wishing he had a newspaper, he settled down to keep watch over her until Terrell showed up. Looking impatiently at his watch, he calculated the time it would take for O'Brien to get on his coat, stagger into the street to the café, and converse with Terrell. Possibly the sandwich was just on the point of being prepared and needed only wrapping. They would wait. He shook his head to shake himself away from this pointless impatience and turned instead to the matter of the hit and run.

The discovery of the car opened up possibilities. Would the owner prove to be the driver? What, he wondered, was this powerful impetus to see justice done in cases like this? After all, it was likely an accident, and doubtless the person who did it must suffer at the thought that he had hit someone on the road. Knowing that would not bring Mr. Gaskell back. He batted away the suddenly intrusive thought that the world wouldn't want him back in any case, with his mistreatment of his child and his poisonous notes, and who knows in what other ways he had been a repellent presence among those who knew him.

Darling shifted in the chair and sat back, crossing his legs. But order and justice were the point. Yes, it might have been an accident, but it was against the law not to stop and render assistance. This alone made the effort of finding the culprit of value. Doubtless he, or she, would get a negligible sentence, but it would send a message: There is order in society. There is right and there is wrong. But what if in the whirling snow conditions the driver had not even been aware that he had hit a person? What if he thought he had hit an animal? He himself had hit a coyote one summer when it had bolted out from under a bush right into his car. He hadn't stopped because he had been responding to a frantic call from a woman who had found her husband dead.

He had just concluded again that Gaskell's death might remain unsolved, and that the major focus should be on solving the assault on Miss Scott, when he heard Dr. Edison's voice in the hall outside.

"Constable Terrell, good afternoon. Your boss is in there waiting."

Darling went out to join them. He would have to bring Terrell up to date. "Constable. Thank you for making good time. Sorry about your sandwich. There will be others. In the meantime, you seem to have sprinkled fairy dust in Miss Scott's eyes. She won't talk to me. Only wants you. According to Dr. Edison here, she was urgently asking to speak to the police. I'm assuming that it's because she remembered something, so if you could step along smartly and find out what it is, I'll give you a lift back and we can get on with getting this sorted before Christmas. Oh, and see if you can get her to tell you where her car is."

Terrell, who had removed his hat and was holding it in

both his hands, nodded and turned to go in to see Miss Scott. Darling and Dr. Edison watched him and then she said, "He's a very nice young man. Where did you find him?"

"Yes, I suppose he is. We had a vacancy and he applied. Came highly recommended by his department in Nova Scotia. Good war record."

"I wonder if he ever feels a bit like a fish out of water here," she said. She smiled. "I know I do at times. It was all very well in the army. People soon stopped thinking of me as a woman, and I became someone who patched people up, and directed others to patch people up. In a small town like this I am certainly an oddity. But at least when I get out of my lab coat I look like any other woman. His colour makes him a beacon wherever he goes."

Darling nodded toward the door of the hospital room. Miss Scott was talking earnestly to Terrell, who was leaning in to listen and nodding encouragingly. "So, apparently, does his charm," he said.

Dr. Edison smiled. "True," she said.

"HE WASN'T THAT scary," Rafe said, as Lane closed the book on Dickens's Christmas ghosts.

"That's interesting, Rafe. Why is that, do you think?"

Rafe looked up for a moment to think about this. Lane could see Gabriella's hand waving at the back.

"Because, it's what you said. Scrooge didn't really go anywhere, and he woke up in his bed, safe and sound."

"Good point. What about you, Gabriella? What do you think?"

"I think he was kind of scary, but what made it not seem

scary after all is that he woke up and it was Christmas Day, and he was happy. He gave money to the poor people and gave away a big turkey to Tiny Tim and then went to his nephew for a nice party, and so he forgot about being afraid."

"It sounds like what you are saying is that when something bad has happened, having good things happen afterward can help you maybe feel a little better?"

Gabriella glanced at Samuel, who had his arm stretched out across his desk and was resting his head on it. "Yes. I think that's true."

Lane looked around at the children. "What does everyone else think about this?" The children nodded solemnly.

Samuel had sat up, and now put his hand up. "Yes, Samuel. What do you think?" Lane could feel herself almost holding her breath. She had not expected him to want to speak.

"I think the ghosts are something inside you."

"That is a very important observation, Samuel. Do you think that makes them more, or less, scary?"

"I think it makes a person sad." She thought he had finished, but in a moment he continued. "But this story makes them sort of come out of you."

When Lane had set them to writing a paragraph to express all of their ideas about the story, she sat at the desk quite filled with wonder. Here was the Greek concept of catharsis right from the mouth of a child. But Samuel's words also reminded her that sorrow and grieving were processes that had to be endured, and even though he was in a safe and loving family, he would still need to go through them. Was it different for children? Perhaps they adapted more quickly than adults, responded more quickly to love and warmth and food. She earnestly hoped it were so.

At noon, all the children were outside, but again Samuel stayed back. Lane, with her coat and boots on, knelt beside his desk. "You don't want to go outside?"

Samuel shook his head. "Where is the other lady, Miss Keeling? She was nice."

Of course! The children had been told nothing, really, about the disappearance of their new teacher. "She's had to go off . . . to see someone." Lane desperately hoped this evasion was true.

"She came to my house that day, before my father didn't come back."

A snowball struck very near the window. Lane winced. Well, too bad. If someone broke a window they'd have to live with the cold as a consequence. "Did she?"

"She was mad. She said he was neg . . . neg . . . I can't remember the word."

"Neglecting?"

"Yes. She said I didn't have enough food and she said she thought he had hit me. They had a big fight."

"Oh, dear. That must have been hard for you to listen to."

Samuel nodded. "He pushed her and said he'd hit her if she didn't go, and then she said she would make sure he didn't hurt me anymore."

ANGELA DROPPED THE post on the dining room table and hesitated over taking off her jacket and settling down to read the mail. A light snowfall was beginning again, and as late as it was getting in the afternoon, her curiosity about the people at the Anscomb house won over her desire to hang Christmas cards. Going to the kitchen door, she called the dogs and slipped back into the boots she had parked on the porch.

The dogs gathered around her wagging their tails and Lassie offered a bark of encouragement as they waited to see where they were bound. She set off toward the barn and then onto the path that issued onto the road about three hundred yards farther up the path. She could see, in spite of the snow that fell in the night, that a vehicle had been along the road. They must be there still. She wondered if she should have brought along some of the ginger snaps she'd made the day before as a welcome present, and then worried that showing up with two rambunctious collies in tow might not be the most advantageous way to greet a newcomer. But, in for a penny.

She strode purposefully up the hill, the dogs running in and out of the bush along the side of the road. She saw the car even before she heard it and just had time to throw herself onto the snow-covered bushes on the side of the road to avoid being hit. Her heart beating frantically, she swore and sat up in time to see the tail end of a large, black, late-model car barrelling down the road at full speed. Her next thought was for the dogs, but they both were running down the middle of the road, barking at the disappearing car.

She struggled up, brushing snow off her trousers and aware of a sharp pain in her hip. She must have landed straight on a large rock, she thought angrily, and gingerly felt for any other pain.

"Who the hell was that?" she said out loud to the dogs, who had given up any thought of pursuit and were now watching their mistress, tails wagging expectantly. Was it the car Mabel had seen?

"Yes, you're a bloody big help!" she said to the dogs. She thought about going home and putting on a pot of coffee, but instead determinedly continued her walk to the house.

Standing before it, Angela was taken aback by how much still had to be done. There were clearly plans for a new wider porch, but the old one had been wrecked and only the skeletal supports for the new one were in evidence. Larger windows were stacked against the house, but no move had been made to replace the ones that were there. She looked down the hill at what the new windows would show and saw that the view would simply be what it already was: a view down the road, a curtain of evergreens, and only the tops of the mountains on the other side of the obscured lake. No water view at all. Angela climbed the stairs and rapped on the door, but already knew that no one was there. There was an eerie stillness to the place that, in spite of the smell of the new wood studs and gathered building materials, almost intensified that sense of abandonment and desolation the house had always had. The person in that car must have spent a cold night, unless whoever it was slept in the car just to get a nap in before taking off again in the morning, she thought.

She put her hands up to the windows and looked inside. The rudiments of furniture occupied the centre of an otherwise empty space: a small hearth rug and an old wingback chair near what was evidently to be a huge stone fireplace, the stones piled on the floor waiting to be put in place. She went around the back of the house to look into the kitchen window to see if there were any interesting new appliances. People with the kind of money to practically rebuild a house would want only the latest gadgets, but aside from the new linoleum and the electric stove that she and Lane had seen before, nothing had yet been touched in the kitchen besides the removal of the old stove.

She turned and looked around the back of the house. Who would want this sad place? she thought. She supposed someone from the city could imagine a picturesque cabin for summer retreats and had bought it sight unseen. Had the new owner come to check on the work and decided it wasn't worth going on? Someone with a lot of money would want a lake view, surely? The dogs were once again sniffing around the coal chute. No doubt some animal had got in and died ages ago. The doors sat at an angle against the house and opened upward. Looking around nervously, Angela considered pulling up one of the doors just to see what the dogs were making such a fuss about. She knew what she would see. An angled chute into the basement where no doubt some coal had been delivered. Or a dead muskrat. Gingerly she lifted one of the doors and peered into the darkness. The dogs moved forward, sniffing eagerly.

"Hello?" She knew it was ridiculous. There would be no one there. And indeed, there was only silence. Very slowly she became aware of a peculiar smell. The cold had prevented her from sensing it right away. What was it? The strong smell of coal was overlaid with a slight smell of stale food and a scent she could only liken to a train-station toilet.

Obviously, the workmen had left food behind to go stale in the basement along with all the other general mess. She shuddered. She wished now she'd made a note of the name of the construction company on the van. She must remember never to call them for anything. She left the door open and turned to go. The dogs had now bolted off into the trees behind the property. "Come on, you two. Let's go home." That's when she saw what she'd missed. Underneath all the disturbance of the snow around the coal chute caused by herself and the dogs, she saw a pale red streak right along the inside edge of the chute. She lifted the other door this time and saw a clear stain of what most certainly looked like blood on the edge of the frame. The imagined muskrat, hurt and trying to escape? One of the workmen? She nervously went toward where the dogs had disappeared behind the woodshed.

A bank of cloud had moved over the already pale winter sun, emphasizing the unutterable dreariness of the whole place. She turned her mind back to the comforts of a pot of coffee in her snug house and the pile of Christmas cards awaiting her.

CHAPTER TWENTY-FOUR

"**I'M NOT SURE ABOUT THE** man, you see. I can't seem to see it."

Terrell nodded. "Not sure you remember the man? Is that what you wanted to tell us?"

"Yes, that's why, you see. I'm not sure anymore about a man." Miss Scott had her hand on Terrell's coat sleeve. She tilted her head and gave a slight smile.

For his part, Terrell was trying gamely to understand. Miss Scott had felt strongly enough about a change in what she remembered to call the police back, but that change was in itself completely confusing.

"Are you saying that you can't remember the man, or you can't remember a man at all?" It could not be possible that there was no man, otherwise how had the house been torn apart? "Do you mean it was a woman?" This would bring them right back to Miss Keeling.

"No, no, no! She wasn't there! I was surprised, you see. That's what I wanted to tell you. I felt so unwell!"

"Miss Keeling was not there?"

Miss Scott became more agitated. "No! I said so. Everything gone. Suitcase, everything. After she promised me! She promised so I could go. It meant I would have to stay, and I couldn't, I just couldn't. I had to get away. Do you see?"

"You were upset because she was gone. You had been out somewhere, and you came back and she was gone, is that right?"

Miss Scott's eyes filled with tears and she nodded.

"Did she leave you a note or anything to explain where she was going?"

"No! Nothing! I looked everywhere. There was nothing!"

Something stirred at the back of Terrell's mind. He wanted to capture it, to clarify it, but it eluded him.

"So, then, you didn't find a note. Do you remember what happened next? You looked everywhere for a note, and then, did someone come to the door?"

He was not prepared for the terror that appeared suddenly in her eyes. "No. No, he couldn't. Not after that, he couldn't." Miss Scott sat up, looking wildly around the room, and then began to rock and cry. "Wendy went to see him. I should have said something. I should have. Now look what happened!" Her sobbing became uncontrollable.

"I think that's all for tonight, Constable. She is very agitated. We'll take over from here. She'll need a draught to calm down and be able to sleep." Dr. Edison was by his side now, showing him the door. "Sister, if you could come in here, please," she called out to the desk in the hall.

Terrell stood in the hall with Darling, watching the

calm but hurried efforts to bring Miss Scott down from her distress.

Darling put on his hat and turned to the door. "And that's that. Hope you got something."

"I got something, sir, but I'm damned if I know what. Nothing about the car though. And I wanted to ask her if she'd received poison-pen notes. She went to pieces before I had a chance to ask either thing. It's becoming an annoying habit. And she kept saying it was all her fault, that she should have said something, that Miss Keeling had gone to see him. Perhaps she meant that she should have warned Miss Keeling not to go see him because he would get so furious about having anyone say anything to him about Samuel."

"Perhaps, indeed." This was interesting. Very interesting. Darling had his hat off already as he pushed open the door of the police station. "Ames here?" he asked O'Brien.

O'Brien gestured at the upper floor with his chin, and then said, "You've had a call, sir, from your lady wife. You're to call back right away. Good to see she's keeping you busy, sir."

Darling looked at his watch. It was barely after three thirty. She must have rushed home from school. He picked up the phone and had a call placed to King's Cove, tapping his fingers on his desk while he waited. It was picked up instantly.

"KC 431. Lane Winslow speaking."

"Darling?"

"Oh, thank you for being so quick. Listen, Samuel told me today that Miss Keeling had visited his father at their house. 'The day before my father left,' he said. That would have made it the Thursday. They had a whopping row." Lane gave him as word perfect a narration as she could remember.

"He said exactly that? She would make sure he didn't hurt him anymore?"

"Yes. But, I don't know. Could a woman like that have taken it to those extremes?"

"I'm afraid you'd be surprised by who is perfectly capable of taking things to those extremes." When he'd hung up, Darling sat for a couple of seconds and then bounded out of his chair and made for Ames's office.

"Miss Keeling went to Gaskell's house the day before he died and threatened him. This matches what garbled information we got from Miss Scott today. We've got to find her. This opens the possibility that she is very much in the picture. Gilly and I have just had a look at an abandoned car a few miles out of Balfour. Call Van Eyck and get them to tow it to the garage and assess the damage to the car. Then run out and have a look at the thing yourself. Report back. It seems to me to be possible it's the car that could have been involved, and that Miss Keeling could have been driving it."

"Sir?" Ames said, trying to still a slight alarm that turning up at the garage would surely look as though he'd asked for the assignment and was using it as a flimsy excuse to see Miss Van Eyck.

"No quibbling. Run along. I'll get Terrell to get back onto the RCMP to redouble their efforts."

Having delivered this instruction to Terrell, Darling sat at his desk, and then swung his chair around to look at the snow-covered street outside his window with his hands behind his head to think about how Miss Keeling could have abandoned the car in an orchard and then disappeared. And whose car was it? In some scenarios either car would work. Here was certainly an even better motive than her upset about the notes aimed at Miss Scott: her anger about Samuel's condition and his abusive treatment of her. If she had the nerve to confront him in his own house, she could have pursued him into town, found him drunk, and run him down with his own car, or she could have used Miss Scott's car. It would need a lot of teasing out.

———

July 1947

THE LONG PORCH at the community hall in Balfour was strung with lights, and the warm evening had driven dancers outside to cool off and smoke. The band members were taking a break and drinking beer at their seats onstage. Lively business was being conducted at the bar and cakes and sandwiches that had weathered the afternoon Dominion Day picnic on the grounds were on offer.

Rose Scott was propped on the railing leaning against a pillar, looking out into the moonlit semi-darkness of the night, past the reach of the building lights toward the lake. A light winked on and off somewhere on the water. Someone who had spent Dominion Day fishing, no doubt, on the way home. She was feeling a kind of relief at the end of the school year. It was her fourth at the Balfour school and she was looking forward to going home, in spite of her mother's constant pressure on her to get married and settle down. She was longing for a cigarette, but that was firmly in the category of things teachers did in private. The moon would be full in the next couple of days. She remembered reading somewhere that some people got a bit crazy as the full moon approached, even more than on the full moon itself. She looked out at the velvet darkness and longed again for a cigarette. The full moon was certainly a reason some of her teacher colleagues used to give for the kids being a little more rambunctious.

Mrs. Bertolli waved at her and pushed her way through the crowd on the porch. "Miss Scott, how lovely! You must be absolutely exhausted after another year with the boys. I can't thank you enough. They seem to really enjoy the lessons."

Miss Scott pulled herself off the railing and smiled. "They're lovely boys, Mrs. Bertolli. I think Philip has the makings of a scientist."

"Well, I'm glad he has the makings of something. They're growing up like wild animals. They'll spend the whole summer up trees and crashing around in the bush. I'm afraid all your hard-won gains will have evaporated by the end of the summer and you'll have to start all over again."

"It's the best way to grow up, surely? And I didn't find that to be true this last year. You are one of the families that supplies the children with books, and they seem to read them, so there's nothing you need to worry about."

"What will you do this summer?" Angela asked.

"I'll go home to Winnipeg, I expect. My mother has a good deal of work on the farm, and I'll help her."

"Well, you see you come back. Here's a little something to thank you." Angela opened her handbag and pulled out a package with green ribbon on it.

"Oh, you shouldn't have." It proved to be a bottle of violet eau de cologne, the scent, Miss Scott thought rebelliously, of unmarried women everywhere. "It's lovely. Thank you."

"Oh, nonsense! Oops, there's David waving at me! I had him take the boys home after the picnic and he's come back for me. See you in September!" Angela waved cheerfully, her gloved hand suddenly animated in the glow thrown by the hanging lights.

The Bertolli family was the only one that gave her a little gift at the end of the year, though many of the children had made her cards, and families plied her with baked goods all year long. Holding the bottle of perfume cradled in her hands, she perched herself back up on the porch railing and prepared not to be approached again. Much to her dismay, this hope was dashed. She had no sooner settled down when a very drunk Mr. Gaskell approached her, cigarette hanging from his mouth.

"Not dancing then?" He leaned on the pillar so that his breath and cigarette smoke were wafting directly onto her face.

She shifted away. "No, Mr. Gaskell. Just looking for a moment's quiet." She was surprised by his approach. They had been at loggerheads about his son, Samuel, for most of the year. Gaskell had told her to mind her own business when she asked if Samuel had a warmer sweater. He had protested angrily that he didn't need charity when she gave the boy an apple at lunch or lent him a book. He pointedly returned the book and sent the boy to school with two apples, one to be paid in cancellation of the debt to the teacher. She wished with each of these interactions that his wife could be the one to come to the school, but she was fearful of suggesting it and creating tension between Gaskell and his wife. She quickly glanced past him. Where was his wife now?

"Mr. Gaskell's a bit formal. How about just Jim, eh? We know all about the army Jezebel, eh?" He pulled his cigarette out of his mouth with one hand and ran his other over her clasped hands, pressing down on them in a way that made her stomach lurch.

She stood up, feeling disgusted and horrified. "I'll say good night, Mr. Gaskell." Miss Scott wound through the crowd gathered on the porch, nodding and saying good night.

"You're not leaving yet?" said Mrs. Bales. She had no children at the school anymore, but she liked Miss Scott.

"I'm afraid I must," Miss Scott muttered.

"Playing hard to get like any army tart!" This outburst from Gaskell silenced the noisy, laughing throng. Miss Scott felt heat pour into her cheeks and she scrambled down the stairs and along the path to where the cars were parked on the baseball field, but instead of going to her car, she walked past the parking lot to the edge of the lake. The gentle ripple of the water curling onto the gravelly sand and the reflection of the moonlight on the dark water soothed her nerves. The noise of the party fell into the distant background and the enveloping silence of the summer night surrounded her. The "hoo" of a great horned owl sounded in the trees behind her, and then the rustle and flapping of wings as it took flight. She had loved it out here. She was sorry to be leaving for the summer because the summers were so lovely, but her mother did need her at the farm. She was even sorrier that her enjoyment of the Dominion Day dance had been ruined by that dreadful man. She sat on a log emitting a great sigh. What had he meant, calling her a Jezebel? Perhaps, like her father, he didn't approve of women in the army. She shook her head and lit up another cigarette, enjoying the blissful solitude, and only then wondered, with jarring disquiet, how he knew she'd even been in the army.

"The nerve of the man!" Angela Bertolli exclaimed to her husband, who'd had to come as far as the porch to collect his wife, as she seemed incapable of escaping all the other parents. "Poor Miss Scott. It's really too bad! I wonder if I should run down to her place and see that she's all right."

"I bet she can hold her own. She's been through the war after all." Back at the car, David rolled down the station wagon window to let in the warm night air.

"I hardly think you can call our children 'the war'!"

"I'm not so sure about that, but that's not what I mean. She was in the army corps, I think, and got quite close to the action. Was a clerk at bases behind enemy lines. She told me that once when I picked the boys up. We were talking about what it takes to be a teacher. She told me to keep mum, though. She didn't seem to want anyone to know."

"No wonder she's so good at controlling that mob of children! But that Gaskell is a horror. You know the boys were telling me the other day that he hits little Samuel. Judging by tonight's behaviour, he's a drunk as well. I hope she doesn't take it to heart. She's worth a thousand of him. It's a crying shame she had to leave the party."

ROSE SCOTT, FEELING more herself after a visit to the water, parked the car at the side of the house as usual. The cottage looked almost sinister, with its dark windows and its isolation. Her feeling of tranquility shaken by a sudden reluctance to leave the safety of her car, she turned her mind to Gaskell. He lived just west of her. Though his house was a quarter mile away, it suddenly felt too close.

Her heart was pounding. She wanted to cry with frustration at her encounter with him but was determined not to. She looked at the cabin, a line of cold light from the nearly full moon along the east part of the roof. When she had moved in, she had liked how the cabin was nestled in the trees, but now these same trees seemed to harbour all that was menacing. It was ridiculous. She was behaving like a child who imagined a bogeyman under the bed!

With resolve, she unlocked her car door, took up her handbag, and walked up the steps. She swallowed an anxious breath as she opened the unlocked door and went inside, wondering if the habit of never locking the cottage door was such a good idea.

The curtains were closed. It was the first thing she noticed, because the house was so dark inside. She anxiously reached for the light switch, but her hand was shaking a little and she had to reach farther than she thought, and she fumbled. She was sure she'd left the curtains open when she'd gone off to the Dominion Day celebrations just after one. She'd never have shut them. She managed the switch and light flooded the little room. Her heart pounding now, she stood by the open doorway and looked around the room. Nothing.

That bastard Gaskell, drunk and insinuating and then shouting obscenities for all to hear, had really frightened her. She closed the door and dropped the hooked latch, and then went to the sink for a glass of water. Her fear was slowly giving way to fury. How dare he? She pulled the kitchen curtain open a little to see the lake and the reflection of the nearly full moon across the water. It would calm her.

The noise came from behind her, right inside the house, and her heart froze. She wheeled around in time to see Gaskell coming out of her bedroom. Something between a gasp and a shriek escaped unbidden from her lips. A particular horror that he'd been in her bedroom swept through her. She saw now that he could have been in her house any number of times, going through her things, touching her clothes. She shuddered convulsively and edged toward the door, her mind already racing ahead to how she could undo the latch without turning her back to him. Faster than she could have imagined possible, he darted at the door and leaned heavily against it, facing her.

"Going somewhere?"

His breath reeked. How drunk was he? She had faced drunks before, in the army, but they had at least had the restraint of facing possible charges from senior officers. This time she felt the deep fear of facing a man absolutely on her own who was both inebriated and had nothing to stop his worst instincts. Hardly knowing how, she had the bread knife in her hand.

"Get out!" She didn't recognize her own voice. "I mean it. I'll use it!"

Gaskell put his hands up and smiled sloppily at her. "You don't mean that. An army whore like you. You've just been waiting for it." He let his arms drop and then reached for her wrist, his expression changing to a kind of leer.

With a cry she lashed at his hand with the knife. She could feel it connecting, sliding off his cuff onto his wrist, slicing into flesh. Gaskell recoiled with a shout of rage, clutching at his cut with his other hand. She could see the blood welling between his fingers.

"Get out! Get out! Get out!" She was screaming now, holding the knife with two hands at chest height.

He looked at his hand and reached for the latch with his left hand, flipping it up, and pulled the door open, still facing her. With a last imprecation that she could scarcely hear with the panicked buzzing in her own ears, he stumbled onto the small porch. She slammed the door and threw the knife on the floor and put the latch down. She found her keys where she'd put them and tried to fit the skeleton key into the lock. She could hear him stumbling down the stairs, swearing. Finally! The key slid in and she tried to calm the shaking of her hands enough to turn it, to hear the click as it took.

She stood for a moment, listening. Gaskell's obscenities were receding. With a sob she collapsed on the floor and leaned back against the door, shuddering and crying with rage.

Thursday, December 4

THE SITTING ROOM in the Shaughnessy house where the Devlins lived was warm from the fire. Light flickered along the walls and highlighted the thick green velvet drapes that kept out the wet December chill. Drinks had been brought and Serena sat with hers on the sofa, leafing through a magazine, while Harry stood looking into the fire, one hand resting on the mantel. Here at least he could forget the vastness of the house around them, full of empty rooms, childless and silent.

"I think it's time you told me what you've been up to, don't you?" Harry turned to Serena, who looked up at him, her expression unreadable.

"Do you? You've never cared before."

"I don't buy that balderdash that you've been to see your mother, something you usually avoid like the plague." He'd give her a chance, wait to see if she came through.

"Mother's not been well."

"I see." Devlin waited. "I had a man come by the office late last month. Scruffy fellow. Said you'd been to see him. Not your type at all, I should have thought." Devlin sat in the chair opposite her and crossed his legs, then he downed his drink and put the glass on the round occasional table with a thunk.

"So, I'm the one with something to hide? The trouble with you is that you're guileless. You go through the world like a puppy with your tongue hanging out, charmingly oblivious to what's good for you. You're an absolute child. I suppose that's what makes you so attractive to the voters. That scruffy man was the husband of the woman you took to bed when you were, what, in your early twenties?" Devlin sat staring at her. He was disoriented suddenly by the feeling that he was just now seeing her for the first time.

Serena gave a little chuckle. "Nothing to say? That's precisely why you need a keeper. Do you think you would have got this far without me? Oh, I see, you're wondering how I knew. It was that woman with the extraordinary eyes on the fishing boat. She must have been a doozy twenty-five years ago. Her workmates were happy to fill me in. After we left, she apparently said she 'knew' you all those years ago. It wasn't hard for them to guess how. They knew she'd left a bad marriage, and even knew she had a grown-up child somewhere that she never talks about. She actually told someone there that her husband was furious at the thought of bringing up someone else's child."

"That can't matter to you in the least, something I did in my youth. You're being ridiculous, and you can't be sure about the child," Devlin finally managed.

"It's the child, I'm concerned about. A love child suddenly springing out of the undergrowth demanding money, or worse, recognition, will be the death knell to your career and utter humiliation to me. I have relatives who specialize in this sort of research, and if I could find it all out in the blink of an eye, so could the opposition."

"That's rubbish." He found he didn't want to ask about her relatives. He thought instead about the girl. "She can't possibly know. Her father took her to live with relatives in some religious community. He told me that." Had Irving told her? Of course, he must have.

"So, you've been talking to someone as well about it. I'm delighted to learn you are smart enough to be concerned." She got up and put her glass down. "I'll have to go see about the cottage. The workmen are impossibly slow. They've gone off, claiming they have another more urgent project. Obviously, I will have to go supervise them in person. I'll leave first thing. With any luck, we'll get through this by-election before this comes out."

AFTER SHE LEFT, Devlin, alone in the sitting room with only the sound of the murmuring fire, turned his thoughts to the daughter. It surprised him that what was uppermost in his mind was that Serena was wrong. It was not the danger his daughter posed, but the thrill of knowing, acknowledging, there was a daughter at all. Denise had drifted out of his life, had never contacted him to tell him about the birth of the baby, and he had forgotten about her and moved on. Only, of course, he hadn't. In the years that followed until he married Serena, beautiful, well-heeled, twenty years his junior, he had never met a woman who affected him as Denise had. Even on the boat, she had refused to tell him anything except that her husband had dispensed with her at some point. It had shocked him that, even now, Denise had the power to unnerve him. He wondered now if this was what love felt like.

———

Friday, December 5

WENDY KEELING WALKED down the hill from the school knowing that she would have to leave here as well. Her heart ached. This was going to be her life. Always on the run.

She had tidied the classroom and put everything in place for whoever came to replace her. She thought about taking the revolver, but it suddenly felt like something too dangerous for her to have. Her rage at Gaskell had taught her that. It frightened her. Anyway, her father knew she was a teacher. He'd look for her at school, if he tracked down where she was. He'd done that last time, in Saanich. She stopped at the store to pick up some flour and milk. She and Rose could have a last weekend together, and she would ask Rose to drive her to the station. She felt a momentary pang for her colleague, who was meant to be leaving the next day. Wendy would go east. Northern Saskatchewan, Ontario. There must be somewhere he would not come for her. She swallowed another rush of anger. Gaskell, her father. Was she never to know any peace?

It was already dark, and the headlights of a single car driving north illuminated the snowy landscape of the road, while the rest of the world was encompassed in inky darkness. She waited until it had passed and then crossed the road and walked south toward the turnoff to the cottage. The dark bulk of a car was parked a hundred yards farther ahead on the side of the main road at the top of their neighbour's drive. There appeared to be no one in it. Perhaps the driver hadn't wanted to attempt the rough and slippery descent to the house. She felt a flash of worry

311

and hurried more quickly down their drive to the cottage, returning her thoughts to the business of packing, and how Rose would take the news of her leaving. Well, it couldn't be helped. They'd get someone in soon, and the two of them could get on with their lives, she with her fleeing, something that in this, her third time, she felt almost adept at, and Rose to her marriage.

It was the strangeness of finding the house empty that caused her first anxiety; where was Rose? The car was gone, the stove was unlit, and the silence inside the cottage almost reverberated. She put the groceries on the counter and felt the press of fear returning. Now the car parked up on the main road suddenly loomed large in her mind. Why would someone park there? Rose had told her that their neighbour on that side was an older couple who kept to themselves.

What if there had been someone in the car, watching her? Angry now that she'd left the gun, logic deserted her, and she ran to her room and pulled her suitcase out from under her bed and began yanking clothes off the hangers and out of the drawers. With shaking fingers, she started to try to press the latches on the suitcase and then she remembered her toiletries. She hurried into the bathroom and stopped, trying to get hold of herself. Clutching the sink with both hands, she looked at herself in the mirror. She was shaking and she leaned into the rim of the sink harder to still the trembling. Tears welled up. It was no good. She could bob her hair, change her name, find a calling that she loved, that made her independent and free from them, none of it made any difference. She was always evil, always the carrier of her mother's sin. They would always be looking for her.

She took up the hairbrush on the shelf beside the sink, and in the grip of an impotent rage struck the mirror so that it cracked through the middle. She could see her own face, reflected now in the jagged edges, distorted, angry, irreparably broken.

It was only when she'd pushed the last of her possessions into the suitcase and was thinking about calling a taxi to come from Nelson to get her that she heard the car coming slowly down the road. She saw the headlights sweep around, causing the surrounding trees and bush to appear for a brief moment and then disappear again into the darkness. The car came to rest facing the house, like some fire-breathing demon that would not leave without her.

——

Tuesday, December 16

LANE STOOD ON the steps of the school watching the Bertolli boys playing in the snow while they waited to be picked up. She was smiling, remembering her own palpable relief when lessons were over as a child, that burst of freedom to go and play. Even in the rarefied world of the tutors and governesses that had passed as schooling for her and her sister, the sense of freedom from grown-ups, at least until dinnertime, was wonderful.

Indeed, she was feeling a bit of relief and even triumph that she'd survived the last few days as a schoolteacher. Finally, she heard the car coming up the hill. "Okay, boys, you'd better brush yourselves off; your mum is here!" she called out.

The station wagon pulled up and instead of waiting, as she usually did, for the boys to pile in, Angela got out and waved her friend over. Lane came down the steps, wishing she'd put her jacket on if she was going to stand around talking in the snow and darkening afternoon.

Angela drew near and practically whispered, "There's something very strange going on up at that house! The dogs and I were nearly killed by that car! And I saw blood. I guess it was an animal looking to get into the coal chute, but it was creepy." She looked nervously toward where the boys, having completely ignored Lane's exhortation to brush off the snow and get ready to go home, were now darting in and out of the underbrush avoiding snowballs.

"Goodness. Slow down! You went up to the Anscomb house, and someone was up there? What car?"

"Yes, that's what I'm saying. I was halfway up the road and a car plowed down at speed. They didn't even see me. I had to jump into a snowbank."

"They?" asked Lane. "Did you see who was in the car?"

Angela shook her head ruefully. "I was too busy cracking my hip on a rock buried in the snow."

"What kind of car was it? Surely it was the builders?"

"Not in a car like that! All I saw was a black car . . . oh . . . and maybe a flash of red. Like a red insignia. Anyway, I went up to the house, and the dogs were back at that coal shuttle, sniffing and making noises. I opened it . . ."

"You never! You're as bad as I am!"

"I did, and a very peculiar smell was coming from it, I can tell you. I know, I know, it's only the workmen."

Lane smiled. "It could just be one of the workmen

popping behind the house to relieve himself."

"Oh. I hadn't thought of that. But why should they if there's perfectly good plumbing inside? Unless they haven't finished putting it in. It just seems strange. Of course, I've always thought that house was a bit spooky."

Lane shook her head. "I wouldn't worry too much about the blood. Perhaps the builder cut his hand. Maybe he was rushing off in the car to get it seen to. But I tell you what. I'll go with you on Saturday and we can have a good look. It's so close to Christmas now, I doubt the builders will be back till the holiday is over."

She wondered, as she watched Angela drive down the hill and was enveloped in the blissful silence that she and her boys left behind, if she was a bad influence on Angela. Still, she thought, turning back into the school, it was odd. It wasn't the builders' van that had run her friend off the road; it was a black car, and plainly in a hurry. Was this the same car that had been seen outside the teacher's cottage?

CHAPTER TWENTY-FIVE

DARLING STOOD LOOKING OUT AT the darkness, his hands in his pockets. The Franklin was going, the wood crackling in a comforting way, and the lamp on the low bookshelf threw a soft light across the room. Something in the kitchen smelled good, and he sighed contentedly. He had thought he would be unhappy with the commute up the lake and back every day, especially now, when the snow put the trip at well over an hour. In fact, though, he was finding a benefit he had never imagined. The time on the road gave him an opportunity to think about his day, to look at things from different angles. Admittedly the "aha!" light bulb had yet to illuminate, but he was certain his unconscious liked the mulling time. He could arrive home at last, his thoughts in order, and not feel driven to spend his nights trying to mentally sort through work things.

He wandered back into the brighter light of the kitchen where Lane was looking critically at a pot on the stove. It was then that he smelled a slight whiff of burning.

"I might have let the potatoes burn," she said. "The question is, are they too burned?" She pulled the pot forward and offered it for his inspection.

Darling looked at the contents and nodded thoughtfully. "Are we just having potatoes?" he asked.

"No, I have a little chicken roasting. I mean, they aren't too bad. Just a little charred on the bottom, but they might taste of burn all the way through. The beans are all right."

"Chicken and beans. Just what I was dreaming of all the way home." He took the pot from Lane, pushed open the French door against the snow that had piled up on the porch, and put the pot outside, then closed the door and brushed his hands with satisfaction.

"My mother used to do that," he said. "Then she used to get the pot in the morning and boil it with something to get the char off the bottom."

"Good grief. You married a girl just like dear old Ma!"

"I did," he said. "It's much the best formula."

Lane looked out at the pot that was rapidly melting the snow it sat in. "And what did she boil in the pot to clean it?"

Darling shook his head. "I've no idea. I suppose I had the blithe ignorance of any teenaged boy about the workings of the kitchen. Or I put such things out of my mind after she died."

It surprised Lane to realize in that moment that he had never told her very much about his mother's death. "You were so young when she died."

He nodded. "I was. Sixteen. I was quite devastated, I think. She was a bit of a softening influence. My father withdrew and I think expected me to deal with my brother

John. He was twelve and bewildered and trying hard to put a brave face on it."

"My poor darling," Lane said, taking his hand. "No wonder you're so kind." She kissed him. "I suppose losing our mothers early is something we have in common. I was five, and I'm afraid I fell into a permanently gloomy state. I'm sure I did nothing to help my baby sister."

He laughed suddenly. "I'm not at all kind, and if you see any evidence of it, you're to keep it to yourself. I trade on my reputation as the gruff inspector. Take today's work. I sent Ames off to deal with the Van Eycks to get an abandoned car towed to their garage. I couldn't help myself. Now then, how was your day?"

"You're right. You're completely horrible. But it might backfire. They might reconnect and then you'll have him constantly down at the garage visiting her instead of labouring at the police station. It will serve you right." She sighed. "My day? It's all becoming a bit of a pattern. I think I'll just be able to make it through to the end of the week. I gave everyone a very good mark on their essays about Scrooge, we studied a little bit of science, did some penmanship, and finished up with arithmetic. I thought Samuel had a very good idea for a science experiment." Lane said this as she opened the oven and pulled out the chicken.

Darling, who had set the table and had a bottle of white ready to open, took up the carving knife. "My dear old da was entrusted with cutting up the bird. May I?"

"Certainly. I'll open the wine while I tell you about the experiment and, of course, about Angela's adventure today."

The chicken was excellent and not a bit burned. After

a few moments of happy munching, during which Lane tried to imagine what Darling's mother would have used to remove the burn from a saucepan, Darling said, "The science experiment?"

"Oh, yes. Well, as you can imagine, it's mighty cold in the schoolhouse when I get there in the morning, so I make like a scullery maid and light the fire to warm the place up before the children arrive. When they were getting ready to go outside, they were all crowded into the little kitchen area where their outdoor clothes are, and someone noticed how much hotter it seemed in there with everyone in the room than when he'd gone in by himself earlier to get a glass of water. Samuel had the idea that I not light the stove when I get in, and we would see how much warmer having everyone in the schoolroom would make it. Oh, I'll have to take that thermometer, I guess." Lane pointed at the porch door where a thermometer was hanging outside the window registering twenty-four degrees.

"Very commendable. A practical science experiment. One would honestly think you'd been made for the job. More, say, than being made to nose around my cases. You should consider it."

"Thank you, I'm sure. Now, listen to what happened to Angela."

Darling listened to Angela's story and when it was over put down his fork and took up his glass. "It's a bit *Northanger Abbey*, the whole thing, isn't it? Angela's seen something that seems out of place and she's inventing a Gothic tale around it, obviously set off by nearly being hit by an unknown speeding black car. Do you think there's anything in it that ought to worry people around here?"

Lane considered. "Probably not. I mean everyone was worried about who'd bought the house and what changes it will make to the place, and now that word's gotten around that the contractors have downed tools and haven't come back, I imagine they are worried that the place will be left all of a heap, and it will be an eyesore. Not that it wasn't before, mind you."

"True. Luckily it's tucked way up that road, so no one really sees it. What I didn't tell you when you called is that I visited Miss Scott today. I went to the hospital on the off chance she'd recovered her wits enough to talk to me, and was told I'd arrived very fast, considering they'd just called, as Miss Scott thought she'd remembered something. In the event, however, she didn't want to talk to me; she only wanted to talk to Terrell."

"How sweet!" Lane said, beaming.

"Yes, very. Just what I said when I was standing around trying to make awkward conversation with the doctor while we waited for Terrell to turn up. I wanted to go back to the station, but I was afraid she might start to fade before Terrell got there, and I'd have to extract information from her anyway. My only satisfaction is that I may have separated him from the sandwich he'd been about to eat when I called the station. Unfortunately, la Scott faded before she could be asked about her car, or indeed if she'd been the recipient of the letters from Gaskell. Except this. She said Miss Keeling had visited Gaskell."

"Confirming what Samuel said! I wish I didn't feel like this puts Miss Keeling in the frame, as it were."

BY THE TIME he'd recalled, to the best of his ability, the garbled communication Miss Scott had provided to Terrell, they had finished dinner, stacked the plates, and refrigerated the leftover chicken. They now moved into the sitting room and Darling shoved another piece of wood into the Franklin and collapsed in his chair.

"Any more headway on the hit and run?" Lane so wanted not to think it was Miss Keeling.

"Not so far. We advertised for information about his car and of course appealed for the driver to come forward. Maybe it's a bit much to hope for altruism in the general public, but I'm hoping whoever it is gets eaten up with guilt and will pick up the telephone. And in the meantime, we had two lost cars, and have now found one, if it is indeed one of the ones we'd lost. I'm hoping by morning I will learn whom it belongs to." And if Miss Keeling could have been driving it, he thought grimly.

"What about Christmas?" Lane said, shifting the conversation suddenly.

Darling frowned. "Christmas?" he asked warily. "I imagine it will come and go as it has every year. Are we expecting it to do something different this year?"

"Last year we all had a lovely long luncheon at the Hugheses', complete with vicar. But this is our first Christmas together."

"Sort of. As you'll recall, I broke into your house last year and was here awkwardly waiting for you when you got back from that luncheon. We drank whisky and ate mincemeat tarts, which, as I remember, you swiped from your hostess."

Lane smiled. "Yes. That was very sweet. You didn't really break in. The door was unlocked, but I did wonder why you'd come all that way."

"Believe me, I did too. Looking back, it seems precipitous and foolish to have driven for an hour and a half in the snow only to find you gone. I had no idea what kind of reception I'd get. I must have been mad!"

"You were, of course. But I am willing to confess this one thing. When I saw you standing in the sitting room, the fire lit, that beribboned bottle of whisky in hand, and that sheepish expression, my heart turned over. It might have been the beginning for me, against all odds. As you know, I was quite finished with love."

Darling leaned across and kissed her. "Thank you. Again. Now what about Christmas, lest we sink into more maudlin revelations."

"Well, as it's our first Christmas together, I wondered about having a little drinks party on Christmas Eve. Just a little something to nibble and a glass of wine sort of thing."

Darling sat up and stared at her. "I'm sorry. Could you say that again?"

———

Friday, December 5

THE BAR WAS full and smoky, the noise filling the place with the jovial abandon characteristic of workers on a Friday night. Mackenzie stood on the street outside looking at the row of cars parked in the snow. He should go to the Metropol. He'd gone into the Legion and seen Gaskell in his usual corner, morosely nursing a pint with a cigarette hanging out of his mouth. He looked like a man who was just waiting for a fight. Mackenzie shoved his hands in his pockets and hunched up against the cold and started toward the Metropol.

And then he saw the car. The bastard's car was parked right there at the end of the street, nose into Baker. He looked around at the empty streets: the shops dark, snow blowing desolately along the sidewalk. The car door was unlocked. He slid into the driver's seat with the almost boyish joy he'd had as a youth when he'd wired cars with his friends. He felt around under the seat and then in the glovebox. Gaskell might have left extra keys. Nothing. He sat on, thinking of hot-wiring the thing. He hadn't done it for years. He leaned over and felt under the panel, and that's when he saw them. The idiot had left the keys in the ignition. Mackenzie laughed. Gaskell must have started drinking the minute he got off shift. He started up the engine and let it run for a bit. He could run the car into a ditch. That would serve him right. Or he could move it and park somewhere where Mackenzie could see his face when he came for his car and couldn't find it.

THE DOOR OPENED and light and smoke poured onto the street. Men lit up new cigarettes for the cold walk home, shouted farewells, or slunk sullenly off, fearing the reception they'd get from the wife, depending on their circumstances. Gaskell was a sullen slinker. He walked down the street, unbalanced already, never mind the slippery footing, steadying himself with one hand on the wall of the Hudson's Bay store. He stopped at the corner, his face contorted with the effort of remembering. He had parked it here. He remembered it exactly. He reached into his coat pocket to finger his keys, as if that might somehow make the car appear, but they weren't there. He turned and started east on Baker toward Ward Street. He must have left it down by the lake and walked up to the Legion after his shift. There was a car behind him, moving slowly. He was still struggling to remember actually leaving the car, feeling in his pockets for the keys again, when the car pulled up beside him. "Hey, do you need a lift?"

———

ALL THE WAY into town the next morning Darling considered married life. His wife's tendency to socialize had evinced itself a bit during their honeymoon, but he quite frankly never imagined that it could reach the level of filling their house with people on Christmas Eve. For one thing, it went against her love of solitude. Was it some sort of mad counterbalance he'd not been aware of? His argument that people would be organizing for the next day seemed to hold no weight with her. In fact, she took it as supporting evidence. Angela would be wanting to get the boys home and no doubt the Armstrongs wouldn't want to leave Alexandra on her own for long, so the whole thing was bound to be very short.

"And the children?" Darling had said. "Do they drink wine too, then?"

Consequently, when he kicked the snow off his boots

just inside the police station door, there was a vigour in the action that alerted O'Brien straight away that the boss was fractious.

"Good morning, sir," he said. "Terrell and Ames both have asked to see you."

"My cup runneth over," Darling said glumly.

"I'll send Terrell up, then, sir?" O'Brien asked. "Ames is already upstairs."

"Yes. Send everyone, why don't you? That seems to be the way things are done nowadays."

Upstairs, Darling was taking off his coat as he passed Ames's office.

"Oh, you're here, sir," said Ames, jumping up.

"You *are* quick." Darling threw his coat onto the coat rack and tossed his hat after it, where it lodged on the top. He collapsed into his chair. "What have you got?"

"We got a call from Gaskell's supervisor, Begley, this morning. He said he remembered something, and didn't know if it was important," Ames said, consulting his notes. "He said he read our piece in the paper asking for information from anyone who might have seen Gaskell on that Friday night, and it occurred to him that sometime last month he'd found Gaskell and one of the other men at shift change in what looked like an argument. He'd gone to get the other fellow, Art Mackenzie, because he was supposed to be on the ferry starting his shift, and he found the two of them looking daggers at each other just below the docks. It looked like they might come to blows, or already had. He said it wasn't unusual for Gaskell to be having words with one of the men or the other because he was not popular, so he didn't think much more about it. Mackenzie lives just at the edge of town, just before the road out of town toward Castlegar. We should go see him."

Darling nodded. "Yes, we should. Let us away."

They nearly knocked Terrell off the stairs on the way down.

"You wanted to see me, sir?"

"Sorry!" said Darling. "It can wait."

"Sir," said Terrell. This glum news could wait, he knew. He'd had a call from the RCMP in Prince George. That was where Samuel Gaskell's mother had disappeared to. She had gone to work as a cook in a logging camp under an assumed name and had died in a freak accident when a logging truck's brakes had failed. It was only after going through her things that they had found her real name. They were surprised the Nelson Police were asking, because they had notified her husband back in November once they had discovered who she was.

Sitting at his desk, Terrell tapped his fingers in a continuous roll on the wooden desk. She had died in early November. Obviously, Gaskell had not told his son that his mother was dead. He grudgingly owned that this might be some scant sign of humanity on his part. But had Gaskell's drinking become even worse as a result? Had the number of times he left young Samuel on his own been accelerating? It was difficult for Terrell to imagine the man caring that much for someone else, but he had been told often enough by his grandmother when he had been outraged by someone's behavior that you can never know what is in someone's heart.

Samuel was in Terrell's heart at the moment. The RCMP had tried to track down any relations, but it appeared he was well and truly an orphan. What did that mean about his future? Would good sense reign, and the boy be placed officially with the Benjamins? And how was he meant to cope once he learned his mother was gone as well? Thank the lord for Gabriella and her parents. They, at least, seemed genuinely to love him.

MACKENZIE'S HOUSE PROVED to be a tiny dilapidated cottage with peeling paint and a great deal of refuse on the long porch. The mounds under the snow suggested more flotsam and jetsam littering the small yard. Next to the house, a black Ford coupé sat, vintage 1939 or so, partially snowed under.

Smoke floated from the chimney, suggesting someone was home. Darling and Ames were about to climb up to the porch, skirting a pile of bent stovepipes, when Ames put his hand out and stopped Darling.

"Sir. That plate. It looks like Gaskell's plate number. We've had an appeal out for it and haven't had a response." He bent over and brushed the little buildup of snow on the corner of the licence plate. "Yup. It's his."

"That is very interesting. Let's see what Mr. Mackenzie has to say about that."

Darling pulled open the screen door, which was hanging off its top hinge, and knocked on the inner door. Silence. He knocked again, louder. Finally, a shuffling sound from inside. The door opened tentatively, revealing a man in singlet, frowning. An unpleasant smell, a combination of cigarette smoke and poorly burned coal suggesting something amiss with the furnace, wafted out. As if to demonstrate the unwholesomeness of the air, the man coughed before he spoke.

"Yes?"

"Nelson Police, sir. We've come to ask you a couple of questions, including some about that car out there." Ames pulled out his warrant card and held it up.

The man made no move to open the door wider. "I tried to call him about that. I borrowed it from Gaskell. He's a workmate of mine. He never came to get it."

Darling spoke. "I wonder if we might just step inside. We'd just like to go over the details."

Oozing reluctance, the man stood back to let them in. They could smell the strong residue of the previous night's bender on his breath as they passed him. He did not ask them to sit but stood facing them with his hands in his trouser pockets like a schoolboy prepared to defy the principal.

"Now then, sir. Your boss phoned in this morning in response to a newspaper request for information. He said he remembered you and Gaskell having an argument earlier in the month."

"So? He could have remembered us having an argument any day of the week."

"I see. You didn't get along, then. What was the argument about?"

"None of your business," Mackenzie said sourly.

"Gaskell's dead and you were seen having a fight. I think you'll find it is our business," Darling said.

Mackenzie moved across to the table and scrabbled among the dirty cups and dried food stains until he found a packet of cigarettes. "I owed him a bit of money. He wanted it back."

"How much?" asked Ames.

"A couple of hundred bucks. I got behind on my car payments." He lit a cigarette without offering them the packet.

"What happened to your car?" Ames asked.

"It was repossessed."

"Can you just go over again the circumstance of your having his car?" Darling said.

Mackenzie looked nervous. "I told you, I asked Gaskell if I could borrow it to pick up my mother in Castlegar. The next day I tried to phone him to arrange to give it back. He wasn't there."

"What day did you borrow it?"

"Friday. Not last Friday, the one before."

"I see. The fifth, then. Can you describe that Friday night again? You saw Gaskell where?" Darling asked. Ames had taken out his notebook.

"I saw him outside the Legion. He was on his way in for his usual Friday night. My . . . my mom had called to say the pipes broke and I wanted to get her to come stay with me till I got them fixed."

"You knew he'd be there?"

Mackenzie snorted. "Is the pope Catholic? Where else would he be on a Friday?"

"So, he handed over his keys and you drove off to Castlegar to pick up your mother, and he went in for his usual Friday evening."

"That's about the size of it."

"See, what I don't understand is why you didn't pick up your mother and return the car that same night. How was he meant to get home?"

Mackenzie frowned and shifted his weight from one foot to the other. "I don't know," he said hesitantly. "He never told me that. In fact," he added, more sure now, "it was his idea to bring the car back the next day. That was it. I figured he had a ride or something already arranged."

"You know Gaskell died right around then?"

Mackenzie jerked his face to one side and then looked down. "Yeah. I heard from the boss."

"And you didn't think to alert the police about his car? You were likely the last person to see him alive on Friday night."

"I . . . I didn't think it would . . ."

"No, I daresay not. Quite useful for you to keep the car. If you'll give us the keys, we're going to have to take it to the station."

Looking defeated, Mackenzie went to the fireplace, took the key off the mantel, and handed it to Ames, who had his hand out to take it.

Darling turned back to Mackenzie as they went out the door. "Your mother's pipes all fixed up now?"

"What? Oh. Yes. I took care of it. She's back home."

Driven in your conveniently acquired car, Darling thought.

"Ames, get that thing back to the station. I'll meet you there."

Darling drove off, and Ames swept the snow off the windshield of Gaskell's car, knowing Mackenzie was no doubt watching him through the murky kitchen window. The door took extra effort to open because it had sat in the cold, but the engine, much to his relief, started up just fine. It wasn't until he'd parked it in the alley behind the station that he saw, with the snow blown off the hood by the drive to the station, that the car was pretty battered up. Could be the effects, Ames thought, of one or the other of them driving around under the influence, or, perhaps on closer inspection, they might find evidence of Mackenzie knocking someone to his death on a snowy night.

BACK AT THE station, Darling mused about their conversation with Mackenzie. He'd borrowed the car, he said. Okay. Fair enough. But that phone call on the Saturday. "Ames!"

"Sir? I'm just off to the Van Eycks' to see about that car."

"Mackenzie said he called on Saturday to see if Gaskell was home but got no answer, and several times after that, but never got an answer."

"Because Gaskell was dead by that time. But wait. Little Samuel was in the house all through the weekend," Ames said.

"Wouldn't he have told us if someone had called?"

"He didn't remember, sir?"

Darling leaped up. "No. Samuel would forget nothing. Especially if he'd had a long cold night on his own. And he would have answered the phone in a flash because he was waiting for his father. Something doesn't add up." He followed Ames down the stairs. "Off you go, then. I just remembered Terrell wanted a word before we left." After that, he'd have Mackenzie brought in. He was lying like a rug.

CHAPTER TWENTY-SIX

AMES SLOWED THE CAR TO take the sharp turn down to the Van Eyck garage. He very nearly stopped altogether, so daunted was he to be once again facing Tina Van Eyck, but he reminded himself this was work. His job was to find out about the damage to the car that had been found. O'Brien was back at the station, finally tracking down the licence plate.

He pulled up in front of the garage and could see the lights inside the bay through the small windows at the top of the bay doors. The tow truck was parked at one side of the garage. They must have already backed the car in, and he hoped they were looking at it now. He took a deep breath, and then got out, grateful that the parking area and the path to the door were beaten down so he wouldn't get snow inside his rubber overshoes.

He pushed open the door to the office attached to the working bay, and called out, "Hello? Mr. Van Eyck?"

"In here," Van Eyck said. He extracted himself from

under the hood of the car and came forward, wiping his hands on an oily rag. "Sergeant Ames. Good to see you. Tina, it's Sergeant Ames!" he called out toward the back of the shop.

Ames removed his hat. His eyes had to adjust to the dark of the repair bay. "Is that the car?"

"That's the one. Tina and I pulled it out of the snowdrift. A bit of a mess inside. The grill was smashed in and it damaged the radiator, which in turn pushed into the fan."

"Ah," said Ames. "Oh, hello, Miss Van Eyck." Tina had come out of the shadows and now stood just behind her father.

Flashing him a massive smile that did nothing for Ames's determination to be professional, Tina nodded. "Sergeant."

"So," continued Ames, "the car must have hit something nearby? Wouldn't all that damage have stopped it in its tracks?"

The mechanic was about to answer when the phone rang in the office behind Ames. "I'd better get that. Tina, show the sergeant the damage and explain." He hurried past Ames to pick up the phone on the desk.

"You better come through, then," Tina said. She was wearing coveralls and a thick wool shirt, and her hair was mostly obscured by her usual workaday turban.

Ames pulled his eyes away from the blond curls that had escaped the turban, and reminded himself firmly that this avenue of possible romance had long since left the barn, or perhaps, he amended, the garage, and tried to focus on the engine into which she now shone the trouble light.

"In answer to your question, no. The car could have

gone on for some distance. As you see, the radiator was beat up, and this pushed against the fan, here." She pushed the light farther into the engine and pointed. Ames leaned in to look.

"And there," she continued, "the housing for the fan belt is a little bent, but the belt held on. And the water didn't drain all at once from the radiator, so there was still a bit of life in her."

Ames was about to stand up when he looked at the fan belt again, and then went to move the trouble light closer, managing to graze Miss Van Eyck's hand in the process. "Oh, sorry," he said. With a glance, Tina gave him the light to hold, and looked toward where he pointed. "The fan belt is quite worn along here, on this one side. Could that be a sign that the car was driven some distance, rubbing against the bent housing?"

Tina stood up and beamed at Ames. "Bingo! Well done, Sergeant. That's exactly right. My guess is it was driven with the belt sawing away on the bent housing, until the radiator emptied. Now, I couldn't say how it got into that ridiculous position off the road. The driver could have driven off on purpose, but why? Or the driver could have lost control of the vehicle trying to keep it going when it was dying, or just simply skidded and lost control. The conditions certainly have been bad, especially for inexperienced drivers, for example."

"It might depend," Ames said, handing back the trouble light, "on whether the driver wanted to hide the car or not, say, if it were stolen. At least until the snow cleared up, and they'd gotten clean away. What is your speculation about what the car could have hit?"

"Dad and I thought about that, didn't we, Dad?" Mr. Van Eyck had rejoined them and was nodding.

"It wasn't something stationary like a tree. You can see the dent in the bumper, here," he said as Tina shone the light to where her father pointed. "It's a good strong bumper, to be sure, but whatever it hit flew up, landed on the hood, and cracked the windshield."

Ames saw the windshield properly in the light for the first time. Whatever it was had hit the windshield mainly on the passenger side, but the cracks continued right across to the driver side. "It must have been hard for him to see where he was going," he suggested.

"One headlight out as well," said Van Eyck, showing Ames where Tina was now shining the light. The passenger-side headlight glass was broken, and the bulb inside cracked.

"So it hit something that was not stationary: an animal, a person?"

"That's about the size of it, Sergeant. Have you got the other half of this accident somewhere?"

Ames nodded. "We may have. A man from just a ways up the road was found dead. We think it was a hit and run. I mean, he wasn't found dead here, he was found dead on the other side of town; that's why I wondered about how far it could travel with that damage. Well, thank you, both. I'd best get back and let the inspector know. Trouble is, we have another car in town that's banged up as well." Ames put on his hat. One of them was bound to be the one. He'd have to have a closer look at the car they'd taken from Gaskell's workmate. "At least I feel like I know what to look for."

"I can come and have a look at it for you, if you like," Tina offered, glancing at her father.

"Oh. Would you? That would be helpful." Ames tried to rein in his enthusiasm for this idea.

"Yup. I can go up to town and meet you after I've cleaned up here. Will that do?"

"Gosh, yes. Thank you!"

"Won't you stay and have a cup of coffee, Sergeant? We were just going to take a break ourselves," Van Eyck said.

"Thanks all the same," Ames said with genuine regret. "Inspector Darling will want to get my report."

Tina walked Ames out to the car. "Thanks for attending to it so quickly," he said.

"All part of the service. What's on at the movies?"

"Oh," said Ames, his hand on the door handle. "I'm not sure. I . . ."

"Well, why don't you find out? I might want to stay on and see it after I've looked at the car and had a bit of dinner," Tina said.

"WELL," SAID TINA, cocking her head thoughtfully. "This one has been through the wars as well. You can see that whoever drove it ran into things all the time. Dents and scratches along the sides, a dent in the back bumper. I'd say he backed into a post rather than got rear-ended. That would look different."

They were standing in the alley behind the police station where Gaskell's car had been towed. It was rapidly getting dark and a wind had whipped up and was tunnelling through the alley. Tina's green winter coat hem was lifting, and she had her arms crossed to keep the heat in. Ames's hat was pulled down and he had his hands in the pockets of his coat.

"It wouldn't surprise me. From what we know of him I'd be amazed to learn he was ever sober, including when he was on the road. What about this, in the front? The fender is bent badly right here and there's a crack along the bottom of the windshield, though nothing wrong with the grill like we saw in the other one."

Tina nodded. "It is possible it hit an animal or something. This bend on the right side of the hood could have come from something landing on it. Too bad there's no way to tell when it might have happened. But you want to know if he could have hit your dead guy."

"Well, yes, as a matter of fact."

"Let me go on record as saying this car could have hit someone, but given the damage on the other car, I'd bet on that one."

"Hmm. Right. That's something anyway. Let's get inside out of this gale." He took her elbow gently and guided her along the slippery alleyway around to the street and the front door of the station, where the lights were already on, giving it an almost cheerful air.

"This car was borrowed by a workmate of the victim's," he said, stamping his feet on the mat just inside the door. "They weren't on very good terms."

O'Brien, who was packing up to go home, looked up as they came in, and nodded, with a slight lift of the eyebrows indicating his surprise at seeing Ames and the woman he thought of as "the lady mechanic" together, she in a very becoming red hat. In the corner, Terrell was at his desk with the phone receiver to his ear. He hung up the phone and jumped up, waving at Ames and almost betraying excitement.

"Miss Van Eyck, how nice to see you," he said, approaching them. "Sergeant, here's something interesting. Thanks to Sergeant O'Brien we've finally found out who that car is registered to!"

O'Brien, not wanting to let Terrell have any of the credit, said, "Miss Rose Scott. Now then. What do you think of that?"

"Miss Scott?" Ames frowned. "That accounts for her missing car, anyway. Does the inspector know this?"

Shaking his head, O'Brien took his hat off the stand. "You won't find him, I'm afraid. Already decamped. And the night man is not in yet, so one of you will have to hold the fort. Good night, everyone." He was not known to stay past his appointed quitting time. His wife had dinner on the table at five, and O'Brien never liked to miss a meal.

When the door had closed on the desk sergeant, Ames, Tina, and Terrell stood uncomfortably for a moment in silence.

"It's good to see you, too, Constable Terrell," Tina said finally. "I hope the sergeant here isn't working you too hard." She had a soft spot for Terrell because he'd handled a situation she'd found herself in the previous month with extraordinary delicacy. She wondered for a moment why she wasn't contemplating going out to dinner and a film with him instead of Ames, who, she maintained, had been an absolute ass on that occasion.

338

"He only works me as hard as he works himself," Terrell said gallantly. Another silence.

"Listen, I'll get myself off. I can see your day isn't over yet. Dad will be happy to see me back in time for dinner after all," Tina said. She was holding her handbag in both hands, looking from Ames to Terrell, and then turned to leave.

Ames leaped to open the door. "I could—"

"No, you couldn't," she said, smiling. "You heard him. You only work him as hard as you work yourself. You can't leave him alone here after that testimonial. However, I am prepared to give this another try. How are you fixed for Saturday? I'll drive in and meet you."

"No, no. I'll come and pick you up." He pulled himself into a more confident pose. "Look, if this is to be a proper date"—there, he'd said it—"then I pick you up, and I take you back."

"Are we calling it that? A date?"

"We are," he said, more bravely than he felt. She was quite capable of pulling the rug out even after she'd invited him to stand on it.

"Fine, then. See you on Saturday at six. Don't be late." She turned to go. "Oh, and I feel I should warn you. I'm not the easiest person in the world."

"Things seem to be all right with you and Miss Van Eyck," Terrell observed when Ames was back inside.

"She's not actually snapping my head off, if that's what you mean." Not that he didn't have some misgivings about what "not the easiest person" might mean, or why she'd produced that observation just now. "Now, what does this all mean?" Ames plunked himself into O'Brien's chair. He felt a combination of bitter disappointment that he was not heading off to dinner and a film with Tina Van Eyck right then and elation that he'd had the sheer face to insist that Saturday would be a proper date. A date between two people who liked each other. She hadn't objected. That was something. And he had a fleeting thought that for once it wasn't so clear who had actually had the upper hand in the conversation. "Miss Van Eyck had a look at Gaskell's car, and it, too, could have hit someone, though she felt the car we now know is registered to Miss Scott is the more likely candidate. Now, that is one for the books. But, we have two cars, either one of which could have killed Gaskell. One puts Mackenzie in the frame, especially as he owed Gaskell money; the other puts . . . who in the frame? Miss Scott? But surely not, because she is knocked out on the floor of her cottage at the time. Miss Keeling? We now know she threatened him."

Terrell pulled up a chair. "It is more logical, on the face of it, that it was Mackenzie. They might easily have gotten into a quarrel when they'd been drinking, there was the rankling money issue, and who knows what insults were traded, and God knows what else. If on the other hand it's Miss Scott's car that's done the hit and run, we have to look for a Mr., or Miss, if we like Keeling, X. Someone who hit Miss Scott and stole her car. Then, sometime in the course of the night, drove it all the way to town and beyond, hit Gaskell, and then drove the car most of the way back, abandoned it, and went . . . where? Are we back to looking for the elusive Miss Keeling?"

"It's a sorry old world if people go around running each other over because they've borrowed money and haven't returned it," commented Ames. "I'm not sure about Miss Keeling, but I certainly had the feeling that Mackenzie was not telling the whole truth. The car is damaged in the right sort of way, or right enough, anyway. He drove the car to Castlegar, and our corpse met his end on the road between Castlegar and Nelson. That's a lot of coincidence gathering in one place. I'll bring him in for questioning tomorrow. It's a confounded nuisance that Miss Scott can't remember things properly, and we still have no idea where Miss Keeling is!"

CHAPTER TWENTY-SEVEN

Friday, December 5

WENDY LOOKED OUT THE WINDOW. It wasn't Rose. A woman got out of the car. She'd left the engine running and the headlights on. She was just a dark shape in the glare of the light. She could see her coat and the outline of a pillbox hat with netting pulled across her face. Wendy turned away from the window, perplexed. Who was this? It must be someone coming for Rose. Relieved now, she went toward the door, just as it burst open.

"I didn't bother to knock," the woman said. She stood in the doorway and shook her head. "So, it's little Miss Wendy, at last!"

Wendy could only stare at her, her brain scrabbling around trying to make sense of what was happening. In a thousand years she would not have expected a woman to come looking for her. If she'd been sent by either her father or her uncle, she certainly didn't look the part in those fancy clothes. She desperately wished she could see her face. Then she saw that a stocky man in a thick camel coat and a black fedora pulled low over his eyes stood behind the woman holding a revolver. She heard herself say, "Oh," and could feel the blood draining from her face. The desk with the telephone was just behind her. If she could talk to whoever these people were, delay them. She backed up two steps.

"Who are you? I don't think I know you." Another step.

"You don't need to know me."

"Do you want Miss Scott? Only she's not here."

Another step. "Uh-uh. No, you don't!" The woman darted forward. "Get away from there." In a flash she was by the phone and yanked the cord hard so that it loosed somewhere inside the wall and came up in her hand. She threw the damaged cord down so that it fell behind the desk. She looked quickly around the room and saw the suitcase standing by the table. "Going somewhere? How convenient. I'll take you. Get that." She waved her gloved hand at the suitcase. The man with the gun was standing in the room now, with his weapon trained right on Wendy's midriff.

Wendy bent to take up the suitcase and in the same moment that she thought of swinging it at her attacker the woman must have thought the same thing. She reached over and pulled it from her hand.

"Give that to me. Now go. Hands up, and out the door."

Unable to think of another tactic, Wendy went slowly out the door and stood, looking at the car. If I get into that, I may never come back, she thought.

"Move it!" the man said. She felt the gun through her coat and went slowly down the three stairs.

"I don't understand. Who are you? Did they send you?"

"I have no idea what you mean. Get in," the woman ordered.

"But where are you taking me? Who are you?" I should shut up, Wendy thought desperately. I will only make her mad.

"It doesn't matter who I am. I'm afraid that what matters here is who you are. You've been hard to track down."

The man handed his gun to the woman and pulled some silk rope out of his pocket and pushed Wendy around so that she was almost lying face down on the hood of the car. With terrifying efficiency he bound her hands behind her, and then yanked her upright and shoved her into the back of the car. Wendy managed to duck just in time to avoid hitting her head. She fell sideways so that she was sprawled across the back seat, and then struggled to right herself.

The man got into the driver's seat, and the woman got in beside him. She turned to face Wendy, training the gun on her. Wendy, upright now and slumped against the window of the back door, stared at her captors. She desperately wished she could see the woman's face.

The car started, and immediately the wheels began to spin. The driver swore and took his foot off the gas, and then repeated the procedure with the same result. The woman turned her graceful head in his direction and said, "For God's sake, Arnie!"

"It's easy for you to say; you don't have to drive in this crap!"

"Just back up into new snow and then drive forward slowly. We're not in the Le Mans here," the woman said impatiently. She turned to face the front and put the gun on her lap, as if she had no further concern about the prisoner in the back. Somehow Arnie managed to begin a slow and steady crawl up to the main road.

Wendy eyed the woman, her mind desperately trying to understand who she might be. Had her father finally found her? The thought of this added to her fear. "Is this about my father? My uncle? Did they send you?"

The woman glanced back at her and then back at the road. "I thought so," she said with a kind of triumph. "You do know!"

"I do know what? Where are we going?" She could hear her own voice high-pitched with fear. Arnie was driving way too fast for the snowy conditions. She had felt the beginnings of a skid several times. Even the headlights seemed to barely make a dent in the inky darkness of the night. She looked at the woman, trying to assess her. Even in the dim light emanating from the dashboard, she could see that her clothes were expensive, and she wore pearl and diamond earrings. Only now could she smell an expensive scent over the cigar smell oozing from Arnie's coat. Chanel. Lizzy at her rooming house had had a precious bottle of it, and she used to let Wendy sniff it.

"Don't play stupid with me." The woman was angry, and she turned to glare at Wendy as the car swerved.

Who was she? Wendy looked at Arnie. Who was he for that matter? For a wild moment she thought it must be a case of mistaken identity. This woman must want someone else. But how had she found her way so specifically to the cottage? Had she mistaken her for Miss Scott? Did this woman mean to kidnap Rose for some reason? Wendy took a deep breath and closed her eyes. But no. The woman had said, "So it's little Miss Wendy, at last," when she had burst into the cottage, with that thug waving his pistol. How could this woman be from her father or her uncle? It made no sense. She had to find a centre of calm; if she could only get her to talk, to explain.

———

"SIR, THAT CAR is battered up enough that it's possible Mackenzie could have hit Gaskell." Ames was standing in the doorway of Darling's office the next morning, still holding his hat and coat. "I'd like to bring him in."

"You think he hit him just to keep his car and avoid paying him back? That seems a little desperate on the face of it. But they both are heavy drinkers."

"Well, yes. But think about it. Gaskell is hit on the Castlegar road, as if for some reason he's walking back to town from there. Mackenzie is off supposedly picking up his mom, so he's kind of in the right place and it's kind of the right time. But what if none of that is true? What if they'd both been drinking as usual, and gotten into another fight?"

"'Kind of' doesn't bring home the bacon. Why is Gaskell out there, to start with?"

Ames warmed up to his topic. "Mackenzie has taken him. He doesn't want to lend Mackenzie the car, so Gaskell drives him to Castlegar to pick up the mother and is going to drive him back."

"And then Mackenzie says to him, 'Just hop out so I can

346

take the wheel and run you down.' Search the car, bring him in, by all means."

"Right, sir."

"And what about the other car? Nothing on that? I thought the Van Eycks were going to look at it."

"Oh, yes. Sorry, sir, they did. That car, by the way, belongs to Miss Scott. Terrell tracked that down last night. Anyway, it too hit something, in fact, so badly that the radiator was damaged. Miss Van Eyck thinks the damage on Miss Scott's car is more consistent with having hit someone, but it is a much bigger problem. Gaskell has a damaged car, right place, right time, and he's been in a dispute with Mackenzie. But Miss Scott was busy being knocked out, which means someone must have swiped her car, maybe Keeling."

"Who popped out to the Castlegar road to mow down Gaskell," concluded Darling, with a touch of sarcasm. "I think I like the Mackenzie theory better."

"Whoever was driving Miss Scott's car appeared to be returning it, and probably had it break down right where we found it. Could be Miss Keeling. We still don't know where she is. And let's not forget her real name is likely Irving, for whatever that's worth."

"It could be worth something, or maybe not. Nothing was found against her as either person. But there's a first time for everything, including homicide. If she was driving, where did she go after she abandoned the car? There was no suitcase in it, and we know that she cleared out all her things. Was her anger about Samuel reason enough to want Gaskell dead? She'd only been here a couple of weeks. Could she have worked herself into a murderous rage at him in that time? Yes, but Mackenzie is much more likely. It's a lot less complicated, and he was in all the right places, as you've pointed out, and they seem to have had a long-running dispute of some sort. Well, go get him, then," Darling said impatiently. The phone on his desk jingled.

It was O'Brien. "Sir, there's someone down here about the teacher business up the lake. He wants to see someone in charge."

Darling couldn't remember ever feeling less in charge of any case. "Go on, then. Send him up." He could hear O'Brien saying, "Mr. Irving, you . . ." as he hung up the phone.

He stood up as a weather-beaten man in his late fifties knocked on the door and peered in tentatively. He could, Darling thought, amending his initial impression, have still been in his late forties; he'd clearly had a hard life. Deep bags under his eyes, clothes that looked frayed. He'd not shaved in a couple of days.

"Come in. I'm Inspector Darling. How can I help?" Darling said, indicating the seat in front of his desk.

"Irving. I've come about Miss Wendy Keeling. I saw a missing persons notice. She might be my daughter. That is, she isn't my daughter. But she might be in trouble."

Absolutely grand, thought Darling. More completely incomprehensible, nonsensical material to add to this case. Stifling a wince, he said, "I see. Can you say what you mean when you say she is your daughter, but also is not? And what sort of trouble? Wait—Irving. Your daughter is Wendy Irving?"

"She was my wife's daughter by . . . never mind about that. I took her to live with my brother in Williams Lake who's a bit of a holy roller, and she ran away when she was sixteen because they were going to marry her off to some old reprobate who already had a wife. Can't say I blame her. My brother tried to get me to help bring her back, but I decided the best thing I could do is warn her they were looking for her. I did find her finally earlier this year. I tracked her to a rooming house initially, but the woman there wouldn't give me the time of day. I waited and asked one of the other girls. She told me Wendy was calling herself Keeling. I think I decided in that moment to just leave her alone. If she had the will to get away and set herself up in a new life, then more power to her. But I guess with the years I still wanted to find out. She was teaching in Saanich, on the Island there. Didn't want anything to do with me. Smart girl, as it turned out. I'd cleaned up my act by then, gone off the booze, but she wasn't to know that."

"But you're not her father. Who is?"

"My wife apparently wasn't happy with me, well, again, looking back I can't blame her either, what with the drinking. Anyway, she took up with this guy, and then came running back when she was up the spout. Expected me to bring up the brat. And then she buggered off. I couldn't handle the kid on my own. That's why we went to my brother. My family belongs to a pretty religious group, but the trouble is my brother went off the deep end. Said he'd been hearing God talking to him and told him to keep his wife and kids on the farm. They never went anywhere, even to school. My Wendy was the one teaching them."

349

"She ran away at sixteen. And you're convinced that the missing Miss Keeling is the same person."

"This bloody woman tracked me down to try to get me to tell her where Wendy was back in November. I didn't trust her and kept mum, but she suspected Wendy had changed her name too, so she had a pretty good network, I imagine. My brother had tried for a while to find Wendy when she first ran away, but then gave it up. The old guy was plenty mad, but in the end, my brother was just happy he'd got rid of her. He was convinced she was full of sin because of her mother. It makes me laugh that his own two children have run away from that nut farm as well!"

"Who is the woman who came to see you?"

"Turned out it was Devlin's wife. Rolling in dough. You know, Harry Devlin. He's running for parliament. I didn't even know who my wife's lover had been till that woman came around."

Darling tried to brush aside the Byzantine details of the man's story to search his own memory. His brother in Vancouver might have mentioned Harry Devlin the last time he'd had a letter from him. *He* was Miss Keeling's father? That opened up who knew what possibilities.

"So what you're saying is that this Devlin is Miss Keeling's father, and his wife has been trying to track her down."

"Looks that way. I didn't even know she had moved here. Doesn't surprise me. The point is that woman, Mrs. Devlin, seemed pretty intent on finding her. I went to see Harry Devlin himself to find out what was up, and to see what sort of man my wife thought was worth wrecking our marriage for. Pretty confident sort of bastard. Running as a Tory, in a by-election. No surprise there. What surprised me is that he didn't even seem to know about her, Wendy, I mean, or at least the fact that his wife was looking for her.

"Next day I got hold of someone in the Education Department, and they told me she'd been assigned to a school out here somewhere. I thought if I telephoned her, I could just warn her, but it took some work to get the number and then they said the phone was out because of the snow or something, and then I just dropped it because I knew she wouldn't thank me for tracking her down. Then I saw the missing persons notice a couple of days ago in an old paper. I got a bit worried. Thought I better come out."

"Was that on Saturday the sixth?"

"That's right."

Darling did not control his wince this time. "So, you are suggesting Mrs. Devlin has spirited her away? For what purpose?"

"That must be obvious! For some reason she got it into her head that my daughter knows who she is and will make trouble while Devlin's running for office. That woman is ruthless and ambitious. I wouldn't put anything past her. I think Wendy might be in real danger."

Afterward Darling sat in contemplation, his chair swivelled around so that he could look at Elephant Mountain, as he often did when he wanted to move his thinking along. This man, Irving, said he had tried to call his daughter twice and was told the phone was down. When Lane had talked to Lucy, the telephonist, she had said there had been a call from a woman the afternoon before. This call took on a new significance.

"Ah. Mr. Devlin. This is Inspector Darling from the Nelson Police. Do you have a couple of moments?"

"The what police?"

"Nelson, in the West Kootenay. I'm hoping you might be able to help us with a case we are working on."

Devlin frowned at the view of English Bay. A steady rain had been falling and the bay was buried in mist. He had a brass desk lamp that threw a warm light across the papers he had been working on when Darling's call had been put through. It provided a little cheer.

"Yes?"

"I wonder if you are familiar with a Miss Wendy Keeling?"

"No, I don't think so. I'm the head of a large firm and I'm in the middle of a political campaign. I meet a lot of people, so I don't say it's impossible, but I don't remember that name."

Was he being evasive? It was hard to tell on the telephone.

"She's a young woman who teaches at one of the local schools and she's disappeared."

Devlin thought he understood, and he wheeled his chair around so that he could lean forward on his desk and reach for his fountain pen. "Ah, I see. You are hoping I have some political clout in your area. That I can do something to get more law enforcement to help with the search? It's not my district, but I can certainly see if there's anything I can usefully do." Helping out with a missing person couldn't hurt his profile with the voters.

"Ah. No, I haven't made myself clear. I beg your pardon. Miss Keeling is the young woman's assumed name. She was, in fact, Wendy Irving. Does that help?"

The pen dropped with a soft thud on Devlin's gold-tooled leather desk pad. Something that had been scratching at the edge of his consciousness since the inspector had first said the name now came home with a sickening whoosh. Wendy.

"What do you mean she's missing?"

"Are you familiar with the name, Mr. Devlin?"

"I don't know the woman, if that's what you're asking. What do you mean she's disappeared?" He felt an anxious pressure building in his chest. Where the devil had Serena said she was going? To do something about the cottage she'd bought and was fixing up. Was it near a lake? He tried with one part of his mind to remember that last conversation. Said she'd be gone a few days.

Darling was speaking. ". . . Last seen on Friday the fifth. We were wondering if she'd come to you or made herself known to your wife."

"Come to me? Why on earth should she come to me? Certainly not my wife. She would have nothing to do with this." What the blazes was the inspector trying to imply?

"It struck me as a possibility that you had made yourself known to her as her father and had arranged for her to go to Vancouver." Darling wondered what Devlin might have meant by "nothing to do with this." With what?

Devlin fell utterly silent. He gripped the receiver and stared straight ahead. What would this mean? It could be the end of everything. His fantasy about being reunited one day with a long-lost daughter melted and showed itself as naive in the heat of the wave of fear he now felt. What had Serena done?

"Mr. Devlin?" The silence had gone on for so long that Darling wondered if they'd been disconnected. What did Devlin's silence mean? Guilt? The shock of being found out?

"Uh . . . yes, sorry, Inspector. My secretary just stepped in to drop off some papers. What were you saying?"

"Look, Mr. Devlin. It's a bit awkward doing this over the phone. I'll phone the Vancouver Police and have someone stop by your office to collect whatever information you can give us. If she hasn't found her way to you, it's possible we have reason to be concerned."

"No. No, don't do that. I'll get all the information I can and give you a call back. My secretary has your number. No need to trouble the police." He could not have the police swarming around. The press would pick it up in a second.

"No trouble at all. It's what they're trained for," Darling said affably. "Good day. Oh, sorry, sir. One last question: Is your wife available on the telephone at home?" Darling sat musing when he'd hung up the phone. He tapped the top of the receiver with a pencil. Either Devlin knew and was evading, or he was surprised. Surprised about his daughter being missing. Or surprised that anyone knew he had a daughter. According to Irving, that was something Devlin might fear. And there was the business of the wife. Irving had said it was not Devlin but his wife who had come around to see him. The businessman-cum-politician was certainly covering something up, whether because he didn't want scandal attached to him, or because he, or indeed his wife, had been responsible for the young woman's disappearance.

MACKENZIE CUT A poor figure, leaning defiantly back in the chair he'd been told to sit in. He'd been drinking heavily the night before, so the whole interview room reeked. He'd clearly not shaved for several days. Ames looked at him and wondered how he kept his job at the ferry. Terrell sat with his notebook a little behind Mackenzie, against the wall.

"Could you state your name and address for the record, Mr. Mackenzie?" Ames said.

"You know my bloody name and address," Mackenzie said sullenly.

"Nevertheless."

This done, Ames said, "Now then, before we get started, I have discovered you have had your driving licence revoked for drunk driving, so you're already in a bit of hot water if you've been driving Gaskell's car around. It will help you if you could be as truthful as possible in answering our questions. Could you just go over your movements on the afternoon and evening of Friday the fifth of December?"

"I told you. I borrowed Gaskell's car and drove to Castlegar to help my mother with the plumbing. What's this about? I was just about to get a new licence."

"Now, what time would you have driven out there?"

"I don't know. I went down to the ferry to get Gaskell to give me his car around two or so. After lunch, anyway. I had to wait till he brought the ferry back to this side. I asked him, he gave me the keys, and that was it. Told me to get it back to him at the Legion that night."

Ames considered this. "When we last spoke with you, you said he wanted it the next day."

"I don't know. That night, the next day. What does it matter?"

It mattered, thought Ames, because Gaskell was without a car that night. "If he didn't want it till the next day, did he tell you how he planned to get home from the Legion that night?"

"How the hell should I know?"

"He told you or he didn't."

"I can't bloody remember what he told me."

"So." Ames shifted gears. Mackenzie was lying. "You got to your mother's when?"

"Maybe three or so. I wanted to get there before it got dark. The lighting in her house is lousy." Mackenzie ran his tongue over his teeth and moved forward in his seat to lean on the table.

Ames stifled an impulse to back away from the smell of Mackenzie's breath. "Your mother could verify this?"

"Don't you go bothering my mother. She's got a weak heart!"

Having you as her only son, I don't doubt it, Ames thought. "So your mother was there with you while you fixed her plumbing? Did she make you a meal afterward?"

"Yes. No." Mackenzie put his hand up to his forehead as if he was combatting an oncoming headache. "No. It was too late for that. I just wanted to fix the plumbing and get the hell home."

"I see. So how late would you say you stayed at her house in Castlegar?"

"I don't remember, okay? I'd had a lot to drink."

Ames nodded. He bet there was hardly a moment when

Mackenzie was sober. Perhaps he really didn't remember. "Okay then. You fixed her plumbing and drove back to town. It's surprising you wouldn't have visited with her a little bit. She is your mother."

"Look, I took her out to the diner for a bit of a meal, dropped her off, came back. All I can tell you is that it was ten thirty, eleven, when I got back."

Ames nodded. "Oh, good. You took her to the diner. That's decent. Are you sure about the time? You seem to have forgotten some other details about that night. You'd still have plenty of time to get to the Legion, meet Gaskell, maybe give back the car."

Terrell lowered his head to cover a smile. He wouldn't have credited Ames with that slight touch of sarcasm. Ames, to him, had been the picture of the youthful, almost frat-boy sergeant. Bright enough, certainly, cheerful, but predictable. A young man who'd had few challenges. Charming, but not a lot of depth. The quintessential nice guy. Perhaps there would be more to learn about him. He turned his attention back to Mackenzie.

"I didn't try to steal his bloody car, if that's what this is all about. I was tired, and had quite a bit to drink, and I just wanted to go to bed."

Ames saw Terrell glance up, and then get back to his notes. "No one mentioned stealing, Mr. Mackenzie. Should we be asking you if you stole the car? That might account for why you never reported it to the police." Mackenzie said nothing, and instead occupied himself chewing on the cuticle of his very unclean thumb. "Right. Let's get back to your drive back from Castlegar. Did you see anyone on the road: traffic, people?"

"Barely. Look, what's this for? I drove to Castlegar, fixed my mother's plumbing, and came home. When did that become a federal crime?" Mackenzie was becoming impatient. "And I got a shift I have to get to in an hour."

"Traffic on the road that night," persisted Ames.

"I don't remember. Not much, I can tell you that, the snow was blowing and whatever traffic there was, including me, was going at a snail's pace. Except for that ass that passed me going way too fast for the conditions."

Terrell shifted in his chair and glanced at Ames. Ames nodded almost imperceptibly. An ass going too fast might be something.

"Tell me about that," Ames said.

"Nothing to tell. He whizzed past and disappeared around a bend."

"You didn't see the car again, farther along the road? Where, roughly, did it pass you?"

"No, I didn't see the car again, and I couldn't tell you where. It took me another twenty-five at least to get to town, but I was pretty close by then, past the falls."

"Bonnington Falls."

"That's right. Now, can I go? I've answered all your questions."

"Not quite. Are you sure it wasn't you going too fast for the conditions? That car is pretty banged up. Did you hit something that night?"

"No, I did not! That car was a mess when I got it. Gaskell hit some animal on the road in the summer. He had the luck of the Irish he didn't kill himself, the way he drank."

Ames nodded. Judging by Mackenzie's condition, there was a lot of Irish luck going around. "Can you tell me anything about the car that passed you?"

"Not a thing."

"ALL OVER THE map," remarked Ames, when Mackenzie had been put back in the cell. They had gone upstairs to Ames's office to get away from the smell left by their guest.

"I couldn't tell if he was being slippery because he really couldn't remember what he'd said before, or if he genuinely can't remember anything, or if he remembers perfectly well and is making a mess of trying to cover up. It occurred to me when he protested that he wasn't trying to steal the car that he thought he was in trouble for keeping it. And he was much too quick to agree that he'd seen the speeding car at Bonnington Falls. I had the feeling he'd agree to anything if he thought it would get him out of here."

"That's probably right. I expect his brain is like Swiss cheese, the way he drinks. Except, I bet his is the speeding car."

"It sounds like you like him for the hit and run, sir."

"Very much, I confess. He'd certainly have been drunk enough to do it and not remember, and if what he says is true, he did go to Castlegar that day, so it puts him right in the right place. I think we've got enough to charge him."

CHAPTER TWENTY-EIGHT

Friday, December 5

THE MAN WAVED THE GUN. "Get down there." They were standing at the top of some narrow stairs. The kitchen they were standing in was icy. The woman had flicked on a light that had momentarily blinded Wendy after the darkness. There was the smell of fresh sawdust. She'd tried to figure out where they were, but she'd lost track of the turns in the road. Wendy hesitated, terrified. There was absolute blackness at the bottom of those stairs.

"Wh . . ." she began. She turned to look at the woman. She could just see her chin and the lower part of her mouth. The rest was obscured by the veil. It amazed her that what struck her in this terrifying circumstance was how perfect the woman's skin was. She wanted to ask her again who she was, what she wanted with her.

"Oh, stop making such a fuss. It's only for a few days. Down! You can scream all you want when you get down there. No one will hear you. There's an army cot on the right. You can lie down there. I've put some food there. And don't think you can escape. Arnie will be right here looking after you."

Wendy looked down into the blackness and considered one more appeal, but the gun had the upper hand. She took two steps down, her hand on the cold wall. It was enough. The door slammed behind her, nearly stopping her heart. She could hear a key in the lock and then footsteps. The light from the kitchen still shone under the door. She waited, still in a state of desperate hope. Banging on the door now, she shouted.

"Don't leave me here! Let me out!" Only silence came back, and then even the thin line of light was gone. She'd been there, Wendy thought, listening to her, waiting, and then she'd turned off the light and gone. Wendy strained her ears to try to hear the car leaving but could hear only the loud ringing in her own ears.

After she knew not how long, overcome by the cold, she felt her way down the stairs, and scrabbled carefully around in the darkness looking for the cot. She tripped on a bucket. The rudimentary sanitation facilities? She shuddered. Then she found the cot. It was low enough that she banged her shin on it. It shifted on its metal legs. There were some rough blankets piled at one end. She imagined khaki-coloured army blankets. She sat down, trying without success to adjust her eyes to the dark. Finally, exhausted by fear and bewilderment, she lay down and pulled the blankets over her. Only for a few days? Why? And why her?

——

HOW MANY DAYS had she been there? She'd lost track. Certainly more than a few. She was very close to losing hope. She could hear someone upstairs. He put food at the top of the stairs every now and then, and then disappeared. Sometimes she heard a car leaving. At those times she frantically battered at the door, trying to get out. She'd found a door in the dark of the basement and it opened, but only into a tiny coal room. Once she'd managed to scramble up to try to push the doors of the chute, but they were locked tight. Then suddenly that day, the woman had come again, calling down the stairs that it wouldn't be long now, before slamming the door and driving away. She lay on her side, unwilling to climb in the dark to the top of the stairs, and drifted into sleep. She awoke, always in the dark. She sat up. Something had woken her. It was then she felt a blast of cold, fresh air coming from somewhere. She had explored every corner of her prison. Besides the locked door at the top of the stairs, there was only the coal room door. The cold air was coming from under that door. Choking back sobs of hope, she stumbled to the door into the coal room and pushed it open and looked up to see stars that appeared to be whirling like dervishes above the tops of the trees.

AS SHE WAS about to light the fire in the stove at the school, Lane remembered that the children would be expecting the experiment. A bit sorry now that she'd have the extra hour of cold until the students got there, she went to the desk and opened her bag to extract the thermometer she'd taken off the outside of the kitchen window at home. She began to look around the classroom to see where it might be best to locate it, when she heard a cough from the kitchen area.

She nearly dropped the thermometer in her shock at the sound. It was decidedly a human cough. Had a child come early for some reason?

"Hello?" she called out, moving slowly toward the kitchen. "Who's there?" She pushed the door open carefully. She stepped back with a gasp at the unexpected sight. A woman lay along the bench where the children sat to take off their boots and scarves. She was lying under a grey wool blanket and did not look at all well. Her face, covered in black smudges, registered surprise and fear, and she sat up slowly, pulling the blanket to her chest with both hands.

Lane rushed forward. "Goodness! You must be absolutely frozen." She took off her own coat and put it around the woman's shoulders. She could see that the woman's hands were abraded, bloody spots showing through the black soot that covered them.

The woman put up her hand to protest. "No, no. I'm all right." But she clearly was not. The woman was pale and had begun to shiver violently. "You're not her," she managed.

"Listen, this won't do at all. Can you walk? I've got a car outside. The children won't be here for another hour so I've time to get you to warmth."

The woman tried hesitantly to rise. She hadn't taken her shoes off, and Lane could see they'd been soaked through. Finding she could stand, she made one last attempt to return Lane's coat to her, to which Lane responded by insisting she put it on properly and then doing up the buttons.

"I'm Wendy Keeling," the woman said hesitantly. "My schoolhouse . . ." She looked around the room. She sounded rueful. "Who are you?"

Lane was full of questions, but she continued to steer the woman toward the door. "I'm Lane Winslow. I'm just covering until you get back. In fact, I'm relieved to see you. The children will be ecstatic. They think you're the bee's knees."

They negotiated the stairs and Lane settled Wendy Keeling into the car and went around to the driver's side. She started up the car, happy that the heater would work quickly since she herself had only just arrived at the school. She glanced over at her passenger as she turned to back the car up. Miss Keeling had collapsed against the back of the seat with her eyes closed, her breath coming in uneven flutters.

Driving as quickly as she could, Lane made for King's Cove. She'd take her to the Armstrongs. There she was certain to be warmed up, fed, cared for in every way. Questions tumbled about in her mind about the sudden appearance of the missing teacher in this terrible condition—cold, unwashed, and damp still from her time in the snow finding her way from wherever it was to the schoolhouse.

They were driving up the hill toward the turnoff down to the post office when Wendy said in a weak voice, "I was so surprised to see the school. I had been stumbling in the bush all night and had no idea where I was, but there it was, suddenly. I cried with relief."

"Yes, I'm glad you did, too. Everyone has been terribly worried about you." Lane looked at her, but Wendy had turned her face away and was looking listlessly out the window.

Then she turned back to Lane, frowning. "But where is Miss Scott? Oh . . . no, of course, she must have left."

Lane debated whether to tell her anything or just leave her with the impression for the time being that Miss Scott had simply gone off as planned. She could learn everything later. She pulled up in front of the post office. Too early, thank heaven, for anyone coming for mail. "Stay here just a second," she instructed, and Miss Keeling rushed to the front door and knocked urgently.

Eleanor pulled the door open and looked alarmed at Lane's expression. "What is it, my dear? What's happened?"

"It's Miss Keeling. She's turned up in a dreadful state. I have her in the car. Do you mind awfully just having her here to warm up and get some food down her?"

"Goodness!" cried Eleanor looking past Lane at the car. "Kenny, come help!"

At this point Alexandra emerged from somewhere at the back of the cottage and began to bark, alarmed perhaps by the worry in the voice of her mistress.

Between them Kenny and Lane supported Miss Keeling into the cottage where Eleanor took over with blankets and slippers and cups of tea. Kenny walked Lane back out to the car.

"Can you phone my husband straight away? Something dreadful has happened to her, but she wants looking after before she is made to talk. And . . ." Lane hesitated. "And she may be needed to help the police with their investigation into that hit and run."

"Oh. Well, you don't worry about a thing. You go along now. We'll look after everything."

Suffused with the warmth and utter reassurance of having the Armstrongs as her neighbours, able, she was sure, to handle absolutely any crisis, Lane made her way back to the school in a perplexity of questions. Uppermost in her mind was, where had Miss Keeling been for more than a week?

NO CHILDREN HAD yet arrived at the school when Lane returned, so she continued with her preparations for the morning. She decided on the blackboard for the thermometer, and she hung it on a nail and wrote down the temperature as it was now, when only she was in the school, shuddering at the low number: forty degrees. She walked briskly back and forth, trying to keep warm, setting out the foolscap, pencils, and rulers, with a view to making a graph to map the changes in temperature in the hour from when school started.

DARLING AND AMES stood looking at the road map that covered the distance between Castlegar and Nelson. "We found Gaskell's body about a mile this side of the falls," Darling said, pointing. "So the hit and run was behind where Mackenzie claimed he was when that car sped by. If he was telling the truth, which I doubt. He could be throwing a speeding car at us to put us off the scent."

Ames considered. "That's true, sir. That's exactly how I see it. I think we've got enough to charge him."

"Do you indeed? You're pretty confident."

"He's clearly lying about something, sir. And he was in the right place at the right time."

Darling nodded and made a "hmm" noise. "Unless he's lying about something else. Do you believe his story about borrowing the car?"

"No. I think he took it, collected a very drunk Gaskell, and somehow managed to get him out of the car and run him down. As I said, right time, right place, car all banged up."

"Go ahead and charge him. I think you're right. It still leaves the pesky problem of Miss Scott's car, abandoned and banged up."

Ames had gone back to his office, and Terrell now stood at Darling's door. "Sir, it occurs to me that if it wasn't Mackenzie who hit Gaskell—"

"So you believed Mackenzie?"

"I wouldn't go that far, sir. But we have to take into account the possibility that there was indeed a speeding car. I'm just wondering if it is Mr. X or, indeed, Miss Keeling in Scott's car."

"Granted. You were saying?"

"Yes, sir. If it wasn't him, and it was someone driving Miss Scott's car, then to get back to where the car was abandoned, they'd have to take the ferry from Nelson to get to the north shore. Shall I go check with whoever was on shift that night? Mackenzie said he got back to town around ten thirty, so that should help establish when that speeding car would have gotten the ferry."

"Yes. Why not?"

367

"AMES!" DARLING SHOUTED ten minutes later, slamming down the phone, and getting up so hurriedly that his chair nearly toppled backward. It fell back onto its front legs with a bang and Darling reached for his coat and hat.

"Sir?" Ames was in the doorway.

"Yes, blocking the doorway. Very useful in an emergency. Hat! Coat! Keys! Miss Keeling has been found. Now maybe we'll get to the bottom of this schoolteacher business, at last."

Ames, who had just been on the point of putting everything in place to charge Mackenzie, stumbled back and then turned to get his things from his office and follow his boss down the stairs. "Who found her?"

"We're off up the lake to King's Cove," Darling snapped to O'Brien who had halfway lifted his bulk off the stool.

Once in the car, and moving along Baker Street, Ames tried again. "Who—" he began.

Darling pulled his coat impatiently across his chest. "Do you have to ask?"

"No! Really, sir? Miss Winslow? Golly, that is—"

"Just drive, Ames. If I need any insightful observations from you, I'll ask for them."

Darling maintained his silence until they were off the ferry on the north side of the lake. "If you must know, she found Miss Keeling sleeping in the school this morning. She took her to the Armstrongs', where she now is, apparently recovering from cold and hunger."

"In the school! That means she's been nearby the whole time. I wonder where she's been? And why she went away?"

"Let's not wonder. Let's pick up the pace a bit and go find out, shall we?"

Darling wanted quiet to consider the situation. No matter what he was working on, there was Lane. Doing the right thing, of course. He would concede that. She got the woman to safety and did not try to find out anything. She had her priorities right. But honestly, it was diabolical.

Miss Keeling was sleeping in the Armstrongs' bed when Darling and Ames arrived, more than an hour after they set off. Ames had doggedly refused to speed beyond what the chains and packed snow on the road would allow for safety.

"Oh, do come in, Inspector, Sergeant," Eleanor said when they arrived at the door. "Shh, Alexandra, they're not here for you!" She took Darling by the elbow and ushered him in and stood by to let Ames duck through the door. "The poor woman was in a frightful state. We've fed her and she's had a hot bath and is asleep now. I've resisted the urge to throw out her clothes. Please. Sit down. I've got the kettle hot and some lovely raisin bread we can toast."

Darling could almost feel Ames lighting up at the suggestion of a snack and settled his own expression along more dour lines in contrast. The Armstrongs kept a couple of rattan chairs in the kitchen where they normally spent their leisure time in front of the stove, and Darling and Ames were now invited to sit in them. "Did she say much about what happened to her?" Darling asked.

"We didn't want to press her too much. She was shivering and then got a bit weepy, poor thing," Kenny said. He was at the counter cutting the promised slices off a loaf of bread.

Eleanor busied herself with the tea, and then set cups

and saucers on the table for the policemen. "I gather she must have been forced in some way. She kept asking where she was and looking out the window as if she expected to be found by someone. Of course no one's going to find anyone here in King's Cove!"

"She did mention this was better than the basement she'd been in. She wondered what day it was. She said you lose track of time in the dark." Kenny had put the slices of raisin bread into the wings of the toaster, and now watched them closely.

"Basement?" Darling said, surprised. "She's been kept locked in a basement. Whose? No mention of how she might have got away?"

"Nothing, I'm afraid. I didn't like to ask. She seemed quite traumatized."

Darling stirred his tea thoughtfully. Had she been beaten? Was this some sort of sordid sex crime? If Gaskell were still alive, he might have supposed him quite capable of such a crime. Unless he had kidnapped her, but got himself killed before he could, what, kill her? Certainly if he'd kidnapped her and then got himself killed, she'd have been abandoned until someone found her, or she died of starvation. "Did she say anything about the man who kidnapped her?"

"Oh!" said Eleanor with a little cry. "But that's odd, you see, because when she was looking so anxiously out the window, she did say, 'What if she finds me again?' She. I didn't think till just now how peculiar that is."

"A woman?" exclaimed Ames. He nodded gratefully at Kenny who had put a plate with a fat slab of perfectly toasted raisin bread before him and pushed a plate of butter and some raspberry jam after it. "Well, there's one for the records!"

Darling took in a thoughtful breath. Who would kidnap Mrs. Devlin? According to Irving, she had an uncle who might have been capable. But why after all this time? They'd driven all the way out to King's Cove, and he didn't want to spend hours waiting for Miss Keeling to wake up. There was nothing for it. They'd have to wake her. She could sleep after they'd gone. "I think—" he began, but he was interrupted by the appearance of Miss Keeling herself at the door to the kitchen.

She was dressed and had a thick cardigan pulled around her that seemed miles too big and was wearing a pair of slippers obviously lent her by the Armstrongs.

"I expect you want to talk to me."

If she'd been weepy and shivering before, she certainly appeared self-contained now, Darling thought. He stood up and offered his chair and pulled out a wooden kitchen chair for himself.

"More tea, my dear?" offered Eleanor.

"You've been so kind. I'm all right for now. It's been heavenly to have a hot bath! I feel almost myself again."

"This is Inspector Darling of the Nelson Police, and Sergeant Ames. Why don't you have a little chat? I've a good deal to see to in the mailroom," Eleanor continued. She nodded fiercely at Kenny, who got up as well and put on his hat and thick wool sweater.

"That pile of wood out there won't split itself!"

Alexandra looked from one to the other and opted to

follow Eleanor through to the post office.

Darling cleared his throat. "I understand you are Miss Wendy Keeling, teacher at the Balfour school?"

"Yes, that's right. My real name is Irving, but I've used Keeling since I was sixteen. I'd run away from home, you see, and didn't want to be found." She shuddered. "I thought I'd been found when that car turned up, always waiting near the school. I was packed, ready to leave. Then, well, she came. I still have no idea who she is, or why she wanted me locked away."

Ames took notes and Darling coaxed the story out of the teacher. It came in fits and starts. And culminated in her being pushed down into a basement. Yes, food had been left for her, and she'd found a four-quart can of water. A man who had been left to guard her gave her more food from time to time, but he didn't talk to her except to tell her to be quiet. "I was terrified that he was going to attack me, but he seemed more interested in doing anything else but sit around guarding me. He kept driving off somewhere."

No explanation had been given except that it would be over in a few days. It had certainly lasted longer than that.

"Did you know what she meant by a few days?" Darling asked.

Keeling shook her head. "I had no idea what that meant, and less idea who she was. She was rich, I can tell you that. The car was expensive, her clothes were expensive. She seemed to have some fixation about my father, but I couldn't make sense of it. I asked if my father had sent her, but in reality I couldn't imagine in a million years how my father, a man with no money and addicted to drink, would even know someone like her, let alone have the wherewithal to 'send' her to get me. But she did seem very focused on my father. I ran away from a very religious family when I was sixteen. I was sure it must have something to do with that. I've been afraid of that for all these years because I feared they might kill me for running away. Then I began to remind myself that that was the fear of a child. Through the years when nothing happened, I began to feel I was safe, after all, but then my father followed me to Saanich. I wouldn't talk to him. I got this job and thought I was safe here, and then I began to see someone was watching me. I was terrified all over again. I was about to run away. I'm embarrassed to say it, but I couldn't control my fear. Then she turned up."

"How did you get out?"

"I began to be really frightened, besides being filthy and cold, because the idea of being left or forgotten there became more and more terrifying. She went away and left me there, and I honestly had no idea how long it was. Her thuggy sidekick was often not there, and I always feared he'd drive away one day and never come back, and I'd be left to starve. I dreamed that I heard people outside once, talking, and I tried to call out, you know how you do in a nightmare, and then I forced myself awake, but there was nothing. There were no windows, but last evening I felt a cold breeze coming from the door to the coal cellar, and one of the doors to the coal chute was open. It wasn't before. I'd tried so many times to push it, but it felt as though it had a bar across it to keep it shut and I couldn't budge it, and now, suddenly it was open. I managed to crawl out.

I didn't want to go down the road in case she or that man came back so I thought if I could go through the woods, I was bound to find something, a house, another road. I covered up my tracks from the house to a sort of shed and then clambered around in the snow for what felt like most of the night."

Darling thought about the sheer folly of going into the bush in an out-of-the-way place like this in the dark but said nothing. She'd been very, very lucky. She described how she'd climbed for a good part of the night, when the terrain had started to descend and then she saw the schoolhouse through the trees close to dawn. She thought she'd get down to the store to get help, but she knew the store wouldn't be open, and she'd been exhausted. She'd been terrified the woman would look for her there after finding her gone, and knew nothing until that new teacher came, who appeared to be handling the school now.

"Miss Winslow," Ames offered helpfully. "She's the inspector's wife."

"Yes, thank you, Sergeant," Darling said repressively. He was contemplating the nearly inadmissible thought that the wife of a very wealthy and well-known businessman had somehow engineered the capture of Miss Keeling. Under his orders? Was Devlin directing the proceedings? Was Serena Devlin acting on some desperate idea that she had to get Miss Keeling out of the way?

CHAPTER TWENTY-NINE

ERRELL SAT MUSING AT HIS desk. The person who'd manned the ferry the night of the fifth had said there'd been a bit of a rush in the period between ten and eleven that night. He assumed people, seeing the increase in the snow, were probably deciding to get back home and not stay in town as long as they usually might. He wasn't watching too closely because he was pretty bundled up himself. He thought that he'd seen a car with a dent in the bumper getting off on the north shore, as he stood on the side of the ramp holding the chain. No, he hadn't seen the driver, or even given it much thought. It was just that the dent was pretty substantial and stood out in the headlights.

Terrell thought it safe to assume that might have been Miss Scott's car. Mackenzie, also driving a dented car, would have had no reason to cross to the north shore. But who was driving it? Not Miss Scott, lying knocked out. Miss Keeling? Frustrated that the ferryman had not seen the driver, Terrell went to the front to see O'Brien.

"Where is everyone?"

"Dashed off up the lake. Apparently that missing teacher has turned up."

THE CHILDREN WERE very keen on the thermometer experiment. They pushed together to see if having all of them standing right around the thermometer would cause the air to warm up more quickly. Finding that the thermometer had crept up a bit, they were at their desks copying the graph Lane had put on the blackboard. Lane smiled at the ability of the children to feed off each other's enthusiasm. Randy put up his hand. "Can I try writing with ink? I never got to before."

Lane considered. Drawing a graph might be a messy proposition in ink. "I tell you what. I'll prepare the ink and pen, and let's see how you get on in pencil, and then you can do it over in ink."

Happy with this, Randy set back to work and Lane went to her desk to open the bottle and prepare the pen.

"Remember, it started out at forty degrees when I was here by myself. Rafe, can you check now?"

Rafe peered at the thermometer from his front-row desk, and then got up to look more closely. "It's fifty-two!"

"Excellent. After you've done this, let's see if we can make it even warmer by jumping up and down. Why might that make it warmer?"

"'Cause you get hot when you jump around?" suggested Rolfie.

"That sounds right," Lane said. "Maybe if we get warm, we'll warm the room up even more." She went to stand by the window. It was a lovely winter's day, drifts of snow with sun reflecting exuberant light through the trees.

Happily, it would soon be time to light the stove. As novel as the experiment was, she was cold, and the ever-present thought of Miss Keeling spending an icy night on the bench added to her desire to light the stove and get back into the routine.

Where had Miss Keeling been? She hadn't appeared to have any idea. Somewhere within walking distance, though, Lane thought. She wished now that she'd at least ascertained which direction she'd come from. She would do it after school. Even with the children messing around outside during their break, she should find the trail of the teacher's progress coming out of the woods.

She was about to turn away to see how Randy was getting along with his pencil, when she saw a car driving toward the school. She'd just begun to speculate who might be coming to the school at this time of the morning, when it stopped a good hundred yards away on the road, and a man got out. He wore a long camel coat and a black fedora. It struck her momentarily that the clothes looked expensive, but he didn't. Any contemplation of his grizzled facial features was wiped away in an instant. He had reached his gloved hand into his pocket and removed a revolver. The man who'd kidnapped Miss Keeling had come to find her.

Lane took a deep breath and turned to look at the children. She moved quickly to the front of the room and said in a loud whisper, "Class!" and then put her finger firmly to her lips. One of the younger girls began to say something and Rolfie put his hand out to stop her.

377

Urgently Lane indicated through gestures that they were to move quickly and silently into the kitchen area. Every scrape of desk and chair made her flinch, but somehow she got them gathered there. Shutting the door to the classroom, she whispered, "Listen carefully. There's someone outside who I think might be dangerous. Button up your coats now, quick as you can."

The few who had unbuttoned their coats quickly did them up and put their mittens back on. Rafe whispered, "Wait till Mommy hears about this!" with enthusiasm. Lane was relieved to see Gabriella and Philip, the two eldest, do their coats up quickly and begin to help the younger children. Again, she thought with relief, the students were feeding off the earnest calm those two children were exhibiting.

"Philip and Gabriella. Get everyone out the back door and into the woods behind the school as fast as you can. Go around through the trees over that way and down toward the store, do you understand? Stay out of sight, but don't lose sight of the road and get onto it when you are well past the car that is there. Philip," she turned to whisper to him, "I want you to run ahead and get Mr. Bales to phone the police. Tell them there is a man with a gun at the school and they must come. Do you understand? But don't go anywhere near the road till you're past that car. Is that clear?" Darling might have come out already to interview Miss Keeling, but someone at the station would know that.

A footfall on the steps made Lane turn convulsively to look toward the door to the classroom and then back at the children, who clustered by the door, suddenly unsure. "Now!"

Philip, who'd been shushing the children who'd over-heard and gasped at the mention of the man with the gun, nodded. Gabriella had already opened the back door and was ushering the others out into the snow and waving them into the trees behind the school. Philip pulled up the rear and, when the last child was out, made for the woods with them. Lane breathed out, relieved that the children had some chance of safety, just as she heard the man take the last two steps and pause in front of the door.

She darted to the back of the classroom and stood behind the door, desperately looking around for something to strike the man with. She must delay him until the children were fully out of danger. There was still no movement on the steps. She imagined the man looking cautiously around to make sure no one was near. She prayed he wasn't seeing the children. She wished now she'd had the presence of mind to tell Philip or Gabriella to keep the children still and quiet until the man had gone into the school. Where was that damn revolver from the kitchen when she needed it? With a whimper of exultation she saw the broom leaning in the corner. She seized it, sorry it wasn't more substantial, like a cricket bat, and waited.

The door handle rattled and then turned, and the door was pushed open slowly. She heard the man step over the threshold. She would have to wait until he was fully in and was out where she could see him to get a really good swing in. She could feel her heart pounding as she waited. The man stopped. He would be surveying the classroom.

Finally, she could hear him walking forward. When he came into view, she kicked the door out of the way and aimed the broomstick at the back of his head.

He must have heard the sound, because he was halfway turned toward her when the broomstick struck him across the ear and side of his face. His hat flew off and he yelped. Lane could hear the gun fall noisily and rattle across the floor. Almost unconsciously she tried to make out where it might have slid, while she swung her arms back to strike him again. She managed to hit him on the chest, and he grabbed the broom and pulled hard. She yanked back and then let the broom go so that he stumbled back and fell over a desk.

The gun. She had to get the gun. How far would the children have gotten by now? If she could only be sure they were well out of the way, she could make a run for it herself through the open door, but she couldn't risk it.

The man, hampered by his voluminous coat, was making heavy weather of getting up. He was bleeding copiously from the ear and was letting out a stream of obscenities. Lane saw the gun, not quite under the bookshelf, but behind him. She'd have to get past him. She ran at him and pushed hard at the desk he was using to pull himself up so that he stumbled back again.

He saw what she was up to and he lunged at the gun from where he had fallen and managed to get it into his hand. He scrambled up and came at Lane, pushing at her hard so that she fell against the teacher desk. She spun and fell forward, clutching at the top of the desk to stay on her feet. Her right ribs struck painfully against the edge of the desk, and the wound she'd sustained from a gunshot on her honeymoon screamed in protest. She gasped at the pain but managed to push herself upright and turn to face him.

GABRIELLA WATCHED PHILIP sprint down the road, and then she turned to the other children. "I know it looks safe now, but you have to shush and go fast." They had plowed through snow that for some of the children was nearly thigh high, with Gabriella leading and the others following behind, until they were standing well below the parked car, covered in snow.

"Will we be able to take our Christmas cards home?" Amy whispered anxiously. Samuel was holding her hand.

He nodded solemnly. "Don't worry. We'll get them. Miss Winslow will make sure they're safe."

Philip arrived at the intersection and waited for a car to go by, and then with a last push he ran across the road and burst through the door of the shop, causing the bell at the top of the door to ring frenetically.

"Mr. Bales, Mr. Bales! You gotta phone the police right away!"

"Whoa, there, young man," Bales said, coming out from where he was organizing something in the freezer. "Where's the fire?"

"It's not a fire, sir. It's a guy with a gun. Miss Winslow is up there. She made us escape. She said you had to phone them."

Bales didn't wait. "Lucy, get the Nelson Police on the phone, this instant!"

When O'Brien's voice came on the other end, Bales

didn't let him finish his greeting.

"I need Inspector Darling. It's an emergency."

"Well, I'm sorry, sir, you won't get him. He's up the lake in King's Cove interviewing someone. What's the emergency? I've got another officer I can send."

"No, no, no. That's fine. If he's at King's Cove, it's closer. There's a man with a gun holding up the schoolteacher at the schoolhouse. Where is he, exactly?"

O'Brien looked at the paper on the desk. "The post office. I'll put the call through right away. Don't you try to do anything, sir. He can be there in two shakes."

Bales hadn't had time to think concretely yet about what he could do, but O'Brien's injunction not to do anything set him on a rebellious train of thought. He had a hunting rifle. He could get to the school before the police.

He went into the cupboard where he kept a small safe, a hunting rifle, and ammunition, and unlocked it. The rifle was leaning against the wall. He took it out and broke it. Not loaded. He was reaching onto the shelf when he heard the door open and close. Philip had gone outside and was shouting something. He took the box of bullets out and put it on the counter with the gun. Lucy was out standing by the counter.

"Do you want me to load it?" she asked. Bales was by the door watching the children crossing toward the store.

He turned and looked at her, appalled. "No, absolutely not." He opened the door wide and was calling out to them to come in quickly.

"Why not? I go hunting with my dad. I know how," Lucy was saying, aggrieved.

Bales seized the rifle and the box of bullets. "You make sure these kiddies are all right. Give them something hot, tea or cocoa, and give them each a chocolate bar, and don't let them out of your sight. And don't let anyone in here unless you know them, is that clear? And lock the door behind me."

"AND SHE NEVER gave you any indication of why she was holding you?" Darling asked.

Miss Keeling shook her head wearily. "I haven't the first idea. I can't understand any of it. I've always thought that one day my father or my uncle might come after me because I ran away from a marriage they'd arranged for me. I was told that if I tried to run away, I would be beaten and brought back. They came to Vancouver once, right after I ran away, and were asking for me at all the rooming houses on Cardero Street, where I was living. Mrs. Franklin said she sent them away and told me that it was against the law to force me to marry someone I didn't want to. I hadn't even known that. I still felt if they'd caught me, I would never be allowed to leave. Then when nothing happened for a few years I felt a bit more relaxed, and then when my father turned up in Saanich all the fear came back. He stopped me outside the school and tried to tell me that he'd changed. I told him to leave me alone and go away. I didn't trust him. I haven't got the first notion who that woman is or what earthly reason she had for taking me, but she was very certain that I knew something about my father, which brings me back full circle. How would my father know someone like her? I mean, I've been gone for ten years and I guess anything could have happened to him, but it just doesn't seem right." She leaned back and put her hand on her brow as if she might somehow clear the confusion and exhaustion away.

"Can you describe the woman, Miss Keeling?" Ames asked.

"Like I said, well dressed. She wore a sort of widow's veil across most of her face, so I never got a good look."

"Miss Keeling, have you heard of Harry Devlin?"

She opened her eyes and then shook her head. "No. Should I have?"

"He's a very wealthy businessman from Vancouver who is running for parliament. It's possible that the woman that kidnapped you was Harry Devlin's wife. Your father knew, and I suspect he was trying to warn you about her. He tried to telephone you that Saturday, the sixth, but was told the line was down." He was going to have to tell her that Harry Devlin was very probably her father and he didn't relish it.

"She pulled the cord out of the wall. But why would she want me? Did she think I was having an affair with her husband? I've never even heard of him." Miss Keeling shook her head, her confusion intensified by this revelation.

At that moment the phone rang. Eleanor, who was tidying up the already perfectly tidy sitting room, waited. It was for them: long, short, long. They could hear her say "Hello? King's Cove Post Office. Eleanor Armstrong speaking." Then silence. As if by unspoken consent, the interview stopped, and they listened to Eleanor's voice.

"Oh, goodness. Yes, right away." They heard the receiver fall onto the phone and then Eleanor hurried in, wringing her hands.

"Inspector, that was the police station. They've had a call from the Balfour general store that, and I want to get this right: 'There's a man with a gun at the school, and the children are all safe. The teacher is there trying to hold him off.' Oh dear, that must be Lane!"

As one, Darling and Ames leaped up, and were out the door without their coats.

"Just turn right up the little road near the store; you'll see the sign!" Eleanor called after them. "Oh, Kenny," she said to her husband. He'd rushed to the door at the commotion of the two policemen running full tilt to the car. "Lane is up at the school with someone with a gun!"

Kenny's eyes widened and he went into the house, almost tripping over the near-hysterical Alexandra, and reached into the corner behind the door.

As Ames was backing the car around, Kenny was outside holding out his rifle. He saw Darling say something to Ames, and Ames stopped the car.

"I don't know if you're armed, Inspector, but you might need this. It's only a .22, but it might scare someone," Kenny said, and Darling opened the door and half stepped out to take it.

Eleanor and Kenny stood outside watching the car tear off up the hill, scattering clumps of icy snow off the chains. Miss Keeling was behind them, standing in the doorway, her arms crossed tightly in front of her.

Eleanor had a hand over her mouth. "Oh my God," she said at last. "What if . . ."

"Don't be silly," Kenny said. "It's our Lane. She'll have thought of something."

CHAPTER THIRTY

———

"**C**ONSTABLE TERRELL? IT'S DR. EDISON. I . . . I think you'd better come to the hospital. It's about Miss Scott."

Terrell frowned. He couldn't imagine Dr. Edison being uncertain about anything, but she sounded uncertain now. "Of course, right away. Is something the matter? Has she taken a turn for the worse?" If she died it would become a murder investigation.

"No, no. Nothing like that, but I just think you'd better come and hear what she has to say."

Terrell, who had been fully preoccupied by what must be happening up the lake with an armed man at the schoolhouse, and the inspector's wife apparently there with him, was almost reluctant to leave the station in case he was needed, or news came in.

He took up his coat and hat and said to O'Brien, "That was the hospital. Apparently there's some development with Miss Scott. I'm going to have to go up there right now. Dr. Edison was very insistent."

"Don't you worry your pretty little head about things. I'll hold the fort." O'Brien sighed. In truth, he was perfectly content to stay right where he was. He'd brewed a cup of tea, and he had a very nice raisin scone his wife had made to go with it.

Realizing that the car was out, Terrell set out on foot, grateful that it wasn't actually snowing, and that his rubber overshoes seemed to work reasonably well on the icy sidewalk. By the time he'd made the top of the hill and was at the hospital entrance, he was overwarm in his overcoat and was hoping crossly that whatever Miss Scott had to say was worth the hike. He thought rebelliously that she had kept them dancing with her constant collapsing just before she got to where she could tell them anything useful. His heart sank when he saw that the reception desk was manned by the same woman who had doubted his credentials on his first visit.

"I'm here to see—"

"Go on up," she said coolly, scarcely glancing at him, her expression suggesting that whatever madness they got up to in the wards was none of her lookout.

"Dr. Edison," Terrell said. He had his hat in his hand and was desperate to fan himself with it.

"Ah, Constable Terrell. Please come through. I've put a chair next to the bed. Miss Scott seems quite collected at the moment, so I hope she'll get through her whole story without another relapse."

Indeed, Miss Scott was sitting up in bed with a dressing gown wrapped neatly around her and her hair done and looking altogether more composed than the last time he'd seen her. She put down the glass of water she'd been sipping and waited. Terrell took off his overcoat and pulled the chair out to sit down.

"Miss Scott. How are you feeling?"

"Much better, thank you. They say I won't have to stay much longer if I keep making progress. That is, if I keep . . ." Her voice trailed off.

"That is good news. I'm glad you're improving. I understand you wished to see me?" He wasn't sure whether she wished to see him, or Dr. Edison wished him to see her.

"It's just that I'm beginning to remember a little . . . about that night."

"Excellent. Do you mind if I write some things down?" Terrell brought out his notebook and pencil and held them up.

"Yes, that's fine." She closed her eyes and leaned back against the pillows that had been plumped up behind her. Terrell waited. Was she giving up already? But then she sat up and began.

"I was out, you see. I had come into town to arrange the train. I was leaving to go home to Manitoba. My mother isn't coping well."

Terrell wondered about the story that she was going off to be married, but he did not want to interrupt her. She seemed to be collecting herself again. She turned and looked at him.

"I had to get away. I had to. It was too much. I scarcely survived the wait till Wendy arrived, and then to have to stay longer to make sure she was settled in . . . I should have left after a couple of days. I could see she wouldn't need me. She is a natural. If only I'd left, none of this . . ." She twisted her hands together and looked away.

"What was it you needed to get away from so urgently?" Terrell asked gently.

She turned back to look at him, tears forming in her eyes. "Him. I had to get away from him."

"Is this the man who was sending you poison-pen notes?" Terrell ventured.

Rose Scott's eye widened. "Yes. How did you know about that? How could you know? I never told anyone, not even Wendy."

"We found the notes. There was one at the schoolhouse in the desk and several in your stove at the cottage. You must have meant to burn them. The teacher there discovered that they were from one of the parents, Mr. Gaskell. How long have you been getting them?" Terrell hoped that laying out what they knew would help Miss Scott struggle less with what she felt she could tell him and what she might still want to keep hidden.

"I was so ashamed and angry. It was a torment. He made my life a nightmare. I'd been so happy. I was nearly sick with the fear I felt every moment. I was desperate to get away, but you can't just walk out on the children. The last one was the last straw. He said next time he would finish what he started. He would, too. I knew it. He . . . he tried . . . before, you see. He was in my house. He tried . . . he tried . . . I had a knife." She put her handkerchief to her eyes and took a long breath.

Terrell made a note. So, Gaskell had taken it further, was threatening to "finish what he'd started." It was no wonder

Miss Scott had been so desperate to leave. Had Gaskell been in the house that night? Was he the one who went on the rampage in it? He struggled to imagine what sort of time frame would have him tossing the house, hitting Miss Scott, and then getting himself killed miles away. He was about to ask.

"It was clever of Wendy to figure it out." She smiled briefly. "I didn't want to tell her. I thought he might have only been after me, you see, and he might just leave her alone. No need to frighten her."

"Oh, it wasn't Miss Keeling who found the note. It was Miss Winslow. She's the inspector's wife. She was holding the fort till Miss Keeling was found. You likely don't remember her, but Miss Winslow is the one that found you in the cottage and brought you to the hospital."

"What do you mean, till Miss Keeling is found? Where is she?"

"She's just been found, Miss Scott. You mentioned before that you came home and found her gone. It upset you." How had she forgotten the very thing that had made her so angry? He wondered now how reliable anything she said might be.

"Oh. You're right." Rose Scott spoke slowly, furrowing her brow as if trying to remember something. "Yes. She wasn't there. She'd taken everything. I was confused, you see. Angry. I think I tried to phone someone, but the phone wouldn't work. Yes, I remember that. I had to phone about the car, but it wouldn't work." She turned to look at him. "Why would she pull the phone out like that? It made me so angry, I can't tell you!"

Terrell could see she was beginning to drift. He thought about what question he should ask to refocus but not alarm her. The question about Gaskell was still uppermost in his mind, and to this was added the sudden revelation that the phone hadn't worked.

"So, you found the phone wouldn't work. What did you do then?"

Tears welled in her eyes. "Yes. Can you imagine? None of it would have happened if only the phone had worked." But then she shook her head. "No, of course. That's not true. It had already happened, hadn't it? When I found her gone, for a minute I thought it must have been him, you see. That he had found her, taken her."

"You were worried he might try to attack Miss Keeling?"

"Of course! He tried with me. He would have succeeded. I . . . I thought, you know, that I was going to die that day. That he would finish me off. I tried to ignore how much he frightened me. I thought when I came back in the fall that it would be all right, but I woke up sick with fear every single day. I felt I would go mad."

Time for a more neutral question. Perhaps she could tell him more about the car. "Miss Scott, did you drive in your car here to Nelson to the train station to make arrangements?"

"Yes, of course I did. How else was I to get here? And I made the arrangements, and I went to the Metro to have dinner, then I drove home, and found she'd left. Yes, that was it. I was very upset. I was cold and tired and wet from the snow."

"But you said your phone didn't work," he pursued. "You wanted to phone someone about your car?" And why was she tired and wet from the snow? The answer was obvious to him. She had abandoned her car in the orchard near her home, but she wasn't saying that. "Had you had an accident? Is that why you were phoning about the car?"

"Yes, that's right. The car stopped working and I went off the road. I had to walk. So when I came and found she'd gone . . . oh, God, what have I done?" She had seized a tissue and had begun to cry.

"Miss Scott, had you hit something with the car?" Terrell was afraid he was losing her.

She looked genuinely confused and stared down at her hands. "Yes, I must have, when the car went off the road, I must have." She leaned back again and closed her eyes.

It was now or never. "Miss Scott, was it Gaskell who came into the house that Friday night and hit you?"

The exhausted woman did not respond immediately. Then she slowly turned to look at Terrell. Her expression was one of complete bewilderment. "Gaskell? No. No. Not in the house. Not again. How can you say such a thing? How could he have?" She closed her eyes again for a moment. "Not then. Before. Oh, I was so angry. I . . . I think I broke something."

That's when the thing that had been at the back of Terrell's mind, that had lodged there the last time he interviewed her, leaped to the front.

In as comforting a tone as he could manage, he said, "Miss Scott, did you get angry and knock everything around in the house? Is that what happened?"

But Miss Scott had closed her eyes and turned her face away from him.

"I think that's about all you'll get. She's worn herself out," Dr. Edison said quietly. She'd been standing just near the door in case her patient relapsed and had come in to check when she heard the voices stop. "Was it any use?"

"Yes, I think so." Terrell got up and went to stand in the hall with the doctor. "It's like putting a jigsaw puzzle together. I'm not sure I paid enough attention to what she said before, but now when I assemble all the pieces, a picture is beginning to emerge, only I'm not fully sure precisely what it's a picture of. I'm not even completely sure that I can believe what she is saying. I don't mean she's lying deliberately. I just think she's lost her grip a bit and isn't sure what's real."

"I expect there may well be an element of that," Dr. Edison said. "She's quite convinced she's on the mend and will leave in the next day or so, but she is far from well. I believe if we can get her physically better, she will still need a long convalescence to recover her emotional health."

She's not saying "in an institution," Terrell thought, but he knew that's what she meant. Still struggling over what he could use to construct a reliable picture of the events on the night of December 5, he made his way down the hill and back to the station to await news.

LANE HAD IN her mind only one thing: to keep this man talking. He was in a decidedly cranky mood after being knocked about and now stood with his hair dishevelled and the gun trained on Lane.

"Who the hell are you? Where's the other one? I had to drag myself through the snow trying to find which direction

394

she went. I'm not getting paid enough for this."

He knew Wendy Keeling had come here. Lane was standing against her desk with her hands up. If only she could delay him long enough to be sure the children were completely safe. If he was here to shoot Miss Keeling, and if he was a professional, he wouldn't want to pile up more bodies than necessary. Her mind turned continually over the space she was standing in, wondering if there was anything she could use as a weapon.

"I'm not sure I know what you mean. There's no one here but me. I'm the schoolteacher here, Lane Winslow. Who are you? Who were you expecting to find?"

He looked at her impatiently. "I don't need any questions. What have you done with her? You tell me or I'll put a bullet in you." He walked toward her, training the gun at her head, his other hand out, ready to take her arm.

God, she thought, he's a trained killer and he's got a one-track mind. As he came nearer, she saw the pin on his coat. A tiny gold maple leaf. "Did you fight with the Third Canadian?" She had put her hands down and pointed at his pin.

In the second it took him to frown and look down at his lapel, she seized the bottle of ink she'd prepared for Samuel and threw its contents in his eyes. She followed it up by throwing the bottle hard at his face. It was a small bottle and did almost no damage, but the man was desperately wiping his eyes. Lane glanced behind her on the desk and found the much heavier bottle of ink the teachers used. She picked it up and swung it hard against the side of his head.

BALES AND THE police arrived at the point where the assassin's car blocked the road at the same time.

Darling shook his head at Bales and his rifle and then reconsidered.

"Are you any good with that?"

"Yes, sir."

"Good. You can cover us from back here. Do NOT come any closer, is that clear?"

Bales nodded, trying to ascertain if he was disappointed or relieved. He watched Darling and Ames advance on the school, and moved in behind them, but keeping a distance. The school looked cold and silent. Not even any smoke from the chimney. Had Miss Winslow not lit the fire that morning? He scanned the woods and thought about the children sneaking away through the snow in the trees adjacent to the building and the road. Darling and Ames took positions in the trees closest to the building. He looked back toward the school abruptly at the sound of Darling's raised voice.

"Come out with your hands up. This is the police and we are armed!"

He heard the loud, clear response in Miss Winslow's voice as the door of the schoolhouse opened.

"Don't shoot." A pause. "Please."

Darling and Ames darted forward and surged up the steps. Darling wanted desperately to take Lane, apparently in one piece, with no evident bullet holes, into his arms, but she shook her head, handed him a revolver, and motioned inside of the schoolhouse. An angry oath-laden groaning could be heard coming from inside.

As the police burst into the building, Lane saw Bales hovering with his rifle near the assassin's car. She hurried down the stairs toward him.

"How are the children?" she asked anxiously. "Did they all arrive in one piece?"

"That they did," he said, lowering his rifle and leaning it against the car. "Those two older children had the situation well in hand. Lucy is back there now, feeding them hot drinks and chocolate bars, compliments of the house."

"Gabriella and Philip," Lane said, smiling, relieved. Out of danger now herself, she could feel a kind of exhaustion stealing over her. "I'm very proud of them, of all of them. Everyone did exactly as they were told, with a minimum of fuss. Do you suppose Lucy thought to call their parents to come pick them up?" She leaned against the car and looked back toward the school. She wondered how Miss Keeling was getting on. "Nice car. The gangland assassin business must be lucrative."

Bales smiled. "You don't see a late-model Lincoln like this around here that often. Though there was a very nice black Packard that stopped for gas, yesterday, was it? That was unusual too."

Lane turned to him. "Black? Who was driving it?" Angela had talked about nearly being knocked over by a black car in a big hurry on the road down from the Anscomb house.

"A very good-looking woman. She snapped at me like I was the help."

"Listen," Lane said, turning to him, "that might be important. Could you remember everything you can about her? I suspect the police will want to know."

The noise of movement on the porch made them both look toward the schoolhouse. Ames was going carefully down the stairs leading the handcuffed assailant, and Darling was close behind.

"Good grief! What did you do to him?" asked Bales. The would-be assassin had a largely blue face, and in addition a sizeable cut on his forehead was bleeding heavily. His camel coat was covered in blue splatters and blood stains.

"It turns out," said Lane, "that the pen really is mightier than the sword."

"ARE YOU SURE you're up to this?" Darling asked, leaning over to look at Lane, who was sitting in the driver's seat of her own car. He longed to be driving back with her, holding her inky hand, but, well, he wasn't sure why, he felt she wouldn't want to be mollycoddled.

"Certainly. Don't be silly. When we're done, I can come back here and tidy up the classroom. The children will be anxious to get their Christmas cards and take their essays home to their parents."

Ames had stowed the handcuffed assistant kidnapper in the back of the police car, where Bales now stood guard over him with a ferocious expression and his rifle at the ready. He came up behind Darling and looked at Lane, his face wreathed in smiles. "You were very brave, if I may say so, Miss Winslow!"

Darling turned back to the police car, muttering, "Here we go."

Lane ignored him. "The children were the brave ones, Sergeant. You should have seen them! They followed my instructions exactly, and Philip and Gabriella just naturally took over, buttoning up the younger children and getting them out. I couldn't be more proud of them. I'm a little less sure how I can reassure parents that their children are safe at school, with gun-wielding assassins pouring in all the time."

Ames was about to comment, but Lane had sat up and was leaning forward looking at the schoolhouse, now peaceful in the waning afternoon. "One thing is certain, a telephone must be installed there over the winter holidays. I can't imagine how no one has thought of it before. I shall get hold of the telephone company first thing. I think a representation from the police about the importance of a phone for the safety of the children would help."

LANE SAT IN Darling's office with him and Ames. Terrell had been invited to join in while Lane was being taken through her story. Darling and Ames would be interviewing their prisoner, who was in a cell and being seen to by a doctor, directly after they were finished with Lane. She filled them in on the sudden appearance of the gunman, how she'd sent the children out, and how she'd managed to subdue him.

"He was on the floor after the ink bottle and looking like he was about to stagger back onto his feet, and then you two, with voices like angels from heaven, 'Come out, we're armed.' I can't tell you how relieved I was, because I wasn't at all sure what to do next. I hadn't any rope to tie him up and I really didn't relish coshing him with the butt of the revolver!"

Ames wrote busily.

"Very quick thinking, ma'am. Not many would have reacted that way," said Terrell.

"Self-preservation is a powerful force!" Lane protested, smiling.

Darling gave a slight shake of the head, signalling perhaps a note of exasperation at Lane's activities. He turned to Terrell. He didn't particularly want to start in on their prisoner, with whom he was inordinately angry, too soon. "You went to see Miss Scott, I understand. Any joy? Now that we've found Miss Keeling, maybe there is some way this all fits together."

Terrell recounted what she'd told him. "If we put it all together, her bits and pieces from the last couple of interviews plus what she told me today, I think I can construct a bare sequence of events. She drives to the town to book her train trip, has dinner at the Metro, drives back, somehow runs her car off the road and down the embankment, and has to walk the rest of the way home. She's cold and in a state about the accident and arrives home to find the cottage dark and cold, and Miss Keeling nowhere to be found. I'm speculating a bit now, but she's upset about Miss Keeling's absence and about her car. She tries to make a phone call but finds the phone is dead. She doesn't know what time it is, only that it is dark and has been since she was having dinner at the Metro. Anything after that she couldn't say, but I am beginning to suspect she might have inflicted most of the damage on the cottage herself. But at the rate she's going, I'm not sure we'll ever know the full truth of what happened there. She says she'll be getting out soon because she's improving so much, but Dr. Edison told me that is definitely not the case, so she's a bit deluded about that as well."

"But I still don't understand about the car," Ames put in. "According to the farmer, none of his trees was hit, and according to Miss Van Eyck, that car was leaking radiator water and had a faulty fan belt for probably quite a number of miles. How did the car get into that state?"

"Hmm," Terrell said. "She said she thought she must have hit one of the trees. She doesn't really remember."

"Doesn't that suggest, if she didn't hit a tree, that she hit something long before that, that damaged the radiator and fan belt?" asked Lane. "And I also wonder if, either with whatever she hit or the sliding into the ditch, she got a head injury that might have kicked off her collapse in the cottage. That doesn't account for someone going through the cottage and knocking everything about unless it was Miss Scott herself, as Constable Terrell is suggesting." She turned to Darling and said, "The mattresses."

"Now, hang on a minute," said Ames. "The bartender at the Legion said he'd kicked Gaskell out and Gaskell said he'd get treated better at the Metro. I know we aren't talking about him, but she had dinner at the Metro. Did they meet up there? Is it a coincidence? Or did he forget that he'd loaned his car to Mackenzie, just like Mackenzie said, and go looking for it? Maybe she saw him then."

Darling looked at him speculatively. "Out of the mouths of babes?" he asked no one in particular. "However, we have charged Mackenzie with the hit and run."

Terrell mused. "And it seems strange that she would have

spoken with Gaskell under any circumstances. She was absolutely terrified of him. She said he'd made an attempt to attack her before," he pointed out. "I wondered, when she told me he'd been in the house, if it was he who had come in that night and knocked the place around, but she looked very puzzled and said it certainly wasn't. 'It couldn't have been,' she said. She seemed very clear about that."

Lane nodded. "You feel certain about Mackenzie? I've seen people with battle fatigue, some people call it shell shock still as they did in the Great War, who block out memories of their experiences in battle. They don't do it on purpose, or course. Perhaps it is some defence mechanism of the body. What if it was that Miss Scott somehow saw Gaskell that night, and followed him, and hit him accidentally, or on purpose, and that's what she just can't get to in her memory?"

CHAPTER THIRTY-ONE

"**WE WERE EXPECTING YOUR WIFE** to be here," Bamfield said. They had settled into the spacious sitting room and were seated on sofas and easy chairs for the war-room meeting. Bamfield was a party executive and was not amused to be short a person. He'd put a pile of papers on the coffee table, and now anticipated the discomfort of leaning forward out of the deep sofa to try to reach them when he needed them. It was undignified. Why hadn't he said they should use the dining room table?

Devlin's campaign manager, Ed Barber, looked in anxious appeal at Devlin.

"She's visiting her mother. She was due back last night. Let's just get started. I can tell her anything we discuss," Devlin said. He was covering his anxiety well, he thought. He had no idea where she was, only that she'd said she'd be back in a few days. She'd taken her car. He'd found her behaviour of late stranger and stranger and had begun to have a vague fear that it might somehow affect his campaign. The call with that inspector from Nelson had rattled him badly.

"We're not here to tell you things, Devlin. We're here to make sure we know everything there is to know about you, so we have no cock-ups during the election. It's a few days away."

"I assure you, there is not a single skeleton in any Devlin closet. You can look till you're blue in the face. In fact, why are we having this meeting? Does every prospective politician have to submit to this sort of nonsense?" Devlin was not as nonchalant as he sounded or looked. His wife's behaviour and the revelation of a grown daughter somewhere were both factors he had not expected, and had no control over.

"Obviously we vetted you," Bamfield said. "It's just that we've found something that might be a matter of concern. And I must say, the fact that you have been mum on the subject is, yes, a concern. What else are you not telling us, I wonder."

Devlin could feel his face redden. Had that bloody Irving said anything to anyone about the girl? "I have absolutely no idea what you're talking about," he said angrily. He got up and went to the decanter on the sideboard and poured himself another scotch. He did not offer it to anyone else.

"Your wife, Devlin."

Amazed, Devlin turned to look at Bamfield. "My wife? What's she got to do with the price of tea in China?" Not the illegitimate daughter?

"Her family. Not *comme il faut*, I think you'll agree. We're going to have to come up with a strategy, that's all. Agree on a story, to put it more crudely."

Barber looked at Devlin's face, and his heart sank. It was abundantly clear that the poor sap had absolutely no idea what Bamfield was getting at. And neither had he, which made it worse. For the first time he began to wonder if he'd hitched his wagon to the wrong star.

Bamfield must have seen the same thing. "For God's sake, sit down, man. You can't be all that ignorant! No need to panic. We just have to come up with a plan." But he was thinking how damaging it would be to have to jettison this candidate. Good-looking, successful, from a sterling business empire, money poured into him already—it would be a bloody shame, that's all.

Devlin was back on the sofa, watching Bamfield, waiting to hear what was coming, his mind going desperately over every meeting he'd ever had with a member of Serena's family. Every dinner, every cocktail party, every Christmas. Of course, he knew some members of her family had their fingers in dubious pies, but had he ever directly heard anything? Had he ever directly benefited? Her father was wealthy and ran a completely respectable furniture-manufacturing company, that much was true. Her mother was a notable society hostess. His own father would have approved of her in every way. They could not possibly imagine he and Serena were directly tainted? A tiny misgiving lurked in the back of his mind. He'd met her at a not particularly respectable club. Would they make something of that?

"They have a good front, the Lees, and if there was only that, we'd be sitting pretty. Unfortunately, there's her

405

brother and, worse, her uncle and cousins. I dug it up in no time, so you can bet the other side are probably already on to it."

"I don't understand. Her brother is a lawyer. He has a very successful firm." Devlin pushed his hair back fretfully.

"He does indeed. The most lucrative part of his practice is defending gangsters," Bamfield said, waving his empty glass at Barber, who hopped up to fetch the decanter of scotch.

"But that's not a crime, surely? An attorney is going to have unsavoury clients. It's part of the deal."

"Yes, it's all very well, but unfortunately some of them are his, and her, relations. In fact, it's worse than that. We suspect that her father is in it up to the gills. His company is a front for a sizeable enterprise—gambling, prostitution, you name it. And at least one probable hit man."

Devlin felt pinned to his seat. How had he not known the extent of her father's "businesses"? Had he been so swept up in her beauty and society connections and busy with work that he hadn't seen? Well, yes, obviously. Or had he known in his heart and just ignored it? He stood up convulsively and began to pace.

"If what you say is true, I can't see how we can possibly cook up a 'story' to cover it. I can't believe what you say is true. Serena must not even know the extent of it, or she would have told me. She would never have let me go this far into a campaign without telling me." But uppermost in his thoughts was this: he'd been a complete fool over her.

The noise of the front door opening caused Devlin to jump. He opened the sitting room door and ducked into the foyer. His wife was there, pulling off her gloves. He had to tell her; she couldn't be ambushed like this.

"You can rest easy about your bastard daughter," she said. Too late he realized he'd left the door open. "I've taken care of her; Oh, don't look at me like that. It's just a couple of days, till after the election."

THE NURSE KNOCKED and then put her head around the door. "You have a visitor, Miss Scott." She was young and cheerful and missed the look of weariness that crossed her patient's face as she lay back and closed her eyes.

"Who is it? If it's that policeman, I don't think I want to see him."

"Rose? It's Wendy." Wendy Keeling, wearing a long, dark blue winter coat and a hat to match, stood by the bed for a moment and then sat on the chair. She took off her gloves and reached for Miss Scott's hand.

"Wendy!" Miss Scott sat up and took both her colleague's hands in hers. "Where did you go? I couldn't find you. I thought he—" She fell back onto the pillows again, tears springing into her eyes. "It's all been so dreadful! A kind of nightmare! When I found you gone, I—"

"Shh, shh. It's all right. You see? We're both in one piece."

"But the children, what happened to the children? I've been in here, and I didn't know where you were."

"It's fine. A very nice woman, a Miss Winslow from King's Cove, has been teaching them. They are all perfectly happy. I will go back after the Christmas holiday. Everything will be as it was. The main thing is for you to get better. Has your fiancé been to see you?" At this Wendy

407

glanced around, as if he might be hiding somewhere.

Miss Scott took her hand and shook her head ruefully. "There is no fiancé. I made him up." She put up her hand to forestall the question she saw forming on Wendy Keeling's lips. "I had to. I knew they wouldn't let me go early unless it was something like marriage, and I had to leave. I had to. I couldn't take it anymore." She brought her sheet up to her eyes to staunch the tears. Wendy pulled open the drawer in the white enamelled side table and found a box of tissues and handed her one.

"The police told me about the horrible notes you were getting. Rose, why didn't you tell me? I had no idea. We could have told the police. He could have been stopped."

Shaking her head, Miss Scott said, "He came into the house last July. I found him there, he nearly—" More tears. Then she turned on Miss Keeling. "Where did you go? How could you have left me to deal with him on my own?"

This outburst was loud enough to cause the nurse to come in and ask if everything was all right, and to remind the visitor that the patient should not be overexcited as it was bad for her heart.

Wendy sat back and wondered what she could possibly say. It would do Rose no good to learn she herself had been kidnapped and would possibly have been killed if she'd not escaped. She leaned forward, laying a comforting hand on the bedclothes. "I am sorry, Rose. I should have told you. I was going to go see my mother. I didn't quite get there, but I will go now, over the holiday."

"Your mother? But you told me your mother was dead." Miss Scott seemed to forget her own troubles for a moment.

"I thought she was, and then I got a note from my father to say she was alive and living on the coast." She had. From the man she had always thought of as her father, Zeke Irving. He had left it with the police in Nelson, because he knew, he said, that she wouldn't want to see him. Not after everything. But he was pleased to see she'd made something of herself and was sorry they couldn't have spent more time together when he saw her last. Apparently the police had located her mother, and he was sure they would tell her where she was. By now, he said, she probably knew he wasn't her real father. He'd tried to phone her to tell her to watch out for Devlin and his wife but hadn't got through. He hoped she'd understand that he had tried his best.

She'd wondered, when Inspector Darling had handed her the envelope from Irving, what she felt now that she knew who her real father was, and she was relieved to find it had not much shaken her view of Zeke Irving or herself. She had spent ten years on her own, constructing a life for herself. But she could not hide from herself that she wanted to see her mother, to ask her why she'd left. She pushed Harry Devlin far away in her mind. Maybe one day. She took a breath and turned back to her friend.

"I'm going to my mother too, as soon as I'm better," Rose Scott said listlessly, turning to look toward the window, where the afternoon was already darkening for another long winter night. "In Manitoba. She's alone on the farm. I doubt I will teach again." She turned back and looked at Wendy. "I'll never marry either. I lost the man I loved. He went missing, you see, in Holland. A friend from my unit wired me last spring to say he was dead. It was at about

409

that time he started up, Gaskell, you know, with his notes and insinuations. I think he'd been in the house before, gone through my drawers, my mail even. He started saying I was an 'army whore.' He must have seen my letters. But it doesn't matter now. He's dead. I killed him."

THE RESTAURANT WAS quiet, with only one older couple sitting at a table near the back.

"That'll be us one day, eating dinner at five o'clock," Darling said, nodding toward the couple. "Hello, Signor Lorenzo, it is good to see you. Do you mind having us descend on you this early?" Darling took off his hat and shook hands with the restaurant owner with something approaching affection. He thought of Lorenzo's restaurant as the place where he had truly begun to be aware that he was falling in love with Lane.

"Inspector, Signora! You can come here any time, any time." He seized Lane's hand and kissed it. "You are more beautiful than even before!"

Lane, embarrassed by the Continental treatment of her hand, and his compliments, said, "My husband says one day we will be old and wanting to eat early like those people, but I was about to tell him that we already are! Something smells wonderful."

She sat in the chair Lorenzo pulled out and brushed a fall of hair away from her eyes. Lorenzo, her coat over his arm, said, "The inspector, he will get old soon with that terrible police job, but you will never get old, Signora."

"That's you told," Lane said, when Lorenzo had disappeared to procure the veal piccata that was today's special. "But you needn't upset yourself. I will still love you when you are old."

"You don't know that. I could become extremely cranky when I get old. You will want to push me over for some perennially cheerful specimen, like Ames."

"I don't know about that. Could your crankiness get any worse than it is already? I haven't pushed you over yet. Now, has anyone been able to get the ink off that poor man's face?"

"Poor man, my umbrella! He's a hired thug. No, it's worse than that; he's not hired. He's a relation of Serena Devlin, the wife of the would-be politician. He owed her a favour, apparently. He's singing like a canary, as I believe our American brethren say. He's a bit cross because he was apparently given the fairly easy job of keeping an eye on Miss Keeling until such time as Serena gave new instructions. However, he went off into town for more cigarettes and whisky, and returned to find her gone. He followed her footsteps in the snow for a fair bit to see which direction she was going, at great inconvenience to himself and his expensive Italian shoes, and realized from his map she was headed toward the school. It was very obliging of the local community to put a jaunty sign at the turnoff saying, "Balfour School." It occurred to him she might seek refuge there. And, by the way, he evinced a grudging respect for your spirited defence. The Vancouver Police are picking up Mrs. Devlin. I don't fancy her husband's chances now. This was all to cover up the fact that he had an illegitimate daughter, or at least delay the news getting out. The by-election is on Friday. She just wanted to get

Miss Keeling out of the way so no one in the opposition or the press dug her up. She would certainly have been better off leaving well enough alone. How are your ribs?"

Lane reached around to feel where she'd been grazed by a bullet on her honeymoon and winced with a quick intake of breath. "It would perhaps have been better if I hadn't fallen over the desk trying to retrieve the gun, but nothing a good glass of wine won't put right." She was sure Lorenzo would have just the thing, in his secret stash.

CHAPTER THIRTY-TWO

THE SCHOOLROOM WAS WARM, AND Lane was feeling a satisfaction that she thought must be what mothers feel when their children are home safe, fed, and tucked up listening to a story. Darling had told her about Samuel's mother, but everyone had agreed that there was nothing to be gained by telling him about it before Christmas, something Lane found herself agreeing with, though she was conscious of an underlying sadness about what was still to come for him. And now, here it was the last day before the Christmas holiday. Eleanor had supplied a lovely tin of chocolate and lemon cookies, and Lane had invited the students to move their desks into a circle so that they could eat cookies and share stories.

"Now then, who wants to start?" she asked.

"You do, Miss Winslow," said Rafe. "What happened after we left?"

Lane smiled. "I was going to suggest the same thing! I'm dying to know all about your adventures in your brilliant escape through the woods!"

"The snow came all the way up to my chest," said Amy, the smallest of the children, exaggerating slightly. "But I wasn't scared!"

"Goodness! You weren't?" asked Lane. "I'm very sure I would have been."

"Were you scared?" asked Samuel in a very soft voice.

It was so unusual for Samuel to speak up that she knew he must really want to know, and that it was critical she be as truthful as possible.

"I was very afraid. You know, it's an interesting thing about fear. It seems like it is a very unpleasant feeling, and nobody wants to feel fear. But it is a perfectly natural thing when someone is in a dangerous situation, and it has a very important job to do. When you are in danger, you know it is important to run away, and fear can sharpen your senses so that you can get away faster. But if you can't get away, those sharper senses can also make you do things to try to keep yourself safe that you might never usually think of."

"Like throwing ink at the guy's face!" said Rolf excitedly. "Mr. Bales told us about that!"

"Yes, exactly like that. I think because I was alert and so aware of the danger, I thought about the ink. I don't usually throw ink at people!"

The children laughed.

"Here's the important thing, since it seems to be my turn after all. You were absolutely wonderful. You did everything just right, and you got to the store safely and in a big hurry, because it felt like the police were here in no time. I could not be more proud of you. And when we have all finished our stories, I think I have very good news indeed for you."

A chorus of "What?" and "Tell us now!" erupted.

"All right. I'll tell you now. After the Christmas break, Miss Keeling will be back!"

Another chorus, this time of questions and delighted exclamations. And just as suddenly as it started, it stopped, and all the children looked at Lane.

Finally Gabriella spoke for all of them. "But what will you do, Miss Winslow? We like having you as our teacher."

"You are very kind to say so. I'm not a real teacher like Miss Keeling. She will prepare you properly to go on to the high school."

"Can you come back and do experiments with us? Those were fun," said Philip.

"Or read to us?" suggested Amy.

Lane smiled. "Are you forgetting that you are the ones who thought of the experiment with the temperature? And as to reading, you should read to each other. That's how good you are! Anyway, I live right nearby, so we are bound to see each other. Now, let's get on with our stories. We have to finish this tin of biscuits and collect all our cards before your parents come for you at noon."

MISS KEELING, WHO would rather be anywhere else, and in any case was catching the afternoon train to the coast, stood at the desk of the police station. "May I speak to the inspector? I'm sorry, I can't remember his name."

O'Brien was on his feet. She was very pretty. "Inspector Darling, miss. I'm afraid he's in a meeting. Is there something I can do?"

She shifted her handbag onto her other arm and put the tips of her gloved fingers on the counter. "I believe it is very urgent and I should speak with him. I am leaving in an hour. Please, can you interrupt him?"

Sighing, the desk sergeant took up the phone. Darling was in the interview room with the very man who had apparently been assigned to kidnap and possibly eliminate this young woman. And Darling was in a bad mood. He'd already had a nasty conversation with both the police in Vancouver and a provincial official who had telephoned to tell him to lay off the case, and did he know how important Harry Devlin was? They couldn't, he'd been told, have some two-bit, small-town policeman messing things up. Consequently, he'd been in a blacker mood than usual as he'd proceeded to the interview room. O'Brien had been advised not to interrupt him, not if the prime minister himself should walk in and demand an audience.

He put down the phone and invited Miss Keeling to take a seat, and then called Terrell over. "Pop down and get the inspector, would you? This young lady says it is urgent."

Terrell glanced over at the bench along the wall just beside the door and raised his eyebrows at O'Brien. "Sir?"

"You heard me. The inspector. Urgent." O'Brien watched Terrell go down the stairs with almost no qualms. After all, what were underlings for? He returned to his seat, smiled at Miss Keeling, and opened a file that he should have begun work on first thing in the morning.

To Miss Keeling's surprise, Darling appeared quite quickly. He opened the gate and showed her upstairs to his office. The only sign of impatience he showed was a tense tenting of his hands under his chin.

"How can I help?"

"I'm sorry to do this. I understood from the man at the desk that you are very busy. I'm on my way to Vancouver but I stopped by to see Miss Scott, and she said something that surprised me very much. So much that I don't know what to make of it. She told me that she had killed the father of one of my students, Samuel Gaskell. Is he dead?"

Darling frowned and bit his lip. "Yes, of course, you were not to know. He is. Are you quite sure that is what she said?" Lane's completely unlikely speculation moved to centre stage in his mind.

"Yes. I told her I had learned that he'd been sending her nasty notes, and she told me that he'd been in the house with the intention of hurting her before . . . I'm not sure before what, but then she said, 'It doesn't matter now. He's dead. I killed him.' And then she just sort of lay back and closed her eyes and wouldn't say any more. I went in search of the nurse because I was worried something was wrong, but she told me Miss Scott was probably exhausted and needed rest. I came straight here." Miss Keeling glanced at her watch. "I feel terrible for her if he'd been persecuting her like that. I had no idea. It's apparently the reason she wanted to leave. She told me she lied about getting married because she was so afraid the education people wouldn't let her leave for anything less. I could have told her I was allowed to leave my last job with no difficulty."

"Thank you, Miss Keeling. You've been very helpful. You are anxious to catch your train. Is there a place we can reach you if something arises out of any of this?"

"I'm going to see my mother at that fishing lodge you told me about, the Aspen Gold. If it's immediately urgent I could be reached there. I'll probably treat myself to a couple of days. I'm sure if the Devlins took holidays there it is bound to be the height of luxury. I think it will take that to wash the stench and memory of that horrible basement out of my mind. But I am coming back after Christmas to take up my job at the Balfour school." She stood up and pulled on her gloves.

"I'm sure the children will be delighted," Darling said, rising and offering his hand. "My wife says you are a great favourite with them."

"Of course, it is your wife that has been holding the fort. Please, thank her for me." She made her way to the door and then turned. "I was about to ask what will become of Miss Scott, but of course I realize you can say nothing."

Darling smiled slightly and nodded. "Will you seek out Harry Devlin while you are on the coast?"

She shook her head, more in puzzlement than negation. "I don't know. I think of Ezekiel Irving as my father. He wasn't much good at it, but he has been more of a father to me than Devlin ever was. Though it's possible Devlin didn't know about me. I'm not sure. If I'm honest, I'm not even sure about seeing my mother. I haven't seen her since I was eight, and I've been on my own since I was sixteen and am quite happy as I am."

Darling watched her go down the stairs and thought how very Lane-like she was. Self-contained, practical, clear, somehow, about who she was.

Now, Miss Scott. He still had Mackenzie, protesting

wildly that he was innocent, in one of the cells. Maybe he was telling the truth about that, at least. "Terrell!" he bellowed when he hit the bottom of the stairs. After all, he had the magic touch with the woman.

IT WAS AN irony, Lane thought, that on Christmas Eve there should be scarcely a drop of snow to be seen except on the tops of the mountains across the lake. It had begun raining two days before, and now, though thankfully it had stopped, King's Cove was enveloped in a misty damp atmosphere more akin to late October than late December. Everyone had arrived on foot and flashlights, umbrellas, and boots littered the area around the front door. Darling had occupied himself collecting people's coats and stacking them on the bed. Now the guests were gathered variously in the sitting room, where the Franklin stove burned merrily and a small Christmas tree with coloured lights shimmered in the corner, or in the kitchen, where Lane had laid out plates of little salmon sandwiches. Eleanor was attending to the alignment of pieces of her Christmas cake on a crystal serving plate that she'd fished out of one of the boxes of Lady Armstrong's things in the attic the day before. The noise of people talking, seemingly all at once, made a hubbub that was unfamiliar to this quiet house.

"I brought these." Lane turned from the sandwiches and saw Alice Mather in the doorway to the kitchen with a round tin and a defiant expression, as if she expected to have her offering rejected.

"Oh, Alice, how lovely!" She'd been about to say, "Are

these the famous sugar cookies?" but then worried that Alice would think she'd been the subject of gossip. Instead, she opened the tin and said, "Shortbread! Splendid! It's just what we need. My biscuits are ghastly, even with Eleanor's guidance. Find Frederick and he'll supply you with a glass of sherry."

"Adroitly done," said Eleanor, winking. "Your short-bread is perfect, by the way. Shall we get these out to the sitting room?"

"THERE'S A FOR SALE sign on the bloody house again," Reg Mather was saying to Kenny. "It's really too bad. The owner disrupts everyone for ages with racket and commotion and then buggers off. Begging your pardon," he added, raising his glass in the direction of Gladys Hughes, who was glaring at him, about to suggest he mind his language.

"He never changes," she grumbled to Mabel. "Shocking language in front of the children!"

"We're sitting ducks out here, really," Gwen was saying to Angela, who was only partially attending, as she had one eye on the children who had gathered in a suspiciously conspiratorial huddle in the corner by the bookshelf. "Any criminal could come along and set up shop on the land around here. We're miles from anywhere."

Angela turned away from the children. "But I still don't understand why it would be a good idea. It's not convenient to anywhere if they are hiding stolen property or drugs."

"But that's the point, isn't it? They could grow that drug, whatever it's called, that they put in reefers, I think

420

they're called. Who would see? Then we'd have those little airplanes that land on the water coming and going all day, or motorboats cluttering up our beautiful cove."

"It's a good thing we have a resident police inspector, then. Boys, what are you up to?" Angela could not subscribe to the idea that their Eden could ever succumb to the dystopia envisioned by Gwen.

"Weren't you nearly run down by a car?" Mabel, who had joined them, asked. "I don't know how you can be so sanguine about it. Gwen's right. We have to be on our toes."

"Oh, yes. I suppose I was. Well, they've gone now. So strange to think an actual gangland criminal was right in our midst! And what they did to poor Miss Keeling! She showed real enterprise, I must say. I'm delighted she'll be back, and so are the boys."

Darling, who'd been talking with Kenny and David about the ins and outs of the local creeks and how to manage them, overheard Angela and sighed. How did everyone get all the details so quickly and accurately? It certainly wasn't from Lane. They just seemed to winkle out information from the air. If he was going to live among these people, he would have to be even more constrained than was his wont. However, Angela had been right to be concerned about what was going on in that house, and about the blood by the coal chute. In fact, he realized, she'd been the means of Miss Keeling's escape when she opened the coal-chute door. He nodded at Kenny and David and went across the room to tell her so.

"Good of you to come along," Gladys said to the vicar, who was standing by the Christmas tree, accepting a top-up from Lane. "You'll just have to plow all the way back here in the morning for the Christmas service."

"I like to spend time with my parishioners, and frankly, my little flock at King's Cove is much the most exciting, with your resident detective Miss Winslow, or ought I to say Mrs. Darling, and the inspector established here now, and murderers and would-be murderers turning up all the time. Better than a fictional English village!"

"Isn't every little community full of secrets?"

The vicar smiled and held up his glass. He'd clearly had several, as it was only once a year. "Not like this one!"

At this moment the three boys came out of their huddle and approached Lane, who was persuading a grumpy Robin Harris to take another sandwich. Rafe, the youngest, had his hands behind his back. Philip pushed him forward. Rolf had his hand over his mouth to suppress his giggles.

"Miss Winslow, we have something for you!"

Lane turned and put the sandwiches down. "Goodness. Have you?"

Rafe produced what looked at first glance like a pile of paper and held it up, and then, like magicians, the boys unrolled a long chain of cut-out dolls, each one coloured differently.

"It's a Christmas decoration for you to put on your mantelpiece!" declared Rolf. "We made it. Even Mommy didn't know we were doing it!"

"It's to thank you," said Philip, suddenly shy. "You were a really good teacher."

"The last one has a blue face!" cried Rafe happily. "You know why!"

Angela caught Dave's eye from across the room, fondness and pride struggling for prominence on her face.

Lane was very nearly speechless. "Oh, it's absolutely beautiful!" she finally managed. "Darling, look at this! It will fit perfectly on our mantel."

CHAPTER THIRTY-THREE

"YOU'D BETTER COME IN," DENISE Irving said, stepping back. Wendy Keeling hesitated, put off slightly by her mother's coolness. She stepped in and looked around the cabin. It gave an impression of airiness that was attractive. Perhaps it was the large front window and the simple furnishings.

"What do I call you?" Wendy asked.

"A bit late for 'Mother.' My fault, I suppose. 'Denise' will do. Let me take your coat. I've just made myself some tea."

Leaning with her elbows on the table, Wendy looked out onto the snowy landscape outside. "It's nice here. Maybe I'll get someone to put a larger window in the teacher's cottage I live in. It's very dark inside."

There was a long silence during which tea was poured, milk and sugar attended to, spoons put down. "I suppose you want to know things," her mother said finally. "Why I left, things about your father. Your real father, I mean." Her tone suggested the conversation might be some kind of necessary ordeal.

Wendy turned to look at her mother. She tried hard to reconstruct what her mother would have looked like as a much younger woman. Even now, though, her mother's beauty was remarkable, with those intense blue eyes. "I'm not sure I do want to know. And I can't even say who I think of as my real father."

Her mother shook her head and smiled ruefully. "Of course, you are reserved with me. I would be too. Would it surprise you to know that I too was brought up without a mother? She died of diphtheria in 1905. I think you must lose something of an instinct for mothering in those circumstances."

Wendy thought about the failings of mothers. Of her mother's, of Samuel's. It would be best, she thought, never to put myself in the way of letting down a child.

Her mother spoke again. "I never stopped thinking of you, wondering how you were doing. I don't say that to excuse myself. It's just how it was. I knew he would take you to your aunt and uncle eventually, so that's where I imagined you, among the chickens. No, don't shake your head like that. I want you to know. You deserve the truth. When I knew I was carrying you, I lied to Zeke and said you were his. But by the time you were five, his drinking had become even worse. I told him then, in a fit of anger. I won't tell you how he responded immediately to that, but life became unbearable. I knew I would have to leave one day, and that he would not let me take you. He did that just to be bloody-minded. I'm not sure he wanted you. I'm sorry if this hurts you. I don't think lies are of any use at this late date, do you? I can tell you one thing. He was a decent man once. Smart, a promising future. The Great War did for him, I'm afraid." She stopped and looked away, then turned back and took her daughter's hand. "It killed me to leave you, but all I could think was that if I didn't, you would be stuck with me in utter poverty. I had no idea how I would make a living or how I could support you. At least he still had a job."

Wendy pulled her hand away and picked up her teacup. It was empty. She put it down. She was surprised that she felt no automatic affection for this woman who was her mother.

"I think I'm sorry for you," she said at last. "I teach these children in a little rural school in the Kootenays. They aren't even mine. And I've really just met them, but I can't bear to leave them. My life was not so bad at the farm. My aunt was kind enough, and I looked after my little cousins and taught them, because we were never allowed away from the property. I barely saw my father. It got so that I didn't know there was another way of life. And then I turned sixteen. My uncle picked out an old man for me to marry. It was to expunge your sin. That's what they told me. That I was forever marked and would become like you. I must have had some vague notion that this wasn't normal, that others didn't live the way we did, because I ran away, and have lived in terror ever since that they would come for me. But I learned about myself. I learned I was strong. I look at you, independent, alone, surrounded with what is yours, and I don't think I'm so different. I guess I should thank you. I don't know what my life would have been if I'd grown up with you and him fighting. I suppose he hit you. One of my students had parents like that. It's unbearable. It's horrible to say, I know, but I feel that student is better off now that his parents are dead, and he lives with people who care for him. And I guess I was better off without you."

Her mother got up and put her hands in the pockets of her wool trousers. "I deserve that." She went to stand looking out the window and then she turned back to Wendy. "Will you see Harry Devlin? I read in the papers his wife has been arrested. His career is in ruins. He could probably use some sympathy." She said this in a manner that suggested he wouldn't be getting any from her.

"If he wants to see me, he knows where I am. It's difficult to forget that his wife might have tried to kill me." She stood up. So, her mother knew and had said not one word about the ordeal she'd been through. "I should go. I promised a friend I would visit."

At the door her mother looked at her and smiled, putting her hand on her daughter's arm. "You're more wonderful than I imagined. Thank you for coming."

As Wendy Keeling drove along the isolated road back toward what she thought of as her own life, she wiped a surprising tear from her eye.

CHRISTMAS MORNING DAWNED sunny and cold. The snow was still staying away, and outside, the damp green of the forest that nudged up to the bedraggled lawn looked decidedly unseasonal. Lane had woken to the sound of her husband's voice in the hall. She had not heard the phone ring. She listened drowsily to his "hmm" and "I see" and

427

then heard him say, "Thank you. I'm sorry you've had to work on Christmas Day. Well, good. Wish them a happy Christmas from me."

This was followed in good time by the smell of coffee, and she was pleased to see it arriving, unbidden, on a tray borne by her husband, accompanied by some buttered Christmas cake. He looked, she thought, extra handsome in his striped pyjamas and new maroon paisley bathrobe, his hair a little tousled. He put the tray down on the bed and got in beside her.

"Happy Christmas," he said, kissing her. She smiled, feeling a warmth and sense of truly being at home that was deeper than anything she remembered in her life. She had her beautiful new fountain pen and leather-bound journal on the table beside her, her half of the Christmas Eve gift exchange, accomplished when the last of their guests had splashed off into the night. They declared their sherry party a successful event, because after all, it had been fun, and because people had lived up to Lane's prediction that they'd all want to rush off early.

"Happy Christmas to you. You'd better tell me who was on the phone."

"Oh, all right. That was Terrell. He was called to the hospital yet again last night. He wasn't able to go because he was the only available copper on duty, but he went up this morning. As you know, you were right about Miss Scott being our hit-and-run artist, and it turns out you and Terrell were right about her trashing the cottage. It's clear she hasn't been in her right mind for some time."

"Will she stand trial, do you think?" Lane was holding

428

her cup cradled in both hands to warm them.

He shrugged. "She's very weak and requires a long convalescence. She said it was an accident. There will be an inquest on the twenty-eighth. That will determine, I suppose, if it will be dropped or followed up on. I'll be honest, I'm inclined to think she did it on purpose. I don't know how, but I imagine somehow she managed to pick him up, drop him in the middle of nowhere, pretend to drive off, and then turn around and come back at him."

"But you don't blame her?" suggested Lane.

He sipped his coffee thoughtfully. "I am not keen on any crime going unpunished. It would unravel society if there was some sort of free-for-all where people who killed others who'd done them harm could get off without a question. It would be the Middle Ages again. But when I think about that child left alone in that freezing house . . ."

She leaned over and kissed him softly. "I know, darling."

"There's something that's been mystifying me. You brought up the Snow Queen in relation to the mirror in the bathroom. What was the significance of that?"

Lane was thoughtful and took several swigs of coffee. "It started, innocently enough, with those beautiful piles of snow we'd been getting. I had a very snowy childhood, and it reminded me of the beautiful Snow Queen I'd been told about. Then I remembered how horrible she really was.

"It really, I'm embarrassed to say, goes back to an incident when I was thirteen. I don't like to reveal what a horror I was at that age, in case you reconsider. I was a very unhappy child, and in a fit of anger on my birthday I smashed the mirror on my dressing table with my hairbrush.

429

I thought I was terribly ugly and unlovable, and somehow seeing myself through that shattered glass seemed to confirm it. A broken mirror plays a pivotal role in 'The Snow Queen'; I can't remember whether she, or a devil, breaks a mirror into millions of shards of glass that shower all over the world so that anyone whose heart is pierced by it is made angry and unhappy. For some reason, 'The Snow Queen'; kidnaps a little boy who's been made miserable by one of the shards, and it takes all the wiles of his innocent sister, who is not affected by the glass, to save him. When I saw that broken mirror in the bathroom, I thought, or at least wondered, if the unhappiness of whoever did the smashing was central to this story." She took a large bite of cake. "And in a way it was central," she continued. "There was Miss Keeling, thinking she'd finally found a place of safety, and then realizing she wasn't safe at all. I could see her blaming herself, thinking she didn't deserve to be happy, and in an angry moment looking at herself and smashing the bathroom mirror. She endured a good deal of rejection as a child, is quite entitled to feel horrible about herself, yet she is a very loving person. Somehow in her growing up, she allowed the good person inside her to save her. I wonder if that is the point. Inside each one of us is the unhappy little boy and the good sister who tries to save him."

"I can't help feeling the Snow Queen story is a bit obscure, and, like so many stories directed at children, essentially hectoring. What is a child meant to make of a tale like that except to go to bed and be afraid to sleep? As to Miss Keeling, broken mirror or not, I was actually struck by how much she reminds me of you. Terribly self-possessed and kind. I feel certain she could overcome any odds," Darling said.

"I'm sure you are exactly right. *A Christmas Carol* was a much better choice for the children. Only ghosts to keep them up at night, and a good clear moral lesson, not struggles with the eternal duality of good and evil. What more did Terrell have to say?"

"I thought you'd never ask! Ames and his mother have invited Terrell for lunch. Now then, what do you think of that? Wait. There's more. Among the guests will be Mr. Van Eyck and the lovely Tina. I'd call that pretty amazing, wouldn't you?"

She smiled warmly, not all that amazed, but happy. Happy for Ames, happy to be looking forward to Christmas lunch with Angela and David. Happy that it was her first Christmas with Darling.

"Amesy!" she said, clinking her coffee cup with his.

ACKNOWLEDGEMENTS

2021.

THE GRATITUDE I FEEL IS especially great this year, because when there was so much else to be uncertain about everyone involved in the creation of a Lane Winslow mystery carried on without skipping a beat. To Sasha Bley-Vroman, Gerald Miller, and Nickie Bertolotti, the first readers, a special debt of gratitude, for it is they who are charged with the responsibility of telling me if I should even go on with it. For this book I am especially indebted to Canadian historian and educator Rebecca Coulter for the time and articles on one-room schoolhouses that she so generously shared with me. I thank Gregg Parsons for again sharing his deep knowledge of vintage cars and their workings.

Editor Claire Philipson somehow magically can see the whole finished book through the weeds and undergrowth, and patiently walks me through with a pair of sturdy clippers to reveal the orderly garden underneath. And to Meg Yamamoto, for her meticulous proofreading. The TouchWood team: Taryn Boyd, for always believing in my books; Tori Elliott, who pushes the book out into the wider world with such unwavering enthusiasm; and Kate Kennedy, full of encouragement and an eagle eye.

Each Margaret Hanson cover has become a star in its own right, exciting admiration wherever it appears. Thanks to Margaret, for giving the books the wonderful face they turn to the world, and to Sydney Barnes, who has made this book a perfect match to the whole set.

And of course, there are not enough thanks in the world to adequately cover the support and belief in me of my wonderful husband, Terry, and the ready ear he always gives when Lane and I need it.

I cannot end without thanking my readers. It is for you I write, and it is because of you that I can continue to do so.

IONA WHISHAW was born in British Columbia. After living her early years in the Kootenays, she spent her formative years living and learning in Mexico, Nicaragua, and the US. She travelled extensively for pleasure and education before settling in the Vancouver area. Throughout her roles as youth worker, social worker, teacher, and award-winning high school principal, her love of writing remained consistent, and compelled her to obtain her master's in creative writing from the University of British Columbia. Iona has published short fiction, poetry, poetry translation, and one children's book, *Henry and the Cow Problem*. *A Killer in King's Cove* was her first adult novel. Her heroine, Lane Winslow, was inspired by Iona's mother who, like her father before her, was a wartime spy. Visit ionawhishaw.com to find out more.